AMONG THE SHADOWS

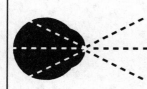

A JOHN BYRON NOVEL

AMONG THE SHADOWS

A DETECTIVE BYRON MYSTERY

BRUCE ROBERT COFFIN

THORNDIKE PRESS
A part of Gale, a Cengage Company

Farmington Hills, Mich • San Francisco • New York • Waterville, Maine
Meriden, Conn • Mason, Ohio • Chicago

LIBRARY OF CONGRESS CIP DATA ON FILE.
CATALOGUING IN PUBLICATION FOR THIS BOOK
IS AVAILABLE FROM THE LIBRARY OF CONGRESS

ISBN-13: 978-1-4328-4775-3 (hardcover)
ISBN-10: 1-4328-4775-9 (hardcover)

Published in 2018 by arrangement with Harper Paperback, an imprint of HarperCollins Publishers

Printed in the United States of America
1 2 3 4 5 6 7 22 21 20 19 18

For Kevin.

The past is never dead. It's not even past.

William Faulkner

CHAPTER ONE

The bitter stench of urine and impending death permeated the small dingy bedroom. Hawk stood next to the bed, looking down at O'Halloran. The ancient warrior lay withered and gaunt. Patches of dull white hair clung to his age-spotted scalp. Eyes, once calculating and sharp, were now yellowed and dim. O'Halloran was dying.

Hawk moved quickly, snatching the pillow from beneath the old man's head. He covered O'Halloran's face and pressed down firmly, his well-developed forearms flexed.

O'Halloran thrashed about, nearly toppling the chrome IV stand, but Hawk caught it easily. Muffled screams vibrated up through the pillow. He held fast as O'Halloran's bony legs slid back and forth like eels under the coverlet, kicking the sheet free on one side. Hawk closed his eyes, attempting to block out the image before him.

9

The old man's feeble struggles, no match for Hawk's strength, tapered off, then ceased.

In the next room a clock chimed, shattering the silence and signifying that the hour was at hand.

Warily, Hawk lifted the pillow. The warrior was gone. O'Halloran's eyes were lifeless and wide, projecting a silent narration of shock and fear. He closed them with a gentle hand, smoothed the disheveled hair, then fluffed the pillow and restored it to its rightful place. Lastly, he slid the old man's bony white foot back under the sheet and retucked the bedding.

Standing upright, he surveyed the room. Everything appeared in its proper place. O'Halloran looked serene, like he'd simply fallen asleep. Satisfied, Hawk walked from the room.

CHAPTER TWO

Detective Sergeant John Byron parked his unmarked Taurus behind a black-and-white cruiser. Neither the heat nor humidity were helping his foul mood. Only seven-thirty in the morning and the temperature displayed atop Congress Street's fourteen-story Chapman Building already read eighty-four degrees. Though September had nearly passed, summer wasn't quite ready to release the city from her sweltering grasp.

Portland autumns were normally cool and comfortable. Normally. Tourists returned to whichever godforsaken corner of the globe they had come, kids returned to the classroom, and the days grew increasingly shorter.

Byron's poor attitude had more to do with the day of the week than the weather. Wednesdays always put him in a bad mood, because it was the day Chief of Police Michael Stanton held his weekly CompStat meeting, a statistical midweek tough-mudder designed to give the upper echelon an opportunity to micromanage. Today's administrative migraine was accompanied by one of Byron's own creation. He knew of no better cure than a little hair of the dog, but nothing would land him in hot water with Lieutenant LeRoyer faster than the scent of Irish on his breath. Instead, he opted for the mystical healing properties of ibuprofen and caffeine, with a breath mint chaser. He closed his eyes and swallowed the pills on a wave of black coffee, pausing a moment before giving up the solitude of his car. On his game as always, in spite of his current condition.

Officer Sean Haggerty sat behind the wheel of another police cruiser, parked further down the street under a shady canopy of maples. The veteran officer was speaking with a young auburn-haired woman. Byron guessed she was the nurse, primarily because she wasn't in hysterics, as most relatives would've been. He was pleased to see Hags on the call. Hags did things by the numbers. The same could not be said of every beat cop. They exchanged nods as Byron headed up the driveway.

A skinny uniformed rookie stood sentry at the side door to the Bartley Street home.

Byron knew they'd crossed paths before, but couldn't recall his name. What had once been a phenomenon was occurring with far greater frequency, a clear indication the cops were either getting younger or he wasn't.

"Morning, Sarge," the rookie said as he recorded Byron's name into the crime scene log.

"O'Donnell," Byron said after stealing a glance at the name tag. He gestured with his thumb toward the street. "That the nurse with Haggerty?"

"Yes, Sir."

"Who's inside?"

"E.T. Pelligrosso and Detective Joyner. First floor, back bedroom."

Evidence Technician Gabriel Pelligrosso, a young, flat-topped, ex-soldier, was known for being methodical, thorough, and dependable, traits Byron's own father had harped on. "If every cop on the job had those qualities, sonny boy, it'd be a sorry fuckin' day to be a criminal." Byron stepped inside.

The odor assaulted him upon entering the kitchen. An all too familiar blend of bladder and excremental expulsion, which, thanks to the humidity, would undoubtedly linger in the fabric of his clothing all day.

He listened to their footsteps on the hardwood floor along with the occasional click of Pelligrosso's camera as they recorded the scene. Not wanting to interrupt them, he waited in the kitchen, making mental notes of everything he saw.

A 2015 Norman Rockwell calendar depicting several boys and a dog running past a No Swimming sign hung on the wall beside the refrigerator. Notations had been made with a red pen in what resembled the flowery script of a woman, perhaps the nurse. The days of the month had been crossed off up to the twenty-third. Someone had been here yesterday. Maybe a family member or one of the nurses. He'd check with Hags.

"Sarge, you out there?" Diane called from down the hall.

Diane Joyner, Portland's first female African-American detective, was a tough-talking New Yorker. Tall and attractive, she'd lulled more than one bad guy into thinking he could get over on her. Prior to arriving in Portland, she'd worked homicides in the Big Apple for seven years. Byron didn't know if it was her confidence or thoroughness that made some of the other officers insecure about working with her, but those very same traits made Diane his first choice for partner on murder cases.

"Just waiting on you," Byron said.

"We're all set in here."

Byron walked down the hall and entered the bedroom. "What've we got?"

"One stinky stiff," Diane said. "Formerly Mr. James O'Halloran."

"O'Halloran?" he asked. Byron had known a James O'Halloran. Was this the same man? The emaciated corpse lying in the bed bore little resemblance to the squared-away Portland police lieutenant from his memory. "Did we find an ID?"

Diane handed him an expired Maine driver's license. The photo, taken seven years and at least a hundred pounds ago, was definitely Jimmy O. The same man who had sat beside him in the church, on the worst day of Byron's life.

"You know this guy?" she asked.

"Retired Portland cop," he said, returning the license. "What's the nurse got to say?"

She referred to her notes. "Nurse Rebecca St. John says she left here yesterday evening around six-thirty, after changing his bedding and giving him his meds for the night. She returned this morning and found him like this."

Byron looked at the IV. "Was he being fed?"

"Still feeding himself. Hospice care."

"And the IV?"

"Pain dope. Keeping him comfortable and waiting for the cancer to do the rest."

"If he was under a doctor's care, why are we here?"

"Nobody's been able to locate the doctor. Sounds like he's away on vacation."

Of course he is, Byron thought.

"St. John said this was expected, just not so soon."

Byron remembered the lieutenant as a chain-smoker. "You said cancer. Lung?"

"And bone," she said. "Pretty shitty way to go out."

"How about the M.E.?"

"I spoke with Dr. Ellis," Pelligrosso said. "Said he'd have the attending physician sign off if we don't find anything."

"I was gonna take care of notifying the next of kin," she said. "Unless you'd like to?"

Byron considered her question. He couldn't imagine anything more enjoyable than breaking the news of death to a loved one, especially on a sweltering day in the middle of Indian summer while still in the grips of one bitch of a hangover. It would be the high point of his day. But it was the right thing to do. "Got a number?"

Diane handed him the scrap of paper the nurse had provided. Written in the same flowery script was the name Susan Atherton along with an out-of-state telephone number. Byron recognized the given name, Jimmy O's daughter, as well as the Florida area code. The surname must be her married name. He wondered why Susie was still in Florida and not here with her dying father. "I'll take care of it," he said.

Adding to Byron's discomfort, his sweat-soaked dress shirt clung to his back. He retreated from the home's stuffy interior to the quiet air-conditioned comfort of the rookie's black-and-white. While the AC in his own car was nonexistent, the air coming from the vents in O'Donnell's cruiser was icy and soothing. Byron noticed a *City of Portland Street Guide,* standard issue for all new officers, sitting atop the dash. He thought back to his first day on the job, when he was issued one of his own. Having grown up on the peninsula, he'd biked or walked every inch of Portland in town and hadn't needed a street guide, at least not until he was assigned to patrol a beat in the Deering section of the city. Bordering the towns of Westbrook and Falmouth, Deering had been as foreign to him as another world.

He despised making death notifications,

all the officers did. And yet it came with the territory. If asked, he wouldn't have dared guess how many he'd made over the years. The short answer was too many. He preferred making the notifications the way he'd been taught, in person. Death was personal and news of it should always be delivered face-to-face. However, in cases where the recipient of the bad news wasn't nearby, he'd occasionally sought help from the local authorities. This notification was different, as he knew Susie personally. As bad as the news of a loved one's death by phone was, he knew it would be far better coming from him than some stranger in uniform. A stranger who likely wouldn't have the best delivery.

He lowered the volume on the cruiser's base radio, then pulled out his cell and dialed Atherton's number.

A woman's voice answered in mid-ring. "Hello."

"I'm looking for Susan Atherton."

"This is she. And whatever you're selling I'm not —"

"Susie, it's John Byron."

There was a brief pause at the other end of the line. "Johnny? Oh my God. How are you?"

He couldn't remember anyone having

called him Johnny since high school. "I'm well. It's good to hear your voice."

"I was about to say the same. It must be, what, thirty years?"

"Listen, Susie, this isn't a social call, and I apologize for dropping this on you. I'm afraid I have some bad news."

Another pause. "Is my father dead?"

"He is."

"Good riddance."

Byron thought he'd experienced every conceivable emotion associated with hearing the news of a loved one's death. Some people fainted, some got angry, some blubbered, some punched things, but he honestly couldn't recall anyone ever telling him they were happy about it.

"Susie, I'm very sorry —"

"Don't be."

He wasn't sure how to proceed. She clearly didn't want his pity. He understood her feelings of resentment toward her father. They were feelings with which he was all too familiar. "Susie, I'm not sure if —"

"We hadn't spoken in years."

"Mind if I ask why?"

"Because he was a son of a bitch, John. A no good, lying, cheating, boozing piece of shit. What I wanted, needed, was a father, and my mother needed a husband. What we got instead was a drunken asshole."

The conversation turned awkward and they both quickly ran out of things to say. Byron thought he heard her voice cracking as she said goodbye.

He was startled by a knock at the window. Haggerty. Byron opened the door and stepped out.

"Hey, Sarge, didn't mean to interrupt, but they're asking for you inside." Haggerty's pained expression suggested whatever they'd found wasn't good. Byron sincerely hoped the phone call he'd just made hadn't been as premature as it now felt. His headache, which had begun to fade, was threatening to return.

"Where's the nurse?"

Haggerty pointed to the side lawn. "Calling her boss."

"Make sure she stays here," Byron said as he slammed the car door and walked back to the house.

They were waiting on him as he returned to the bedroom. "What's up?"

"Think we've got a problem," Pelligrosso said. Wearing white latex gloves he peeled back O'Halloran's lips. "See the purple discoloration?"

Byron saw it and it wasn't the first time. "Bruising?"

"That's what it looks like," Diane said.

"Could it be something else?"

"Maybe," Pelligrosso said. "But I'm certainly not qualified to make that call. And here's another thing." He pulled down the bottom right eyelid. "Petechial hemorrhaging."

Hemorrhaging of the small capillaries around the eyes often appear as dark-colored dots called petechia. Any number of things can cause these vessels to rupture: violent coughing, vomiting, crying, and certain medications. God only knew what medications had been administered to O'Halloran. And, as they were all well aware, petechial hemorrhaging can also be indicative of asphyxiation.

In his twenty years on the job, Byron had only seen two confirmed mercy killings, but this had all the makings of a third.

He phoned Dr. Ellis, deputy medical examiner for the state of Maine. Ellis lived a short distance from the Casco Bay Bridge, in South Portland. With any luck, he hadn't yet left for Augusta.

"John Byron," Ellis said as he picked up on the second ring. "I was just thinking about you. Got something for me?"

"Not sure, Doc. You still in town?"

"On the interstate almost to Falmouth,

but I can turn around and be there in fifteen."

"You need the address?"

"Bartley Street, right? I'll look for the one with all the police cars in front."

"We'll be waiting."

Ellis was something of a throwback. He wore his dark hair slicked back with Elvis-style sideburns. As medical examiners go, he was as thorough as they came, only a bit eccentric. The more peculiar the case, the better Ellis liked it. More than once he'd left his wife sitting alone at a restaurant so he could check out a "weird one."

He arrived wearing shorts, running sneakers, and a black AC/DC T-shirt, which stretched unflatteringly over his ample belly.

"Thanks for coming, Doc," Byron said.

"Morning, John." He set his worn black medical bag down and turned to address the others. "Lady and gentleman. What do we have for Dr. E?"

Diane spoke up. "James O'Halloran, seventy-two, advanced stages of lung and bone cancer. He was found this morning by the agency nurse."

"Uh-huh," Ellis said as he pulled on a pair of blue surgical gloves. "And when was Mr. O last seen alive?"

"Nurse said she left here last night around

six-thirty," Pelligrosso said.

Ellis lifted one of O'Halloran's arms, attempting to bend it. "Not in full rigor yet, but he's getting there. Best guesstimate, he died some time between eight and midnight. Am I correct in assuming this was in-home hospice care?"

"You are," Byron said. "We've still got the nurse outside."

Ellis opened the eyes and confirmed the presence of petechia. "You saw this?"

"We did," Pelligrosso said. "Along with what looks like bruising inside his lips."

Ellis pulled O'Halloran's lips back. "Correct, my boy. Did you check the body for any signs of trauma?"

"Not yet," Pelligrosso said. "Once we found those things, we stopped to wait for you."

Ellis turned to Byron and grinned. "Wish my people were as efficient as yours. Wouldn't consider a trade, would you?"

Byron shook his head. "Think I'll keep what I've got."

Ellis forced the jaw open. It made an unpleasant grinding sound. Diane winced. The doc illuminated the cavity with his penlight. "Uh-huh."

"You find something?" Pelligrosso asked.

Ellis looked back. "Patience, my boy,

patience." Reaching into his black leather bag, he removed a long thin pair of stainless-steel tweezers. Carefully, he probed deep inside the victim's oral cavity. "Here we are," he said as he retracted the instrument and held it up for all to see.

"What's that?" Diane asked.

"That, Detective, is goose down."

"The pillow?" Byron asked.

"That's what it looks like. Most likely inhaled during suffocation. I'll need to perform a full post on Mr. Bones and his pillow to be sure."

Byron looked at Pelligrosso. "The pillow goes to Augusta with us."

Ellis continued his exam, cutting off O'Halloran's pajama bottoms and top. The old man was wearing a soiled adult diaper. There were no obvious signs of trauma on either the torso or legs. Ellis waited for Pelligrosso to snap a couple of photos before proceeding. He looked at Diane, who was still wearing gloves. "Give me a hand rolling him over."

Her face squinted up in disgust. Pelligrosso smiled. O'Halloran's body was stiff enough to make it more like flipping a mattress. Again, Ellis checked his upper torso and legs. Lividity, pooling of the blood, was exactly where it should have been on the victim's back and lower extremities, confirming he'd died lying face up.

"So we know the body hasn't been moved." Ellis said to himself as much as to anyone in the room. "No other obvious signs of trauma," he said, turning to face Byron.

"How soon can you post?"

"How soon can you get him on my table?"

"Sarge, I still gotta dust everything in this room for prints," Pelligrosso said.

"We'll lock down the house and post a uniform outside," Byron said. "You can come back this afternoon after the autopsy. Also, I want elimination prints from everyone who came in here. Anyone who may have touched something, paramedics, cops, nurses, everyone."

"I'll take care of it."

Byron turned to Diane. "Let's get Nurse St. John down to 109. I've got a few questions for her."

CHAPTER THREE

Portland's police department stands at the corner of Middle Street and Franklin Arterial, beside Portland's revitalized Old Port district. The physical address is 109 Middle Street or, as it's more commonly referred to by the rank and file, simply 109.

Byron pulled into in a metered space a little west of 109. Experience told him the rear garage was most likely full, as there were more police vehicles than spaces, but his real reason for parking in front was to piss off Assistant Chief Cross, or Ass Chief Cross, as Byron fondly referred to him. Cross, thanks to a designated spot inside the climate controlled garage beneath the station, had no concept of 109's parking problems. Byron thought of his own glove box, so packed with parking citations it barely closed. Lieutenant LeRoyer was always yelling at him about parking illegally. "They're gonna slap a boot on your car,

John," he'd say. Byron was pretty sure if the parking-control Nazis ever got brazen enough to enforce the scofflaw on his car, they'd skip right past the boot and towing options and proceed directly to the salvage yard, where they'd have it crushed. Time to start throwing the citations in the trunk, he thought. With his battered briefcase in hand and a knowing grin on his face, he ascended the crumbling cement steps toward the plaza and the day's first interview.

The 109 was constructed in the early 1970s as a police station/ community center, replacing an outdated, turn-of-the-century two-story brick-and-granite structure, which once stood around the corner between Newbury and Federal Streets. The new building's façade is brick and mortar with darkened glass windows. In spite of numerous transformations since its grand opening in 1972, the odd-shaped exterior still looks much like a child's attempt at building a southwestern Pueblo from blocks than the headquarters to Maine's largest municipal police agency. Unlike the original police headquarters, which Byron visited frequently when he was a boy, when his dad had still worked a beat, the current is a far cry from stations of old. Missing are the granite steps, lighted glass globes stenciled with the word POLICE, and the large wooden desk inside the foyer from which the duty sergeant could bark orders. In short, it no longer had any character. The veteran officers joked that the character is now on the inside.

O'Halloran's nurse was seated in Interview Room One, waiting for Byron to return with a coffee. She'd readily agreed to an interview. Haggerty had driven her to 109, leaving O'Donnell to sit on the house, which was now officially a crime scene. Diane monitored the interview from the conference room along with Detective Mike Nugent.

Byron returned with two mugs of coffee, closing the door behind him. "Here you are. Careful, it's hot."

"Thanks."

St. John was attractive in a tomboyish way. Cinnamon hair, pulled back into a ponytail, nicely complimented her light blue short-sleeve top and matching pants. Byron caught a glimpse of freckled cleavage as she bent down and removed a package of tissues from her purse.

"Thank you for coming in to talk to me, Ms. St. John. I want to make it clear again, for the record, this is completely voluntary on your part. You understand you're free to

28

leave at any time."

"Becca, please. And it's not a problem. I'm happy to help anyway I can."

Removing a small notebook and pen from his suit jacket, he spent several seconds pretending to read over his notes. "How long have you been in nursing, Becca?"

"Almost ten years. But I've only worked for Pine Tree Hospice the last couple."

"Before that?"

"I worked at Maine Medical Center in the CCU. Sorry, Critical Care Unit."

"I would imagine with the job you have now, you see a great deal of death."

She nodded. "Yes. All of my patients are terminally ill."

"You ever get used to it? Patients dying under your care, I mean."

She shrugged her shoulders. "It's part of the job."

"Must be tough, though," he said.

She appeared to be considering her answer while she toyed with the mug. "Am I suspected of doing something wrong, Sergeant Byron?"

"Why would you ask that?"

"Because, I've already given a statement to the officer at the scene and now you're asking questions about how I deal with the death of my patients. Do you think I killed

Mr. O'Halloran?"

Byron was used to the idiosyncrasies of people when they were being interviewed. Many became combative, lied, or lawyered up, whether they were guilty or not. Seldom were they as direct as St. John. "Did you?"

"Of course not. He was dying and nothing could have prevented it. It's my job to make patients as comfortable as possible while they await the inevitable."

She dabbed at the corners of her eyes with the tissue. Byron knew when it came to people's tears, it was nearly impossible to differentiate between the genuine and the crocodile variety. And he'd learned from experience that women were infinitely better at manufacturing them than their male counterparts. His wife, Kay, certainly had been.

"How long had you been caring for O'Halloran?"

"A few weeks."

"Were you assigned to him every day?"

"Only during the week. Another nurse from the agency covered the weekend shifts."

"Who was that?"

"Frankie Mathers."

"And she was the only nurse covering the weekends?"

St. John rolled her eyes. "Frankie's a guy. Not all nurses are women, Sergeant."

He wasn't in the mood for her feminist sermon, but his headache was threatening to return. Against his better judgment, he let her comment pass. "What about after hours? What happened if O'Halloran needed something after you left?"

"There was a panic button, which automatically dialed up the agency answering service. They'd either call me or another on call if I didn't answer."

"Was that the cord I saw wrapped around the headboard?"

"Yes, red button on the end."

"Do you know if he activated the system during the time you cared for him?"

"I don't believe he did."

"What time did you arrive and depart each day? Was it always the same?"

"It wasn't an all-day visit. I have other patients. Normally, I'd get there around eight o'clock and leave by nine-thirty or ten, depending on his needs. I also made a late-afternoon stop to make sure he had enough pain meds to make it through the night."

Byron made a note in his book and watched as St. John toyed with the tissue. "What medications were you administering to him?"

"I gave him morphine for pain along with several other drugs to control congestion in his lungs."

"How long was he expected to live?"

"His doctor told him he most likely still had two or three months."

"A long time to suffer."

Her eyes narrowed. "Sergeant, I'm not sure where this is headed, but I can assure you I did not kill my patient. My job was to keep him comfortable and clean and that's what I did. The next step would have been palliative sedation."

"Palliative sedation?"

"Yes. It's the term we use for keeping a patient sedated once the pain and symptoms become unbearable. At some point, he would have been kept sedated through the administration of a benzodiazepine until he simply passed away in his sleep."

Byron couldn't remember ever hearing a term that sounded more politically correct than palliative sedation. He supposed it beat medically induced coma. "And you would've been the one to make that determination?"

"No, Sergeant Byron. I'm only a nurse. If I did what you're suggesting, I'd be wearing an orange jumpsuit and residing at the state prison. Mr. O'Halloran would've been the one to make the decision, along with his doctor. If he'd made it that far."

He switched gears. "Did you have your own key to the house?"

"The door was never locked."

"Why would you leave the home unsecured?"

"It was at his request."

"Did he have visitors?"

"There may have been a couple."

"You ever see them?"

"No, but he'd talk about them occasionally."

"Did he mention any names?"

"He probably did, but I don't pay attention to those things. I try not to get too attached. You know?

He remained silent, waiting to see if she would say more.

"You asked me before if it was tough taking care of the dying. Well, only if you let yourself get attached to them. I don't."

Byron saw no sign of tears now, crocodile or otherwise.

"So, what do you think?" Byron asked Diane as he rinsed out the mugs in the sink.

"I didn't get to see all of it, got a call from the D.A. A bit of a bitch, isn't she?"

"Definitely not the most affable I've ever met."

"Think she did it?" she asked as she followed him to his office.

"Too early to say." He grabbed a necktie from one of his desk drawers and quickly began to knot it around his neck. "What time is it?"

"It's late. Pelligrosso's already waiting by your car."

"Damn."

"You lose your razor?"

Byron ran a hand over his stubble. "I forgot."

"Guinness?"

"Bushmills."

"Maybe you could get the Emerald Society to schedule their monthly meetings for a Friday or Saturday night, then you'd be fresh for the weekdays."

"You should consider joining. You must have some Welsh, Scottish, or Irish in you."

"News flash. What I've had in me is none of your business. I never kiss and tell," she said, giving him a wink.

Byron blushed. "LeRoyer in yet?"

"Running late."

"Good. I want to get out of here before he gets in."

"Trying to avoid CompStat, are we?"

"Of course. You and Nuge take care of the canvass?"

"Of course."

"I wanna know if someone might've paid O'Halloran an unexpected visit."

CHAPTER FOUR

The air-conditioning in Byron's aging unmarked needed recharging. His procrastination meant they'd be making the sixty-mile drive up the turnpike to Augusta with the windows down. The hot air blasting through the windows felt like opening an oven door, but at least it was moving. It was a little past noon as he turned into the lower lot and parked next to the brick building housing the offices of Maine's chief medical examiner.

The cavernous exam room was cool and dry, a welcome contrast to the unseasonal heat. Dr. Ellis's workspace consisted of painted concrete walls and subway tile. High ceilings and harsh fluorescent lighting made the pale and waxy skin of his patients look even worse. The walls were lined with white metal cabinets and rows of shelving, each containing various supplies and implements of deconstruction. A half-dozen stainless steel exam tables were scattered throughout the room, each with its own hanging scale used for weighing organs, similar to those found in butcher shops.

Like all seasoned investigators, he and Pelligrosso had both been to countless autopsies and were very familiar with the sights and sounds associated with the procedure. That being said, neither had ever developed a true appreciation for the effect dissecting a corpse had on their olfactory senses.

Ellis had donned green scrubs and now looked the part of the professional medical examiner he was — although, Byron was fairly confident Ellis was still wearing the gray AC/DC shirt underneath.

Ellis's assistant, Nicky, entered the room and nodded at them. The skinny lab technician never spoke unless spoken to, and Byron had never been able to think of a single thing to say to him. His wide eyes made him look like he'd seen a ghost. Given what Nicky did for work, Byron figured it wasn't out of the realm of possibility that he had — perhaps more than one. Dark purplish circles under those wide eyes made him look significantly older than the thirty-something he probably was.

Ellis began the exam by gloving up. He carefully unzipped the bag containing

O'Halloran's remains, permeating the air with the same stench of bodily fluids Byron and Pelligrosso had been savoring for most of the morning. Byron wondered how Ellis could swim in it every day.

The doctor picked up a scalpel, then paused. "He was a Portland police lieutenant?"

"A long time ago," Byron said.

"Did you work with him?"

"My father did."

"I'm sorry."

Byron appreciated the sentiment but found it an odd conversation, considering what Ellis was about to do to O'Halloran's body.

During the half hour following, Ellis worked slowly and methodically, beginning with the Y incision into O'Halloran's bony chest cavity. It was obvious the cancer had been living inside of him for some time. Ellis cut and probed, weighed and sampled, preserving bits of every organ should they be needed later. He paused from time to time to ask questions and to allow Pelligrosso a chance to photograph evidence. He located two more down feathers, one in O'Halloran's trachea and the other in the right lung.

"I've seen this type of thing before," Ellis

said as he removed his gloves. "What did you say the name of the agency was?"

"Pine Tree Hospice," Pelligrosso said.

Ellis nodded.

"Have you seen anything like this with any of their other patients recently?" Byron asked.

"Nah. They've got a pretty good track record. Some of these places don't give very good care. You should see some of the bedsores that come through here. You guys like the nurse for this?"

"Too soon to like anyone," Byron said. "At this point, she's the last person we know of to see him alive."

"How long did you say she's been a nurse?"

"Ten years, give or take. Why?"

"Well, I was thinking, there are certainly easier ways to commit a mercy killing, John. If that's what this is. If Dr. E was going to do it, he sure as hell wouldn't use a pillow and risk leaving all this evidence."

"How would you go about it?" Pelligrosso asked.

"I might up the pain medication, just a bit. If he was already on a high enough dose, it wouldn't take much. Or, even better, I could inject air into his veins and he'd die from an embolism."

Byron looked at Ellis, trying to see if he was serious. His usual smugness was gone. "Remind me never to get on your bad side, Doc."

Ellis smiled and drummed his fingers together.

"So what are you saying?" Byron asked.

"Feels more like someone who didn't know how, a friend or relative maybe."

"And you're officially going with death by asphyxiation?" Pelligrosso asked.

"Yup, pending toxicology of course. Who knows, I may be able to further complicate this case for you guys by finding something else."

"Gee, thanks, Doc," Byron said.

"Gentlemen, as always, it's been a pleasure." Grinning, Ellis bent forward in the exaggerated bow of a stage performer. "See you at the trial."

Pelligrosso drove them toward the pike while Byron made some calls.

Diane answered on the first ring. "Just about to call you."

"Anything from the canvass?"

"Zilch. No one home at half of the houses, the others all claim to keep to themselves. Said they didn't know O'Halloran."

"Nuge fare any better?"

"Nope, but we left a shitload of business cards on doors. Felt like we were running for public office. What's the doc's prognosis?"

"Pending tox. But definitely suffocated. You guys still on the street?"

"We're grabbing a quick burger. What do you need?"

"Do me a favor and swing by Pine Tree Hospice in South Portland. Tell them you want to see St. John's personnel file. I want to know if she's worked any other questionable deaths."

"They're gonna raise holy hell. What do you want us to do if they refuse?"

"I'm calling the attorney general as soon as I hang up. I'll have them draw up a subpoena and fax it directly to them. Don't leave there without her file."

"You got it."

"Also, I want the file on the weekend-duty nurse, Mathers. And find out if anyone else may have filled in or covered an after-hours emergency at O'Halloran's."

"Ten four."

"One last thing, Diane. Get a hold of Tran and have him search in-house and NCIC. I want to know if she's got any history."

"We'll take care of it."

As Byron hung up, he heard his own

stomach's audible protest. Aside from coffee and breath mints, he hadn't eaten since yesterday. "You hungry?" he asked Pelligrosso.

"I could eat a horse."

"Think I can do better than that."

Pelligrosso looked at him as if he was waiting for him to finish his thought.

"My treat."

"Now you're speaking my language."

"Was that Ferguson?" Pelligrosso asked as Byron ended the call.

"None other. The best assistant AG in the state."

"Sounds like he's on board."

"Why do you think he's the best in the state?"

They pulled into the gravel parking lot of Jimmy's Lunch, a hole in the wall located off the Gardiner Exit on Route 126. Prior to Detective Ray Humphrey's retirement, he and Ray always made a habit of stopping at Jimmy's after an autopsy, a custom going back years. This was his first time with Pelligrosso.

Byron liked the young evidence tech. He liked the way Pelligrosso went about his work, taking great pains to be thorough. There was a bit of a dark streak, a brooding quality about him, but Byron chalked it up to the time he'd spent fighting in Afghanistan. Byron figured if Pelligrosso ever wanted to talk about it, he would.

They seated themselves at a booth. Byron commandeered the wall seat, second nature to any veteran officer, which allowed him to watch the door as well as the activities of any other customers. Pelligrosso was fidgety. His discomfort at having his back exposed to the room was obvious.

"Don't worry, Gabe," Byron said. "I've got your six."

Pelligrosso smiled. "I know you do."

They each ordered soft drinks, burgers, and hand-cut fries. Best in the state, according to a greasy sign on the wall.

"Can I ask you a question, Sarge?"

"Shoot."

"You remember the whole Dr. Kevorkian thing?"

Byron already knew where this was headed. "Assisted suicide, yeah."

"Let's say O'Halloran only had a month or two left. Based on the way he looked, I'm probably being generous. If it *was* one of the nurses who suffocated him, maybe they did him a favor."

Byron took a sip out of the red plastic tumbler as he formulated his response. He remembered rooting for Kevorkian himself. "I think this one's a little different, Gabe."

"Why is it?"

"In the Kevorkian case, each of his victims had given up and were seeking a humane end to their suffering. They went to the doctor and asked for his help. He had videos to document their wishes. But in this case, whether it was the nurse or not, there's nothing humane about smothering someone to death with a pillow. And there's nothing left behind to indicate O'Halloran even wanted a way out. This is a murder, plain and simple."

"I guess maybe you're right. I just keep picturing myself lying there, dying from cancer. I'd sure want a way out."

"I probably would, too," Byron said.

Byron pictured a younger, stronger O'Halloran, squared away in his dress uniform, sitting beside him in the front row of the church. Byron had been no more than a scared teenaged kid. O'Halloran had provided the strength Byron needed to get through what had been undoubtedly the toughest day of his young life.

He returned to the here-and-now and looked over at his young evidence tech. "Someone murdered that old man, and I'm gonna find out who."

CHAPTER FIVE

It was nearly three-thirty by the time Byron and Pelligrosso arrived back at 109. Pelligrosso grabbed the evidence van and returned to O'Halloran's in his search for prints and any other trace evidence. Byron headed up to his office on the fourth floor. He was washing up in the CID locker room when LeRoyer walked in.

"Well, that was certainly convenient, John. Did you purposely schedule the autopsy to coincide with CompStat?"

"Hey, I only asked how soon Ellis could do it. The M.E.'s office schedules the exams, not me. Would you rather I sat around the table watching the command staff measure each other's dicks or work a homicide?"

"Easy there, cowboy. I'm part of the command staff."

Lieutenant Martin LeRoyer was affable enough, and although Byron liked him, they frequently butted heads. It went with the territory. The thing that bothered Byron most about LeRoyer was he'd been a boss for so long he'd forgotten what it was like to be an investigator. Gone from LeRoyer's memory were what it meant to eat, sleep, and breathe a case. It was all about statistics now. Byron had never gained a single thing from statistics. Not once in twenty years as a cop could he remember stats helping to crack a case.

Criminals are an unpredictable lot, with diverse motives. The dumb ones were caught, repeatedly, but the intelligent ones sometimes never. What Byron sought were cold, hard facts, not charts and graphs and questions about who got the credit and who got the blame. The most useful investigative knowledge came from digging, fact-checking, and interviews — good old-fashioned police work, not sitting around discussing absurd statistics. As far as Byron was concerned, CompStat was a waste of time and resources.

LeRoyer went to his locker, grabbing his toothbrush and paste. Byron despised the lieutenant's habit of talking with a mouth full of toothpaste foam. It made him look like a rabid dog. "So, what'd you find out?"

"He was suffocated."

"Wasn't he damn near dead anyway?"

"Close."

"We like the nurse?"

He wondered how many times in one day a person could be asked the same question. "No. I don't really care for her. But at the moment, she's made the top two on our list of possible suspects."

"That's good."

"Not really. There's only two names on the list."

"Family?"

"Estranged. I spoke to his only daughter, Susan, by telephone, but she's in Florida. The biggest problem is anyone could've accessed the house. It was always unlocked."

LeRoyer spat into the sink, spraying foam onto the mirror. "Neighbors?"

"Nuge and Diane canvassed, nothing yet. We're checking the nurses' records."

"Yeah, I know. Already got a call from the manager at Happy Hospice. Tim Caron. Big asshole."

"Pine Tree Hospice," Byron said, grinning.

"Whatever." LeRoyer rinsed. "Guy's still an asshole."

"Nothing I'd enjoy more than to hang here all afternoon and chew the fat, Lieu, but I got a case to work."

"Oh, by all means, Sergeant. Don't let me stand in your way. And stop parking in front of 109!"

Detectives Diane Joyner and Mike Nugent were as opposite as the ends of the earth. The tough-talking Joyner was a full six inches taller than her wisecracking, foul-mouthed sometimes partner. Normally, Nugent and his highly reflective dome would've been partnered with Detective Melissa Stevens, but manpower issues had forced her back into the lab on a part-time basis. Byron never worried about Diane, but at times Nugent could be a bit too laid back.

"How'd you make out with the records?" Byron asked.

"We got copies of reviews, training, and thank-you letters for both nurses," Diane said. "Hey, did you know Frankie was a guy?"

Byron, recalling St. John's remark about him being sexist, began to laugh.

"What?"

"It's nothing," he said, waving her off and trying to regain his composure. "Anybody else care for him?"

"According to Pine Tree Hospice, St. John and Mathers were the only nurses who had any contact with O'Halloran."

"The best part was the quality time we got to spend with the hospice manager," Nugent said.

"Asshole," they both said in unison.

"So I've heard. Any indication St. John might previously have been suspected of helping a patient along?"

"Delivery from this mortal coil?" Nugent asked. "None. In fact, when he wasn't threatening us with civil action, Caron did manage to say she'd come highly recommended from Maine Med. Why the hell would she risk everything to do in a patient anyway?"

"I don't know," Byron said. "Why does anyone? Tired of watching people suffer, maybe?"

"She wouldn't be the first," Diane said. "You want us to grab the hospital records as well?"

"Yes, before their legal team starts circling the wagons," Byron said. "I don't want to overlook anything."

"You want us to call Ferguson for another subpoena?" Diane asked.

"No, I'll take care of it. I need to speak with him again anyway. Anything new on the canvass?"

"We're still waiting to hear from a few folks who weren't home," Nugent said.

"Good, let me know if something breaks. I gotta go see Tran."

Dustin Tran was a thirty-year-old bachelor who rode his bicycle to work every morning, regardless of the weather. He was the only detective assigned to the Computer Forensics Lab. A virtuoso on all things computer related, Tran actually preferred working alone. Byron wondered if the loner thing was a result of his acne scars or his odd personality.

Tran's office sat at the end of the third-floor corridor, beside the Regional Crime Lab. He was seated at his desk, which looked more like a display shelf in some big-box store than a detective's workstation. His jet-black hair, glistening with gel, had been molded into something resembling a pompadour. Three oversized, high-definition monitors sat atop his desk while shelves of computer towers whirred away doing God knew what.

"Yo, Sarge," Tran said.

Byron bristled. He'd never quite warmed up to Tran's casual surfer-dude demeanor, but he tolerated it because the detective was good at his job. Had anyone else tried talking to Byron like that, he would have lost it. "Any luck on St. John?"

"Nothing in-house, but NCIC shows one arrest in '93."

Byron's interest peaked. "For?"

"Disorderly conduct. Looks like she was attending a peace rally at the University of New England. Might've gotten out of hand."

Byron wondered if caring for O'Halloran might also have gotten a little out of hand.

"Anything else?"

"If there is, I can't find it."

He flipped open his notepad. "I need you to check on one more person for me."

"Go with it."

"Francis Mathers, DOB two, thirteen, eighty-nine."

"I'll let you know."

Byron stopped as he reached the door. "One more thing."

"Bring it."

"O'Halloran has a daughter named Susan Atherton. See if you can find out if she's been outside of Florida recently. Like, maybe visiting Portland, Maine."

After leaving Tran's office, Byron headed for the privacy afforded by the building's stairwell. He still needed to make a phone call he'd been putting off. Even if Atherton had been on the outs with her father, nobody wants to be informed of their

51

parent's murder.

LeRoyer called Byron into his office. "I just got off the phone with St. John's attorney."

"Let me guess, one of the senior partners at Dewey, Fuckem and Howe?"

"Close. It's Roger Bertram."

Bertram was an arrogant windbag, known for stealing defendants from other attorneys. If the case made a splash, he wanted it; not for any merit it may have had, only for the free publicity. Red-faced and overweight, he got winded riding an elevator. Bertram had crossed paths with Byron on several different occasions, and his disdain for the Portland Police Department was not news.

"Great, so I guess we're done talking with her."

"Nope. She didn't lawyer up."

"Then, why the attorney?"

"She wants a polygraph. Says she's got nothing to hide."

"Wasn't expecting that."

"Me neither."

"I still don't like it," Byron said.

"What's to lose?"

"Everything. You know I don't have any faith in that crap."

"Maybe you should broaden your horizons, John."

"All right, Lieu, let's say she fails the test. We won't be able to use it in court."

"Maybe it'll make her confess."

"You honestly think Bertram would allow that to happen? Then there's the other possibility — she passes it."

"Why would that be a problem?"

"If we do end up finding out she killed O'Halloran, don't think for a second that weasel won't try and get the judge to admit the polygraph results as evidence of her innocence."

"So what do you want to do?"

"Don't have much of a choice, do I? We don't give it to her and Bertram will say we refused to let her clear her name."

Byron knew the polygraph was a double-edged sword. The idea of catching people in lies sounded good on its face, but there was still the monumental problem of getting them to confess if they did fail the test. The inadmissibility of polygraph results meant obtaining a confession would be key. Unlike the desperadoes of stage and screen, the prospect of failing a polygraph never causes the real-life baddies to curl up in a fetal position and give up the goods.

Byron was heading out to find Mathers when he ran into Shirley Grant, the CID office assistant, in the hallway.

"Sergeant Byron," she said fixing him with a disapproving stare. "You haven't been checking your voicemail, have you?"

"Been a little busy, Shirley. What'd I miss?"

She held up her hands and began counting on her fingers. "Well, let's see — your wife called twice, wanting to speak with you. Said it was important."

It always is, he thought.

"And Davis Billingslea has been by twice and called three times about the body you had this morning."

Byron always did his best to avoid the *Portland Herald*'s young, overzealous police-beat reporter. Billingslea seemed to get his hands on information even before Byron himself. "You switched them all to my voicemail?"

"I did, and they're both upset because you haven't returned their calls."

"You're too good to me, Shirley. I promise I'll call them both back as soon as I have two seconds. Okay?"

"Okay," she said, not sounding the least bit convinced.

As he exited the stairwell out onto the plaza, Billingslea was lying in wait.

"Sergeant, you're a hard man to get a hold of," he said, positioning himself between

Byron and the parking garage.

"Davis. What can I do for you?"

"I wanna know about the hospice death you're investigating."

"Nothing to tell. An elderly hospice patient died. It happens all the time."

"Really? 'Cause the way I hear it, you brought a nurse in for questioning. There's a rumor the patient might have been put out of his misery."

"Davis, I don't know where you come up with this stuff, but you know I can't comment on an ongoing investigation."

"So there *is* an ongoing investigation. Can I quote you?"

"No."

A car horn blared from inside the police garage. They both looked up; it was Diane and she was waving frantically. She lowered the passenger window. "Sarge," she shouted, "we just got the call. Come on, we gotta go."

"What call?" Billingslea asked. "Where do you and Detective Joyner have to go?"

"Sorry, Davis."

"Come on, give me something."

"I gotta run," Byron said as he hurried up the steps to her car. "I'll catch up with you later."

"Is this connected to the death?" Billingslea hollered after him.

Byron climbed into Diane's car and closed the door as she put it in gear. "Thanks," he said.

"Don't mention it. Looked like you needed saving."

"The guy's friggin' relentless. How the fuck does he know so much about this case already?"

"Maybe he's psychic."

"More like someone's got a big mouth." Byron adjusted the sun visor. "I thought you were getting the records from the hospital."

"Won't be ready till tomorrow. Wanna bring me up to speed and tell me where we're headed?"

"Five-hundred block of Cumberland. Time to interview O'Halloran's other nurse, Frankie Mathers."

CHAPTER SIX

They scanned three dozen white buttons and the accompanying name tags on the intercom system. "Three F, Mathers," Diane said as she pushed the button.

"Y-ello," a male voice said from the speaker.

"Francis Mathers?" Byron asked.

"Frankie's my name. Who might you be?"

"Mr. Mathers, my name is Detective Sergeant Byron and I'm here with Detective Joyner from the police department. We'd like to come up and speak with you."

"What's this about?"

"It's about one of your hospice patients, James O'Halloran. May we come up?"

"Uh, okay, give me a second."

It took nearly a minute before Mathers finally buzzed them inside. They ascended the stairs to the third floor.

Diane rapped on the door and Mathers answered. The smell of burnt marijuana wafted out into the hallway.

Mathers looked nothing like Byron had imagined. Blocking most of the open doorway, dressed in cutoffs and a blue sleeveless V-neck, he stood about six feet tall and at least two hundred and fifty pounds. Mathers's physical appearance combined with the curly black hair and receding hairline reminded Byron of the *Full Metal Jacket* actor Vincent D'Onofrio. The resemblance was striking.

Byron made the introductions.

"Sergeants, was it? Or detectives?" Private Pile was obviously high. His bloodshot eyes and stoner's smile were a dead giveaway.

"Either is fine," Diane said. "Do you mind if we talk inside?"

"Of course I don't mind. Come on in, detectives and sergeants," he said.

They exchanged a knowing glance and followed him inside. The apartment was surprisingly clean and tidy, despite the strong smell of cannabis. Byron wondered if Le-Royer had been right after all; perhaps Pine Tree Hospice really was Happy Hospice. He also wondered whether or not Tim Caron, asshole extraordinaire, was aware of Nurse Mathers's little secret.

Mathers led them into the living room with its white furniture, white carpet and white walls. Any surface not white was either chrome or glass. He'd lit a scented candle, probably hoping it would mask the odor. It didn't. "Can I get either of you something to drink? Soda or coffee?"

Or maybe a hit off the bong, Byron thought. "I'm fine, thank you."

"How 'bout you?" he asked Diane.

"No, thanks," she said as she sat on the love seat.

Byron, wanting to take his host out of his comfort zone, opted for the Barcalounger, as it looked to be their host's normal relaxation spot. Mathers's sullen expression confirmed it, and he begrudgingly took the couch, the only remaining place to sit.

"So, detectives and sergeants, you said you had questions about Mr. H."

Byron thought about correcting him, but realized in Mathers's current state it was probably pointless.

"That's right," Byron said. "We were told you cared for him on Fridays, Saturdays, and Sundays."

"No, no," Mathers said exaggeratedly, shaking his head. Just Saturdays and Sundays."

His lucid answer confirmed he wasn't too stoned to talk with them.

"My mistake," Byron said.

"Yeah. Bummer, huh? Poor old dude was on the way out anyway, I guess. The big C."

"Big C, yeah," Diane said, her sarcasm evident. "Like you said, a real bummer."

"So when did he die?"

"We're still checking," Byron said. "How did he look to you yesterday? Any change in his condition?"

"I wouldn't know. I'm on days off. Didn't work yesterday or today."

Passed another test. "So Tuesday and Wednesday are your normal days off?"

"Yup, unless I have to cover for a vacationing nurse."

"How long have you worked for Pine Tree, Mr. Mathers?" Diane asked.

" 'Bout five years."

"You ever stop by and check in on your patients when you're not working, Mr. Mathers?" Byron asked.

"Against the rules. Mr. Caron, my boss, he wouldn't like it. Actually, Rebecca would probably go all ape shit too. Especially if she knew about giving him some ganja." Mathers stopped and stared wide-eyed like a cartoon, unable to believe the words he'd just uttered. Both detectives remained silent. "Dudes, I can't believe I just said that. I'm one dumb fuck. I know you're, uh, cops, but I'll get fired if you say anything. *Shit.*"

"You gave your patient marijuana?" Diane asked.

"You a doctor?" Byron asked.

"It's not like — It's medical, ya know."

"It's called furnishing, genius," Byron said.

"I told him it might make his pain go away."

"Did it?" Diane asked.

"Not sure. Maybe."

"Were you trying to put him out of his misery?" Byron asked.

"Yeah. No. Wait. That's not what I meant. You're both F-ing with my head, man. Like I don't believe in that shit."

"What shit?" Byron asked.

"Killing."

"Does Rebecca?" Diane asked.

"I don't know. I don't think so. But, you're okay about the weed, right? I can't lose this job."

A little late for that epiphany, Byron thought. The cannabis probably had made O'Halloran feel better. There were worse things Mathers could have done for a dying man, but that was a doctor's call to make. "We're not here about the weed, Francis."

"Oh, good," he said, exhaling loudly. "Can't afford to get fired, man. Thanks."

Of course, it didn't mean they wouldn't be reporting it later. "Did O'Halloran ever have weekend visitors?" Byron asked.

Mathers closed one eye and looked up at the ceiling with the other as he tried to concentrate, making him look cartoonish once again. "Maybe a couple of times. Friends, I think."

"Male or female?" Byron asked.

"Male."

"Can you describe any of them?" Diane asked.

He shook his head. "I don't pay particular attention to that stuff. We're not supposed to get involved in their private lives, or get too familiar."

"How many different men visited?" she asked.

"Maybe two? I can't really remember."

"Ethnic background? White, Black, Asian?" Byron asked, watching as Mathers scratched his neck.

"White, maybe. Sorry, I'm not sure."

"Would you recognize them if you saw them again?" Diane asked.

Mathers shook his head again.

"How many times did they come by?" Byron asked.

"Maybe once?"

"You're sure?"

"Pretty sure," Mathers said in a tone suggesting he wasn't.

"What about phone calls?" Diane asked.

He shook his head.

"So, no one ever called him while you were there?" Byron asked.

"Nope. Not while I was there. You sure you're cool about the weed thing?"

It was obvious Mathers didn't comprehend that a murder trumped a furnishing charge. "Is there anything else you can think of that might help us?" Byron asked.

"I told you guys everything."

"Where were you last night?" Diane asked.

"Chillaxin' right here."

"All night?" she asked.

"Yup."

"Alone?" Byron asked.

"Nope, I was with my girlfriend, Sunny."

"We're gonna need Sunny's address and phone number," Diane said, handing him a notepad and pen.

"What do you think?" Byron asked as they walked down the sidewalk to her car.

"I think I wanna know how in hell the big Lebowski ever got a nursing license?"

"Maybe hospice nursing isn't as strict," he said. "I mean, their patients are already dying."

"I hope you're kidding," she said as they both climbed into the car. "Where to?"

"Let's grab something to eat. I'm famished."

"What do you feel like?"

"You're driving."

"Thai it is."

Byron made a quick call to Pelligrosso. "How did you make out?"

"I lifted a bunch of prints. Won't know if I've got anything good until I can check them against the elimination prints we've taken. Do you want me to start on those?"

Byron checked his watch. "Mel's in, right?"

"Yeah, she's on until midnight."

"Why don't you go home, hug your wife and kid, and get a good night's sleep. Have Mel start working on the eliminations tonight and we'll get back at it first thing in the morning."

"You sure?"

He knew they'd done about all they could to this point. O'Halloran's murder certainly didn't look much like a whodunit, and they did have St. John scheduled to poly in the morning. "See you tomorrow, Gabe."

"Thanks, Sarge."

Byron and Diane were seated at a table in

the back of the restaurant. Eastern Thai was located at the top of Munjoy Hill, Byron's childhood stomping grounds.

"Bet you came here all the time when you were growing up," she said.

He smiled and shook his head. "Not many Thai restaurants around in those days."

"Too bad. New York was full of them."

"It used to be a butcher shop."

"Really?"

"Yeah. When I was a kid, we had steak once a week. My dad would always bring me down here to pick out the cut."

"That's a pretty cool memory. You must have all sorts, growing up here."

Byron was only half listening. His mind entranced in the vivid childhood memory.

"Penny for your thoughts," she said, twirling some noodles onto her fork.

"Sorry. I was just remembering how good that steak smelled on the barbecue."

"I'll bet."

"That and I keep thinking back to something Ellis said this afternoon."

"Which was?"

"Well, I still like one of the nurses for this, but we do have at least two unidentified males who might have been paying visits to O'Halloran."

"And? You're thinking what? An old

friend?"

"Maybe."

"So what *did* Ellis say?"

"He said it felt like something an amateur would do. He told us if *he* wanted to kill O'Halloran, he would have administered an overdose or injected air into the IV in order to cause an embolism. Something along those lines."

"Comforting thought," she said, ditching the straw in her gin and tonic and lifting the glass to her lips.

"He said anyone with medical experience wouldn't risk leaving the evidence associated with suffocation. Yet we found bruising on the inside of the lips, petechia, even the down feathers he inhaled. I think he may be right. The whole thing feels amateurish."

"Like a family member or old friend," she said, nodding.

"Except his family isn't close. I spoke with his daughter and she sounds like she'd rather he went on suffering."

"Okay, so that leaves old friend."

"Or a nurse wily enough to make it look amateurish."

"Which would certainly rule out Mathers."

It was nearly eight by the time Diane

dropped Byron off at 109 to retrieve his car. He stopped by his office long enough to retrieve the Pine Tree Hospice personnel files on both nurses before driving to his Danforth Street apartment.

He stripped off his jacket and tie, poured himself a tall nightcap, and lay on the couch as close as he could get to the squealing air-conditioner. It was annoying as hell, but the cool air made the small apartment at least bearable.

He wrote a summary of the day's activities on a yellow legal pad. He'd get Shirley Grant to type it later. Some of what he wrote was from memory, the rest from the hieroglyphs he called notes. He finished his summary, then turned to the files. By all accounts both nurses seemed like model employees, except of course Mathers and his marijuana issue. According to their personnel records, neither had ever been reprimanded for anything, not even excessive use of sick time. Considering their line of work, Byron thought that was impressive.

He continued reading until his eyelids became heavy. It was after eleven by the time he finally returned Kay's call. Her cell went directly to voicemail. "Kay, it's John. Sorry I couldn't call sooner. I'm in the middle of a case."

How many times had he said those words to her? Did it now sound as hollow as it felt?

"I'll try you back tomorrow."

He almost said "love you" out of habit more than anything, but caught himself. Did he? Did he still love her? Did she still love him? They hadn't lived together for over nine months, hadn't had a meaningful conversation in six, and hadn't seen each other in at least a month. Whatever they had, it certainly couldn't be mistaken for a marriage. Not anymore.

Byron knew he bore most of responsibility for their separation. He couldn't really blame Kay for wanting some time alone. He was far from a model husband. Juggling the responsibilities of a marriage and the demanding life of a cop hadn't been easy.

Once this case is solved I'll sit down with Kay, he thought. I'll make a real effort this time. We'll even try counseling if she wants.

While contemplating the nature of their relationship, he drifted off to sleep.

CHAPTER SEVEN

Detective Vince Hayward was the official polygraph operator for the Portland Police Department. Although technically a detective, his primary responsibility was interviewing police candidates, both civilian and sworn. Occasionally, and to his great delight, he'd be given the green light to polygraph and interview a suspect in one of the other detectives' cases. Usually, if the case fell as far as Hayward's desk, it was either an outright whodunit or the lead detective was grasping at straws. For many in the bureau, the polygraph was nothing more than a desperate attempt to maintain their clearance rates; and in the land of detectives, nothing was more important than clearance rates. Nobody knew that better than Byron. Unsolved cases, specifically murders, were to a career like ink on a tie.

Byron had never had much use for polygraphs or, for that matter, for Hayward. But even he had to admit, they needed something. If St. John was offering to poly, why not let her? O'Halloran's relatives had all disowned him. During a second phone call, Susan said she'd have preferred it if the "old bastard" had gone on suffering. Not exactly a loving endorsement. None of the neighbors had seen anyone coming or going, aside from the nurses. Much like fighting for yards and a new set of downs on the gridiron — when you can't find what you seek, take what they'll give you. Byron couldn't remember where he'd heard that particular turn of phrase, but it had always stuck with him. He wasn't sure if a football analogy was the best way to describe working a tough murder case, but it was better than nothing.

Byron, Diane, and Nugent were seated in the conference room or, as Nugent referred to it, the "war room." They were briefing Hayward on the case in preparation for St. John's nine-thirty poly.

"I think I've got a pretty good handle on it," Hayward said. "All we need to do now is come up with the questions."

"Let's see if she knows where the Lindbergh baby is buried," Nugent said. Byron, who wasn't in the mood, shot him a disapproving glance.

"We only want to know if she did it, Vince," Diane said. "It's not complicated."

"I understand, but I need to design questions she can't dodge."

"Jesus, Vince," Nugent said. "What a crock of shit. Just ask her if she put the fucking pillow over O'Halloran's face and pressed down on it until he died. How's that design work for ya?"

"Works for me," Hayward said, swallowing nervously.

"Get her to confirm that she was home Tuesday night and not paying a visit to our victim," Diane said.

"How should I ask it?" Hayward asked.

"Ask any way you want," Byron said. "But don't screw this up."

The three detectives monitored the interview from LeRoyer's office, observing as Hayward covered the preliminary questions with St. John. Did you sleep last night? How many hours? Are you on any medication? Each question designed to evaluate her fitness to give accurate responses during the actual test.

"Jesus, his instructions are putting me to sleep," Nugent said. "I oughta have Vince come by my house tonight and fucking talk me to sleep. Ten bucks says it's inconclusive.

Who wants in?"

Byron hid a smile as LeRoyer looked up from his computer, annoyed. "Look, I told you guys, if you're gonna be in here you're gonna have to keep it down. I got work to do. And get your goddamned foot off my desk, Mike."

"Sorry, boss."

It was almost eleven by the time St. John was wired up to the polygraph and answering control questions. Roger Bertram, her attorney, was also in the room, seated right outside of the camera's view. Bertram had made sure he'd seen and approved the questions before they were asked.

"Are you currently in Portland, Maine?" Hayward asked.

"Yes," St. John answered.

"Is your name Rebecca St. John?"

"No."

Hayward continued through the initial battery of questions, asking her to tell the truth on some and lie on others. These simple control questions allowed him to calibrate the instrumentation to most accurately measure her physiological responses. The nurse looked calm and composed, sitting in the black leather chair.

Finally, Hayward began asking the questions they'd all been waiting for.

"Did you cause the death of James O'Halloran?" Hayward asked.

St. John shifted slightly in the chair. "No."

"Remember not to move, okay? Try and sit still."

"I'm sorry."

"Did you cause the death of James O'Halloran?"

"No."

Hayward questioned the nurse for twenty minutes before allowing her a break. He needed time to evaluate the printed charts and to consult with the others.

"So? Did she kill him?" Diane asked.

"She's not showing any deception," Hayward said, pointing to the charts resembling topographic mountain ranges.

"You're saying she didn't do it?" Byron asked.

"I'm saying she believes she's telling the truth when she says she didn't cause O'Halloran's death."

"It was the damned pillow, right?" Nugent said. "You missed your calling, Vince. You shoulda been a fuckin' lawyer."

"Give me the bottom line," Byron said to Hayward.

"I'd be looking at someone else."

Byron would've bet his paycheck the polygraph results would be inconclusive.

But now, assuming Hayward knew what he was talking about, and assuming St. John wasn't a sociopath, they needed to explore other possibilities. Mathers? Nurse Feel Good had already demonstrated no qualms about bending ethical boundaries when it suited him. But bending them and chopping them up into kindling were two entirely different things. Either way, it was time to pay another visit to Frankie Mathers, this time on Byron's turf.

Diane and Nugent headed to the hospital to pick up St. John's records. Byron left a message for Mathers to call him back regarding a follow-up interview. It took the nurse less than five minutes to return the call.

"I thought we were cool," Mathers said.

Cool? Is that what we are? "It's just follow-up, Frankie. We've been talking to Rebecca St. John as well."

"Yeah, I heard. Lie detector. No way am I taking one of those, man."

"I'm not asking you to. Right now all I want is for you to come down to the station and talk with me. Voluntarily."

"At the police station? Not too sure about that, man."

"I only want to talk, Frankie. But if you won't talk to me, I guess maybe I'll have to talk to Tim Caron instead." The other end of the line went silent for what seemed an eternity. Byron could picture Mathers squirming.

"I'll be there in half an hour."

Byron was reading over supplements from the O'Halloran case when his desk phone rang. "Byron."

"Sarge, it's Gabe. You have a sec?"

"Be right down."

He found Pelligrosso seated in front of the AFIS computer. AFIS, short for Automated Fingerprint Identification System, was a one-stop shop for computerized fingerprint indexing and comparison, maintained by the FBI. The benefit of AFIS was that it was a database containing millions of prints, greatly improving the odds of finding a match. The problem: it was a time consuming process. Crime scene prints had to be classified manually into types and converted into an electronic format before they could be uploaded and compared to those already in the database.

"What's up?" Byron asked.

"Remember you asked me to dust O'Halloran's bedroom for prints?"

He nodded.

"Well, I might have something. It's only a

partial, not good enough for a positive ID, but if we develop a suspect, I can at least rule them out or keep them in contention."

"It doesn't match anyone?"

"I took comparison prints from everyone who entered the room, including St. John and the MedCu attendants. This partial doesn't belong to any of them."

"What about the weekend-duty nurse, Mathers?"

"Don't have his prints yet."

"He's on his way in now. I'll call you when he gets here."

"Frankie, this is Officer Pelligrosso," Byron said as he led the nurse into the first-floor interview room and closed the door.

Mathers reached out to shake Pelligrosso's hand, then awkwardly pulled it back when the evidence tech made no effort to return the gesture.

"I've asked him to take your fingerprints, okay?" Byron continued.

"I thought you just wanted to talk, man? Why are you asking for my fingerprints? I haven't done anything."

"We've printed everyone who was known to have been inside O'Halloran's house, Frankie. We're trying to rule people out."

"I gotta tell ya, I'm not real comfortable

with this. You said we were only gonna talk."

Pelligrosso spoke up. "Mr. Mathers, I lifted fingerprints from everything in O'Halloran's room. These are elimination prints so we can rule you out."

Mathers's eyes narrowed with suspicion as he looked back and forth at both cops. "How do I know you're not trying to set me up?"

Byron tried a softer approach. "Frankie, you were caring for O'Halloran as part of your job. You were supposed to be there. We're looking for anyone who wasn't. You've got nothing to worry about if you didn't do anything wrong."

"Yeah, but you already know I did."

"Trust me, this isn't television. We're not trying to set you up."

Mathers glanced over at Pelligrosso. "What about the thing we talked about?"

"We're trying to solve a murder, Frankie," Byron said. "You really think I give a damn about a marijuana charge?"

Byron waited as Mathers thought it over; his distrust of the police was obvious. "Okay. Let's get this over with."

Pelligrosso obtained a full set of fingerprints from Mathers, handed him a short stack of paper towels to wipe the ink off his hands, then left the room.

"Take me through it again, Frankie," Byron said. "From the beginning."

After he had finished, Byron reapproached the subject of the polygraph.

"I told you it's not gonna happen."

"If you didn't kill him, you've got nothing to worry about."

"I got plenty to worry about. I'm no killer, but I'm no angel either."

"Will you at least think about it?"

Mathers continued scrubbing at the black ink stuck to his fingers. "Could I see the questions beforehand?"

"I'll have to check with the expert, but I think it can probably be arranged."

Byron escorted Mathers out of the building, then headed straight up to the lab. "Any luck with Mathers's prints."

"Found him in AFIS on a minor possession charge. Guess they don't screen nurses like they used to."

"There's a shocker. What about the partial? Tell me it's his?"

"No can do. Doesn't match. That print may be the glass slipper, Sarge."

"Okay, Gabe. I'll see if I can find you a Cinderella."

"Where are we at?" LeRoyer asked, looking rather frazzled seated behind his desk.

"Chief Stanton's breathing down my neck."

Byron deposited himself in one of the chairs across from the lieutenant. "In a word? Nowhere. The neighborhood canvass yielded dick. At the moment, both nurses seem in the clear. O'Halloran may have had a couple of male visitors who may have been white, but nobody can identify them or remember what they looked like. Pelligrosso lifted a partial print from the scene, that doesn't match anyone. It's not in the system and probably wouldn't hold up in court even if we could find a match. If this were New York City instead of Portland, Maine, you'd be calling this a misdemeanor homicide by now and telling me to move on."

"What about the nurse who gave O'Halloran the weed, Matthews?"

"It's Mathers, and he's a dumb-ass, more concerned about a furnishing charge and losing his job than anything else. He seems much too "love all, be all" to even think about a mercy killing. Frankly, he's not bright enough to have pulled this off anyway."

"You still think it's a mercy killing?"

"I don't know what to think. What I do know is we seem to have hit a dead end."

"Can we use the press?"

"Sure, if you don't mind the lawsuits that

will likely be filed by both nurses and Pine Tree Hospice."

LeRoyer sighed. "What *do* you suggest?"

"I don't know. Let me think on it."

As Byron entered the stairwell to the rear garage, he pulled out his phone and tried Kay's number again.

"Hello, you've reached Kay's cell. I'm either on the phone or with a client. Leave a message and I will return your call as soon as I'm able. Thanks and have a great day."

"Kay, it's John, again." He checked his watch. "It's about three o'clock. Call me."

He slipped the cell back into his pocket. Exactly what the last few years of marriage had been like, he thought. Never-ending games of phone tag, Kay working late while he either got called in nightly or never made it home. Was it any wonder they were apart?

No sooner had he stepped out onto the plaza when his cell rang.

"Byron," he answered.

"Ah, the illustrious Detective Sergeant John Byron. Greetings from Augusta, Maine. Second home of the world famous and brilliant pathologist Dr. E," Ellis said.

"Hey, Doc. Give me something, anything."

"Alas, I cannot."

"Toxicology?"

Byron's cell began to vibrate with an incoming call. He looked quickly at the number. Kay.

"John, you still with me?" Ellis asked.

"Yeah, sorry about that," he said as he started his car and pulled out of the garage. "I got another call coming in."

"Call me back if you need to take it."

"No, it's okay. Go ahead. You were about to give me the results of the tox screen."

"Indeed, I was. We found four different drugs in his system: morphine, doxepin, gly-copyrrolate and prednisone. All are commonly used to treat dying cancer patients and their symptoms. The levels were also consistent with the norm if you factor in his body weight."

"What about his doctor?"

"You mean the vacationing Dr. Edward Rosenstein? I made contact with him and he confirmed all of the administered meds, their dosage and frequency."

"Thanks, Doc."

"Always a pleasure."

Byron ended the call with Ellis and checked voicemail. No messages. He redialed Kay's number. After several rings, it went to her voicemail again. He hung up without leaving another message. Wishing he'd taken Ellis up on his offer, he continued toward Bartley Avenue.

Retired Detective Ray Humphrey, one of Byron's oldest and dearest friends, had always said: "If you find your train derailing during the course of an investigation, the best thing you can do is go back to the beginning." Humphrey had been his mentor both when Byron first started on the job and again after he made detective. And in a promotional twist of fate, Humphrey had even worked for Byron as a detective during his last few years on the job.

Byron parked his Taurus across the street from O'Halloran's and got out. He used a spare key to unlock the evidence padlock Pelligrosso had installed on the outside of the side-entry door, and stepped inside.

In spite of the day's bright sunshine, the interior of the house was dark, gloomy, and empty, no longer bustling with activity as it had been only thirty-two hours prior. He walked to the center of the kitchen and stood, making a slow three-sixty, taking in everything he saw, checking for anything they might've missed. The ringing of his cell shattered the silence and gave him a start. He looked at the ID. Diane.

"Hey, partner," he said.

"Hey, yourself. You off sleuthing without me again?"

"Busted."

"You're so predictable. I knew exactly where you'd be. Want another set of eyes?"

He walked into the living room and looked through the front window. Diane was leaning against her car, parked directly behind his. "Come on in."

"Any idea what we're looking for?" Diane asked as she stepped into the kitchen and closed the door.

"Nope. How did you make out with St. John's hospital records?"

"Nothing to indicate she was capable of killing her patients. Highly rated employee is the standard jargon on her monthly performance reports."

"You?" Byron asked. "Any luck with Frankie's girlfriend?"

"Sunny Day?"

Byron turned and made eye contact. "You're kidding?"

"Nope, Sunny Day. And she alibied Nurse Mathers."

"Of course she did. So here we are back at square one."

"Okay, talk me through the case again," she said.

They both knew the trick. Detailing the facts of a case out loud to another person added a fresh perspective. Occasionally, something previously overlooked would become apparent.

Byron summarized everything they knew. "Elderly male dying of cancer, lives alone. Family disowns him. He's former military and former cop. Doctor says they can't do anymore for him at the hospital so they send him home. He receives in-home hospice care from a reputable local company. Only two nurses have contact with him. The home is never locked. He may have had a couple of unidentified male visitors during his remaining weeks. Who are we looking for?"

"Family members?" she asked, already knowing the answer.

"Very doubtful. He burned a lot of bridges. And I had Tran check, none are local."

"Friends. Ex-military buddies or cops."

"Good. Where?"

"Address book, fridge notes, or business cards. Something along those lines."

"See, you're not just a pretty face."

Diane smiled. "Damn straight. I'm a lot more than that."

They searched methodically through drawers, cabinets, and tabletops in each room. Diane located a handful of business cards in O'Halloran's top bureau drawer.

The refrigerator yielded a lawn care rep, an oil burner serviceman, and garage mechanic. Byron found a tattered address book inside a desk drawer in O'Halloran's study.

"Hey, look at this," Diane said, holding up a framed photograph. "Looks like an old PPD team photo."

"It's the old SRT," Byron said, referring to Special Reaction Team, PPD's version of a SWAT team.

"How do you know that?"

"That's my dad," he said, pointing to one of the men in the photo.

On the way back to 109, Byron got a call from Tran.

"Sarge, I just heard from the Transportation Security Administration. If Susan Atherton made any recent trips to Maine it must have been by car."

"No record of any flights?"

"Negative, *mon capitaine.* Not for the past two years. Last trip she took was to Phoenix — about as far from Maine as you can get."

"Thanks, Dustin."

"I'm here to serve. Over and out."

Byron hung up and slid the phone into his jacket pocket.

"Well, Lieutenant O'Halloran, if not your

daughter, who *were* you getting visits from?"

CHAPTER EIGHT

The Charles J. Loring AMVETS Post, chartered in 1955, is located on the in-town side of Interstate 295 on Washington Avenue in Portland. Post 25, as it's known to the senior members of the club, is an odd-shaped structure built into the side of a hill that slopes sharply away from the street toward Kennedy Park. The only exception to its flat roof is the peak protruding from the right side where a lighted AMVETS sign is attached to clapboard siding. Two steel doors bookend a long windowless brick-and-mortar façade, separated from the paved road by only a sidewalk.

It was getting late and Cleophus Riordan, or "Cleo" as he was known to his friends, had long since lost track of exactly how many Bacardi-and-Cokes he'd consumed. It was a typical Sunday for Riordan. He always arrived around four in the afternoon, parked his tan Buick in the dirt parking lot across the street, sat at his usual table in the corner, told stories to anyone who would listen, cursed the news on television, and got drunk.

On this particular Sunday night, Riordan had been drinking and telling war stories to an old friend who had strangely shown up that evening.

"Pretty friggin' weird running into you like this, Hawk," Riordan said with a pronounced slur. "Hadn't thought about you in years."

Hawk smiled, but there was no humor in his eyes. From the corner of his eye he watched as Ralph Polowski, the on-duty bartender, walked over toward their table while wiping his hands on the filthy white apron he wore.

"Hey, Ralph," Riordan said. "I got one for ya. How does a Muslim like his pie?"

"I give. How?"

"Allah mode," Riordan said with a cackle. "You get it?"

"Yeah, I get it," Polowski said. "Okay, you two, it's eleven-thirty, time to call it a night."

"Aw, come on Ralphie. Just one more for me and my friend?"

"No, Cleo. I think you've had more than enough for tonight," Polowski said as he laid the handwritten bill on the table.

"See what I mean?" Cleo told Hawk. "Zero respect anymore."

Hawk waited as Riordan awkwardly pushed himself up and out of the chair and began fishing for his wallet.

"I got this," Hawk said, handing four twenties to Polowski.

"Like I said, you're A-OK. Now, I gotta take a piss," Riordan announced to the empty room.

Hawk watched Riordan stagger toward the bathroom and out of sight. Hawk bid good night to Polowski, then turned and headed for the door.

Hawk was standing outside next to the building waiting when Riordan stepped out onto the sidewalk, pausing to light a cigarette. The nighttime air still felt warm and humid. Hawk was watching Riordan dig into his pocket for his keys, wondering how long it would take the old drunk to notice him, when Riordan looked over.

"Hey, Hawk," Riordan said excitedly. "I've got a brand-new bottle at home that needs to be drunk." He laughed at his own bad joke until the laughter tailed off into a series of raspy coughs.

"I don't know, Cleo, it's getting kinda late."

"Nonsense, it's still early. Whatdaya say? That bottle ain't gonna drink itself, ya know."

Hawk pretended to mull it over. "Okay, but I'm driving."

"Done and done. Let's take my car," Riordan said, tossing him the keys.

"Be just as easy to take mine," Hawk said, catching them easily.

"My bottle, my car."

"You're the boss," Hawk said.

The two men walked across the street, although in Riordan's case it was more of an unsteady shuffle, and got into Riordan's LeSabre. Hawk pulled out of the lot and onto Washington Avenue. A faded bumper sticker affixed to the rear bumper read: "Drink Responsibly."

It was nearly one-thirty in the morning. Both men had been drinking at the kitchen table since they'd arrived. Hawk kept getting up to mix their drinks at the counter while Riordan regaled him with stories. Hawk had been giving Riordan nearly pure alcohol while his own glass was mainly soda.

Riordan, well past the point of constructing anything resembling an articulate sentence, was barely able to hold his head up. He didn't seem to notice that the alcohol wasn't affecting Hawk.

The sidearm Riordan had carried while fighting in Vietnam lay on the table next to his glass. "Home protection," he called it. Hawk imagined the old man probably showed it off to anyone who cared to see it, and even a few who didn't.

Hawk studied Riordan as they sat at the table. His eyes were glassy and the road map on his nose told a tale of years of self-abuse. Riordan exhibited the thousand-yard stare only an experienced alcoholic can master.

"Fuckin'-A right!" Riordan announced to no one in particular, before taking another drink.

Realizing that Riordan was close to passing out, and not wanting him to spoil the plan, Hawk excused himself, then headed for the bathroom.

He returned to the kitchen several minutes later, dressed from head to toe in a white Tyvek suit, complete with boots, gloves, and a hood.

"Hey, now, what in the hell are you up to?" Riordan croaked before he was once again overcome by a fit of laughter that gradually morphed into a body-racking cough.

"Just righting a wrong, old man. Righting a wrong."

Hawk snatched the handgun from the table, pressed it against Riordan's temple, and pulled the trigger.

CHAPTER NINE

LeRoyer had been hounding Byron about going down to the firing range all morning. "I know you're working a case. I get it, okay? But Cross has been riding my ass about having the bureau qualify on time, for once. That's how it works, John. He rides my ass and I ride yours."

"Well, there's a picture I'm gonna need therapy to get over," Byron said. "You missed your calling, Lieu. You should've been a writer of porn."

"Gay porn," Diane added.

LeRoyer gave her a disapproving scowl. "Watch yourself, Detective. Look, I'm begging the both of you. Get your asses down there. Now!"

"Well, if you're gonna get all sentimental about it, okay," Byron said.

Sergeant Gary "Cowboy" Mullins was the PD's senior range officer and armorer. Everyone called him Cowboy on account of the thick white handlebar mustache he sported. Too old to effectively work a beat, he was still one of the best sharpshooters on the department. Mullins had instructed Byron during his academy days, when the state's basic police school was still located in the Central Maine town of Waterville.

"Well, as I live and breathe," Mullins said.

"Morning, Cowboy," they said in unison.

"Didn't expect you two till sometime after Christmas."

"We like to keep you on your toes," Diane said.

"And I suspect you could, young lady," Cowboy said with a wink. "You know the drill, empty your mags on the table and unload your guns down range. Grab some eye and ear protection and I'll go hang your targets."

"Thanks, Cowboy," Byron said.

"I aim to please," he said over his shoulder as he walked down to the far end of the range. "Hey, you guys know why there'll never be a range officer named Will?"

Byron and Diane glanced at each other. They'd both heard him tell the joke countless times but neither wanted to burst his bubble. "Why?" Byron hollered down range.

"Ready on the right, ready on the left, fire at Will." Mullins chuckled.

Byron was unloading his magazines when he noticed his hands were shaking. He clenched his fists to try and stop it.

"That happen very often?" Diane asked in a whisper.

He heard the concern in her voice. "Every once in a while. Nothing I can't handle."

She frowned and placed her hands on her hips.

"Really, I'm fine."

Mullins returned. "Jesus, John. When you gonna lose that forty-five caliber dinosaur and get a nine like the young'uns?"

"Can't teach an old dog, I guess."

"Ain't it the truth?"

Mullins ran them through the qualification drills simultaneously, starting at fifty feet and working toward the targets until they'd each exhausted their fifty rounds.

"Okay, let's see how we did," Mullins said. "John, you scored eighty-four percent and Diane, I've got you at ninety. You're both clear to carry."

"God, I'm so relieved," Diane said, holding a hand up to her chest for effect.

"There's cleaning supplies in the next room if you want to take care of it here," Mullins said.

"Thanks, Cowboy," Byron said. "But I've got a funeral to attend. You coming?" he asked Diane.

"I'm gonna give my gun a quick once over. Besides, I've got to catch up on some paperwork."

"Suit yourself."

After Byron left the firing range, Mullins turned to Diane. "You know you're not doing him any favors."

"I don't know what you mean," she said, raising her eyebrows.

Mullins crossed his arms and stood facing her. "Young lady, Byron carries a Glock 30 and you carry a 26. You think I can't tell the difference between a hole made by a forty-five and one made by a nine? I could go and study them if you'd like, but my guess is you gave John the five rounds you missed. I know you, Detective. You almost never miss. Why are you helping him?"

"Because, he's my partner." Diane quickly reassembled and loaded her gun, then headed for the door.

"I hope you don't live to regret that decision," he said.

She stopped at the door and looked back. "Don't worry about me, Cowboy."

"Not you I'm worried about."

It was a couple of minutes after eleven

Tuesday morning and Byron stood in dress uniform at the sparsely attended graveside service of former Lieutenant James O'Halloran. The sky was overcast and the air was still thick with summerlike humidity. He counted maybe a dozen current Portland officers and half as many retirees. Only half listening to the familiar words of the priest as they drifted by on a warm breeze, his thoughts were occupied by other things, not the least of which were the murder and why Kay wasn't returning his calls. She'd obviously wanted something, so why not leave a message saying what it was? He didn't have time for a prolonged game of phone tag.

"A warrior for peace, both here and abroad," the priest said. "James O'Halloran answered the call. Serving his country overseas, then returning stateside where he defended the peace."

Byron had attended many police funerals during the course of his career, but he'd never quite been able to stomach them. Truth was he hated going. It wasn't that he didn't want to show respect for a fallen officer or to honor their service to the community, because he did. His disdain for these funerals went much deeper. Dark thoughts of his own mortality and of those he worked with and cared about would inevitably come creeping in, thoughts he could do without. Memories of his Irish Catholic upbringing intertwined with his father's suicide, the one event that most clearly marked the end of his faith, left behind only anger and distrust for all religion.

Byron had been seventeen years old the day his father committed suicide. It was a warm sunny afternoon, and he had grabbed his bike and peddled over to pop in on old dad. His parents had already split by then. He knew his father would be at home, it was his day off. Byron grabbed his father's uncollected mail from the box out front, then entered the apartment. He yelled out a greeting but got no response. Worried that his father might either be in the midst of an afternoon tryst or drunk, he quietly searched each room. He found his father slumped over the dining room table, his revolver was lying on the floor. The image never left him.

"The Lord is my shepherd," the priest continued.

Byron tried to refocus on the murder. The weekend had been largely uneventful, save for two more pharmacy robberies and Frankie Mathers's decision not to submit to a polygraph test, effectively closing the door on his cooperation in the O'Halloran case. Byron didn't really believe the simpleton stoner was up to the task of a mercy killing anyway, but it might have been nice to put that theory to the test seeing as how St. John had already done her part. Mathers felt like unfinished business and Byron despised anything left undone.

"Surely, goodness and mercy shall follow me . . ."

Byron didn't know about anyone's cup running over, but he was pretty sure he could relate to walking in the valley of the shadow of death. It was after all, his job.

The priest passed along the traditional invite to the home of one of the other retirees for fellowship and refreshment. Byron knew the obligatory post-party was really an excuse to tell war stories, and refreshment meant getting drunk — and while he was never totally averse to the latter, today he wasn't in the mood for either. He walked alone through the cemetery to his car, then drove to the Public Works garage to get the Taurus's air-conditioner recharged.

He was standing in the CID locker room changing out of his sweaty dress uniform and into a wrinkled but dry suit and tie when his phone, still on silent from the service, began to vibrate. He looked at the caller ID. It was dispatch.

"Byron," he answered.

"Hey, handsome, it's Mary."

Police Dispatcher Mary O'Connell was a sweetheart of a lady. She'd been with the department far longer than Byron. Aside from Humphrey, O'Connell was probably the closest thing to family he had. She had taken him under her wing dating back to his first day on the job. When he was a rookie cop, still wet behind the ears and still two years from having earned the respect afforded the officers who'd already completed their probationary period. On more than one occasion, Byron had ended up in the emergency room while O'Connell was working the board. Barroom brawls, motor vehicle accidents, or trying to take a crazed suspect into custody. Each time, after learning O'Connell was beside herself with worry, Byron would stop by dispatch to see her before he went off duty.

"Hey, Mare, what's up?"

"Didn't know if you were tied up at the reception or not. I can call one of your detectives if you'd rather."

"No, I'm available, just changing."

"I'd pay to see that," she said in her deepest, sexiest voice.

Byron laughed.

"Well, since you're available I've got patrol units out at a possible suicide. They're requesting CID."

He copied down the address and asked her to contact Pelligrosso and Joyner.

"Gabe's already on scene and Diane's en route with Nugent. Let me know if you need anything else when you get there, Sarge. I'm on till six."

"Thanks, Mare."

It was one-twenty by the time Byron pulled up in front of the Osgood Street address. The short dead-end street in the Libby Town section of Portland was only a stone's throw from the Westgate Shopping Center. The home, a small gray-shingled Cape, was in serious disrepair. Several faded red shutters had fallen off and were now sitting among the weeds up against the house. Peeling paint gave the siding a distinct brindle-like appearance. The evidence van was parked in the driveway, two unmarks and a black-and-white lined the street in front.

Byron was very aware of unseen eyes peering out from neighbors' windows. They were always there. Others, far less subtle, stood gawking in a small cluster, down the street, hoping to get a good look at whatever had happened. In the great train wreck of life, some folks couldn't get their fill of tragedy.

Officer Sean Haggerty appeared as Byron pried himself from the car. Built like a linebacker, Hags would've been handy to have as a partner during Byron's early years on the beat. If Hags had been at his side, he likely wouldn't have come out on the losing end of so many fights.

"Afternoon, Sarge. We've got to stop meeting like this. People are beginning to talk."

"What do we have?"

"Looks like the homeowner killed himself in the kitchen. Handgun. A real mess."

"Who called it in?"

"Victim's daughter." He looked down at his notepad. "Amy Rubio. Says she came by to visit and found him."

Byron ran the surname through the memory bank in his head but came up empty. "How'd she get in?"

"Key."

"Victim married?"

"Divorced."

"Where's the daughter now?"

"Down the street at a neighbor's," he said, pointing. "She's pretty shaken up. Both

Detective Joyner and the victim advocate are with her."

"Good. Let's make sure she doesn't come back here." He knew her statement might have to wait. "Pelligrosso inside?"

"Pelligrosso and Detective Nugent."

"Who else has been in there?"

He checked the log. "Other than the one MedCu attendant and me, only your folks."

More people than he would have liked, but he'd had to contend with worse. Too often his scenes were trampled by firefighters and paramedics alike. People who only wanted to see the body. CID was fond of referring to the EMS folks as the "Evidence Eradication Unit."

"I want supplements from everyone."

"Already on it. Working on mine. Vickers, the paramedic, told me he'd call when his is ready. Holler if you need anything else. I'll be out here writing."

"Thanks, Hags."

The home's front door was standing open, and Byron walked toward it, taking care to watch where he stepped. Evidence can exist anywhere. He visually inspected the doorframe, as he always did, checking for any signs of forced entry. The casing was intact.

"Gabe, you back there?" he hollered.

"In the kitchen, Sarge."

"Okay to walk in?"

"Yes. I left a box of Tyvek booties inside the front door on the living room floor. You're gonna want them. Hold up when you get to the kitchen doorway."

"Okay."

Byron slipped on the foot protection along with a pair of rubber gloves from his back pocket, deliberately making his way through the living room, careful not to disturb anything as he went. He knew Pelligrosso would've already photographed every room in detail, prior to working the scene where the body was located, but protocol was everything, especially at a suspicious death scene. And suicides by their very nature were suspicious deaths, each one a potential crime. He'd taken more than one officer aside at a crime scene to lecture them on the importance of leaving everything exactly as they'd found it. "There are no mulligans in evidence collection," he'd tell them. What he wouldn't do was tell them twice.

Pelligrosso was busy photographing the kitchen. The victim was seated in a wooden ladder-back. His head was flopped over the back of the chair, like a broken Pez dispenser. The man looked as though he'd simply passed out in the chair, were it not for the blood spatter on everything. In addition to the spatter, there were pieces of skull and brain matter clinging to the cupboard doors, counter, and wall to the victim's left. His arms hung by his sides, nearly touching the floor. A semiautomatic handgun lay on the once-white linoleum beneath his right hand.

Byron noted none of the usual signs of decomposition, and that the larger pools of blood were still reflective, suggesting that the event had probably occurred within the last day or so.

On the table stood a half-empty bottle of Bacardi and a single drinking glass, containing a small amount of liquid, which two houseflies were busy surveying from the rim. Aside from the carnage and the corpse, the kitchen was unremarkable. The scene was typical of a bachelor of advancing years who had opted out of this world, by his own design, rather than waiting to see what the Almighty had in store. Byron had witnessed this ending before.

"What can you tell me so far?" Byron asked.

"Entry wound at the right temple complete with contact burn. Bullet exited out the left side of his skull. I might've found a bullet hole in the wall, above the counter, hard to tell until I remove some Sheetrock."

"What kind of semiauto is that?"

"Browning Hi Power, nine millimeter. I found a spent casing over in the corner by the door. Haven't checked the gun yet. I want to see if there's any other rounds left in it."

"Did we find anything resembling a note?" Byron asked.

"Nothing yet. Nuge is going through the other rooms."

"How about the M.E.?"

"Still waiting on the call."

Byron noticed several window screens were open. "Were the screens like this when you got here, Gabe?

"Nope, that was me, Sarge. Had a few too many flies in here. Figured I'd let them out before they screwed up my pictures. Can I make a suggestion?"

"Go ahead."

"I could use some help with this, if you don't mind."

"Sure, I'll call in one of the new E.T.s."

"Actually, I was hoping for someone more experienced, like Mel. This spatter thing is still new to me."

Byron knew what he was referring to. The lab had been decimated by two retirements in the past year. The replacements were good officers but still new at evidence collection. Detective Melissa Stevens had worked in the lab for years before moving upstairs to CID. She was to blood spatter analysis what Pelligrosso was to fingerprints. On more than one occasion, Byron had been confused by what looked like conflicting physical evidence at a scene only to have Stevens recreate the event to perfection in the lab.

"I'll get her out here." Byron pulled out his notebook as Nugent came in from another room. "Hey, Mike, we get a name yet?"

"Yup, found an ID in the bedroom." Nugent read from his notepad. "Cleophus Riordan."

Byron stopped in mid scribble. "Cleo?"

"Name ring a bell?"

Byron remembered Riordan had a daughter named Amy. Rubio must have been her married name.

"Sarge? You know him?" Nugent asked again.

"Sergeant Cleophus Riordan worked for the fucking department too." When Byron's father Reece was still alive.

"That would explain the pictures I saw," Nugent said.

"What pictures?"

"In the den," Nugent said. "There's pictures of this guy in Vietnam. Army."

"Which would explain the Browning," Pelligrosso said.

"How so?" Byron asked.

"Army Special Forces, the Browning nine was standard issue in Vietnam."

"I also found an old Portland Police SRT photo," Nugent said.

Byron entered the den. Hanging on the wall above a cluttered desk was the very same framed black-and-white print of Portland's SRT displayed in the Byron home when he was a boy. The same one Diane found at O'Halloran's. Byron lifted the picture off of its hanger and held it in his hands. He ran his hand over the glass, removing a thin layer of dust. Ten members of the SRT, four kneeling in front and six standing in the rear, among them were Riordan, Reece Byron, and, standing in the center of the frame, Lieutenant James O'Halloran. Each of the men were dressed in dark-colored fatigues, several holding rifles; and, with the exception of O'Halloran, they were each sporting a mustache. Byron recalled how his mother had disapproved of Reece's facial hair. It wasn't the only thing she'd disapproved of when it came to his father.

Byron pulled out his cell and called Le-Royer.

"Lieu, it's John."

"Dispatch told me you're out at a 10–63. I thought you'd be at O'Halloran's reception by now?"

"Not really in the mood for either."

"I'm almost afraid to ask. What does that mean?"

"It means we just lost another retired Portland cop. Cleo Riordan."

"Jesus. How?"

"Handgun."

"We sure it's a suicide?"

"At this point, I'm not sure of anything. I've got Pelligrosso and Nugent here, and I'm bringing Stevens in to give them a hand."

"You want me out there?"

Byron knew LeRoyer was only trying to be helpful, and they both knew there was little he would've been able to offer at the scene. "No, I've got this covered. You can do me a favor, though."

"Name it."

"I need a heads-up in case the press gets wind of this."

"I'll downplay anything and let you know."

He disconnected the call and pressed the speed dial for Stevens.

■ ■ ■ ■

Davis Billingslea stared into the lunchroom fridge. There was something unappealing about leftover pizza in a Ziploc®. No matter that the slices contained therein were his favorite Otto's Pizzeria offering, mashed potato. The clear plastic had already taken on a slight opacity due to the moisture forming on the inside of the bag. He scanned the other shelves, his eyes stopping on a blue container.

Shit, he thought. Last week's lasagna. I'd forgotten all about that.

"Hey, Billingslea," Will Draper said.

He turned to face his assistant editor. "Yeah, Will."

"You finished at court?"

"Just got back. Not much happening over there. Thinking about lunch."

"Well, think about it on the way to Osgood Street. The PD's got something on. They've sent a couple of detectives and the crime scene van out there."

"Any idea what?"

"If I did, wouldn't need you, would I?"

Byron had walked down the street to speak with Rubio. He was standing on the front walkway as Diane stepped outside to meet him.

"How is she?" he asked.

"Not too good at the moment," Diane said. "Pretty shaken up after seeing her dad like this. Did you know he was on the job in Portland?"

"Yes."

"Coincidence?"

"I sure as hell hope so. Advocate still in there?"

"Yup. You want to speak with Rubio?"

"Yes, but I'd prefer to do it alone."

"I'll get the advocate out of there so you can." Diane led him inside to the home's kitchen. He couldn't help but think of the irony.

"Mrs. Rubio, this is Detective Sergeant John Byron."

"I'm very sorry for your loss, Mrs. Rubio," Byron said.

Rubio looked up through grieving eyes, reaching out instinctively to shake his hand. "Thank you, Sergeant."

Byron nodded to Diane and waited as she led the advocate out of the room. "Mrs. Rubio, I need to ask you a few questions."

"Do we have to do this right now?"

"It's important."

She sighed. "All right. What do you want

to know?"

"When did you see your father last?"

"Last Tuesday, at his house. But I spoke with him by phone on Friday."

"Did he seem depressed?"

"No. And he wasn't taking any pills either. Cleo . . . How do I say this? He self-medicated."

Byron could certainly relate. "Alcohol?"

"Yes. For as long as I can remember."

"Divorced?"

"Five years."

"Your mother?"

"Remarried. She lives in Connecticut."

"How did you happen to stop by today?"

"I make it a point to visit him at least once a week. Or I did."

Realizing she wouldn't be attending to him anymore, she started to cry. Byron waited for her wave of grief to pass. He was familiar with the various stages of grieving. It was a lot like suffering from a serious illness, sometimes the pain was bearable, but at other times it left the griever unable to function.

She slowly pulled herself together. "I'm sorry, Detective. What were we talking about?"

"You said you visited him weekly."

"Yes. I tried to make sure he ate healthy

and that he was getting more into him than just booze."

"I didn't notice a car in the yard. He didn't drive?"

"No, he drove. Sometimes when he shouldn't. He was a regular at the AMVETS, the one near the highway on Washington Avenue. Most likely you'll find his Buick parked up there."

Byron made a note to check with the AMVETS about whether they might have called him a cab or if he'd gotten someone to drive him home. "Was he up there every night?"

"Not every night. But he was up there a lot. I can't believe he's gone." She broke down again and began to cry, loudly enough that Diane poked her head around the corner. Byron gave her a nod and rose from his chair. He placed his hand gently on her back as Diane and the advocate returned. "I'm so sorry, Mrs. Rubio."

Diane followed him outside. "Was she any help?"

"A little. I'm gonna follow up with the AMVETS, where he was a regular. Think you can try and get her written statement?"

"I'll take care of it."

Byron returned to the scene. The black livery-service hearse was parked in the driveway, its rear door stood open like something waiting to be fed. He saw Haggerty talking with someone on the street in front of the home. Billingslea.

"Hey, Sergeant," Billingslea said. "You have a minute?"

"Not for you," Byron said. "Hags, give us a hand inside."

"You got it," Haggerty said.

"Beat it, Davis," Byron said.

"You have a lot of help out here, Sergeant," Billingslea said. "Must be something suspicious about this death, right?"

Byron stopped walking and turned to face the young reporter. "Davis, I get that you have a job to do. But you being in the way just makes my job harder. *Capisce?*"

"Well, if you won't tell me what is going on, maybe I can find a family member to speak to."

Byron felt the muscles in his jaw tighten as he stepped into Billingslea's personal space. "Listen, you little shit. You'll do no such thing. This guy's daughter is upset enough without you sticking your nose in. Leave it alone."

"Yeah, Davis," Haggerty added. "Have a little respect, huh? The guy was a cop for chrissakes."

"Another dead cop, Sergeant?" Billingslea said.

Byron glanced over a Haggerty. "Hags, why don't you head in. I'll meet you there."

Haggerty turned and walked toward the house.

Byron turned back to Billingslea, leaning in until their noses nearly touched. "I'm warning you, Davis. You either get the fuck out of here on your own, or I'll help you."

Byron stood his ground until Billingslea backed away and began walking toward his car.

"The public has a right to know, Sergeant," Billingslea called out over his shoulder. "Maybe I'll just see what your lieutenant has to say about this."

"Yeah, you do that," Byron said under his breath, already knowing whose side LeRoyer would take.

He walked up to the house, slipped into clean booties, and headed inside. Riordan's remains, already zipped into a body bag, were being lifted onto the gurney by the attendants, assisted by Stevens, Pelligrosso, and Nugent.

Haggerty looked at him sheepishly. "Sorry, Sarge."

"No worries."

"Look, Sarge, Mel's got her lab hat on

today," Nugent said.

Stevens waited until they'd finished getting the wheels of the stretcher down before punching him in the shoulder. Normally Nugent's partner on cases, the scrappy detective with the spiky blond hair and the smoker's voice didn't take crap from anyone, especially Mike Nugent.

"Did you see that, Sarge? She's hostile."

"I'll show you hostile."

"She just misses working with you, Nuge," Pelligrosso said.

"I guess that's a no on the M.E.," Byron said.

"I spoke with Ellis," Nugent said. "They're right out straight, but I explained our concerns and he said he'll do the exam tomorrow morning."

They rolled Riordan out to the station wagon and loaded him inside. The driver handed a custody form to Pelligrosso, which he signed.

They stood in the driveway watching as the livery drove away. Byron turned to Pelligrosso and Stevens. "Okay, what's the plan?"

"We'll seal up the house and head in to 109 to tag some of this stuff into evidence," Stevens said. "We'll come back as it gets dark. I wanna hit the scene with luminol and get some more pictures using an alternative light source."

"Mel and I will attend the autopsy tomorrow," Nugent said.

"Good. Diane's getting a statement from the daughter, and I'll follow up on what she told me," Byron said.

"Do you want me to post someone on the house?" Stevens asked.

Byron considered it. He looked at Haggerty. "You mind staying late?"

"Whatever you need, Sarge."

"Hags will stay here, at least until you both get back; then we can install our own locks and tape it up. Let's treat this like a murder until we've proven it isn't." He hoped.

Chapter Ten

Byron drove slowly past the AMVETS on Washington Avenue but didn't see a Buick parked on either side of the road. He made a U-turn and pulled into the dirt lot across the street from the hall. Parked near the middle of the lot was a gray LeSabre. He radioed the registration number to dispatch and they confirmed it was Riordan's car.

He walked up to the car and tried the door. Locked. He looked inside through the side windows. Seeing nothing unusual, he headed across the street.

The lounge with its dingy maroon-colored linoleum floor and long wooden bar comprised the majority of the building's main floor. A dozen wooden tables were scattered about the room, the accompanying chairs stacked upside down on each. A large window overlooking Portland's skyline dominated the far wall. Byron approached the bar where a lone middle-aged male was washing glasses.

"We're not open yet," the man said.

"I'm not here for a drink," Byron said, producing his identification.

"Nice to meet you, Sergeant Byron," Carr said with a tone that didn't sound at all genuine.

"And you are?"

"Melvin Carr, bartender."

"Well, Melvin Carr, bartender, would you happen to know Cleophus Riordan?"

"Yeah, I know Cleo. He's a regular," Carr said as he rinsed another glass, setting it up on the bar to dry with the others.

"Remember the last time you saw him?" Byron asked.

"Sometime last week, I guess. He definitely would have been in Sunday night, though."

"Did you see him Sunday?"

"No. I was off last weekend."

"So how do you know he was in?"

"Because he always comes in on Sunday," Carr said. "Why are you asking all these questions about Cleo? He in some kind of trouble?"

"He's dead."

Carr's head snapped up. He nearly dropped a glass on the floor. "He's dead?"

"Yeah," Byron said, taking a certain satisfaction in having deflated Carr's surly attitude.

"How?"

"That's what I'm trying to find out. Who tended bar Sunday night?"

"That would've been Ralph. Ralph Polowski," Carr said, suddenly much more helpful. "If you wanna talk to him, he'll be in tomorrow afternoon, 'round three."

"Any chance you've got his number?"

"I don't. But I can check the sign-in book for you."

"Sign-in book? For Polowski?"

"No, for Riordan. All our members gotta sign in. Club rules." Carr pulled the black leather-bound book out from under the counter. It looked to Byron like an accounting ledger. "Here he is, right here," he said, pointing to Riordan's signature.

"Can you tell if he was here with someone?"

"No. All the signatures are stand-alone. You'd have to speak with Ralph."

"You happen to know where he lives?"

Byron got Polowski's Morning Street address from Carr and drove up Congress Street to Munjoy Hill. He climbed up a common stairwell to the second floor. The flowered carpet runner was so tattered it was nonexistent on some of the steps. He skirted several boxes of returnables and one large green trash bag before knocking on the door to apartment three. The smell of burnt food permeated the hallway. He'd knocked several times and was about to give up and leave his card when the door opened.

"Ya," Polowski said. He looked like he'd just woken up, standing there unshaven in a grubby T-shirt and underwear, scratching his greasy head.

"Ralph Polowski?"

"Ya. What do you want?"

"Mr. Polowski, I'm Detective Sergeant Byron, Portland Police Department. I'd like to ask you a few questions about a case I'm working on. Would you mind if I came in, so we can talk?"

"Nope. Come on in." Polowski stepped back, allowing Byron to enter. The small apartment was cluttered and dark. Blankets had been hung over the windows, presumably to make it easier for Polowski to sleep during daylight hours. Byron followed him into the kitchen and pulled out his notepad.

"Coffee?" Polowski asked.

"I'm fine. Thanks."

"You sure? I gotta make some anyway."

Coffee at the hands of the great unwashed was the last thing he wanted, but he didn't want to offend his ticket to information about Riordan's last hours. "Sure, if it isn't too much trouble."

"No trouble." Polowski pressed the brew button, then sat down at the kitchen table across from Byron. "So, you said something about a case."

"I need to confirm your employment," Byron said as he flipped to a fresh page.

"Got two jobs. I tend bar at the AMVETS two or three nights a week and work at Vinnie's Variety on Congress Street the others.

"Where did you work Sunday night?"

"The AMVETS. From one till about midnight."

"How long have you worked there?"

"I don't know. Ten years maybe."

"Do you know Cleophus Riordan?"

"Cleo? Sure I know him. He's one of our regulars."

"Was he in last Sunday night?"

Polowski laughed, causing Byron to look up from his notebook. "He's in every Sunday."

"Do you remember anything different about last Sunday?"

He thought for a moment, then shook his head. "Nope, nothing jumps out. Why you asking?"

"Did he come in with anyone?"

"Yeah, now you mention it, he did come in with a guy."

"Do you know the guy's name?"

He shook his head. "Sorry."

"You recognize him?"

"Nope, never seen him before. I took him to be a friend of Cleo's. Think they go back a ways."

"What makes you say that?"

"Just the way they were talking. Nothing in particular, just seemed like they'd known each other awhile."

"Can you describe him?" Byron asked.

"Sure, white guy, late fifties, rugged build, about your height I'd say. Six foot plus."

"Hair?"

"Gray, at least what little I could see of it."

"What do you mean?"

"He was wearing a ball cap."

"Do you remember what the hat looked like? Logo?" Polowski shook his head. "How about facial hair, beard, mustache?"

"Goatee, trimmed up real neat."

"Can you remember what time they arrived?"

"Early evening I guess, but they closed the place. I kicked them out about eleven-thirty."

123

"Have you seen either of them since Sunday night?"

"No. But I haven't worked there since Sunday." Byron watched as Polowski reached up under his T-shirt and scratched deep into an armpit. "They in some kind of trouble?"

"Riordan's dead." As if to punctuate this statement, the coffee maker beeped, signaling it was done. Byron studied the bartender's face. His expression was one of indifference.

Polowski got up and poured the coffee. "Heart attack?"

"Possible suicide."

"Wouldn't have seen that coming." He opened the fridge. "How do you take it?"

"Black, thanks. Why do you say that?"

He handed the mug to Byron, then sat down. "Cleo used to be a Portland cop. You know him?"

"I know of him."

"Well, he was one of the most confident men I've ever met."

"Confident?"

"Yeah, I'm being kind. Full of himself, I guess you'd say. Liked to drink, a lot. Turned into an asshole when he drank. Didn't have many friends."

"Sounds like he might've had one."

"Maybe. This other guy, is he in some kind of trouble?"

Not an unusual question, Byron thought. But it was also exactly the sort of question a friend of Mr. Baseball Cap might ask. "No," Byron said, handing the bartender a business card. "But if he should happen to come in again, give me call."

"Sure thing."

The sun had crept below the horizon by the time Byron returned to Riordan's. Stevens and Pelligrosso were busy photographing the kitchen. The blood spatter that appeared as brownish maroon stains by daylight now glowed eerily in the darkened room. The luminol cast a bluish light, reminding him of a child's glow stick. Normally, investigators spray the chemical, which reacts with minerals contained in blood, on any surface suspected of having been cleaned by a suspect. In the case of Riordan's kitchen, where no attempt had been made to hide the blood, it simply made photographing the smaller blood droplets easier.

"What do you think?" Byron asked Stevens.

"I think we've got a problem."

"How so?"

"I don't think he was alone when this happened."

"How can you tell?"

"Check this out." She had Pelligrosso hold a flashlight from the side and shine it across the kitchen table. "I was checking for blood spatter detail on the table when I found these."

Byron bent down and looked closely at the tabletop. "What am I looking at?"

"See these marks?" she asked, pointing to several circular patterns on the table.

"Are those rings from Cleo's glass?"

"Not Cleo's. His are over here. There was another person drinking with him. Probably took the glass from the scene."

"How do we know the rings weren't already there, from some other time?"

"Follow me." Stevens led him to the next room where she'd set up her laptop. "I downloaded some of the pictures to my computer already. This is a picture looking toward the door from the table. I wanted a shot of the floor showing the back spatter from the entry wound. Everything was enhanced with luminol. Can you see it?"

"I see some fine spray, but that's it."

"That's all we could see at first. This is the same photo, but I enhanced the contrast. Do you see it now?"

"There's nothing in the middle."

"Bingo. Something blocked the blowback spatter," Stevens said, referring to the fine spray of blood droplets typical of bullet-entry wounds. The blood spatter travels in an ever-expanding pattern, moving in the opposite direction from the bullet.

"Something or someone?" Byron asked.

"My guess? Someone was standing right here beside Riordan when the gun went off," Stevens said, pointing to the screen.

Byron felt the hair stand up on the back of his neck. He knew the presence of another person didn't necessarily mean Riordan's death wasn't a suicide. But he also knew the death of two former SRT members, under suspicious circumstances, inside of a week, wasn't a coincidence. If this was a murder, it meant that they'd been looking at O'Halloran's death all wrong. It wasn't some misguided attempt to put a dying man out of his misery. Someone was making a statement and their target, or targets, was becoming clearer by the moment.

He pulled out his cell and dialed Diane.

"Hey, Sarge."

"Diane, I need you to do something else for me."

"Name it."

"Grab Nuge and canvass Riordan's entire neighborhood. I want to know if anyone remembers him having a visitor in the last day or two."

Byron drove to 109 and found LeRoyer pacing in front of the snack box.

"You know that crap will kill ya, Marty."

"So will this job. Remember when this stuff only cost a quarter?"

"No, I don't."

"Well, it did." He pulled a bill out of his pocket. "Don't suppose you got change for a five."

"Sorry. Why don't you write an IOU like everybody else?"

LeRoyer's face lit up and he grabbed a Milky Way. "Good idea," he said, pocketing the money. "Billingslea called. Says you threatened to physically remove him from a public street."

"I was just explaining his options."

"Jesus, John. You can't go around threatening reporters. Like it or not, he's the police-beat guy."

"Doesn't give him the right to fuck up an investigation. He was gonna try and talk with Riordan's daughter. Don't suppose he mentioned that, did he?"

"Just ease up on the guy, okay? So, give

me some good news. Make my friggin' day and tell me this is just a suicide and isn't linked to O'Halloran's death in any way."

"Okay, but I'd be lying."

LeRoyer returned the unopened candy bar to the snack box. "There goes my appetite."

They walked through CID toward LeRoyer's office while Byron filled him in.

"So we still don't know what we have yet?" LeRoyer asked hopefully.

"We'll know more tomorrow."

"Great, another sleepless night. Donna's already peeved at me. I fell asleep during our anniversary dinner the other night."

"Happy anniversary."

"Yeah, thanks." LeRoyer's cell chimed with an incoming message. He removed it from his suit coat pocket and looked at it. "Speak of the devil."

"Stanton?" Byron asked.

"No, it's my other boss. She wants to know if I'm ever coming home tonight."

"You might as well. We're not gonna be able to do much more tonight. I'm waitin' on the last of my people."

LeRoyer stood up and grabbed his suit jacket off the back of his chair. "You're right. I'll call Stanton on the way home. Oh, almost forgot. Billingslea has already begun poking around, and don't forget we've got

CompStat tomorrow."

"And?"

"And you're up."

Byron rubbed his temples. "You're just full of good news."

CHAPTER ELEVEN

It was nearly one o'clock Wednesday afternoon when Byron headed down to the police department's first-floor conference room for the weekly CompStat meeting. As usual, he avoided the elevator, favoring instead the solitude of a darkened stairwell. It wasn't a fear of elevators that motivated him as much as the likelihood of sharing one with someone boorish. Worse still, being stuck in one with such a person. He'd never quite developed a knack for suffering fools.

The conference room was two stories high with walls constructed of exposed brick and Sheetrock. The floor was tiled in an earthy rust-colored terrazzo. Two large wood-framed windows overlooked the plaza, which lead to the rear parking garage. At the center of the room stood a massive wooden table, fifteen feet long, surrounded by more than a dozen padded black-metal chairs. Byron sat down in his usual seat at the far right side of the table closest to one of the conference room doors, just as the others began to arrive. The meetings always made him feel like he was sitting down to dinner as part of some dysfunctional Earl Hamner television family, living in the Blue Ridge Mountains of West Virginia during the Great Depression. Mind passing me the murders, Grandpa?

CompStat had come to Portland, Maine, by way of a young, stat-happy police captain, shortly after he'd earned his master's in police administration. When the idea was first implemented, the brain trust at City Hall, unable to contain their giddiness, held a joint press conference at which they trumpeted loudly about things like "leading the Portland Police Department into the twenty-first century" and "cutting-edge crime fighting." Byron wondered what century they'd thought the police had been fighting crime in. Not surprisingly, the captain's rhetoric about saving Portland was really nothing more than a way to garner regional attention for himself in his bid to become a chief. Following that captain's departure, to fix whatever might be ailing some other police agency, Portland PD was left with CompStat, and Byron and his cohorts were left to suffer through the tedious Wednesday afternoon meetings each week.

CompStat meetings were usually comprised of the same personnel: the Chief, Assistant Chief, Commander, CID Lieutenant, CID Sergeants, Captain of Patrol, Community Policing Lieutenant and Sergeant, Crime Analyst, and several Senior Lead Officers. Each attendee was provided with a copy of the weekly Crime Analyst Report showing violent crimes, property crimes, and calls for service. Each report was broken down into subcategories like murder, gross sexual assault, aggravated assault, robbery, etc. Also factored in were things like location within the city where the crime occurred, time of day, day of the week, and so on. An increase in any given area would require an explanation, along with a plan to fix the problem. Any decrease in criminal activity and somebody would undoubtedly take credit, usually somebody of greater rank and importance than a sergeant.

Byron knew he'd be occupying the hot seat at today's meeting. All anyone wanted to talk about was the murder investigation and why it hadn't been solved. The chief's protocol was to make the supervisor about to be served up as the main course wait until last before being called upon, allowing adequate time for basting the goose.

After everyone was seated, Chief Stanton, the master of ceremonies, started the meeting, beginning with Detective Sergeant Peterson, supervisor of the property crime unit. Peterson covered each of the property crime categories in agonizing detail, at least as far as Byron was concerned. He knew there was zero hope of being called away from the meeting, unless the world came to an end. Next, Stanton called for Detective Sergeant Crosby's report on current drug investigations. And so it went until finally Byron was called upon.

He wanted to keep his cards as close to the vest as possible while still providing something for the group and satisfying Stanton's infernal need to know. The last thing he needed was one of the CompStat attendees leaking valuable case information to a news media vulture like Davis Billingslea, and not for the first time. Byron explained how they'd spent most of the previous week trying to establish whether or not O'Halloran's death was at the hands of one of his nurses.

He could see Assistant Chief Reginald Cross salivating to add his two cents. Cross suffered from what Diane referred to as "stater of the obvious syndrome." He always led with the same worn out caveats: "I don't want to tell you how to investigate cases, but —" and "Wouldn't it be better if — ?" Cross wasn't alone in telling Byron how to go about being a detective, but he was the second-highest ranking know-it-all.

"I don't understand why you're trying to connect these two cases," Cross said. "Cleo's death was a suicide, wasn't it?"

"Inconclusive. We still can't say he didn't take his own life, but we *have* established he wasn't alone when he died."

"Doesn't mean someone else killed him. Maybe there was someone there and they didn't want to get dragged into a police investigation. I don't suppose that occurred to you?"

Byron bit his tongue, trying to keep his real thoughts to himself. "It has. But we're keeping all possibilities on the table until we can say with certainty it was a suicide."

"Sounds to me like you're attempting to make a link where there isn't one," Cross said, playing to Stanton and the rest of the room. "If I were you I'd be focusing my efforts on solving O'Halloran's murder, instead of searching for some conspiracy."

Byron was fighting exasperation. He

glanced over at LeRoyer, who was giving him a watch-yourself look. "As I said, Chief, we still need to prove Riordan wasn't murdered."

"Seems pretty friggin' clear to me."

As the sage advice from all corners of the room faded into a dull pointless hum, Byron imagined how great a dram of the Irish would be at that very moment. He made eye contact with Sergeant Peterson, who was sporting a large shit-eating grin, apparently enjoying Byron's quandary. He glanced down at his vibrating cell. The text from Peterson read: "Looks like somebody needs a big steaming cup of shut-the-fuck-up!" It was all Byron could do not to laugh out loud.

Homicide 101 continued ad nauseam. He needed to check in on his people and get back to the case. What he didn't need or have time for was more useless advice.

CompStat mercifully concluded with a promise from Lieutenant LeRoyer that CID would continue to put all of its resources toward the O'Halloran homicide.

LeRoyer and Byron rode the elevator up to the fourth floor. "Thoughts?" LeRoyer asked, breaking the silence.

He looked up, glaring at the lieutenant. "You don't want to hear them."

The doors opened and they were immediately confronted by a mousy-looking young man. His hair was slicked back and he wore a dark pinstriped suit. His general appearance screamed attorney. "Which one of you is John Byron?" pinstripe asked, skipping right past the customary formalities.

Byron was pretty sure he had suits older than the man standing before him. "I'm Byron. Who are you?"

"John Byron, you've been served," striped-suit said as he quickly slipped a manila envelope into Byron's hand and escaped into the elevator just as the doors were closing.

"I'm guessing it's not good news," LeRoyer said.

Byron opened the envelope and unfolded its contents.

"Who's it from? Another happy customer getting ready to sue?" LeRoyer asked with a chuckle as he peered over Byron's shoulder.

Byron turned and stared at his lieutenant.

"Well, who's it from?" LeRoyer asked.

"Kay's lawyer. She's filed for divorce."

Byron unlocked the door and stepped inside his cozy first-floor Danforth Street apartment. A savvy realtor friend had once told him that "cozy," a favorite adjective among their ilk, actually meant a place too small to swing a cat. He'd found the description rather disturbing, and he didn't own a cat. A maze of cardboard boxes occupied the floor in each of the four rooms. Some were open but none had been emptied. He removed things as he needed, rather than unpack.

It'd been nine months since Kay announced she wanted a trial separation. Calling it a separation had been her way of letting him down easy. He was pretty sure he'd known even then their marriage was over, but he hadn't been ready for the feeling of finality the act of unpacking would have brought with it. It wasn't optimistic pretense as much as living in denial and hoping things might still work out.

He dragged out a stool and sat down at the kitchen counter with the envelope containing Kay's divorce papers. He pulled out the documents and flipped through them. A twenty-year marriage dissolved by one stroke of a pen. It was absurd, and would've been laughable had it not hurt so badly.

One by one all of the things they had talked about, all of the dreams for their future, everything had fallen apart. The children, the camp at the lake, the grandchildren, retiring to Florida. All of those bullshit greeting card moments gone. What had happened? Where had they gone wrong? Was it his career? Hers? Or was it just the picture-perfect dreams of two starry-eyed kids looking for something more than their parents had had? Was it really anyone's fault? Or had they simply paid the price for a lifetime of dreaming.

"Looks pretty fuckin' official now, John," he said aloud as he scanned the room. Somehow, in the short span of five minutes, his living space had grown even more depressing. All his meager belongings stacked up like they were about to go into storage or off to the Salvation Army. The sum of his life reduced to a dozen or so boxes in a shitty little one-bedroom-efficiency. No longer a temporary home, it was now his future.

As if on cue, the secondhand air-conditioner, given to him by Humphrey, began making the horrible squealing noise to which it had lately become prone. The AC wasn't doing much to cool the tiny living space, but it was better than nothing. Besides, when autumn finally did make an appearance, he would no longer need it. He got up, walked over to the window, and gave a hard rap with his knuckles to the side of the aging appliance. The squealing stopped. He returned to the kitchen, rinsed out a dirty juice glass, and poured himself two fingers of Jameson Irish whiskey. The strong smell of the liquor filled his nostrils and the slow soothing burn caressed his throat. He closed his eyes, savoring the restorative powers of the bottle.

He gave a start at the unexpected ringing of his cell. "Yeah," he answered without checking to see who it was.

"John, it's Kay."

He paused before responding. Unsure of what to say, he said nothing.

"I know you were served today. I'm sorry about doing it like this."

He felt the anger swelling inside. "Not too sorry to file them, though."

"I know you're upset. I guess I probably would be too."

"No you don't know," he snapped. "You don't know because you're not me. We couldn't even talk about this in person? Really, Kay? Is this how two responsible adults handle things? Through an attorney?"

"I couldn't tell you in person. I knew how upset you'd get."

"Upset? You're goddamned right I'm upset! Twenty years of marriage and you couldn't even tell me to my face. You asked me to give you some space and I did. You said you needed time and I gave it to you. I gave you everything you asked for, and for what? What the fuck did it get me?"

"John, please —"

"I'll tell you what it got me, nothing. Do you have any idea how goddamned humiliating it is to have some pimply-faced attorney wannabe serve you with divorce papers, at work? In front of my boss. Really?"

"John —"

"I hope you're happy." He hung up and threw his phone across the room, striking the air-conditioner. "Fuck," he announced to the empty apartment.

The squealing began again, in earnest, like fingernails on a chalkboard. He set his glass down, walked slowly but purposefully to the window, and delivered a forceful side kick to the metal casing. The same kick he'd delivered to scores of doors during his early years on the job. There was a loud cracking noise before the AC tumbled out of its frame. The wire pigtail popped from the wall outlet and gave chase. He heard it crash onto the ground below. Only an empty window frame remained. He slammed the window shut and calmly returned to the bottle.

■ ■ ■ ■

Diane stood on the doorstep to Byron's apartment, waiting. She'd already knocked several times but hadn't gotten a response. She knew from prior visits that the button to the ancient doorbell was probably still broken, but she pressed it anyway.

Byron had already departed 109 by the time Shirley Grant told Diane about the divorce papers. He wasn't answering her calls and she was worried. Worried about what her partner might do to himself. For all his tough talk and posturing, she knew that his crumbling marriage bothered him more than he let on. She wasn't sure if he still held a place in his heart for Kay or if he just hated to fail at anything.

She knew Byron well enough to know that he'd want to be alone as he sorted things out, but she also knew how self-destructive he could be. The alcohol seemed to be getting the better of him. And she knew first-hand what addiction could do to a person, having gone through it with her brother. The truth was she wanted to be with John. In spite of his many faults, he was a good man, with a good heart, and she had feelings for him. But he was an old-fashioned guy who had, at least until now, still considered himself married. Probably why she hadn't acted on those feelings.

"John, you in there?" She turned to the sound of giggling behind her on the sidewalk. Two young girls laughing uncontrollably about something, staggering drunkenly by under the cone of light cast by a streetlamp. Diane waited until they were gone, then knocked again. "John."

There was a light on in the front room, the living room. She couldn't see inside the apartment from the stairs, and the windows were too high to look into from the sidewalk. She hadn't seen his car parked anywhere nearby, but given the late hour and the lack of on-street parking, she knew he might have parked blocks away. Diane pounded on the door one last time. She pulled out her cell and sent him a text, then reluctantly returned to her car and drove home.

It was still dark out when Byron awoke. The throbbing pain in his head was only slightly less uncomfortable than the pressure in his bladder. Unsure of his surroundings, he took a moment to gather himself. He was seated in a car, his Taurus, and it was running. He wondered how long he'd been there. Cool air poured from the dashboard vents. An empty bottle lay on the seat next to him. Blacked out. Again. He dragged himself out of the car and staggered to the rear. Leaning against the trunk to steady himself, he urinated on the grass. He was standing near Munjoy Hill's East End Beach, still attired in the previous day's clothing. Moonbeams sparkled brilliantly across the surface of Casco Bay. Breaking waves and gulls crying were the only sounds. He struggled to reconstruct the previous hours, as he had countless times before. He remembered Kay's divorce papers, followed by his impromptu home air-conditioner repair, after that it became fuzzy. Byron assumed that his visit from Saint Jameson must have come next. He must have opted for the cool car over his sweltering apartment with its broken AC. He returned to the car on unsteady legs and checked his cell. Only three-thirty. He'd missed three calls and a text message: one call from Kay and two more from Diane. The text was also from Diane. "Heard what happened. U OK? Call me."

"Just fucking dandy," he said.

He put the car in gear and drove slowly to his apartment.

Dawn came far too soon. The intoxicating

effects of the whiskey had mostly departed, but there was still a price to be paid. Shedding his clothes, Byron stepped into the shower. He spent the next twenty minutes trying to wash all of it away, the self-pity, failed marriage, stalled murder investigation, his shitty little apartment, all of it.

After showering he shaved, dressed in clean but wrinkled clothes and a tie, made coffee, and washed down three Tylenol, then swallowed one more for good measure. Pausing in front of the mirror, he studied the dark recesses of his eyes. The purplish black circles told the story of a man haunted by self-destructive habits. A man determined to walk a different path than his father. A man failing.

Get it together, John, the voice inside his head told him. He was surprised by how much it sounded like something Diane might have said.

"Enough with the mothering, already," he said aloud. "I'm handling it. Like always."

Are you? The voice asked. *Are you handling it? The same way you handled Kay's call last night?*

He looked at the divorce documents lying on the counter. Sooner or later he'd have to deal with this. In spite of how she'd blindsided him, he did owe Kay an apology for being such an asshole. If he was being honest with himself, he owed her many apologies for the countless times he'd been an asshole. A drunken asshole. He opened the cupboard where his booze was hidden, a habit left over from his married days. Four unopened bottles of whiskey sat on the shelf behind the boxes of mac-and-cheese. One by one he removed them from the cupboard, uncapped them, and poured them down the sink. His career in the bureau was in jeopardy. Hell, his career in general was in jeopardy. His drinking wasn't the best kept secret, and he knew both Stanton and Cross would like nothing more than to replace him. If not for LeRoyer running interference, they likely would have already. Probably with some rumpswab like Crosby, who would do anything they asked, like some damned puppet. With Kay gone, only two things made his life worth living: the job and the bottle. And the first was being fucked hard by the second. He unsealed the last bottle and emptied it out.

He knew this simple act was largely symbolic. But he also knew that getting his shit together began by taking a first step. Cleaning out the reserves was his first step.

The voice was unrelenting. *How is this going to help? You'll only buy more, like always.*

He snapped a lid on his travel mug and walked out the door, ignoring the voice.

"Wow, you look like shit," Diane said as she entered Byron's office and plopped down in the chair across from him.

He squinted his eyes at her. "Gee, thanks."

"I heard about your visit from Kay's lawyer yesterday. I'm sorry, John."

"Thanks again."

"Didn't you get my text?"

"I was busy."

"I stopped by your apartment on my way home."

"I was out."

"Self-medicating?"

He stopped reading a case supplement and looked up at her. Aware that the voice from earlier had taken on a physical form. "You're not really gonna sit there and lecture me, are you?"

"Would you listen if I did?"

"No. Did you come in here to bust my balls or do you have something for me?"

"Both," she said with a sly smirk. "We might've actually gotten something useful from the canvass."

"Wouldn't that be novel? What?"

"Alice Keagan. I just got off the phone with her. She's an elderly neighbor of

Riordan's. Sounds like she's the neighbor-hood busy-body. Told me she suffers from insomnia, stays up most nights sitting by the window so she can see what's happening. Said she remembers seeing two people get out of Riordan's car after it pulled into his driveway Sunday night."

"She get a look at who?" he asked, now fully attentive.

"Told me it was too dark to make out any detail, but she's confident it was Riordan, and another man."

"She remember what time it was?"

"Around midnight."

"How about hearing a gunshot?"

Diane shook her head. "Said she didn't hear anything, but she's hard of hearing."

"Did she see anything else?"

"Yeah. She saw Riordan's car being driven away a little before two."

CHAPTER TWELVE

Byron drove out Washington Avenue, past the old J. J. Nissen bread factory toward Tukey's Bridge, looking for something he should have checked before. He'd erroneously assumed Riordan had either been given a ride home or taken a cab. The possibility that the killer might have driven Riordan's car never even occurred to him. It didn't make sense. Why wouldn't the killer have driven his own car? He pulled into the lot across from the AMVETS, parking where he had the previous afternoon. Riordan's Buick was still parked in the same spot. He contacted dispatch and requested the beat officer to his location.

He stepped out of his car and scanned the lot until he spotted it. A security camera mounted atop one of the nearby light poles. The parking lot appeared to belong to the adjoining industrial-style gray-steel building. The only business currently occupying the large building was Bay City Florist.

A bell chimed as he opened the glass door to the business and stepped inside. A young blond girl wearing a nose stud stood behind the counter. She was chomping on gum and texting. He waited for her to finish, noticing her purple lipstick and matching eye shadow.

"Good morning," she said, finally lowering the phone.

"Morning."

Like an automaton, she delivered the company's catch phrase, "If you're looking for flowers for a special someone, you've come to the right place."

It was all he could do not to laugh in her face as he thought of how his special someone had just gifted him with a divorce. He wondered if they sold an arrangement for that. He held out his credentials. "Actually, I'm trying to find out who owns the pole camera outside."

She furrowed her brow as she checked his ID. "That would be us. This is my uncle's business. I'm Dorothy Webber. Guess you'd call me the manager."

"Detective Sergeant John Byron," he said, extending his hand. "Pleased to meet you."

"Likewise," she said with a firm but quick shake of her hand. Following the customary greeting, Webber resumed her previous activity.

Byron, noting that her nails were also purple, wondered if a purchase might help her to focus. "Does the security camera work or is it only for show?"

"It works," she said without looking up. "We put it in the last time we had a break-in. Dropped our insurance rates, a little."

"Any chance you've still got the footage from Sunday night into Monday morning?"

"We did, but I already gave the video to one of your detectives yesterday."

Byron stared at her as if she were joking. "One of my detectives? I didn't send anyone over here."

"Well, he showed me a badge and said he worked for the police department."

"The Portland Police Department?"

She shrugged. "I guess."

"What time was that?"

"Around ten-thirty, I'd say. Late morning anyway."

Observing her phone hypnosis, with some amazement he realized exactly how ludicrous his next question would likely seem. "Can you remember what he looked like or what he drove?"

"I didn't see what he was driving, 'cause I was working on a big order, but he was a little shorter than you and maybe a bit older."

"How old would you guess?"

"Fifties maybe. I'm not real good with people's ages."

Too bad the mystery man hadn't texted her his picture. "Anything else you can remember about the way he looked: hair, eyes, anything?"

She shook her head. "Sorry." Ms. iPhone looked up momentarily, giving Byron the once over. "He was wearing a suit, like you."

"Anything else?"

"Nope. I don't pay very close attention, sorry." *Back to the phone.*

Byron was working hard to maintain his composure and thanking God he didn't have to deal with a teenager of his own. "Did anyone else see him? Maybe your uncle?"

"I was here by myself when he came in."

"Think you might recognize him if you saw him again?"

"Maybe," she said, snapping her gum.

Byron wrote down her information and handed her a card after jotting the number of his cell on the back. He returned to the parking lot as the beat officer was pulling in.

"Hey, Sarge," the officer said. "Fancy seeing you again."

O'Donnell. The same officer who'd kept the crime log at O'Halloran's. "Morning, O'Donnell. See the Buick parked over there?"

The officer nodded.

"I want you to tow it to the basement of 109 for processing."

"Happy to help."

"Make sure it's secured in the cage."

"Yes, sir."

Byron pulled out his cell and called Diane.

"Joyner," she answered.

"Diane, it's Byron."

"What's up?"

"I need you to drive out to Bay City Florist on Washington Avenue and take a statement from the florist shop manager, Dorothy Webber."

"Sure thing. What do you want in her statement?"

"A guy went in there yesterday morning, identified himself as a detective, and made off with their security video."

"You're kidding."

"Not in a kidding mood."

"On my way."

"One more thing. Bring Dustin with you and see if there's anything he can do to recover whatever was on their surveillance system."

"I'll take care of it."

Byron's next call was to Sergeant Peterson, the property crimes supervisor.

"George. You didn't happen to send any of your people over to the AMVETS yesterday, did you? The one on Washington Avenue?"

"Nope. Why?"

"Or maybe Bay City Florist?"

"No. Neither one of those businesses are even on the current case board. Why?"

"Someone playing detective just made off with my surveillance video from the florist shop."

Byron returned to 109 to meet up with Pelligrosso and Stevens.

"Sarge," Stevens greeted as he entered the lab. "Good timing. We were about to call you. Think we've got something you'll wanna see."

"I've got something for you too. Riordan's car is being towed down to our basement. I need it processed."

"I'll take care of it," Pelligrosso said. "What are you searching for?"

"It's possible our victim's mystery guest may have driven Riordan's car back to the

AMVETS after the suicide."

"Well, that's interesting," Stevens said.

"What did you find?" Byron asked.

"Riordan's death wasn't a suicide."

Pelligrosso placed two old police department photos of Riordan on the table. "These."

Byron looked at them. "What am I supposed to see?"

"Riordan was a southpaw, Sarge. Problem is he was shot in the right temple."

Byron looked from one picture to the other. Riordan's holster was on his left hip in both. "Shit."

Dustin Tran was the answer guy. When it came to gathering background information quickly, there was no one better. Byron knew they needed as much information as possible in order to find whatever else linked O'Halloran and Riordan. Interviewing the officers who were being targeted would be key to establishing the killer's motive but pointless if they didn't know which ones were targets or what questions to ask. With the lives of former cops at stake, they couldn't afford to guess.

"Hey, striped dude," Tran said as Byron stepped into the computer lab and closed the door. "I looked at their surveillance system like you asked, but it's pretty anti-quated."

"I thought they just had the camera installed?"

"They did. The camera was new, but they didn't want to shell out for a new recorder. Still using a top-load VHS. Probably an old tape too. I checked the video in the machine and reviewed your arrival this morning, and the image was so grainy I couldn't tell what kind of car you were driving or even if it was you I was looking at. If I had to guess, they haven't replaced those tapes in at least two years. Whoever made off with the tape you were after probably didn't need to."

"What about video of our mystery man?"

Tran shook his head. "They didn't start recording again until after he left."

"Okay, thanks for checking. Now drop everything else you're working on. What I'm about to give you takes top priority."

"Must be *muy importante.*"

"It is."

Tran grabbed a pen and paper. "Tell me what you need."

"Someone has murdered two former Portland police officers, James O'Halloran and Cleophus Riordan. The obvious link is that they were both members of our Special Reaction Team during the early eighties, but so were a number of others." He handed Tran a copy of the photo taken from Riordan's home. "I've written the names of each officer on the back. I need you to keep an open mind as you search for a link. A number of these guys were former military. Check everything. My gut is telling me this has something to do with the SRT, but it could also be something totally unrelated."

"What are you thinking as far as motive? Someone out for revenge? Maybe just out of prison?"

"Could be that simple." Although he knew it rarely was.

"Anything else?"

"That's all I have at this point. Look for cases that link both of them and look for anything linking them to other SRT members.

"Worry not, number one. I'm on the case."

But worried he was. Someone had murdered two former Portland cops, and he had no idea why. If the goal was to go on killing, the clock was ticking and the killer already had a big head start.

"Christ, John," LeRoyer said. "Tell me you're not serious."

Byron said nothing.

"Who would target ex-cops?"

157

"I don't know." He watched as LeRoyer ran his fingers through his hair, a nervous tic the lieutenant probably wasn't even aware of. Behind his back, the detectives referred to LeRoyer as "Lieutenant Einstein." The good-natured nickname had nothing to do with brilliance and everything to do with how his hair looked on particularly stressful days.

"Where do we start?"

"I want to work this with a small team."

"Why not take the entire unit? You can borrow some of Peterson's detectives."

"I don't want extra bodies. This will quickly get out of hand."

"Many hands make quick work, John. Maybe you've heard that one?"

"Yeah, and they also lead to sensitive information leaks, freelancing, and grandstanding. No, I only want Diane, Nuge, Dustin, Mel, and Gabe."

"They're your people, John. You telling me or asking me?"

"I'm telling you who's on the team, but I'm asking for freedom from all other tasks and the autonomy to investigate this as I see fit."

"Autonomy?"

"I don't want politics to get in the way, not on this one. Our victims were Portland cops; there's no telling where this thing may go. Do we have an agreement?"

"Unencumbered and unfettered, is that it? Chain of command be damned."

"That's the idea." Byron waited while LeRoyer considered it.

"Okay, John. Have it your way. I'll try and keep the wolves at bay. Just promise me you'll catch this guy before he kills another cop."

Byron slid a copy of the SRT photo they'd taken from Riordan's home across the lieutenant's desk. "We're going to need to find and interview each one of these guys."

LeRoyer picked up the picture and studied it. "Jesus, that's Cross."

"Beginning with him."

CHAPTER THIRTEEN

Byron took the elevator to the basement, only because the stairwell at this end of the building ended at the first floor. The overhead garage door was closed and the lights were out. At first he thought someone had tripped a breaker until he saw the familiar blue glow. The evidence techs frequently used an alternate light source (ALS) to locate latent trace evidence. The high-intensity lamp was capable of emitting light at different frequencies or colors. When used correctly, the ALS often made visible hairs, fibers, and prints, which had previously been invisible, visible to the naked eye.

He walked down the ramp to the caged area used for securing and processing larger pieces of evidence, like vehicles.

"Anything, Gabe?" Byron asked.

Pelligrosso shook his head. "I've lifted a couple of prints, but I'm guessing they're yours."

"Why?"

"Because they're all from the outside handle of the driver's door."

"What about inside, the steering wheel or rearview mirror?"

"Wiped clean."

"Everything?"

"Whoever returned this thing to the parking lot knew exactly what they were doing."

Wiped it clean and came back for the video. Byron checked his watch, one-thirty. "I'm planning a team meeting in the CID conference room at three, will you be done by then?"

Pelligrosso looked at his own watch. "No, but I can be done by four."

It was four-fifteen before they were all seated in the CID conference room. Tran had written the pertinent case facts in his ridiculously neat script on the large whiteboard dominating one of the room's longer walls. On the opposite wall, he'd posted a three-foot enlargement of the black-and-white SRT photo. Next to this, he'd hung four colored mug shots that were faded with age.

"Okay, everybody, listen up," Byron said. "I've asked Dustin to give us a rundown on all the information he's gathered so far. Go ahead, Dustin."

"Bonjour, my fellow crime fighting compatriots. You've all seen the photograph taken from Cleo Riordan's home, depicting the Portland Police Department Special Reaction Team as it looked in 1985. As you can see, the team was comprised of ten members. Starting in the back row from left to right they are Sergeant Cleophus Riordan, Officer Dominic Beaudreau, Officer Bruce Gagnon, Lieutenant James O'Halloran, Sergeant Christopher Falcone, Officer Reece Byron, Sergeant Reginald Cross, Sergeant Eric Williams, Officer Ray Humphrey, and finally Officer Anthony Perrigo."

Tran was sounding a bit hoarse. He paused long enough to sip some water from his lime green Nalgene bottle and continued. "I conducted a global history search using internal records, news archives, and link searches. My goal was to find one incident involving several if not all of these officers. Some singular event that could be the catalyst for these murders. The first thing I discovered was how short a period of time this grouping of officers served together. Portland PD didn't even have an SRT until 1981, this group began working together at the end of '83 and remained cohesive until the death of Reece Byron in November 1985. Byron took his own life." As soon as the words were out of his mouth, he stopped and turned toward Byron. All the color had drained from Tran's face. "Sergeant, I'm so sorry. I didn't mean to sound —"

"No worries, Dustin," Byron said, raising a hand. "I know you didn't. Please, continue."

Tran cleared his throat and continued. "I managed to locate several major arrests involving four or five of the officers. Their assignments at that time were varied, with some assigned to Patrol, some to Traffic and some to CID. Most of them only worked together when they were acting in an SRT capacity. Even some of the SRT call-outs didn't involve the entire team. Things like vacations, training, and illness kept them apart. But I did find one incident that involved every single one of them, and these four men" — pointing to the old booking photos — "they are: Nicholas Andreas, Fredrick Ellis, Marvin Rotolo, and Leslie James Warren."

"Nice uni-brow," Nugent said, referencing Warren's Neanderthal-like appearance.

"The incident in question was a robbery arrest gone bad. Back in '85, these last four

163

were suspects in a Boston armored car robbery. As you're all aware, Officer Bruce Gagnon was the last Portland officer killed in the line of duty. He died on October nineteenth, 1985, during this SRT call-out. They were attempting to take these guys into custody when Gagnon was shot and killed. Subsequently, Warren, Ellis, and Rotolo were killed by officers during the exchange."

"What happened to the fourth guy, Andreas?" Diane asked.

"It appears he avoided capture. And here's an interesting factoid: none of the money was ever recovered."

"How much money was taken? Stevens asked.

"According to the news articles, about one point four million."

Nugent whistled. "I'd say that might qualify as motive."

"None of it was recovered?" Byron asked.

"Nope. And this shooting was by far the biggest thing to happen involving all of the officers in this photo."

Byron's cell phone rang. He stepped into the next room and took the call. "Byron."

"Sergeant, it's Shirley. Do you have a moment?"

"Not really, I'm in the middle of a meeting," he said, trying hard to hide his annoyance with the secretary. "Can it wait till we're through?"

"It's important. I've got something you need to see. It's about the case you're working."

Byron stood next to Shirley, both of them staring at the photocopies lying on her desk.

"These just came?" he asked.

"Yup, couple of minutes ago. There's the envelope, addressed to the Portland Police Detective Bureau at 109 Middle Street. No return address. I didn't dare to touch anything once I saw what it was."

Someone had mailed a photocopy of a newspaper article pertaining to the shoot-out Tran had described, along with the SRT photo. Red Xs were marked across the faces of O'Halloran and Riordan. Byron looked at Shirley. "Have you got a clean file folder?"

"Sure, right here," she said, handing it to him.

Carefully he slid the envelope into it, followed by the photocopies. "Thanks, Shirley. Would you scratch out a quick case supplement?"

"Of course," she said in a tone suggesting he needn't have asked.

He was hurrying back to the conference room when LeRoyer stopped him. "You got a sec, John?"

"Not really. I've got two things going right now."

"Look me up when you're done. It's about Stanton's press conference."

He frowned. "Press conference? Little early for that, isn't it?"

"Come find me when you're done."

So much for keeping the wolves at bay, he thought as he continued toward the conference room.

Tran wrote the letter *D* in red marker next to the name of each decedent on the list. He stopped and took another swig from his water bottle before continuing.

"If I'm right, and this is the event linking these two murders, someone may well be planning to kill the remaining members of the 1985 Special Reaction Team."

"Looks like you are right," Byron said.

"I am?" Tran said, sounding surprised.

Byron had donned a pair of white rubber gloves. He opened the folder and set it on the table. "Someone just mailed this to us."

Everyone bent to look.

"Shit," Nugent said.

"Shit is right," Stevens agreed.

"Gabe, I'll need you to dust these for prints when we're through here."

"I'll take care of it."

"Okay, so who's left?" Diane asked Tran.

"As far as I can tell, there are six officers still alive: Beaudreau, Perrigo, Falcone, Williams, Humphrey, and Cross." He circled each of the survivor's names in black then added one additional red *D* beside the name of Reece Byron.

"What about Nicholas Andreas?" Diane asked. "Is he still alive?"

"As I said, Andreas managed to avoid capture. He wasn't present when the shootout occurred and he's still on the FBI's most wanted list," Tran said. "Although, his ranking dropped significantly after September eleventh."

"That would make him our best suspect at this point," Pelligrosso said.

"How in hell are we supposed to find a guy the FBI hasn't been able to locate in thirty years?" Nugent asked.

"I don't know," Tran said. "But isn't the more important thing locating the other officers, before Andreas or whoever does?"

"Dustin's right," Byron said. "We've gotta find these guys before the killer does. Looks like we have the target, and with the missing money, at least a possible motive. The press doesn't have this information yet, but it's only a matter of time."

"I'm almost afraid to ask," Diane said.

167

"Stanton's already planning a press conference."

Several of the detectives groaned.

"Here come the bullshit leads," Nugent said, throwing his hands up. "Detective, I think this is the work of aliens. You know, little green men."

Byron continued. "I've no idea what the chief is gonna say, but once this thing breaks, we'll likely be hampered by more than a few bogus leads. We've got to do as much as we can before the case goes public. Diane, I want you and Dustin to locate addresses for Beaudreau, Perrigo, Falcone, and Williams."

"We're on it," she said.

"What about the Ass Chief?" Nugent asked.

"I'll handle Cross," Byron said.

"I got a question, Sarge," Pelligrosso said. "Some of these guys have been gone from the PD for a long time. They might not be so easy to find. Most cops have unlisted numbers and P.O.s for addresses."

"I'll check with the State Retirement System," Diane said. "They'll have records for these guys."

"Or at least the ones who actually retired," Stevens added.

Byron looked at his watch. "It's almost

five. I highly doubt anyone working for the retirement system will still be at work."

"There are ways around that," Tran said.

Byron stared at him. "I probably don't want to ask."

"You don't," Tran agreed with a shake of his head.

"Nuge, I want you to hit the basement archives and pull the shooting case file."

"Mold city, goodie for me," he said hunching his shoulders and rubbing his hands together in mock excitement.

Byron shot him a look of disapproval.

"On my way, Sarge."

Byron turned his attention to Pelligrosso. "Anything from the car?"

"Everything I found either belongs to Riordan himself or you. Whoever this guy is, he's good at covering his tracks."

"Mel, I want you and Gabe to compare the partial from the O'Halloran case with the seven names on the board."

"Done," she said.

"Are we thinking one of the cops is responsible?" Nugent asked. "Or are we just ruling all of them out?"

"Both," Byron said. "Someone returned to the location Riordan's car was dumped, pretended to be a cop, and grabbed potential evidence. Let's do exactly what we'd do on any other case, assume everyone is a suspect. I want each of you to report directly to me. Hand off or back-burner anything else you're working on. This takes top priority."

It was obvious to each of them their free time had evaporated before their very eyes. None of them would be having anything close to a personal life for the foreseeable future. Such is the life of a homicide investigator.

Byron found LeRoyer in his office. "Well?"

"Well what?"

"Did you tell Cross I want to interview him?"

"Yes. He said he'd get back to you. Said he couldn't do it tonight."

"Why not?"

"Because he's got a budget meeting with the city council."

"A budget meeting? Are you kidding me? How, exactly, is that more important than solving a murder? Strike that. Two murders."

"John, I don't know what to tell you. I'm only a lieutenant, I've got people to answer to, just like you."

"Well, that's just dandy."

"Stanton wants me to start writing up key

170

talking points for his press conference. Any thoughts on what you want released?"

"Yeah. Nothing. A press conference is the last thing we need right now. We've still got people to find and interview."

"Are you absolutely sure the target is the SRT?"

"I am now."

"Afternoon," said a voice from the hall. "Hope I'm not interrupting."

They both looked toward the doorway where Davis Billingslea stood, salivating like a rabid dog.

Byron departed for his own office, leaving LeRoyer to joust with Billingslea. He made a quick call to Ray Humphrey, who readily agreed to meet and suggested the Black Gull, a West End watering hole they'd often frequented.

Humphrey was his closest confidant and oldest friend. A history buff, Humphrey knew more about Portland than anyone Byron had ever known. He'd taken Byron under his wing, mentoring him, first as an officer then as a fledgling detective. Prior to retiring from the police department, he'd worked under Byron as a detective. His wife Wendy's yearlong battle with cancer had ended unsuccessfully. Her death had devastated him and was one of the reasons he'd laid down his shield.

Byron parked about a block from the Black Gull, as parking in the West End was hard to come by. There were several Portland bars known as cop hangouts. The Gull wasn't one of them. The Black Gull catered toward the working-class.outlaw type. Byron couldn't remember ever having seen another cop there, which was precisely why they both liked it. Humphrey was already there, seated at a corner table. He waved Byron over.

"Sarge. It's good to see you," he said as he stood, giving Byron an awkward combination of a handshake and bear hug.

"How've you been, Ray?"

"Never better, my friend. Never better. Take a seat." He signaled the barmaid to their table. "Whatdaya have?"

Byron held up his hand. "Nothing for me. I'm on the clock."

"What's this?" Humphrey said with a raised brow. "John Byron turning down a pint?"

"I'm afraid so."

"At the risk of being hit by lightning — *soda*?"

"Diet." ·

Humphrey turned to the shapely, freckle-faced girl. "Young lady, I'll have another Guinness and a *diet* for my friend."

"Did you want to order some food?" she asked Byron.

He shook his head. "No, thanks. I'm fine."

Humphrey leered at her as she walked away. "If only I was twenty years younger."

"Don't you mean thirty?"

Humphrey turned to face him and winked.

"How's the PI business, Ray?"

"Great. Busy, busy, busy. Cheating spouses, corporate theft, background work, all the usual."

"Pays the bills, huh?"

"It does a lot more than that, my friend. This business is a gold mine. Shoulda done this years ago."

Shortly after retiring from the PD, Humphrey had gone into the private investigations business with an old military buddy.

"You're not gonna ask me to come work with you again, are you?" Byron asked.

"Nah. A guy can only take being rejected so many times." Humphrey picked up the fresh pint from the table and motioned for Byron to do the same. "A toast. To friendship."

"Sláinte."

"How's the love life? You and Kay patch

things up yet?"

"Ah, hell no. It's over. She served the papers on me yesterday."

"Jeez, I'm sorry. Always thought you kids were good for each other."

"I don't want to talk about it."

Humphrey took a healthy swig from his glass, then wiped the foam from his upper lip. "So, what did you want to talk to me about?"

"A case."

"Ah, this is official business," he said, exaggerating the act of sitting up straight in his chair. "What can I do for my old sergeant?"

Byron reached into his suit pocket and removed a folded piece of paper. He unfolded it and laid it on the table in front of Humphrey. "Think we've got a serial killer."

Humphrey picked up the photocopy of the old SRT and studied it. "Someone's crossed out Jimmy O and Cleo. Are they — ?"

"Both dead."

Humphrey looked up at Byron. "How?"

"O'Halloran was suffocated. Cleo was shot in the head."

"Murdered?

Byron nodded.

"Holy shit." Humphrey resumed studying

the photo. "And you think what, I'm next?"

"I don't know, Ray. All I know is it looks like someone is targeting the guys in that picture."

"Why?"

"I was hoping you could tell me."

"Haven't got a clue, Sarge. I haven't seen most of them in years."

"How about Cleo or Jimmy O?"

"Not since I left the job anyway. What's that, four years?"

"About."

"And you have no idea why we're being targeted?"

"The only thing that stands out is that shooting in '85 with the armored car robbers. Same year the photo was taken."

Humphrey returned the photo to the table and took another drink. "You think it could be the guy we didn't get? Maybe he's pissed about us killing his three buddies."

"Andreas. It's possible."

"Did he just get out or something?"

"No. They never found him."

"Ever?"

"No."

"Great. If the feds couldn't find this guy, how are you supposed to?"

"I'm working on it. We want to offer you protection."

Humphrey shook his head. "I never needed protection before, Sarge. Not gonna start now." He patted the bulge under his jacket. "I can take care of myself."

Byron, anticipating his response, pressed on. "I know you can, Ray. But until I can get a handle on this, I'd feel better if we were watching all of you."

"Have you spoken to any of the others?"

"You're the first."

"Ten bucks says they won't want protection either. I'll help you anyway I can, you know that. But I won't be babysat like some damn civilian. How sure are you it's the guy who got away? I remember something at the time about the robbers being connected."

"Organized crime?"

"Yeah. Being a Boston armored car job, talk in the bureau was that they might've worked for Riccio. He ran everything in Beantown."

"We're talking with the feds. I'm considering every possibility."

The two men chatted for several minutes before Humphrey finished his beer and stood up. "I appreciate the heads-up, Sarge. I know you're trying to look out for me, but I'm a big boy."

"Watch your back, Ray," he said as he

stood and embraced his old friend.

Byron had hoped to get more from Humphrey, something that might point them in the right direction. As he drove to the station, he took out his cell and dialed a number from memory. Information was what they needed to piece this thing together, and he knew exactly where to look.

"Collier."

"Sam? It's John Byron."

"John, you old hound dog. What are you up to?"

FBI Special Agent Sam Collier, a staple in the Portland law enforcement community for more years than Byron could remember, was his go-to guy in the bureau. Tall and thin with wire-rimmed glasses, Collier looked more like an investment banker or an accountant than an FBI Agent. He'd always displayed an easygoing demeanor, but beneath his pleasant and calm veneer was a tenacious investigator. When he sank his teeth into a case, he never let go. His specialty was white-collar crime, but his investigations ran the gamut. In addition to Collier's tenacity, the quality Byron most admired was his trustworthiness. Whenever Byron had needed to run something sensitive by Collier, it had always remained between them. The same could not always be said for some of his coworkers at 109.

"You know me, Sam, working my tail off. How high are those stacks on your desk now?"

"About two feet and rising," Collier said, laughing out loud. "You know me too well. And what about your caseload? Rumor has it you're into something pretty big."

"Actually, that's why I'm calling."

"Anything you can gift wrap and send over so I can take all the credit?" Collier said.

"Not this time, I'm afraid. I've got two dead former officers and no clear motive."

"Shit. Anything I can do?"

"Any chance you might be able to lay your hands on a 1985 Boston armored-car robbery case file?"

"I remember that one. Might take me a few days. All of the 302s on a case that old would most likely be at headquarters in D.C., but I can put in a request if you want." A 302 was the federal government's document-designation number for case-agent supplements associated with all criminal investigations.

"I need this to stay quiet, Sam. None of my superiors know I'm reaching out and I'd like it to stay that way, if you know what

I mean."

"Indeed, I do. Don't want to see this on the front page, huh? Actually, I'm good friends with one of the section chiefs at HQ. I might be able to backdoor the request and keep it off the books. Make sure I get it back in the same condition as I gave it, my friend, or we will both, quite literally, be screwed."

"You don't happen to remember who the lead was on the case, do you?"

"Actually, I do. Name's Pritchard, bigwig. Worked most of his career out of the Boston field office. He worked his way up to Organized Crime Section Chief in D.C. Retired from the bureau last year as an Assistant Special Agent in Charge in Boston. Moved up here to Maine. Lives in Cape Elizabeth."

"Good guy?"

"From what I hear. Don't really know him. He was pretty dialed-in back in the day. Solved quite a few high-profile Boston cases. Made quite a name for himself. Ex-military."

"Jarhead like you?"

"Ha! Nothing so squared away. He's an old army dog. You want me to get you his contact info?"

"That'd be great."

"Okay, I'll get back to you on both."

"Thanks, Sam. I owe ya."

Byron pulled into the rear garage of 109 and parked his car. He hoped he was wrong about this being only the beginning. But if he was right, if this was the work of some twisted ex-con seeking revenge, who was next on the killer's list?

CHAPTER FOURTEEN

Dustin Tran had only managed to find addresses for Perrigo and Williams. Both were local. Diane and Byron drove to Falmouth to interview Perrigo while Tran and Nugent went searching for Williams.

It was seven-thirty by the time Byron and Diane pulled into the Falmouth Foreside driveway of Casa de Perrigo. They got out and surveyed the small two-story estate.

"Looks like someone does pretty well on a police pension," Diane said. "It's a little bigger than your apartment."

"Hey, my apartment's nothing to sneeze at."

Byron rang the doorbell. A well-kept middle-aged woman wearing a tan pantsuit opened the door. Her bright orange hair matched her manicured nails.

"Mrs. Perrigo?" Byron asked.

"Yes. May I help you?"

They both displayed their IDs. "Mrs. Perrigo, my name is Detective Sergeant John Byron and this is my partner Detective Diane Joyner."

"Vickie Perrigo," she said as she shook hands with both of them.

"Pleased to meet you, Vickie," Diane said.

"We'd like to speak to your husband, if he's around?" Byron asked.

"He is. Come right in, Detectives."

"I hope we're not catching you at a bad time," Diane said.

"Nonsense," she said with a wave of her hand. "We're just watching television."

"You have a lovely home, Vickie," Diane said.

"Thank you, it was left to us by my parents." Mrs. Perrigo led them through the foyer down a hallway into the living room. "Honey, we have company. This is Detective Sergeant Byron and Detective —"

"Joyner."

"That's right," Perrigo said. "This is my husband, Tony."

Byron immediately recognized the tanned, rugged face as one he'd seen at O'Halloran's funeral service.

After they'd been introduced, Vickie suggested they move into the dining room. "Can I get either of you something to drink?" she asked. "Wine or a beer?"

"We're still on the clock," Byron said. "Coffee?"

"That would be great," Diane said as they sat down at the dining room table.

"You're Reece's son, aren't you?" Perrigo asked.

"I am."

"He was a cop's cop."

"So I've heard. Thank you."

The mutual pleasantries and small talk continued until they were all seated at the table and the two detectives began to fill them in as to the reason for their visit.

"Jesus, I just attended Jimmy O'Halloran's funeral," Perrigo said. "I thought it was the cancer?"

"That's what we all thought initially," Byron said.

"So, what, you think I'm in some kind of danger?" Perrigo asked.

"It's a distinct possibility," Diané said.

"We believe someone may be targeting every member of the Special Reaction Team, as it existed in 1985," Byron said.

"Who would want to kill my Tony?" Vickie asked.

"We were hoping you might be able to shed some light on that," Byron said, addressing Perrigo.

"Me? I have no idea. The guys on my team

were all hard chargers. We put our share of criminals in prison and a few in the morgue."

"We think it may have something to do with a shooting you were involved in that year," Byron said.

"The only shooting any of us had in '85 was on Ocean Avenue. When Gagnon was killed."

"That's right," Byron said. "We think it could be the catalyst for what's happening now. Can you think of a reason someone might want all of you dead?"

Perrigo shook his head. "Nothing I can think of. We were trying to arrest four assholes wanted in connection with an out-of-state armored car robbery when the shooting happened. There were only three men in the house and we shot and killed them all. Maybe it's the other guy. The one who got away."

"We're checking into that," Byron said. "News reports of the incident said no money was recovered when you guys raided the house."

"Correct. We never found it."

"How much money was taken?" Vickie asked.

"One point four million," Diane said.

Byron had been casually observing the

highly accessorized Vickie Perrigo. One adjective came to mind: high-maintenance. Dangling from her lobes were a pair of expensive diamond earrings and adorning one ring finger was a large rock mounted in a gold setting, which Byron guessed was at least a carat. He couldn't even imagine the weekly cost of maintaining her hair and nails. "A lot of money, even by today's standards. Any idea what might've happened to it?"

Perrigo cocked his head slightly. "Sort of an antagonistic question isn't it, Sergeant Byron? You're not insinuating we helped ourselves, are you?"

"I'm not insinuating anything, Mr. Perrigo. We are looking at this from every angle, trying to establish motive. That much money might motivate some folks to do almost anything. We're only trying to determine where it went."

"I'm afraid I can't help you with that," Perrigo said curtly. "Perhaps the other robber made off with it."

"Maybe." Byron studied Perrigo's face, wondering why the former cop wasn't protesting more forcefully. Perrigo seemed much too calm.

"Have any of the other members of the team reached out to you, Mr. Perrigo?" Diane asked, trying to relieve some of the tension from the room.

He shifted his gaze toward Diane. "No, I haven't talked with any of them."

Both detectives also noticed a brief but obvious exchange of eye contact between husband and wife. The kind of nonverbal communication that meant: "Don't say a word, I've got this."

"Well, I wish I could be of more help to you both," Perrigo said as he stood up, sending a clear signal his participation in the interview was over. "But I'm afraid I don't know any more than I've already told you."

Byron remained seated and looked toward Vickie for help, but she also got up and began clearing the table, refusing to make eye contact with either one of them.

"We'd like to offer you both some protection, as a precaution," Diane said.

"Don't you mean surveillance?" Perrigo asked.

"Not at all," Byron said. "We want to protect you."

"Thanks, but we don't need any protection," Perrigo said. "I'm fully capable of protecting myself and my family."

"Here's my card in case either of you think of anything." Byron stood and attempted to hand the card to Vicki but she was staring out the window, ignoring him.

"Just leave it on the table, Sergeant," Perrigo said coldly.

"What do you think?" Diane asked as Byron backed the Taurus out of the driveway and onto Route 88.

"He's lying. He knew we'd be coming. They both knew."

"How would he know?"

"He was a cop. He's not as stupid as he'd have us believe."

"You think he's spoken to one of the others?" she asked.

"Probably." Byron turned to look at her. "I would."

"You're such a cynic."

"Took me twenty years."

"Think there's any hope for me?"

He grinned. "None."

Byron and Diane were headed to 109 when her cell rang.

"Hey, Nuge," she said as she put it on speaker. "How did you guys make out?"

"Williams wasn't home. I left a card in the door. You?"

"Perrigo knows more than he's saying," Byron said. "I actually think the wife knows, too."

"Did he want protection?" Nugent asked.

"Nope," Diane said. "Too damned proud."

"Yeah. Until the next one gets killed," Byron said.

"We're heading in to 109. What do you want us to do?" Nugent asked.

Byron glanced at the dashboard clock. Eight-thirty. "Why don't you and Dustin call it a night? We'll regroup in the morning."

"You're the boss. Oh, I left the PD-shooting file box in your office."

"Thanks, Nuge."

"Oh yeah, the Tran man said to tell you he'll resume his search for the others first thing, Sarge," Nugent said.

"Sounds good."

"Night guys." Diane ended the call and looked at Byron. "What do you say we grab the files, some dinner, and do some light reading?"

The thought of going to his empty apartment and the unpacked moving boxes was nearly unbearable. "Your place?"

"Of course."

"You're on."

They ate pizza and breadsticks and poured over the reports until well past midnight. Nothing they read seemed to provide any new information. Byron was having difficulty focusing on the task at hand. His distraction was mainly due to the outfit that Diane had changed into. Her tight-fitting sweatpants and T-shirt left little to the imagination. He knew it was time to leave when he noticed Diane yawning.

As Byron drove into Portland, he forced his mind away from Diane and back to the case. Something had changed to bring about these murders. But what? Why now, after twenty years, was someone going after former Portland cops? If it was Andreas, where had he been all this time? It certainly wasn't prison. Byron knew that even if Andreas had given a fake name, following an arrest, his fingerprints would have been cross-checked against state and federal databases. Even the smallest of towns would have seen to that, and if not, the department of corrections surely would have. Unless he had gotten arrested outside of the U.S., in some other country. It was possible, especially if he had gotten away with the robbery money. But how could he have reentered the country without being detected? And why would he come back?

Byron whipped the car into a Port City Savings Bank lot and jammed the gearshift into park. He opened the door and leaned out just as his stomach convulsed up the pizza. He pulled the car forward, grabbed a handful of napkins from the console, and stepped out. His head was pounding and he was sweating profusely. *Something I ate?* But he knew better. He leaned against the side of the car until the feeling passed, then got back into the car and exited the lot. He lowered the windows as he drove, letting the night air blow on his face. He didn't need this right now. There were still too many unanswered questions. What he needed were answers. What he didn't need were the DTs or another dead cop.

CHAPTER FIFTEEN

Friday morning brought fog and a cold, steady drizzle. Autumn had finally arrived. At six-thirty, Byron pulled up in front of 109, still a half hour before any of the other detectives were scheduled to arrive. Sleep had been sporadic. Thoughts of the investigation kept him awake for most of the night as did another bout of nausea. He felt tired but not nearly as tired as he should have. He credited this feeling to the adrenaline gun that went off each and every time he found himself on the hunt — and with a cop-killing psycho on the loose, he was definitely on the hunt.

At his desk, he checked both voice and emails, impatiently waiting until seven before calling LeRoyer. "What time can I expect to interview Cross?" Byron asked.

"And good morning to you too, Sergeant."

"Well?"

"I'll talk to him first thing. I promise."

"I don't want him controlling this, Marty. He's going to submit to an interview just like everyone else. We both know, if these guys did something they shouldn't have, they'll be circling the wagons."

LeRoyer let out an audible sigh. "John, at this very moment I'm driving my kids to school. After I drop them off, I'll be heading in to work. When I get to 109, I'll follow-up with him. Okay?"

"Fine."

As Byron was hanging up, Tran knocked on his open office door. "Morning, Sarge. Got a second?"

He wondered why his tech-savvy detective appeared so somber. It was unlike Tran not to lead with something witty like, "Hey, striped dude."

"Sure, Dustin. What's up?"

"I think I've located a couple more of the guys on the list."

"Good. Who've we got?" he asked with pen and notebook at the ready.

"Falcone and Beaudreau. Falcone is living in Damariscotta at a place called Down East Senior Care. It's an assisted-living facility."

Byron scribbled down the info. "What about Beaudreau?"

"I couldn't find a home address for him, but it looks like he might be the owner of a

Westbrook strip club called the Unicorn."

He looked up from his notes with a grin. "An unappreciated career path, I'm sure."

"I guess. Only thing is, it looks like he's traveling at the moment. He's not due back until Monday."

"How do we know that?"

"TSA. He flew out of Portland yesterday, round-trip to Atlanta."

"Thanks, Dustin."

"Sarge, I want to apologize again for yesterday. Sometimes I get a little too cavalier and say insensitive things without really thinking."

"If this is about my father, don't worry about it."

"You're not mad?"

"Dustin, if I let it bother me every time someone made an insensitive remark, *I'd* have to find a new career path. And I don't really see myself as the strip club type," he said with a wink. "Thanks for the information, number one son."

Tran smiled. "My pleasure, striped dude."

Byron was on his way to the third floor to find Pelligrosso when his cell phone rang. "Byron."

"I knew you'd be hot on the trail already," Collier said.

"Been at it for hours, slacker. Not everyone gets to sleep in like you feds. You got something for me?"

"Of course. I only call with good news. The case files you requested should be here on Saturday."

"Tomorrow?"

"Probably not until late morning."

"That was quick."

"Told you, I know people. I'll call you as soon as they arrive. Also, I've got Terry Pritchard's home number. He's expecting your call. Prepared to copy?"

"Go with it."

Byron wrote the number on his palm and thanked Collier for the quick response. He ended the call as he was walking into the lab. Pelligrosso was seated in front of the AFIS computer.

"Hey, Gabe."

"Sarge."

"Any luck matching our partial?"

"Not yet. I did manage to locate Williams's and Beaudreau's prints on file in the old concealed-weapon permit files. Neither are a match."

"What about Ray Humphrey? He's a P.I. He must be licensed to carry."

"Probably carrying as a retired officer, no prints required. The state most likely has

194

his prints on file, but it's gonna take some time. I've submitted dozens of requests I'm still waiting on. Some I made months ago."

"Do the best you can."

"Any idea where I might find Falcone's prints?"

"No, but I found out he's in assisted living. Probably not O'Halloran's mystery guest anyway."

"You planning to meet this morning?"

"Eight-thirty, conference room."

"I'll be there."

"Happy Friday, Sergeant," Shirley said as Byron walked by her desk.

"Morning, Shirley."

"Need anything typed?"

He knew she was only reminding him to keep up with the paperwork. She complained whenever any of his detectives dumped a pile of reports in her in-bin for typing. He also knew she hated being out of the loop. If Grant had her way, he'd be giving her the case updates before LeRoyer. "I'm all set right now, thanks. But you might want to check with Nuge and Diane."

"Okay. Because you know how much I hate getting behind, right?"

"I hear you." He disappeared around the corner and out of her sight. He was walking toward LeRoyer's office when he caught a quick glimpse of Cross scurrying down the rear hallway.

LeRoyer was seated at his desk checking voicemail. Before Byron could ask, he held up his hand like a traffic cop. "Don't start. I just spoke with him, John."

"Yeah, I saw him sneaking out."

"He's got appointments all morning, but said he'd come by your office at ten-thirty."

"Probably because he knows it's easier to leave my office than to kick me out of his."

LeRoyer didn't respond to the comment.

"What's the word on delaying the chief's press conference?" Byron asked.

"You might be in luck."

"How so?"

"Stanton is considering waiting until Monday."

"At the risk of looking a gift horse in the mouth, why?"

"Big news always plays better on Mondays. Friday's are shitty days for press conferences. People are already thinking about or starting their weekends. Everybody watches the news on Monday night."

"So this fortuitous decision to wait is all about his friggin' ratings?"

"Like you said, don't look a gift horse in the mouth. Besides, now you've got the whole weekend to solve this case."

"Gee, thanks."

"You okay, John? You're kinda pale."

"I'm fine," Byron snapped without meaning to, worried that his stomach might have another surprise in store. "Think maybe I'm fighting something off. I'll be fine."

"You sure?"

"Yes."

"How'd you make out with last night's interviews?"

"O and one. Williams wasn't home and Perrigo wasn't talking."

"He wouldn't talk to you?"

"No, he talked. But he didn't say anything."

"You think he's got something to hide?"

"I think somebody does. We're meeting at eight-thirty to go over the case. Wanna sit in?"

"I'd love to, but I've got to meet with the City Appropriations Committee about some budget changes. You wanna keep chasing bad guys, I've gotta keep beggin' for scraps. I'll catch up with you later." Byron turned to leave. "Oh, and John."

"Yeah?"

"Play nice with Cross, okay?"

"You know me."

"Yeah. That's exactly why I said it."

The rain had stopped. The sun was fighting to burn through the shroud of fog still holding Portland in its grip. Byron ran across the street to the Middle Street Delicatessen. He wanted to recaffeinate, thinking coffee might help settle his stomach. He also wanted to check the *Portland Herald.* Billingslea had been ghosting him all week, and it would be so like him to try and break a story before everyone else. Even if it meant being reckless. A quick scan of the headlines on both the front page and local section turned up nothing. Satisfied, he placed the paper back in the rack, grabbed a large coffee, and returned to 109.

It was nine o'clock by the time they'd wrapped up the meeting. Each of them was up to speed on the latest developments, or lack thereof. Diane and Nugent headed out to try and locate Williams again while Tran returned to his office to try and locate a work address for Williams on the off chance he still wasn't at home. Pelligrosso and Stevens returned to the mountain of work awaiting them in the lab, to include finding a match for the partial print. Byron returned to his office and closed the door. He was feeling quite a bit better. He still had Cross's interview to prepare for as well as a pile of mildew-covered officer-involved shooting reports to slog through, but first he had a phone call to make to former Special Agent Terry Pritchard.

"Terry, it's John Byron. I appreciate your taking my call."

"Not at all, Sergeant Byron. Happy to help, if I can."

"And *John* is fine. Okay if I put you on speaker? I wanna take some notes while we talk."

"Fine by me."

Byron opened his notepad and changed the setting on the phone. "Can you hear me okay?"

"Five by five. Collier told me you've requested the Boston armored-car case file."

"A little light reading."

Pritchard laughed. "Until your eyes cross, you mean. You forget, I know how many man hours went into that case. For the first two months there was a team of us, after that, when the trail went cold, it was only me and one other agent. I literally worked that case for a year. At least officially."

"Meaning?"

"Meaning, I continued to work it on my own time until I retired. You know what it's like when you've got that case, the itch you can't seem to scratch."

Byron knew exactly what he meant.

"I couldn't let it go. The powers that be wouldn't let me continue to log any more hours on it, not after the Beirut bombings at the end of '83."

"I don't understand what Beirut has to do with it."

"Resources. Everything became about fighting terrorists after Lebanon. No one gave a damn about an armored car robbery. I was lucky to get as much time as I got. Do your bosses know you've reached out?"

"No. And they wouldn't understand. I'm already getting too much resistance."

"Not surprised. You and I might've worked well together, John. So, where do you want to start?"

"What have you got that's not in the file?"

"Ha. You're asking me if I kept my own private notes outside of the case file, which would have been in direct violation of bureau policy?"

Byron knew if Pritchard was half the investigator Collier said he was, he'd never show all his cards to his superiors. "Yes, I am."

"Of course I did. Dug them out before you called. Got 'em right here."

The two men dissected the investigation, discussing everything from the missing money, the missing robber, and the seemingly impenetrable thin blue line.

"What do you think happened to the money?" Byron asked.

"I really don't know, but my gut always told me some of the cops might've taken it."

"You don't think the missing robber made off with it?"

"Andreas? It's certainly possible."

"But? You don't sound like you believe it."

"I just don't think it's all that likely."

"Why?"

"A couple of reasons. Not one of those four could spell Mensa, even if you'd handed them the letters in the right order. They were strictly small-time thugs, lucky to pull off a job like that in the first place. Who knows, two different guards and maybe they never even get their hands on the money. But even an idiot would know better than to let one guy leave the safe house with all the money."

"But suppose they were dumb enough. With that much money, couldn't he have simply disappeared?"

"Perhaps, but it's more likely he went to the wrong people for help and was killed for it."

"Did you ever find any evidence to suggest it was the cops?"

"No, but I couldn't find anything to exonerate them either. The cops on that team were as tight a group as I've ever seen."

"The department reports mentioned a confidential informant, did you ever find out who it was?"

"No. O'Halloran was in charge of the detectives, and he made his case to the U.S. attorney, telling him the CI was too valuable to the department to take a chance on divulging the identity. The U.S. attorney agreed, saying unless the matter was going to trial, there was no need to release the name to the FBI."

"Three dead suspects and one missing doesn't make for much of a trial, I guess."

"Exactly."

"Was there ever a reward offered?"

"You'll see all of this in our files when you get them, but the short answer is yes. The First Bank of Boston put up fifty thousand."

"Was there ever any attempt to claim the money by the CI or anyone else?"

"Oddly enough, no."

Byron's hand was beginning to cramp from note-taking. He checked his watch. Ten-thirty. "Terry, I hate to end our conversation, but I've gotta get to an interview."

"No problem. You've got my number. Let

me know if I can be of any further help to you."

Byron hung up the phone and grabbed his notepad. *Time for the Ass Chief to answer a few questions.*

CHAPTER SIXTEEN

"Thanks for agreeing to speak with me, Chief," Byron said, unable to keep the sarcasm from his voice.

"Let's cut the crap, Byron," Cross said, his arms crossed defensively. "I'm here because Stanton ordered me to talk to you, period. Don't fool yourself into thinking you have any influence with me. I'm a busy man. If you've got questions, ask them."

Outwardly, Byron maintained his poker face, but inside he wore a smile a mile wide, enjoying the reversal of roles and the irony that accompanied getting Cross into an interview room. "What can you tell me about the night of October nineteenth, 1985?"

Cross shrugged. "What's to tell? You've read the reports."

Byron nodded. "I've read them. But as we both know, not everything ends up on paper. I'm trying to establish a motive. Why, after more than thirty years, would someone start killing the cops who were involved in a shooting?"

"I've no idea. You're the detective. You tell me." Cross gave no indication he was nervous, but Byron always found it difficult to get a glimpse past his pompous and arrogant façade.

"The reports indicate you were acting on information from a confidential informant. Whose CI was it?"

"I don't remember. O'Halloran was the CID lieutenant at the time. I assume it was one of his contacts."

"Who else would know?"

"I've no idea," he said, his mouth twisting into the smug little smirk that Byron hated. Cross had predicted the question in advance and Byron knew it. Giving the one answer he couldn't follow-up on, as O'Halloran was dead.

"Oh, I guess I was wrong, then."

"About what?"

"I just thought since you were one of the SRT supervisors, you might've been privy to more of the intel." Cross's irritating smirk vanished. Byron took some satisfaction in knocking him down a peg. "Take me through the information that led you to the Ocean Avenue address."

Cross checked his watch. "I have an eleven o'clock appointment I won't be late for."

"I don't expect this to take that long. Do you need me to repeat the question?"

Cross glared at him. "No, *Sergeant.* I think I've got it. The CI told us several of the men responsible for the First Bank of Boston armored car robbery were hiding out on Ocean Avenue in Portland. According to the CI, they needed help laundering the money. They were worried some of the bills had been marked."

"Were they?"

"Not according to the feds. They told us they'd released misinformation to the media in an attempt to make it more difficult for the robbers to escape. Along with the reward."

"That's right," Byron said, pretending he'd forgotten. "The reward. How much was it?"

"Fifty thousand."

"Hmm. So, if your CI helped you find these guys —"

"I already told you, he wasn't my CI."

Byron jotted a quick note on his legal pad. "Wouldn't he have been eligible to collect the reward?"

"I suppose."

"But no one ever came forward to collect." Byron tapped his pen on the table for emphasis. "Didn't that seem a little strange?"

Cross unfolded his arms and leaned forward over the table. His big red jowls had darkened a shade or two. "I suppose it did. But as I've already told you, it wasn't my CI."

"Don't you mean him?"

"What?" Cross asked, his irritation obvious.

Byron looked down at his note pad. "*He* wasn't my CI" is what you said. If you didn't know who the CI was, how do you know it was a male?"

Cross leaned back in his chair, trying to regain some of his composure. "I said *he* out of habit. I assumed it was a male CI, but I don't know for sure. You could always check with Jimmy O," he said, his smirk returning.

Byron had a sudden urge to climb over the table and knock some cooperation back into the Ass Chief, but he resisted the impulse. "That would seem unlikely, but I appreciate your keen insight."

Cross's eyes narrowed, never leaving Byron's.

"Why didn't anyone contact the FBI about this intel? It was their case after all."

"Wasn't my call to make. Like you, Sergeant, I was only a supervisor. I knew my place. Besides, we had no way of knowing if the intel was any good. The plan was to set up on the house and see what we could find out."

"Didn't work out too well, did it?"

"Once we confirmed the presence of armed and dangerous criminals we had no choice but to breach. They fired at us and we returned fire."

"Kind of convenient, wouldn't you say?"

"Convenient, Sergeant? Not really a word I'd use to describe losing one of our own."

"And all three suspects."

"They made that choice, not us."

"And the money was never found?"

"I have no idea. *We* never found it. You'd have to check with the feds."

"I did. It's still missing."

Cross shrugged indifferently.

"What do you think happened to it?"

"Not a clue. Word on the street was the last robber took off to Canada with it."

"You're talking about Andreas?"

"The one they never found," Cross said in his most condescending tone.

Byron tried shifting gears. "Who do you think is responsible for murdering O'Halloran and Riordan?"

"Once again, you're the detective. You tell me. Maybe it's Andreas, seeking revenge for us killing his buddies."

"Why would he wait thirty years?"

Cross seemed to consider the question. "Maybe he ran out of money. How the fuck would I know?" He checked his watch again and stood up. "Speaking of running out, I'm out of time. Sorry." His smirk returned. "Gotta run to my eleven o'clock."

Byron remained seated. "I'll let you know if I think of any more questions."

"I think I'm done with you," Cross said as he headed toward the door.

"One more thing, Chief."

Cross turned back to face him, his expression one of annoyance.

"Have you had recent contact with any of the others on the SRT?"

"No." Cross turned toward the door, then stopped. "Oh, and before you ask, because I know how concerned you are about my safety, I don't have any need of your protection detail. I hope, for your sake, you start making some progress on this case, Sergeant. Be a real shame to have to reassign it."

Byron stopped into the locker room to splash some cold water on his face. What he

209

really wanted was a long hot shower to wash the stress away. But for now the locker room sink would have to do. As he dried his face and neck with a couple of paper towels, he could hear Kenny Crosby regaling one of the newer detectives on the property side of CID with his indefatigable wisdom. He'd never had much use for Crosby. The muscled-up drug detective had always been something of a wiseass, and everyone knew he was Cross's errand boy. Doing the chief's bidding was how he'd earned the coveted drug investigator's job with the Maine Drug Enforcement Administration (MDEA).

"See, kid, if you're not careful about splitting your time equally between work and home, you'll wind up like Sergeant Byron over there. He's a glory boy when it comes to solving high-profile cases, but it don't mean shit at home." The young detective didn't say a word. "John spends so much time with New York's finest, it's no wonder his wife threw him out."

Byron saw red. He threw the wet towels into the trash and marched around the bank of lockers. Crosby was just out of the shower and stood wrapped only in a towel. The barrel-chested detective sergeant lived in the PPD gym and it showed. Big arms, big chest. And a midsection showing the effects of too much beer.

"Hey, John. I didn't know you were in here," he said.

Byron walked up until their noses were nearly touching. "What'd you say, Kenny?"

"What?" Crosby wore a shit-eating grin. He held his hands up in a mock surrender. "I didn't say anything, Johnny boy. No need to get your panties all in a bunch."

Byron maintained eye contact until Crosby looked away. "Just as I thought," he said as he turned to walk away.

"I was only explaining to the new kid here how you were probably tapping that sweet African ass."

Byron didn't think or hesitate, he reacted. Stepping in so his weight would be behind it, he delivered the first punch to the large detective's beer-softened midsection. His second punch connected with Crosby's jaw, knocking him backward over the wooden bench. Crashing into the lockers, his feet slipping out from under him on the wet floor, he fell hard, momentarily pinned between the bench and lockers. Byron knew he'd gotten lucky. He also knew if Crosby got back on his feet, the second round wasn't likely to go as well as the first.

The door to the locker room burst open and LeRoyer stormed in. "What the hell is going on in here?"

Neither Byron nor Crosby said a word as they scowled at each other. The junior detective stood wide-eyed.

"Well?" LeRoyer shouted. "I asked you both a question."

Crosby was the first to speak as he struggled to regain his feet and straighten his towel. "Nothing's going on, Lieu. I was just talking to the rookie here. Guess I musta slipped on the wet floor. Clumsy, huh?"

LeRoyer turned to the new kid on the block. "Is that what happened, Detective?"

"I — I didn't see anything, Sir."

"Of course you didn't. Get the hell outta here."

The rookie detective disappeared out the door like a shot. LeRoyer looked from Byron to Crosby, then back to Byron. "Well?"

"Like Kenny said Lieu, he musta slipped."

Byron was turning left onto Middle Street from the parking garage when he saw Diane walking down the steps of 109. He pulled the car up next to the curb and stopped.

"How did it go with Cross?" Diane asked, as she leaned in the open window.

"How do you think?" Byron asked.

"He didn't tell you anything we didn't

already know. And he was arrogant."

"Don't forget prick. He was an arrogant prick." Byron inhaled, held it for a moment, and then tried to expel his frustration.

"Where you headed, sailor?" she asked.

"Lunch. Need to get out of here before I punch someone."

"Mind if I join you? For the lunch not the punch."

He smiled. "Sure. Hop in."

She pointed to his hand as he pulled away from the curb. "You're bleeding."

He lifted his fingers off the steering wheel and saw she was right. "I cut myself in the kitchen this morning."

She tilted her head in disbelief.

"Before I left for work."

"Huh. I don't recall seeing it." She dug through the console for a napkin and handed one to him. "You sure it's not from your school yard altercation with Kenny?"

He raised his eyebrows, surprised. "How'd you hear about that?"

"I'm a detective, remember? Wanna tell me what it was about?"

"Nope."

"Are you crazy?"

"How do you mean?"

"The guy's huge, John. What the hell were you thinking?"

"Guess I wasn't."

"Word is you took him down with one punch."

A smile crept across his face in spite of his attempt to hide it. "If you must know, it was two."

"My hero," she said, batting her lashes. "Where did you learn to fight like that?"

"I'm Irish, remember? There are two things the Irish do well."

"I'll bet in your case it's three," she said, giving him a seductive grin. She reached for her seat belt. "What were you thinking for lunch?"

"Hadn't really. You have a preference?"

"I could go for a really greasy burger and fries."

"I know a place."

Dotty's Lunch was a greasy spoon located in West Falmouth, just outside of Portland, well known for tasty food and reasonable prices. The drive allowed Byron a chance to cool down a bit before giving himself indigestion.

They took their food and drinks outside, taking advantage of the cooler weather and bright sunshine. There were a half-dozen picnic tables scattered across the rear lawn. They commandeered the one closest to the wood line and sat next to each other, facing the road.

"So what to do you think?" she asked, sucking the melted cheese from her thumb.

Byron swallowed the large bite of burger he'd been chewing. "About the burger?"

"No, silly. About Cross?"

"Ah." He took a long drink from his soda straw. "I think he's lying. Or at the very least holding back."

"About?"

"How they came by the information in the first place. He said the same thing about the CI we read in the reports."

"It did look like they'd intentionally glossed over it."

"That's what I mean. He put it on O'Halloran. Said it was one of the lieutenant's snitches who gave them the info. Told me he didn't know who the CI was."

"You don't believe him?"

"Nope. Felt like he was toying with me. Like he knew I couldn't prove otherwise." Byron took another handful of fries. "Pretty sure he slipped up at one point."

"How so?"

"He referred to the CI as *he*."

"Did you call him on it?"

"I did. Told me he was only generalizing. Said he didn't know who gave the information to O'Halloran. Any luck finding Williams?"

"Nope. We left another business card. Nuge's card was gone, so he's probably been home and gone already. Tran's still trying to find out where he works."

"Sounds like he's avoiding us."

"Did you talk to Pritchard?"

"I did," Byron said, wiping the ketchup from his chin with a napkin.

"And?"

"And, I think he may be able to help."

Former Portland Police Sergeant Eric Williams was killing time with a cigarette as he waited for Ray Humphrey to arrive. Williams stood leaning against the front end of a dark blue Escalade SUV, with chrome rims and dealer plates. He had parked here, at the Westbrook commuter lot between exits 47 and 48 off the Maine Turnpike, an hour after he had telephoned Humphrey at his office on Commercial Street and requested a face-to-face. Humphrey had readily agreed. It was nearly one o'clock when Humphrey drove into the lot and parked beside him.

"Ray," Williams said as his former colleague got out of the car. "Thanks for meeting with me."

"I'm glad you reached out, Eric," Humphrey said as they shook hands. "So, you wanna fill me in on what the hell is happening here?"

"I don't know. But someone is sending a pretty clear message." Williams dropped the cigarette butt on the pavement and twisted it under his black wing-tip, then pulled a fresh one from the pack in his suit coat and lit it. "So far they've taken out O'Halloran and Riordan. Byron approach you yet?" Williams watched his reaction closely, knowing he was tight with the younger Byron.

"He did."

"What did he ask you?"

"He asked about the shooting. Showed me the group SRT photo he took from Jimmy O's house."

Williams shoved the lighter back in his pocket.

"What did you tell him?"

"Only what I had to."

"Does he know anything?"

"I don't think so. Sounds like he only knows what was reported. Has he talked with you?"

"Not yet. But one of his people stuck a business card in the door at my house. It won't be long." He inhaled then blew out a smoke ring. "I know I don't have to remind

217

you what's at stake here. Right?"

"You don't. But what the hell are we supposed to do? I'm not gonna wait around and see if I'm next. Someone's coming after us, Eric, and we don't have a fucking clue who."

"I'm working on it. In the meantime, keep your eyes and ears open and your mouth shut. Remember, if one of us says anything stupid, we all go down."

"Do you want me to reach out to any of the others?"

"No. I'll be your contact," Williams said, handing him a business card. "My personal cell is on the back. And don't reach out to me unless you hear something."

"Okay."

"Oh, one more thing, if Byron asks, you haven't seen me."

It was seven-thirty. Margaret and Reginald Cross were finishing dinner.

"Did you want seconds, hon?" she said as she got up from the table.

"Did you make anything for desert?

"I made apple crisp. Your favorite."

"Then, no, on the seconds," he said, rubbing his stomach. "I've gotta save room."

The home phone rang. "I got it," Margaret hollered from the kitchen. "It's probably our Wendy. Said she'd call tonight."

Cross finished the last couple of bites. He could hear his wife talking in the next room but couldn't make out what she was saying.

"Hon," she said, "it's for you."

"Who is it?"

"Jimmy from dispatch."

"Okay, I'll pick it up in the other room." He made his way to his study. "All right, Marge, I've got it," he said, picking up the receiver. He waited until she'd hung up before speaking. "This is Chief Cross."

"It's been too long, Reg."

"Who is this?" But he recognized the voice immediately.

"Oh, I think you know who this is, and you should know why I'm calling. One question. Do you have control of this thing or not?"

"I do," he said, the pitch of his voice increasing by two full octaves. He turned and closed the door to the den. "I've got wheels in motion as we speak. There's nothing to worry about." Cross waited nervously, holding his breath. He heard nothing but silence from the other end of the line. "Did you hear me?"

"Let me assure you, Reggie, if I'm forced to get involved you will not like how things turn out."

"You won't. I'm handling every —" He heard a click as the line was disconnected.

CHAPTER SEVENTEEN

Saturday morning came with a quick meeting at 109. Following the meeting, Byron sent Diane and Nugent north to Damariscotta to try their luck with Falcone while he paid a visit to Williams. Tran had finally located the former SRT supervisor, working at a car dealership in York County. Byron figured the former sergeant would be far less likely to try bullying tactics if another supervisor conducted the interview.

At one in the afternoon, Byron was seated in a maroon faux-leather chair across from Williams's secretary, Dixie. Dixie sported the shortest skirt, longest legs, and blondest hair to ever come out of a bottle. Byron suspected she was a bit more than Williams's personal assistant.

He sipped coffee, which tasted suspiciously like thirty-weight motor oil. He was perusing, but not actually reading, a magazine from the glass coffee table. The glossy cover depicted a showdown between the newest Cadillac Escalade and Lincoln Navigator. Byron, who'd never have a financial portfolio worthy of either, wondered how anyone could possibly care.

As air tools whirred noisily in the nearby service bays, Byron scanned a wall covered in awards of excellence for sales and service. Hiding a knowing smile, he wondered how every dealership he'd ever been in had earned the exact same awards from their corporate entities.

Dixie was doing her best to look seductive, twirling her pen through her dyed curls while she talked on the phone. Based on what little he could hear, her call was of a personal nature. Growing impatient, he checked the time again. Ten past the hour. Power play, plain and simple. Williams was projecting his importance.

At precisely one-fifteen, the general sales manager of southern Maine's largest Cadillac dealership walked in. "My apologies for making you wait, Sergeant," Williams said in a booming baritone as he stuck out his hand.

Byron stood and firmly shook his hand. "Not at all. I appreciate your willingness to meet with me, Mr. Williams."

In the time it took the two men to shake

hands, Byron had sized him up. Williams wore dark gray suit pants and a white dress shirt open at the collar, sleeves rolled up. The suit coat and tie he'd long since discarded, in favor of the down-to-business look. He was sporting a gold Rolex watch, too much aftershave, and a pair of glossy black dress shoes. He maintained eye contact and flashed a smile of bleached teeth. Byron didn't like him, not one bit.

"Please, call me Eric," he said, gesturing for Byron to follow him into his private office. "Dixie, hold my calls, would you, hon?"

Williams grabbed a couple of bottled waters out of a small fridge, handing one to Byron. When they were seated, he said, "So, what can I do for my brothers at the police department?"

"Well, Eric, we're looking into two murders. We have reason to believe they're connected."

"Really, John? Is it okay if I call you John?" Williams asked, cozying up to Byron as if they were embarking on a newfound friendship.

"That's fine," Byron said.

"How exactly can I help?"

Everything about the guy screamed fake. Something below the surface of this well-rehearsed former cop's act was all wrong. It felt like something more than a typical car salesman persona.

"The victims were both former colleagues of yours."

"You're kidding? Who?"

"James O'Halloran and Cleophus Riordan. I'm surprised you haven't heard about it."

"Working seventy to eighty hours a week, I don't have time to keep up on the news. Jeez, Cleo and Jimmy O, I haven't thought about either of them in years. Murdered? I can't believe it. What do you need from me?"

"We believe these murders are connected to the 1985 Boston armored car robbery and the SRT shooting that followed. You were a part of that, right?"

"Yeah, yeah, I was. It was a long time ago, though; some days I have trouble remembering what I ate for breakfast." Williams flashed another a fake smile. "What do you want to know?"

He bet Williams didn't have any trouble remembering bottom line cost to the dealership on the gold Cadillac CTS parked out on the showroom floor or, for that matter, the length of Ms. Dixie Rose's inseam. "Anything you can recall might be helpful."

"Sure, sure, let me think." Mr. Snake Oil

leaned back and stared up at the suspended ceiling. "Well, the entire team was there that night. We were pretty jacked up. These guys we were after were real desperadoes, robbed an armored car in broad daylight. We'd been training on the outdoor range all day. Got the call-out early evening. The robbers were holed up in a house on Ocean Avenue. Lieutenant O'Halloran briefed us at 109. That's what we used to call police headquarters."

"Still do. Do you remember where the information came from?"

"Sure, it was one of . . . No, wait, different case. I can't remember exactly. But I do remember that one of the bad guys' girlfriends owned the house where they were hiding, or something like that. Anyway, once we were all in place, O'Halloran gave the signal to take the house. I was part of the four-man entry team. We used flash bangs, to distract them, before breaching the door."

"Who else was on the entry team?"

"Reg, Dom, and Bruce."

"You're talking about Cross, Beaudreau, and Gagnon, correct?"

"Yeah, sorry. So, we took the door and went in hot. Immediately everything turned to shit. It was like a fucking war zone. They were shooting at us and we dove for cover and returned fire. The smoke was so thick you could barely see."

Byron watched Williams's eyes glaze over as he relayed the story. He knew from experience the former sergeant was now back in the house on Ocean Avenue and no longer seated in his office. Officers recalling traumatic events often find themselves on a time-travel trip of the mind.

"After it was over, Bruce was dead, shot in the throat. We'd killed three of the robbers. The fourth guy was missing."

Williams's recall was far better than he'd been led to believe. "What happened after that?"

"We secured everything, searched the house, and put out an ATL for the missing robber," he said, referring to an attempt to locate.

"Did you find any of the money?"

He shook his head. "No. It wasn't in the house. We figured the other robber took off with it."

Byron noted a change in his demeanor. The glazed eyes were gone, replaced by the predatory look of a salesman. Williams had returned to the here and now, his former smooth façade up and running. "Anything else?" Byron asked.

"That's about all I can really remember."

"Have you had contact with any of the other members of your team recently?"

"No, not recently. Once or twice at Christmas parties after I retired, I guess, but it's been years since I've run into any of them."

"Really, not even a phone call?"

"Nope, not even a call, John."

Everyone lies to cops. It's an indisputable fact. Their reasons might vary, but the end result is always the same. The lies make every investigation infinitely more difficult. Some people lie to cover up involvement, some because they're asked to, some lie by embellishing the truth in their own misguided attempt at being helpful, but most lie because they think it's their duty to fuck with the police, no matter what. Byron, who knew this better than most, knew Williams was lying. What he didn't know was why. He wasn't surprised, the guy was in charge of a car dealership after all. If his lips were in motion, it meant he was probably slinging the bull.

Was Williams behind these deaths, or was it something else entirely? He decided not to challenge him right now. He'd save it for a later conversation.

"You really think someone is targeting everyone who was there that night?" Williams asked.

"Yes, we do. Any idea who we should be looking at?"

"I remember there was some talk about Jack Riccio, the mobster. They thought he might've been behind the robbery. That the guys who ripped off the armored car may have worked for him."

"Do you remember where you heard that?"

He shook his head. "No. It could have been the feds or our guys in CID. I can't really remember."

"Anyone else you can think of?"

"What about the other robber? I can't remember his name. That's probably who you're searching for. Was he ever caught?"

"Andreas. No, he's still missing." He studied Williams's face for a reaction but saw none. "You mentioned earlier that one of the robbers' girlfriends owned the house on Ocean Avenue. Was she ever interviewed?"

"Dunno. You'd have to check with one of the guys who worked CID."

Byron made a mental note to do exactly that. "Can you think of any other reason someone might want you guys dead?"

"Jeez, no." Williams fidgeted with the plastic cap from his open water bottle. "So, you think this guy is going to try and come after me too?"

"It would seem likely. Until we know why this is happening, we have to assume you're all possible targets. We're recommending each of you allow us to set up a protection detail."

"You mean surveillance."

"Yes. To try and protect you." He watched as Williams pretended to ponder the idea, but Byron already knew what his answer would be.

"No, John. I really appreciate the offer, but I think I can handle it myself. I've still got my permit to carry. I like my chances."

Williams's desk phone rang. "Okay, tell him I'll be right there." He hung up. "Sorry about this, John, but duty calls. I've got to go put out a fire for Mr. Dushambeaux, the GM." His toothy bleached smile reappeared as he stood. "Sorry I couldn't be of more help."

"I appreciate your time. Let me know if you think of anything else."

"I will."

Williams walked Byron out of the dealership, shook hands with him, and reentered the business.

Byron waited for a minute or two before walking back inside. As he approached Dixie's desk, she looked up and smiled.

"Well, hello again, Officer."

"Sorry to bother you, but I forgot to give Mr. Williams my card and I don't want to interrupt him while he's in with the GM," Byron said, motioning toward the empty office.

Dixie gave him a puzzled look. "Mr. Dushambeaux? But he's vacationing in the Caribbean."

"Oh, perhaps I misunderstood," he said, giving her his most disarming smile. "Could you see he gets this?"

Down East Senior Care, located less than a mile from the picturesque seaside village of Damariscotta on the banks of the river bearing the same name, was the assisted-living facility Tran had identified as Falcone's address. It was nearly two by the time Diane parked the car in the lot and walked inside with Nugent.

Falcone, it turned out, was suffering from Alzheimer's disease. Neither detective knew what to expect from the former Portland cop, but Diane was hoping his dementia hadn't progressed too far.

The first thing she noticed upon entering his room was the absence of any sign of family visitors or friends. There were no flowers, no cards, no photos, and no homey touches of any kind. He'd either outlived his friends and family or was on the outs with all of them. Given what she knew about cops, Diane guessed it was the latter.

Falcone was lying propped up in an adjustable stainless steel hospital bed, watching television. The elderly, white-haired ex-cop turned his head and looked at the two detectives but remained silent.

"Mr. Falcone," she began, "my name is Detective Joyner and this is my partner Detective Nugent." They both showed him their gold badges.

"Like Columbo?" Falcone asked, his eyes widening with childlike fascination.

"Yes, like Columbo," Nugent said with only a hint of his usual sarcasm.

"Piss off, cop," Falcone said, staring directly at him.

"Mr. Falcone, we aren't here to upset you," Diane said softly, attempting to calm him. She pulled a chair up close to his bed and sat down.

Falcone looked over at her and smiled. "Pretty lady, you can call me Joe."

"All right, Joe. We're from the Portland Police Department and we'd like to ask you a few questions, if that's okay with you."

"You can ask me anything, beautiful," he said, patting her hand.

"Your name is Christopher," Nugent corrected.

Falcone looked up at Nugent, squinting until his eyes were barely open. "I don't like you, copper. Get out of my room."

Nugent looked at Diane. She nodded her approval. "I'll be right outside the door, if you need me."

As soon as Nugent had retreated to the hall, she began again. "I want to ask you about your time on the job, Joe."

"Job?" Falcone asked with a puzzled look on his face.

"Yes, when you were a police officer in Portland."

"I don't remember. Was I a police officer?"

"Isn't this you, Joe?" she asked, handing him a copy of the SRT photograph and pointing to his face.

"I don't know. I can't remember. Do you like my flowers?" he asked, pointing at the windowsill.

She glanced around the room again, reaffirming it was devoid of plant life.

"I raised them all myself," he said. "I think the bougainvillea are my favorite. Do you like them?"

"They're beautiful."

Falcone smiled again and continued patting her hand.

She spent the next twenty minutes unsuccessfully trying to get him to remember his time on the job. Finally, she excused herself, telling him she had to get back to work.

"Your new boyfriend provide anything useful?" Nugent asked after they were down the hall and out of earshot.

"No, and he doesn't appear to have enough of his memory left to be of any help to us. It's so sad, Mike. He has no idea who or even what he was."

"I don't know," Nugent said. "He may not remember who he was, but he seemed pretty happy to me."

"He's tending imaginary flowers. It's just so sad," she repeated.

He opened the lobby door for her. "Well, there's one good thing about Falcone."

"What's that?" she asked, stepping out onto the front walkway.

"He'll be easy to surveil."

"What do you mean he called to complain about me?" Byron asked incredulously. "Did you talk to him?"

"No," LeRoyer said. "He called and spoke directly to Stanton, who is now furious with you. In fact, Sergeant, so am I."

"Lieu, I have absolutely no idea what the

hell you're talking about. I just came from Williams's office. We spoke for about a half hour, tops. No problem whatsoever."

As their voices raised, so did the curiosity of the two weekend property detectives whose desks were located in close proximity to LeRoyer's office.

"You're telling me you didn't harass him or threaten him with a warrant or surveillance?"

"Of course I didn't. Jesus Christ. I mentioned surveillance to him but only in the context of protection. The same conversation we've had with all the others. I'm telling you, nothing happened. This guy's full of shit. Do you want me to call the chief?" Byron asked.

"No, I don't. You'll only make it worse. I'll talk with him myself after he's had a chance to cool down a little."

"This is total bullshit, Lieu. Maybe there's a reason Williams doesn't want us poking around. Did you think of that?" Byron stormed out of the office before he said or did something he could be reprimanded for.

Both nearby property detectives pretended to be on the phone as Byron flew by.

Williams was manipulating things, that much was clear. Did he have a direct link to the chief? Or had he just decided to go directly to the top of the food chain? Regardless, Byron knew he must have hit a nerve when he interviewed Williams.

He was just getting back to his office when his cell rang. "Byron."

"Ask and ye shall receive," Special Agent Collier said.

"Hey, Sam. You've got my files, I assume."

"Four boxes, ready and waiting."

"I'll be right over."

Byron stashed two of the boxes at his apartment, burying them in the bedroom closet. The other two he left in his trunk, figuring he'd have Diane take them and split the reading. He was sweating profusely and his stomach was churning. He sat down on the bed for a second and closed his eyes, waiting for it to pass. He hadn't heard from either Diane or Nugent yet and knew it would still be a couple more hours before they returned to Portland.

Jack Riccio. That name kept coming up. *Could he have something to do with these murders?*

He opened his eyes and made a quick call to Pritchard.

"Hey, John. I was thinking about you. How goes the hunt?"

"Slow and steady. Listen, I've got something I want to run by you. You available for a quick meet?"

"Sure. Where were you thinking?"

"Sam told me you're out in the Cape. How about someplace near you?"

"I know just the place."

It was three-fifteen as Byron walked into the Route 77 Diner. "Wooly Bully" was playing on the sound system. He found Pritchard seated alone at a booth.

"Terry?"

"You must be Sergeant Byron," Pritchard said as he stood and extended his hand. "It's a pleasure to meet you."

At six foot three, Pritchard was every inch as tall as Byron but at least forty pounds heavier and none of it was flab. Byron guessed him to be a very fit early sixties. His jet-black hair was parted in the middle with just a trace of gray creeping around the sides.

"Thanks for meeting with me on such short notice."

"Happy to help." Both men sat down. "Can I get you something?" he asked, pointing to his coffee.

"No, I'm good thanks."

Pritchard waved off the waitress who'd started in their direction. He pointed up at a ceiling speaker. "You know who this is?"

"Sam the Sham and the Pharaohs," Byron said without hesitation.

Pritchard grinned and nodded. "I'm likin' you already. So, you said you had something to run by me. Shoot."

"We've started interviewing everyone in earnest. I spoke with Williams this afternoon and Humphrey and Cross the other day. One name keeps coming up. They keep mentioning Riccio."

"Ah, Jack Riccio."

"You've dealt with him?"

"Our paths have crossed. Currently serving consecutive life sentences in a federal pen. Badass mob boss, worked primarily in the greater Boston area. Prostitution, loansharking, drugs, guns, bribing public officials, murder — you name it and Riccio was probably running it."

"A couple of the ex-cops theorized Riccio might've been the brains behind the robbery."

"It's possible. I already told you there wasn't a brain among the guys who pulled the job."

"Any proof of Riccio's involvement?"

"No. But we couldn't disprove it either. We figured one of the robbers either worked for him or was related."

"But no link was ever established?"

"None that I know of. I'm confident they didn't work for him, but the relative thing is a whole other can of worms."

"Why? Seems like it would've been easy to make the connection if one of them had been related to Riccio."

"You'd think so, but a guy like Riccio had women everywhere. He was married, sure, but the life of a Mafia boss is a little different. You familiar with the term goomah?"

"Yeah. It's Italian slang for girlfriend, right?"

"Mistress. And Jack Riccio had a number of them. Some we knew and some we didn't. If he fathered a son by one of the unknown goomahs, we'd have never made the connection."

"So it's entirely possible one of the four was related."

Pritchard nodded. "It is."

"Giving Riccio motivation to want revenge for his death?"

"I don't know. Seems pretty unlikely after all these years, but still, it is possible."

Byron shook his head and sighed. "This thing's a nightmare."

"John, there's something I haven't told you yet," Pritchard said. "Something you need to know."

Byron studied him, wondering what he'd held back. And why?

"I'm gonna tell you something that isn't in the case file. You're the first person, outside of the FBI, that I've ever told, but I think you should know. After the shootout in Portland, we spent two weeks up here processing the scene, working with the Maine attorney general, interviewing witnesses, cops, everybody. It was exhausting. I'm sure you can imagine how popular we were, poking around the police department. The nosy feds who wouldn't go away."

"Probably about as popular as you'd be if you were doing it today."

"I suspect that's true. Anyway, after the initial investigation was done in Portland, we returned to Boston. There was still plenty of work to be done and I was getting pressure from my bosses to lay off the cops. I'd only been back for a couple of days when I got a message to call Reece Byron."

"What did he want?"

"I never found out. He left his home number. I tried calling a few times, but he never answered. Finally, I called the department and found out he was dead. Suicide."

"What the hell are you saying?"

"I don't know what I'm saying, John. I only know I couldn't get right with it. And it still gnaws at me."

"Why didn't you tell me this before?"

"I couldn't decide if I should. I didn't want to upset you."

"So you really don't have any idea why my dad called you?" Byron asked, sounding more defensive than he'd meant to.

"No, you're right. I don't."

Byron's imagination was off and running like some feral equine. He didn't dare verbalize what he was thinking to Pritchard, but the thoughts came just the same. "Let me ask you something. Do you honestly believe there's any chance the murderer is the missing robber, Andreas?"

"Honestly? No, I don't. I think Andreas is most likely dead. He was lucky to pull off the robbery. There's no way he's managed to avoid detection all these years, especially while being on the bureau's most-wanted list."

"Riccio manage to avoid capture for years," Byron countered.

"Yeah, he did. But Andreas isn't Jack Riccio. Riccio is cunning, well educated, and dangerous."

"What if he made it out of the country? He certainly had enough money to disappear for a while. Why couldn't he have reentered the states undetected? Illegals do it all the time."

"Yes, but it's easier for illegals. It's much harder to pull it off if you were born in the states like Andreas was. The paper trail is too long to hide from. Especially since 9/11."

"If not Andreas, who do you think is behind this?"

Pritchard didn't answer right away. He appeared to be considering how to answer the question. "John, I think there are most likely only two possibilities. Either Riccio sent someone to settle the score or —"

"Or?"

"Or it's one of your own."

CHAPTER EIGHTEEN

As with everything at the Portland Police Department, the Records Division had undergone a number of major changes over the years. One of those had been the death of the antiquated card-filing system. At one time, index cards were created for every suspect, victim, and address relevant to police contact. The cards had been maintained for decades as a way of cataloguing and retrieving police data, finally becoming obsolete with the advent of the computer.

Byron spent the better part of an hour inside the stuffy and cramped back room of 109's Records Division going through the index card filing cabinets before finally managing to locate a case number for his father's suicide report.

Prior to handing over the key, Rachel, the elderly clerk in records, provided him with a stern warning about leaving the archives in disarray.

"If I had a nickel for every time I've had to go down there and fix things because they weren't put back in their proper place, well, I wouldn't need to work here anymore. Now, I know I can trust you, right, Sergeant Byron?"

He didn't know if it was her tone or the way she peered over her wire-rimmed glasses at him, but he couldn't help but feel like a schoolboy being chastised by the librarian. He assured her he was trustworthy, even raising his hand in salute with the Scout's honor sign. Byron had never been a Boy Scout, but he'd seen a picture of the hand salute once and did his best to emulate it. It worked and she handed over the key.

Five minutes later, he found himself in the damp basement of 109. The cavernous and dimly lit storage vault was lined with long rusty metal shelves, each of them ten feet high and twice as long, packed with musty cardboard boxes containing decades of Portland police case files and reports dating back to the 1940s.

There didn't appear to be any rhyme or reason to the filing system. He wondered when exactly Rachel had put things in their "proper place." It took several minutes before he located the boxes marked 1985

243

and systematically began to dig through thousands of mildewed reports. Eventually, he found the one he'd been searching for: the death investigation of Officer Reece Byron.

He sat down on a box, staring blankly at the yellowed face-sheet. This was the first time he'd ever seen the police reports of his father's death. He could feel his emotions tugging him in several directions. On the one hand, he might well find something to help break the current investigation wide open, but on the other . . . He took a deep breath, slowly exhaled, and began reading, looking for anything out of the ordinary.

According to the report, his father was suspected of having killed himself the night before he'd been found. The detective assigned to the case had done all of the usual follow-up, and the medical examiner confirmed the cause of death was from a self-inflicted gunshot wound to the head. The toxicology report attached showed he'd been drinking at the time, but the level was only .15, far from overly intoxicated, especially for a man as proficient at the art of imbibing as his father had been. So if he wasn't drunk, he had to have been thinking clearly at the time, Byron reasoned. Why then would he have called and left a message for Pritchard if he was about to commit suicide? It didn't make sense. Did he call out of guilt? Was he going to confess to taking the money? Was there something else he needed to get off his chest?

He flipped back to the face sheet. The investigating detective was Jeffrey Irving. Byron wasn't familiar with the name, but he was familiar with the supervisor who signed off on the case, Sergeant Reginald Cross. Why would they have allowed Cross to supervise the death investigation of one of his own team members? It certainly wouldn't fly today. He couldn't talk with O'Halloran, and Cross wasn't giving him anything but grief. He needed to find Irving.

It was after five by the time Diane and Nugent returned to Portland. Byron had just located an address for Jeffrey Irving in Windham when the two detectives walked into CID. Irving would have to wait. He copied the address in his notebook, then powered off his computer. They met briefly in the conference room, sharing the details of their respective interviews.

"Falcone is useless to us, then?" Byron asked.

"He's a plant, Sarge," Nugent said.

"Don't be such an asshole, Mike," Diane said.

"Hey, I'm not the one who kicked me out of the room. He threw me out, Sarge. I don't think he liked me."

"He's a good judge of character," Diane said.

"Seriously, he can't help?" Byron asked.

"He didn't even remember having been a cop," she said.

Byron wondered if maybe Falcone had only been having a bad day. He'd read somewhere that there was still a great deal not known about the disease. The effects of Alzheimer's could seemingly worsen or improve from one day to the next. He tucked away a mental reminder to revisit Falcone at a later date.

"What about Williams?" Nugent asked.

"Did he give you anything?" Diane asked.

"Sure, he gave me the runaround. He's a car salesman. I asked where the Ocean Avenue information had come from and he started to tell me."

"But?" Nugent asked.

"He pulled back, said he didn't know, like he was confusing cases."

"You think he was confused?" Diane asked.

"Not a chance. I think he caught himself."

"Maybe he really doesn't remember," Nugent said. "I mean, it has been over thirty years."

"If you'd heard how detailed his account of the event was, you'd know what I mean."

The three of them drove out to Diane's, ordered Chinese takeout, and spent the rest of the evening reading the FBI case files. It was a little before eleven-thirty when Nugent fell asleep in the chair, but he drove home shortly after. Byron got up from the couch and was about to follow suit when Diane stopped him.

"Where are you off to?" she asked. "Got a hot date?"

"Hardly. Thought I'd head home and let you get a few hours of sleep."

Diane stood in front of him, putting her hand gently on his chest. "No one said you had to go, John."

She was less than a foot away, making direct eye contact. The smell of her perfume and the feel of her touch were having an effect on him. Arousing something he hadn't felt for a long time.

"Unless you don't want to stay?" she said.

"It isn't that," he said, feeling too much like an awkward teenager. "It's just —"

She removed her hand and stepped away from him. "Or I could make up the couch for you."

"Don't go to any trouble on my account," he said, relieved that the moment had passed.

"No trouble at all."

Sleep eluded Byron once again. He was lying on the couch, staring at the ceiling, his brain racing in a thousand different directions. The murders, his failed marriage to Kay, the booze, and now he was actually considering sleeping with his partner. No, not just his partner, his subordinate. His friend. He wasn't sure how it had happened. How did it ever happen? Incrementally, he supposed. Working on murder cases, long hours together, shared feelings, an obvious mutual attraction. He realized that Diane probably knew more about his feelings than Kay had. How had things gotten so fucked up? And what was it his dad had wanted to tell Pritchard? Why not tell him before the agent returned to Boston? Was it something he'd found out after Pritchard left? Did it have something to do with the money? If it was the money, did Reece find out who had it? Was he involved? The questions kept coming.

The meeting with Pritchard had been meant to answer some questions not create more. He felt like Dorothy standing where the yellow brick road diverged, only instead of two different directions, this case felt like it could go in a dozen. One thing was certain: he wouldn't find any answers lying there. He needed to talk to Irving. He got up and resumed reading the case files.

It was after three A.M. and Byron was seated in a wingback chair with only a low-wattage floor lamp to read by when Diane padded barefoot into the room. The skimpy white nightshirt she wore, emblazoned with I Love NY across the front, did little to hide her curves.

"Hey," she croaked, rubbing the sleep from her eyes. "Can't sleep?"

"Never could," he said with a smile. "Sorry if I woke you."

"It's okay. I had to pee anyway." She sat down crossed-legged on the floor between the file boxes. Her shirt rode up over her thighs. "Whatcha thinking about, besides this case?"

"My dad."

"This thing has stirred up a lot of memories, huh?"

"In spite of my best attempts at repression."

"You know, in addition to being a great detective and gourmet chef, I'm also a pretty fair listener."

"Don't forget incredibly humble."

"Wanna share?" she asked.

He looked up and smiled. "Not particularly."

She put her hands on her hips. "You know, I spent a whole day with Mike because of you, John Byron."

"Nuge isn't that bad, is he?" he asked, half kidding.

"You've obviously never spent an entire day listening to his bad jokes. You owe me."

"That how you see it?"

"You've never told me what happened to your dad."

He removed his reading glasses and folded them up. "No, I haven't."

"Sometimes it helps to talk about it."

"You're not gonna let this go are you?"

"Nope. I'll make us some coffee."

"Is that a bribe?"

"Yup." She bounced up from the floor with a dexterity Byron couldn't remember ever having, and headed for the kitchen. "Come on. I'll even cut you a brownie."

"All right."

They sat across from each other at the table, each with a steaming mug of coffee. Diane listened intently as Byron recounted his tale.

"I was sixteen when my parents split. An impressionable age, so they told me. Not sure exactly what age is the best for parents to break up. As you can imagine, I didn't take it well. Went to live with my mom on the West End. She left because of my dad's two problems."

"Two problems?"

"Yeah, drinking and infidelity. Ironic, considering how religious he was. He made me go to church every Sunday, Saint Peter's on Federal Street. All the Catholic kids from the Hill went there."

"The Hill?"

"Munjoy."

She nodded.

"I knew he had his issues, but I still looked up to him."

"Of course, he was your dad."

Byron took a drink of his coffee while Diane cut each of them another brownie.

"I liked visiting him when he had his cop buddies over. They treated me like I was one of them. They told the best stories and I got to stay up late. My parents didn't move too far apart, so I could still bike over to see my dad after school, if I wanted. I was seventeen the day it happened. I headed over to see my dad as soon as school let out. I opened the door to his apartment and

251

walked inside."

Byron grew quiet as he toyed with the brownie, picking at it but not eating. Diane waited for him to continue.

"I hollered for him but he didn't answer. I was afraid he might be entertaining a lady friend or something; it had happened before. He wasn't. I found him sitting in the dining room with his head down on the table. At first I thought he was passed out, but then I saw the blood. There was so much of it. His gun was on the floor next to his chair. I had no idea what to do, so I ran outside and started yelling for help."

Diane reached across the table and wrapped her hand around his.

"I'd never seen anything like it. The police came to the house. Ray Humphrey was one of the first officers to show up. I remember I couldn't stop crying. Ray got me out of there, drove me around for a while in his cruiser. I don't recall exactly what he said to me, but whatever it was it made me feel better. He's always been able to do that. He finally drove me home and told my mother what'd happened."

"I'm so sorry," Diane said. Tears streamed down her cheeks.

"The following week was a blur. Mom kept me out of school. Relatives stopped by with food. We ended up throwing most of it out. The service was coming right up and I didn't have a suit to wear. Ray took me shopping at a clothier on Congress Street, paid for it out of his own pocket. At the funeral mass, I sat at the front of the church between my mom and Lieutenant O'Halloran. I couldn't believe my dad would take his own life. Still can't."

Diane got up and walked behind his chair, wrapping her arms around him tightly. "No one should have to see something like that. Especially a teenager. What about your mom? I've never heard you mention her?"

Byron hesitated a moment before answering. "She's gone."

"I'm sorry, John."

"I went through the archives today, looking for his suicide report," he said, getting back on topic.

"Oh, John. Why?"

"I think I located the detective who investigated it. I'm gonna go talk to him today."

"Why would you wanna reopen that wound?"

"I want to tell you something Pritchard shared with me."

Diane released him from her embrace and returned to her chair.

"Terry told me he got a message from my

dad about a week after he and his team returned to Boston to finish up work on the actual robbery. My dad said he wanted to talk."

"What about?"

"He didn't say. Terry said he tried several times to get back in touch with my dad before learning of his death."

"What do you think your dad wanted to tell him?"

He shook his head. "I don't know."

"Maybe I should meet this guy."

It was a bit past twelve-thirty Sunday afternoon when the two detectives walked into the dining room of the Foreside Bistro. Decorated with hurricane lamps, dark wood paneling, and cloth-covered tables, the bistro was a charming little restaurant located in Falmouth at the water's edge. Pritchard had requested they meet him for lunch, his treat.

Pritchard, who was seated at the far end of the dining room, stood as they approached. "Hey, John."

"Terry, I'd like to introduce my partner, Detective Diane Joyner. Diane, this is Assistant Special Agent in Charge Terry Pritchard."

"Pleased to meet you, Agent Pritchard,"

Diane said as she offered her hand.

"The pleasure is all mine," he said, shaking firmly and smiling warmly. "And it's *Terry*. I am retired after all." He gestured to the empty chairs. "Please have a seat."

They sat down as their waiter approached the table. "Good afternoon, my name is Carleton and I'll be taking care of you. Can I start you off with something from the wine list or the bar?"

Pritchard and Diane each ordered a Stella. Byron, trying hard to remain focused, ordered a diet soda. Following the waiter's departure, they resumed their conversation.

"So, Terry, John said you solved some pretty important cases for the FBI over the years."

"I got lucky a few times."

"More than a few," Byron said. "He's being modest."

"Luck is it? John told me about solving the Katzenberg kidnapping and recovering two stolen Renoirs. I'd say there isn't any need for modesty," Diane said.

"Well, I had a lot of help. Worked with some damn fine agents. Feels like all I did at the end of my career was polish a chair with my ass."

"Is that the technical job description for an ASAC?" Byron asked.

Pritchard nodded and smiled.

"What's the job description for SAC?" Diane asked.

"I'm too much of a gentleman to say."

Carlton returned with their drinks. "Have you had a chance to look over our menu?"

"I think we're going to need a few more minutes," Pritchard said.

"Not a problem. Signal me when you're ready."

"So, anything new in the investigation?" Pritchard asked as he tasted the cold beer.

"Not really," Byron said. "We've spoken with a number of the officers, but nobody's been very helpful."

"Yeah, they either really don't know anything or they're circling the wagons and just don't want to talk to us," Diane said.

"Well, that's interesting," Pritchard said. "Why do you suppose they wouldn't want to talk with you?"

"Makes me think you might be right about the money," Byron said. "Something's definitely wrong."

"Do you think they know who's behind the murders?" Pritchard asked.

"No. I think they're as in the dark as we are," Byron said.

"Have any of them outright lied to you?" Pritchard asked.

"I think a couple of them have," Diane said. "They're all claiming they haven't been in contact with one another, but I don't buy it."

"Have you tried dumping their cell phones?"

"We'd need a court order and we haven't got anything approaching probable cause to request one," Byron said.

"Where are my manners? I invited you both here for lunch," Pritchard said. "What say we eat first? You can't investigate on an empty stomach. Am I right?"

They dined on seared Faroe Island salmon, red quinoa salad with cilantro lime vinaigrette, and fingerling potatoes. After they'd finished the meal, Carleton brought a tray with coffee and creamers.

"That was excellent, Terry. Thank you," Diane said.

"I don't often eat like this," Byron admitted. "Normally, it's fast food, Thai takeout, or leftovers."

"It's my pleasure. Although, I must admit, inviting you here is purely a selfish move on my part."

"What do you mean?" Diane asked.

"Working with you is allowing me to feel as if I'm back in the hunt. Haven't felt like this since hanging up my spurs a few years ago."

"Unfinished business," Byron said.

"Precisely."

"Well, we both appreciate your insight into this case," Byron said.

"John mentioned you thought Andreas might be dead," Diane said. "A gut feeling or something more?"

"Intuition, I guess. At the time I thought he might have gotten lucky. Might've been somewhere else when the PD raided the place. But why would the other three allow him sole possession of the money?"

"I'm not following," Diane said.

"According to the police reports, none of the money was recovered. So where was it? Did they stash it somewhere away from the hideout? Andreas could have been out trying to fence the money, I suppose, but would he have gone alone and taken it all with him? And would the others really have trusted him with it?"

"I wouldn't have," Byron said.

"Nor I."

"Why would they need to fence cash?" Diane asked.

"Because the FBI floated a story to the press about the bills being marked," Byron said.

"They weren't, of course," Pritchard said. "But we knew if we put it out there, they wouldn't dare to spend it. They'd be forced to find someone to help them. Pay them so much on the dollar. We'd hoped our little piece of misinformation might help us catch them."

"How did the PD locate their safe house?" Diane asked.

"According to O'Halloran, who was the CID commander at the time, they got a tip from a longtime reliable informant."

"Who?" Diane asked.

"We were never able to find out. O'Halloran wouldn't tell us. Our legal guys tried unsuccessfully to force them to reveal the source."

"Why weren't they able to?" Diane asked. "It's not like the case was going to court. Not with three of the robbers dead."

"No, that's true. But there were legitimate concerns surrounding the possibility the robbers had organized crime connections. The PD countered that even releasing the name of their CI to the FBI would compromise and possibly endanger an important asset. They were right of course; we would've fought just as hard to protect one of our sources. But I always wanted to know where the information came from."

"What about the woman who owned the house?" Diane asked.

"Warren's girlfriend?" Pritchard said. "Tina Hewitt. We checked her out. She was a stripper. Traveled a lot and was out of state when all of this happened. They'd only been dating for a few months. I'm pretty sure Warren was just using her."

"No chance she was the source?" Diane asked.

Pritchard shook his head. "None."

"At some point I'll want to pay a visit to Riccio," Byron said.

"I figured you would," Pritchard said. "You want me to reach out to my contacts at the prison?"

"Not yet. If he is behind this, no sense taking the chance of tipping him off ahead of time. We've still got boxes to check right here."

"Just say the word."

"John told me about his dad reaching out to you right before he died," Diane said.

Pritchard looked over at Byron, who nodded. "He left a message for me shortly after my return to Boston. Before I could find out what he wanted, he killed himself."

"Any idea what it might have been?" she asked.

"I'm afraid we could speculate forever and

not come up with answers. It's always bothered me, though. I thought John should know."

It was two-thirty before they parted ways. Byron and Diane headed to Windham to try and locate Irving while Pritchard headed back into retirement.

"What do you think?" Byron asked as he turned onto Route 9.

"Of Pritchard or the information?"

"Either."

"I like him. He's charming and intelligent. Reminds me of someone else I know."

Byron looked over, exchanging an awkward glance with her.

"But the information? I don't know. Seems like it raises more questions than it answers."

"I think that's it," Diane said, pointing to a quaint single-story log cabin. Byron turned into the driveway. A silver-haired man was cutting the grass on a riding mower. Dressed in jeans and a plaid shirt, he looked like a model straight off the cover of a John Deere catalogue. He waved a gloved hand. They returned the salutation and waited for him to complete his loop around the front lawn.

"You sure you want to do this?" Diane asked.

"I don't have much of a choice do I? Anyway, it's too late now."

The man brought the tractor to a stop near the driveway and killed the engine.

"Are you Jeffrey Irving?" Byron asked.

"That I am," Irving said as he climbed off the mower. "You're either cops or you're selling something."

"My name is John Byron, Mr. Irving. I'm a detective sergeant with the Portland Police Department and this is my partner, Detective Diane Joyner."

"Your car is a dead giveaway," Irving said with a grin and two firm handshakes. "What can I do you for?"

"Sorry to interrupt your yard work. We were hoping to ask you some questions about a case you worked in the eighties."

"Ah, no bother. Think all I'm doing is pushing leaves around anyway. Come on up to the porch. I'll get us some iced tea."

"Don't go to any trouble, Mr. Irving," Diane said.

"It's Jeff," he said with a wink. "And it's no trouble. Have a seat. I'll be right back."

They sat down in two of the porch rockers. Byron loosened his tie.

Irving came outside and handed each of them a tall glass of iced tea before sitting in the chair next to Byron. "So, you've got me intrigued. What case could I have worked on that would bring you two out to see me after all these years?"

"My father's suicide."

Irving looked at him as if he were joking. "John Byron? Your father was Reece Byron?"

"Yes."

"I'm sorry. I didn't recognize the name."

"It's okay. It was a long time ago."

"I'm sorry just the same."

"Thanks. So what can you tell me about your investigation?"

"Well, let me think for a minute. I was sent there for a report of a self-inflicted gunshot wound. Didn't know it was one of ours until I arrived." He looked directly at Byron. "You were the teenager who found him, weren't you?"

"Yes."

"I remember talking to you briefly before one of the officers took you away."

"Ray Humphrey."

"Yeah, Ray."

"Can you remember anything specific about the scene?" Diane asked.

"That's a tough one after so many years. He was in the dining room, his gun lying on the floor next to him. I remembered thinking how messed up it was for him to die by his own hand only weeks after surviving a shootout."

"Do you remember being assigned?" Byron asked.

"Yeah, I do actually. I remember because it was odd for them to assign a suicide to me in the first place."

"Why?" Diane asked.

"Well, because at the time I was a property crimes detective. I worked mostly motor vehicle thefts."

"Do you remember who assigned the case to you?" Diane asked.

"I do. It was the supervisor of Special Crimes, Sergeant Cross."

"Had you ever worked a suicide before?" Byron asked.

Irving rubbed his chin and stared out at the lawn. "Come to think of it, no. That's why it was strange for them to assign me. It was my first and only in the bureau. Normally, the Crimes Against Persons Unit wouldn't have let any of the detectives from our side near a death investigation."

"Why was Cross assigning a case to you if he was in another unit?" Byron asked.

"I think my sergeant might have been away on vacation or something."

"Anything else you can remember about that case?" Diane asked.

Irving shook his head. "No. I just remember how bad I felt." He turned to look at Byron. "I'm truly sorry."

They politely finished their tea and made small talk about Irving's retired life, but it was obvious that the former cop had nothing else they needed.

Byron had driven nearly a mile in silence when Diane spoke up. "Why would Cross assign something as sensitive as a cop's suicide to a detective as inexperienced as Irving?"

"He wouldn't. Cross doesn't do anything without a reason. Something's definitely wrong here," he said.

"What are you thinking?"

He thought for a moment before answering. "We keep this latest find to ourselves."

Diane looked over at him. "Why?"

"Because I'm no longer sure who's on our side."

CHAPTER NINETEEN

The day of Stanton's press conference arrived, promising a larger display of fireworks than the even Fourth of July had seen. Byron could count on one hand the number of mornings in which not a single detective had stopped by his office to speak with him or ask for a favor. This morning, however, the tension was palpable, and even the detectives who were not involved knew enough to give him a wide berth.

He'd spent the entire morning briefing either Stanton himself or one of the chief's subordinates. Byron thought of the word *briefing* as an attempt to withhold critical information from one's superiors. Information one didn't want the media getting their hands on. Murder sells newspapers, but a serial murder brought in network television. And a serial killer of cops meant the story would go viral on the Internet. Stanton would be the grand marshal of his own media circus. The chief lived for this stuff, feeding on it like some well-dressed, egomaniacal parasite. Byron withheld as much information from Stanton as he could, knowing that once the chief got on a roll, he wouldn't be able to contain himself.

Chief Stanton had contacted the Federal Bureau of Investigation almost immediately. Byron wasn't sure if the chief was really seeking assistance from Club Fed or if this was only a calculated political move to make his press conference look more official. Either way, Byron was less than pleased. It wasn't that he didn't have many friends in the FBI, because he did; and it wasn't that he hadn't worked well with them in the past, because he had. It was really about effectively managing the investigation. The problem was too many fingers in the pie. Experience had taught him there was no quicker way to lose control of an investigation than to have too many people trying to run it. As his father had been fond of saying: "Too many chiefs and not enough Indians." Byron was the lead investigator and the supervisor on this homicide case, but the food chain above him included several investigator wannabes. If he wasn't careful, he risked losing control of the whole thing.

It was after eleven. Byron sat in LeRoyer's office while the lieutenant frantically typed talking points for Stanton's press conference. Byron knew LeRoyer was attempting to placate him, but he wasn't in the mood.

"That's way too much information, Marty," Byron said as he threw a draft of the press release on LeRoyer's desk. "We might as well give away the entire case. Did Stanton just reassign my case to Cross or did Cross assign himself as the damn lead? Or, better yet, are we handing it over to the FBI to solve for us?"

"We're not handing it to the FBI, John," LeRoyer said, sounding exasperated. "And you're still the lead investigator."

"Oh good, because as the lead I certainly wouldn't tell the press about the entire Special Reaction Team being targeted," Byron said, raising his voice for effect. "Not only will our killer know what we're up to, but everyone else will too. Jesus, as it is this press conference will bring out every wing nut who thinks they saw something. We're liable to end up with copycat killings, or worse. And it's not just the nuts. What if one of the remaining six gets jumpy and kills an innocent person. Have you even thought of that?"

"Yes, Sergeant. *I have,*" LeRoyer snapped.

"I want surveillance on these guys, and that's going to be pretty friggin' hard to do if everyone knows who they are. Speaking of which, how soon can I have officers assigned?"

LeRoyer threw his reading glasses down on the desk. "Fuck, John, I've been fighting all morning to try and get this thing to go the way you want. In case you've forgotten, I'm not a miracle worker. I don't run this department. I have to answer to people just like you're supposed to answer to me."

"I haven't forgotten, *Lieutenant,*" Byron said sarcastically, emphasizing the last word.

"Good. I'm glad to hear it." LeRoyer picked up his glasses and returned to typing. "Let me get this Christly press conference out of the way first. Okay?"

LeRoyer had managed to win several battles during the course of the morning. But he'd also lost some, thanks to Assistant Chief Cross, who seemed to thrive on this kind of politicking. The losses were the only things on which Byron was focused.

"Look, John, I'll take another shot at the chief as soon as he's finished meeting with Supervisory Special Resident Agent Ridley."

Byron knew Ridley, having worked closely with him before. Ridley didn't aspire to climb any higher on the Federal Ladder, as he still saw himself as an investigator and not a company man. The Portland Resident Agency of the FBI would likely be his last command, and SSRA Ridley was no fan of Chief Stanton, which suited Byron fine.

"And I'll try and get his approval for the surveillance overtime. Okay?"

"Thank you."

Byron rose from his chair, looking down at his frazzled boss, who'd removed his jacket and loosened his tie. LeRoyer's blue-and-white pinstriped dress shirt was soaked through at the armpits, and he'd run his fingers through his hair no less than a dozen times since Byron had walked into the office. Byron realized he was only browbeating an ally. "Lieu, I'm sorry about being such a prick, but I've got a lot riding on this."

LeRoyer looked up from his computer. "We all do, John."

Reporters and videographers began pouring into 109 at a quarter past eleven. A colorful caravan of news vans were parked in front. Some were equipped with telescoping antennas for live video feeds to their networks. It didn't take much imagination to see the circus had indeed come to town.

The Portland Police Department press conferences were generally cozy affairs held on the first floor, but every once in a while the scope of the news being released necessitated the use of the second-floor auditorium to accommodate a larger turnout. This was one of those occasions.

Byron stood at the rear of the auditorium along with his crew of detectives, trying to be as inconspicuous as possible. A bank of microphone stands and a maze of cables, resembling some absurd electronic octopus, nearly obscured the podium and its colored PPD insignia from view. The video cameras and lights bore logos from every local newspaper, network, and several of the national affiliates. He noted, with some amusement, that the sports channels were the only networks not represented.

The auditorium was both packed and sweltering, with most people choosing to stand. Byron could feel the beads of sweat running down his back and was thankful he'd kept his suit coat on to hide his own quickly dampening dress shirt. He didn't need to check his watch to know Stanton intended on being fashionably late. He had attended enough of these dog and pony shows over the years to accurately predict a start time of about five past the hour. The chief adored basking in the spotlight the media provided.

"Sergeant Byron."

He turned and saw Billingslea had taken a spot beside him. "Davis."

"You're not gonna threaten me again, are you, Sergeant?"

"You're not gonna give me a reason to, are you?"

"Care to make a statement before the statement?"

"Nope."

"The way I hear it, you're investigating the deaths of two former Portland SWAT cops. Any idea why someone would want to kill these officers?"

"We don't have a SWAT team."

"Semantics, Sergeant. All right, Special Reaction Team."

"If you're gonna ask the question, at least get the terminology right."

"So? Any comment?"

"You want a quote?"

Billingslea's eyes sparkled. "You mean it?"

"Sure. Get your pen ready."

Billingslea pulled out his notebook and pen. "Okay, what can you tell me?"

Byron leaned in close and lowered his voice. "I don't like reporters."

The reporter lowered the pen and paper.

"That's your statement?"

"Yup. And you can quote me." Byron moved away, finding a spot between Nugent and Diane.

At precisely 12:05, Chief Stanton strolled into the room, followed by Assistant Chief Cross, LeRoyer, and Special Agent Ridley. Byron attempted to establish eye contact with LeRoyer as they passed, but his boss's gaze was fixed straight ahead, leaving him to wonder in which direction the last meeting had gone.

Byron's phone vibrated with an incoming call. He pulled his cell out and checked it. Kay. He pressed ignore and returned the phone to his jacket pocket.

Stanton took his spot behind the podium, shuffled some papers, took out his reading glasses, looked up and surveyed the room. He waited patiently until everyone had quieted down before speaking.

"Ladies and gentleman, members of the press, good afternoon and thank you all for coming. I've prepared a brief statement from which I will now read. Following this, I will attempt to answer a few of your questions. I would ask you to please be patient and refrain from asking any questions until I've finished."

Stanton laid out the facts as he knew

them. "The Portland Police Department Criminal Investigation Division is currently investigating several homicides we believe are connected. This is an ongoing investigation and as such I am not at liberty to release certain facts of the case."

The chief continued for several more minutes, and, to Byron's delight, the rest of his speech was as dry and devoid of specifics as the opening had been. The only obstacle remaining was the barrage of questions that would inevitably ensue.

"That concludes my statement," Stanton said. "I'll now take a few of your questions."

No sooner had Stanton finished before the crowd of reporters morphed into a crazed mob, more closely resembling traders on the floor of the New York Stock Exchange during a run than civilized professionals. Each of them waved their arms and shouted, trying desperately to catch the attention of the chief. Byron looked over at Diane, she rolled her eyes. Stanton pointed to a dark-haired male reporter from one of the national news channels.

"Chief. Chief. There's been some speculation that the killer has been targeting officers from your own department. Can you confirm this?"

"We don't deal with rumors or speculation at this agency. We deal in facts. As I stated to all of you previously, I'm not at liberty to discuss certain aspects of this investigation. Next question."

"But Chief Stanton," the reporter continued, "you didn't answer my question. Is the killer targeting the Portland Police Department or not?"

Byron could feel his stomach knotting up as he waited for Stanton to respond.

Stanton glared over his reading glasses at the arrogant young reporter. "No comment! Next question."

Byron was pleased the chief hadn't caved to the reporter's badgering, but he knew a "no comment" response would likely only fuel the media speculation surrounding the target. As far as the victims' identities were concerned, Stanton confirmed at least one of the victims had a law enforcement background, but refused to elaborate further.

And so it went, one question after another, some were original, although predictable, while others were only thinly veiled attempts to ask the same question in a different way. The goal, of course, was to try and get Stanton to trip up and give something away. Not all that different from police interrogation strategy.

Stanton introduced SSRA Ridley, who

confirmed the FBI had offered their assistance to the police department.

The press conference concluded at 12:35, and Byron made a beeline for the auditorium doors, avoiding the stampede. He was tired and frustrated, but mostly he was hungry. He checked his cell to see if Kay had left a voicemail message. She hadn't. He walked west down Middle Street along the uneven brick sidewalk toward Calluzzo's Bistro, alone.

"Come right in, Detective Joyner," Assistant Chief Cross said with a twinkle in his eye. The twinkle was accompanied by one of those large toothy smiles she so despised. The insincerity of his smile called to mind Lewis Carroll's Cheshire cat. She half expected to see him wink out of existence, leaving only his grin floating above the desk. "Close the door."

She hadn't a clue why the assistant chief wanted to see her, but he was never this jovial unless he was making someone's life miserable. Diane had a sneaking suspicion she knew whose life it was apt to be.

"Have a seat, Detective."

"What's this about, Chief? Am I in some kind of trouble?"

Cross let out a hearty laugh. "You? Absolutely not. How's the investigation going?"

"I think we're making headway. Sergeant Byron and the rest of us have all been putting in some long hours on this."

Cross finally dropped the joyful façade. His expression turned serious as he leaned over the desk. "I'm glad you brought him up. I want to talk to you about Sergeant Byron."

"What about him?" she asked, fighting to keep her expression stoic.

"I'm concerned about a number of things I've been hearing. I've been on the job for a long time and seen many good officers go off the rails. Byron wouldn't be the first."

"Off the rails, Chief? Afraid I don't know what you mean."

"Really?" he asked, raising his eyebrows for effect. "I'd like you to read something." Cross handed her a piece of paper.

She looked at it. It was a statement from Sergeant Kenny Crosby accusing Byron of assault. She looked over at Cross. His smile had returned.

He gestured toward the statement. "Please, continue."

She finished reading Crosby's statement, then returned it to Cross. "With all due respect to Sergeant Crosby, Chief, that isn't exactly what happened." She watched him lean back in his chair and put his hands together, tenting his fingers like some egocentric potentate.

"And you'd know that how? Were you in the men's locker room?"

"No, sir. I wasn't. But I know —"

"What you know," he said, cutting her off, "is only what John told you. Only his version of what happened. Nothing more."

She opened her mouth to protest and he raised his hand to silence her.

"Let's look at the facts, shall we. Your partner told you something different, probably said Kenny instigated it. But how reliable is his word? Isn't this the same John Byron who's been observed, on several different occasions, passed out drunk in his city-owned vehicle?"

"Chief, I don't know what you've heard but —"

He leaned over the desk toward her, cutting her off once again. "What I've *heard* is that two of my detectives have been — how should I say this? — fraternizing with each other. As I'm sure you are aware, it's a clear violation of this department's standard operating procedure for two members of the same unit to engage in any fraternization. Furthermore, if this were taking place, I'd be forced to transfer one of them out of the unit. But you already know this, right detective?"

"Yes, sir. I do."

"Have you anything to add?"

She didn't know how much of what Cross was saying he could prove, but it was obvious he'd set his sights on John and that was bad enough. "No, sir. I don't."

Cross raised his brows. "Are you telling me that you and Sergeant Byron aren't involved?"

She gave him her best eye contact. "We are not involved, sir. I'm not sure where any of this is coming from."

He sat back in his chair, the grin gradually reappeared. "Well, I'm so relieved to hear it. In that case, Detective, why don't you bring me up to speed on the murder investigation."

CHAPTER TWENTY

An old proverb warns against dwelling on things that have already happened. A good police investigator is the exception to the rule. John Byron was an excellent investigator, unable to let go of anything that had already happened. Ever. He was alone in the conference room, updating the whiteboard and scrutinizing it for anything they might've missed, when Shirley Grant poked her head into the room.

"Excuse me, Sarge. I don't suppose you have a second, do you?"

He turned toward her. "What do you need?"

"There's a sweet old lady in the waiting room. She's been waiting for over an hour to meet with Detective Joyner, but she's tied up."

Now that Stanton's press conference had aired, Byron suspected the wing nuts were already coming out of the woodwork. "Have one of the other detectives help her."

"I can't. She says she'll only talk to Detective Joyner."

"Any idea what she wants?"

"Apparently, Diane left a business card in her door."

"Okay, give me a minute. I'll come out and get her."

"Thank you, Sergeant. Her name is Ginny Anderson."

"Got it."

Byron opened the door to the glassed-in waiting area of CID and stepped inside. Seated alone was a well-dressed diminutive woman. He guessed eighty, at least. She looked up from her magazine as he spoke. "Mrs. Anderson?"

"Yes."

"I'm Detective Sergeant Byron. I understand you're waiting to speak to a detective."

"Yes. I'm waiting on Detective Joyner," she said, examining the card in her hand. "I found this in my door."

"She's busy at the moment. It could be a while. Maybe I can help you."

"Are you her supervisor?"

"I am actually," he said with a smile.

"I suppose it would be okay, then." She started to get out of her chair.

"We can talk here if you'd like."

Anderson's expression turned serious. "Sergeant, I am going to be eighty-three next month and this is the first time I've ever stepped foot inside a precinct house. But I watch television and I know how this is supposed to work. If you want my information, we will need to speak in an interview room."

"You're absolutely right, Mrs. Anderson," he said, doing his best to hide his amusement and impart a solemn tone of voice. "I apologize. Right this way."

They walked through the maze of desks toward the interview rooms. Byron caught the curious gaze of LeRoyer as they passed by and gave him a wink. LeRoyer grinned.

The bright blue doors of the three CID interview rooms had always reminded Byron of the television game show *Let's Make a Deal.* And unlike the usual visitors to the interview rooms, Byron highly doubted Mrs. Anderson would have any need to utter those words. He led her to room number three, as it was the only one not currently in use. "Is this okay?" he asked.

"It's fine," she said as she sat down and set her purse on the table directly in front of her.

"Can I get you something to drink?" he

asked. "Water maybe?"

"I'm fine, thank you."

Byron closed the door and sat down across from her. "So, Mrs. Anderson, what do you have for me?"

"Don't you have to read me my rights?"

He smiled again. "Actually, we only do it when we're interrogating a suspect. Unless you've done something you need to confess, I feel comfortable we can skip the Miranda warning."

"Well, okay. You're the expert."

"Do you have some information for me?" he asked, hoping this wasn't a waste of his time.

"I think so. I live across the way from a nice young man by the name of James O'Halloran."

Byron was no longer amused by his visitor. He'd been waiting for a break and realized, however unlikely, she might be it. "Do you know what happened to him?"

"I just found out he was murdered in his home."

"That's right. And we're investigating his murder. We canvassed the entire neighborhood a week ago, Mrs. Anderson. Why did you wait to come in?"

"I've been away visiting my daughter and her family since last Wednesday. I came home and saw the card in my door. I didn't know why the police would have left a card in my door until I saw the news about Mr. O'Halloran. Did you know he was a police officer?"

"Yes, I'm aware. You said you had something to tell us. Do you know something about his death?"

"Well, I'm not sure if this is anything helpful, but I kind of keep an eye on things in our neighborhood. I guess some people might say I'm a bit of a nosy parker, but I don't think it's a crime to care about what's going on around you. Right?"

"You're absolutely right. Better safe than sorry."

"That's what I think. Like the kids at the middle school, sometimes they cut through our yards and do mischief. Mrs. Yankowski's fence got vandalized last year and I saw the boys who did it."

"Did you see something that might help us on the O'Halloran case?"

"Well, I'm not sure. I know he was sick with cancer. He had nurses come to the house every day. During the week it was a cute little redhead girl and on the weekends it was a healthy young man."

"Healthy?"

"I don't want to say he was fat. He was

big-boned. You know, healthy."

Byron nodded his understanding while still doing his best to suppress a grin.

"I got used to seeing both nurses come and go and was familiar with what they drove," Anderson continued. "But the night before I left, let me see, it would have been last Tuesday, I saw a man park out on the street in front of Mr. O'Halloran's and go inside."

"Did you get a good look at him?"

"No, it was too dark, but I know he was a good-sized man."

"How do you know he went inside the house?"

"I watched him."

"Did you see what he was driving?"

"Yes, it was a light-colored Honda van. Maybe silver. It's always so hard to tell at night."

"You didn't happen to see the plate number, did you?"

"No, I'm afraid I didn't."

"Had you seen that vehicle there before? Could it have been one of the nurses?"

"No, it was the only time I'd seen it since he's been out of the hospital. The nurses don't drive vans. The cute little red-haired girl drives a light green Subaru wagon and the healthy young man has a black mini

Jeep. I think it's called a Liberty."

"How do you know so much about cars, Mrs. Anderson?"

"I was an insurance adjuster for forty years. I know my cars, Sergeant Byron."

"I guess you would. Did you see the man leave?"

"I did. He got there around eight. I'd say, give or take, and left a little after nine-thirty."

"Was he alone both times you saw him?"

"Yes, he was."

"Did you see or hear anything strange while he was there?"

"No. He came, stayed for a little while, then left."

"And you're sure this was last Tuesday night?"

"Yes, because I left for my daughter's house in Massachusetts first thing on Wednesday morning, about six o'clock. I can't believe someone would hurt such a sweet man. He was a police officer you know."

After taking Mrs. Anderson's information and walking her back to the elevators, Byron called Tran.

"Dustin, I need you to run 10–28 checks on our list of former SRT. I want a list of every vehicle currently registered to them and their spouses."

"Sure thing, Sarge. What am I searching for?"

"I want to know which one has a tan or silver Honda van."

"What the fuck is your problem?" Diane said as she marched into the police gym.

Crosby, who'd had the gym to himself, was doing standing curls in front of a large mirror. "You'd better not be talking to me, Detective."

"Can't find anyone your own size to pick on?" she said, ignoring his warning.

He set the barbell on the rack with a loud clang, picked up a towel, and wiped the perspiration from his face. "I can only assume you think I've slighted you somehow. And you've lost your good sense. That's the only thing I can come up with to explain your insubordinate tone."

"Why are you fucking with John?"

"If you're talking about Sergeant Byron, I've done nothing to him. Don't have any reason to."

"Really? The bruise on the side of your face says differently. Heard he knocked you on your ass."

"Don't believe everything you hear." Crosby walked over to the bench, where he already had a bar loaded up with steel plates, and sat down.

Diane followed him. "I thought you were tough, but I guess you're nothing but a big pussy. Getting the chief to fight your battles for you?"

"You don't know what the hell you're talking about."

"Don't I? I read your statement accusing John of assaulting you."

"So you read my statement, big deal. He attacked me."

"Huh. I'm curious why that would be? I noticed there wasn't any mention of what led to you getting knocked on your ass."

"Call it a disagreement between sergeants. Nothing that concerns you, *Detective.*"

"Doesn't it? Who I decide to sleep with sure as hell sounds like my business."

"I don't know what you're talking about."

"You don't? That's strange, because the way I heard it, you asked John if he was tapping my, quote, 'sweet African ass,' end quote."

Crosby blushed. "Look, I was only kidding. I wanted to get a reaction from him. I didn't mean anything by it."

"Well, congratulations, you got a reaction, from both of us. Now, *Sergeant Crosby,* I'll tell you what's gonna happen. You'll go see

Cross first thing in the morning and tell him you were mistaken about what happened. Then you're going to drop your assault charge against John."

"And why would I do that?"

"Because if you don't, by the time tomorrow is over I'll have filed a complaint against you charging racial and sexual discrimination in the workplace."

"You're bluffing. You won't do it."

"Try me."

"It's my word against John's, what happened in there."

"You're forgetting about the new property detective."

Crosby laughed. "He won't say anything."

She held up a handwritten statement. "He already did." She watched as the color ran out of his face. "Don't forget, *Sergeant,* first thing tomorrow morning."

Responding to the lieutenant's text, Byron walked to his office and sat down.

"Stanton approved your overtime request for the surveillance," LeRoyer said.

"Great. I want to have those details up and running tonight."

"What did granny want?"

"Might be a lead on O'Halloran."

"Seriously?"

"So how many officers did he approve?"

"One per night."

Byron sighed. It was about what he'd expected. "I guess it's better than nothing. Did he approve all of them?"

"All but one."

"Which one?"

"Cross."

"What the fuck, Marty?"

"Hey, you're lucky you got Williams. Cross tried to nix that one too."

"This is total crap."

LeRoyer sat back in his chair, staring at Byron. "Gee, thanks, Lieutenant, for getting all but one of them approved. You're awesome. I don't know how you do it, but you always seem to come through for me. Oh, it's nothing, John. I'm am here for you, after all."

"Thanks, Lieu."

"Don't mention it."

Byron's cell rang, it was Tran. "That was fast. What've you got?"

"A big fat goose egg. None of our folks have anything close to an Odyssey."

Would've been too easy anyway, Byron thought.

"Assuming she's right," Tran continued, "they either borrowed a vehicle or we're barking up the wrong tree."

"Check the local rental companies," Byron said.

"Sure thing. Might take me a while."

"Let me know." Byron hung up and got up to leave LeRoyer's office.

"Oh, John, before you go. You're familiar with the department's policy on fraternization, right?"

Byron had written the surveillance OT request and was leaving the shift commander's office when he received a text from Diane.

"We need 2 talk. Pick U up out front in 5?"

This can't be good. He typed the letter *K* and hit send.

"He asked if we were involved," Diane said after filling him in on her meeting with Cross.

"LeRoyer gave me some shit too," Byron said. "What'd you say?"

"I said we weren't. It's none of his damn business anyway. Think Cross put Kenny up to it?"

"Probably. Taught him to sit and stay too. He's trying to trump up stuff so he can have me suspended."

"How the hell can he do this, John?"

"He's the Ass Chief. It would appear he can do most anything he wants. Besides it's not like I haven't given him plenty of ammunition."

"He can't suspend you without due process."

"He hasn't suspended me yet. And it's not my suspension he's after anyway. He's trying to get me thrown off this case."

"Why?"

"I'm not sure, but he's been blocking my every move. He convinced Stanton not to let us set up surveillance on him. Where are we going anyway?"

"Coffee."

"Okay," he said.

"I just had to get out of there. This is total bullshit."

He turned to her and smiled. "There's the New York 'tude I love."

"So are we only gonna run surveillance on the others?"

"Hell no. I figure between Nuge, Mel, and the both of us we can watch all of them without their blessing. But, we've gotta be careful."

"Think he'll keep coming after you?"

"Bet on it. It might not be so bad if he succeeds, though."

"How do you figure?"

"If he suspends me, I'll have plenty of free time to work, unencumbered by the rules of law."

"If Cross caught you working this case after being suspended, he'd have you fired."

Byron grinned. "Gotta catch me first."

CHAPTER TWENTY-ONE

The Unicorn advertised itself as a gentleman's club. Byron had never truly understood the terminology associated with calling a strip club a gentleman's club any more than he'd understood the term adult entertainment. He'd never been able to figure out what was so mature about men and women shedding their clothing for money. He wasn't a prude, far from it; he found the sensuous curves of the opposite sex extremely enticing. It was the drugs and the prostitution he could do without. No matter how erotic the dancers appeared on stage, eventually, by the light of day, they all looked the same: hard miles, hard drugs, and bad endings.

Why a former cop would involve himself in a business as sleazy as the Unicorn, Byron couldn't guess. He assumed Beaudreau probably hadn't been all that ethically inclined when he was on the job. It takes all kinds.

He walked into the dimly lit lobby and was immediately ensconced in the deep repetitive bass notes of a DJ dance mix and the sultry feminine scent of perfume. A svelte blonde of undetermined age, wearing pasties and a leather miniskirt, stood by the entry door to the inner sanctum. She was flanked on both sides by muscle-bound gym rats. Both wore T-shirts, adorned with the Unicorn logo, at least two sizes too small. The woman greeted Byron with a well-rehearsed seductive smile, comprised of twin rows of bleached teeth. "Good evening, handsome," she said. "Are you here for the party?"

"Not really. I'm looking for someone," Byron said, flashing his badge. "Dominic Beaudreau."

Miniskirt looked to the rat on her right and nodded. The rat disappeared to the other side of the door, momentarily allowing some of the higher pitched musical notes to leak through. She turned her attention to Byron. "I'll see if he's available. Would you care for a beverage while you wait?"

"I'm fine, thank you." He stepped aside as two well-dressed men in their thirties walked in on the arms of a scantily clad boisterous and slightly drunk older woman. Byron gave her the once-over. What little clothing there was appeared to be of the same caliber as the jewelry she wore. Expensive. He took a second look at the young men, escorts he imagined. She caught his eye and blew him a kiss. The ménage à trois continued through the lobby and Miniskirt repeated her well-rehearsed greeting. As he waited, Byron turned his attention to the posters adorning each wall, depicting headliners from the video world of adult entertainment.

"I'm Dominic Beaudreau," a male voice said from behind him. "May I help you?"

Byron turned and extended his hand. "Detective Sergeant John Byron."

"What can I do for you, Sergeant?"

"I wonder if there's someplace we can talk?"

Beaudreau led the way to his private office on the upper level. The office was soundproof, with a large window overlooking the main stage below. "Can I get you something to wet your whistle, Sergeant Byron? Maybe some scotch?"

He looked at Beaudreau's well-stocked private bar. "No, thank you," he said, needing every ounce of his willpower not to accept. "This is quite an operation you've got here."

"I'm only a partner, I'm afraid. Wish it were all mine."

"Connected, are you?"

Beaudreau smiled politely, ignoring the question. "How can I help the police?"

"I know you were once a cop and I'm searching for information about a shooting you were involved in."

Beaudreau sat down in a chair across from him. Byron noted the odor of expensive aftershave, the dyed black hair, and the heavy gold necklace gleaming from his open-collared shirt. The man was a walking, talking cliché. "Had a few of those. Maybe you could be a little more specific?"

"The armored car robbery shootout in '85."

Beaudreau stuck a finger in his drink, toying with the ice. "That was one for the books. Lost one of our own, as I'm sure you already know."

"Bruce Gagnon."

"Yeah, tough loss. Young guy, full of piss and vinegar. But, a win is still a win."

"How was that a win?" Byron asked, barely masking his annoyance.

"Good guys three, bad guys one. You weren't in the military, were you Sergeant

Byron?"

"Joined the department right out of college."

"Ah, the pursuit of higher education. Well, I got my education in the jungles of Vietnam. Anytime we killed three to their one was a victory."

Byron wondered if Beaudreau had really seen any combat or if he was one of those who enjoyed portraying himself as John Rambo. "I suppose that makes sense."

"Why are you asking about the shooting anyway?"

"Because, as I'm sure you've heard, we're investigating the murders of two of your old partners, James O'Halloran and Cleophus Riordan."

"Murder? I'd heard Jimmy was down with cancer and Riordan killed himself."

"Not exactly," Byron said. "Had you seen either of them recently?

"No."

"Who told you that Riordan killed himself?"

"Hmm. You know I can't remember. Word on the street, I guess," Beaudreau said, grinning.

Byron, not liking Beaudreau's smug attitude, switched to a more direct approach. "Well, regardless of what you heard, they were both murdered."

"So what are you telling me, someone is coming after me?"

"Would they have reason to?"

Beaudreau's face twisted into a scowl. "What exactly is that supposed to mean?"

"What happened to the money?"

"Money?"

"The money taken during the armored car robbery."

"I don't think I like where this is going. If you've got something to say, I suggest you say it."

"Did you guys take the money?"

"Pretty sure I remember answering that question years ago. When the FBI asked it."

"Not really an answer."

"Of course we didn't. I'm not saying I wouldn't have thought about it, but we never found any of it and we turned the house upside down. Believe me."

Byron waited, creating the uncomfortable silence he'd learned to use so effectively. A silence some people couldn't stand, usually those people who had something to hide.

Beaudreau broke that silence. "Assuming you're right, and someone did kill Jimmy and Cleo, what does it have to do with the shooting? What makes you think it's related?"

Byron reached into his jacket pocket and pulled out a folded piece of paper. He unfolded it and handed it to Beaudreau. "We received this in the mail, right after the second murder."

Beaudreau studied the photocopy of the article as he got up and walked over to his desk.

"Has anyone reached out to you recently, maybe one of the others on your team?"

"No." He didn't even wait until Byron finished the question before answering. "I run in a slightly different circle now, Sergeant."

"Organized circle, is it?"

Again, Beaudreau ignored the question.

"So you've had no contact with any of your old partners?"

"Didn't I just say that?" Beaudreau reached down and pushed an intercom button on the desk. "Send Freddie up here."

"Guess this means we're done," Byron said as he stood up from his chair.

The office door opened and in walked one of the gym rats from the lobby. "Unless you want a lap dance before you go? I could hook you up with one of my personal assistants."

"No, thanks," Byron said. "He's not really my type." He turned his attention toward

Freddie. "Let me guess, Thing One? Or are you Thing Two?"

"Here," Beaudreau said. "You can take your article with you."

"Keep it. I've got others."

"Freddie, show Sergeant Byron the door."

"My pleasure," Freddie said with a grin.

"Good luck with your investigation, Sergeant. I hope you catch whoever is doing this."

"Thanks. I'm sure I will."

Byron slid behind the wheel and started the car. He knew Beaudreau had lied to him about contact. But why? Why would each of them lie about having contact with the others? If someone really was trying to settle a score by killing all of them, wouldn't it make sense for them to reach out to one another? What were they hiding?

He drove back into Portland on Brighton Avenue, stopping prior to the St. John Street intersection as the red lights at the railroad crossing began to flash and the gates came down, blocking the roadway. He stopped the Taurus short of the gate. While he waited, he put the car in park, pulled out his cell, and dialed Diane.

He was waiting for her to pick up, aware of the rumble of the approaching train,

301

when his head snapped back in the seat. Something had bumped his car from behind. He looked in the rearview but all he could see were high beams and the grille of a pickup. His car was jolted again. This time, the truck kept moving forward, pushing the Taurus toward the tracks. Byron pressed down firmly on the brake pedal, trying to hold his ground, but the truck was a much larger vehicle and the brakes weren't stopping his forward momentum.

The headlight of the approaching train illuminated the interior of his car like a searchlight. Dropping the phone, Byron struggled to move the transmission lever out of park. Helpless, he watched the front end of the car inching closer to the tracks. The Ford's windshield snapped off the red and white crossing gate. The broken board clattered down the hood onto the ground. The train was nearly on top of him now and the nose of his car was well out over the rails. The sound of the train's horn split the air. He'd never heard anything so loud before. He knew the time for jumping out had passed. "Come on, come on," he shouted as he pressed both feet on the brake and slammed the shifter into drive. The train was less than thirty feet away as he stomped down on the accelerator. The drive wheel squealed on the pavement until finally it caught and the Taurus shot forward over the tracks just as the train struck. The big diesel tore off the rear bumper and sent the car spinning like a child's toy. Byron gripped the steering wheel as hard as he could until the spinning ceased and the front end of his car rolled back toward the tracks. He slammed his foot down on the brake pedal again. Sparks flew from the tracks as the engineer applied the train's emergency brakes. Finally, the car came to a halt, mere feet from the giant steel wheels of the passing train. Byron sat in the stalled car shaking, his face illuminated by the instrument panel warning lights, his heart hammering in his chest.

"John, are you there?" It was Diane. He'd forgotten all about the phone. "John, can you hear me?"

With trembling hands, he felt around blindly on the floor until he located it.

"Diane," he said as his lifted the cell to his ear.

"What's all the noise? You okay?"

He leaned his head back against the seat and closed his eyes. "I lost a game of chicken with the Boston-Maine."

Byron was leaning against the side of a

black-and-white in the lot of Izzy's Sandwich Shop, getting checked out by a MedCu attendant, when Diane pulled in and jumped out of her car. She hurried over to where he stood.

"Holy hell, John. Are you all right?"

"I'm okay."

"You're bleeding," she said as the paramedic cleaned the wound on his forehead.

"Only a scratch. Didn't think a little thing like a train would stop me, did you?"

"Will he need stitches?" she asked the young attendant.

"It's up to him," he said, looking at Byron. "I can put a butterfly bandage on it or we can transport you up to the hospital and have it properly stitched."

"I'll take the bandage."

"You are one hardheaded man, John Byron," Diane said, disapproving of his decision. "Did they find the other driver?"

"No, and I couldn't give them much to go on. I know it was a dark full-sized pickup, but beyond that I couldn't tell."

"It's gotta have some front-end damage," she said.

"Doubt it. Not enough to identify it anyway. Pretty sure it had one of those crash bars on the front."

Diane sighed as she scanned the surrounding area. "What about the gas station?" she asked, pointing across the street. "Don't they have a security camera?"

"Already had a uniform check it. Outside camera only gets the pumps, it doesn't pick up the street."

"Of course it doesn't," she said, her frustration obvious.

"Sarge, the wrecker's here," a uniformed officer said. "You need to retrieve anything before they take it?"

"Yeah, I've got some things in the trunk. Or what's left of it. And my briefcase is on the floor on the passenger side."

"John, why don't I grab that stuff while the paramedic finishes up with you?" Diane said.

"Thanks."

Byron let her talk him into crashing at her place for the night. If someone was trying to send him into early retirement, the last thing he wanted was to make himself easier to find.

"What time is it anyway?" he asked as she pulled into the driveway.

"Almost eleven."

"God, all I want is a shower and a few hours of sleep."

She unlocked the side door and led him inside.

"Make yourself at home," she said as she closed the door behind him. "Towels are in the hall closet."

"Thanks."

"You want me to fix us something to eat?"

"Don't go to any trouble."

"It's no trouble. I'll see if I can find something you'd like."

Byron closed the bathroom door and started the shower to give the water time to get nice and hot. His skin felt clammy, the way it used to when the sweat dried following a strenuous workout, something he realized he desperately needed to get back to. He shed his clothes, dropping them on the floor and wishing he had clean socks and underwear to change into. He stepped into the tub, the water spray was strong and hot. It felt great as it cascaded down his body, soothing his tired and aching muscles. He was careful not to wet the handiwork of Portland's Bravest.

He'd spent countless hours at Diane's going over the FBI case file, but this was only his second time staying overnight. He was wondering what the sleeping arrangements would be when he heard the sound of the shower curtain being pulled back. Before he could rinse the soap from his face, he felt the tender caress of her fingertips on his back. Slowly, she traced around to the front of his torso.

"Thought you might need some help," she said. "I always have such a hard time reaching my back when I shower."

"What a coincidence," he said, grinning as he turned and faced her, seeing her naked for the first time. "So do I."

Her ebony skin glistened in the water. She toyed with the salt-and-pepper hair on his chest, the touch of her fingers electric.

"Like what you see?" she asked, gazing up at him with her big brown eyes.

"Very much."

As she moved in toward him, he pulled back. "You really think this is a good idea?"

She leered at him. "They already think we're doing it. Right? What harm can come from taking it for a spin around the block?"

Given his current state, Byron couldn't argue with her logic. He nodded.

"Now shut up and kiss me."

They embraced under the stream from the showerhead, exploring each other with hands and tongues. After several moments, she pulled back from him. "Have you ever made love to a black woman before, Sergeant Byron?"

His voice cracked, like a nervous teenager. "Ah, no. This is actually a first for me."

"Well then, I guess this is a night for firsts." She pulled him close again and pressed her lips to his.

Byron awoke refreshed, ready to take on whatever the day had in store. Only six-thirty, but the sun was already shining brightly through the window. Following the evening's passionate activity, he'd slept better than he had in months. He stretched, yawned loudly, and looked over at Diane's side of the bed. Empty. He rolled over onto his back, staring up at the ceiling as he recalled the details of the previous night. A night that had started with someone trying to kill him. He remembered his life flashing before his eyes as the locomotive bore down on him, the flashing red lights of the crossing signal, and the air horn blast of the train. It was all so surreal. A near-death experience was followed by the sweetness of having the night end sharing not only the shower but the bed of his partner. He closed his eyes and breathed in deeply. The pleasing aroma of coffee brewing wafted in from the kitchen.

"Hey, sleepyhead," Diane said from the bedroom doorway, already dressed, with a smile on her face and a steaming mug of coffee in her hand. "How're you feeling?"

He grinned. "Not too bad. A little stiff."

"You can say that again. You fell asleep on me last night."

He looked over at her. "Sorry," he said, feeling his cheeks blush. He swung his feet out from under the covers and sat on the edge of the bed rubbing his neck and checking his head to see if the bandage was still in place. It was. The wound was already beginning to itch.

"Luckily for you, you managed to take care of some pressing business beforehand."

"Did I?"

"Oh, yeah." She handed him the coffee and bent down, delivering a lingering kiss.

His body, already reacting to her touch, was in conflict with his mind. He knew Le-Royer would come unglued if he found out what was going on. Fraternization within the same unit of the police department was a big no-no. If their relationship was discovered, one of them would be transferred. "You know this is totally against the rules, right?"

"Uh-huh," she said, leaning in and giving him another prolonged kiss.

She pulled away and looked at him. "Relax, Romeo. I'm not looking for a committed relationship. We are two discreet and consenting adults. Friends with benefits." She picked up his shirt and tossed it at him. "Now, stop teasing me and put some clothes on before I forget we've got a case to work and a bad guy to catch."

Diane drove them to 109, stopping at his Danforth Street apartment long enough for Byron to brush his teeth and change clothes.

At eight o'clock Byron walked into LeRoyer's office. "I need a car."

"So I heard. How many does that make this year?"

"This one wasn't my fault."

"That's what you always say. It's never your fault. Nice bandage," he said, pointing at Byron's head.

"Itches like hell."

"What happened this time, John? Overserved? Did you close down the Gull?"

"I was stone-cold sober."

"Uh-huh."

"Seriously. Somebody pushed me in front of a train, Lieu."

"What'd you do, give 'em the finger?"

The lieutenant was obviously enjoying this. Not believing for a second that someone had really tried to punch his ticket. "I need the keys to another car."

LeRoyer stood up and walked over to the metal wall cabinet where the fleet keys were stored. He scanned the rows with his finger before finally making a selection. "Here," he said, tossing him a pair of keys.

"What do these go to?" Byron asked, not recognizing the shape of them.

LeRoyer grinned. "You know the old gray Jetta the drug guys seized?"

"You're kidding, right?"

LeRoyer shook his head and returned to his chair. "Nope."

"Come on, Lieu. The car's a piece of shit. It's got an inch of dust on it from sitting in the garage. It probably won't even start."

"So, get someone to jump it. Look, you wanted a car, that's a car. It's all I've got. Take it or leave it."

"That's just fucking dandy."

"Hey, look at it this way, at least you won't get towed by Parking Control. You've got a clean plate, John. Given your track record for never listening to me when I've told you to stay out of no-parking zones, I figure you've probably got till the end of the week before you're in violation of the scofflaw again."

"Thanks a lot."

"You're welcome."

■ ■ ■ ■

Byron was in the rear garage pouring a bottle of Poland Spring water over the Jetta's windshield, attempting to rinse off enough of the grime to get to a car wash, when Diane pulled up next to him.

"What are you doing with that piece of crap?" she asked.

He turned to look at her. "You don't like it? It's my good-driving award from Le-Royer."

"I don't know where you're planning on going in that thing, but if I were you I'd rather walk."

"Trust me, I've thought about it, but Harvard, Massachusetts, is a bit too far for me to hoof it."

"What's in Harvard?"

"Jack Riccio."

"Do you really think he was behind what happened last night?"

"Only one way to find out."

"Okay, hop in sailor. I'll give you a ride."

"Mind if I drive?" he said, tossing the bottle at the Jetta.

"Yeah, I do. I've seen the way you drive."

Federal Medical Center, Devens, located

less than forty miles west of Boston, is a federal prison housing male inmates with special medical needs. FMC Devens houses everything from minimum security–status prisoners to those serving multiple life sentences. Jack "The Velvet Hammer" Riccio was firmly in the latter category. A high-ranking boss in the Regalli crime family, with operations based in Boston and New York City, Riccio was convicted in 2005 of racketeering and for his involvement in the murders of several people including one prominent Boston attorney. The U.S. attorney hadn't been able to prove he'd actually pulled the trigger, but the beauty of the federal racketeering law was he didn't have to. Conspiracy is far easier to prove.

It was nearly noon by the time they reached Harvard. Byron figured the prison would be in lock-down until after the lunch hour, so he allowed Diane to talk him into stopping for food.

She took a bite of her sandwich, then set it down. "Have you thought about how you'll ask him?"

"No."

"Hello, Mr. Riccio. I'm curious, did you try and have me whacked?"

"Okay, you're so smart. How would you ask him?"

"I'd bat my eyes at him and be as cute as I could." She proceeded to demonstrate the procedure. "He'd be so enamored with me, he'd have to call it off."

Byron was feeling pretty enamored with her himself. "Only a guess, but it probably won't work for me."

"Oh, I don't know, John, he's been in for a while. You might just light the old boy's candle."

They ate in silence for a few minutes before Diane broke the spell.

"Something on your mind?" she asked.

"Yeah. I know you drove me all the way down here, but I'd rather you didn't sit in on the interview."

"You afraid I'll distract him?"

"No, I'm serious. If he really was behind what happened last night, I don't want to risk you becoming a target."

"You really think he could have done it?"

"I know he could. You've read the same files I have. They always suspected he was behind the robbery. Riccio's a bad guy, Diane. Even having you with me today may have exposed you."

"I am second on this case, John. Are you ordering me not to sit in?"

"No, I'm asking you. Please, sit this one out."

314

"So what am I supposed to do, sit on my thumbs?"

"Check the prison visitor logs for me."

"You're gonna owe me."

They finished eating and drove to the prison.

Byron didn't really expect Riccio to spill his guts if he was involved, but after the obvious attempt at derailing his life, he figured a face-to-face visit with the crime boss himself was in order. Riccio was in his late seventies and living on borrowed time. He'd had two heart attacks and was now suffering from high blood pressure, diabetes, and rheumatoid arthritis. A normal man in his condition wouldn't have been seen as a threat to anyone, but the Velvet Hammer was no ordinary man. The reach of his tentacles was impressive, and, incarcerated or not, he was still extremely dangerous. Byron knew if Riccio had ordered the hit on him, it was only a matter of time.

Inmates were only allowed six visitors per month, but visits by law enforcement weren't counted against the tally. Wanting his visit to be a surprise, Byron hadn't called ahead. After nearly three hours of driving and thirty minutes of the usual corrections red tape, he was finally seated inside the locked interview room. He looked around, wondering how many confessions he'd have obtained if Portland's interview rooms were as cold and bare as this. It had no windows, a concrete floor, gray cinder block walls, stainless steel table and chairs. The table and one of the chairs were bolted to the floor. A security camera hung from the ceiling.

A shackled Jack Riccio shuffled into the room, accompanied by two large, no-nonsense prison guards. Dressed in a bright orange jump suit, the frail inmate bore little resemblance to the slick-talking gangster in the three-piece suit Byron had seen during news coverage of the trial. His once raven-colored hair had grayed and receded. Brown age spots tattooed the backs of his hands. The only thing that hadn't changed were Riccio's steel blue eyes. Sharp and calculating, they already appeared to be sizing up his unexpected visitor.

"Holler if you need us," the bald guard said after seating Riccio in the chair directly across from Byron. He nodded his understanding as both guards stepped out of the room, closing the heavy steel door behind them with a loud clang.

Riccio's expression remained stoic, even as Byron introduced himself.

"Mr. Riccio, my name is Detective Sergeant John Byron. I'm from the Portland Police Department."

"Oregon?"

"Portland, Maine."

"I imagine the foliage is nice right about now."

"It's getting there," Byron said. Each man sized up the other, like a mongoose and a cobra, neither one breaking eye contact.

"Little out of your jurisdiction, aren't you, Detective Sergeant Byron?"

"I go where the case takes me."

"You're here about a case, then?"

"A murder."

"Interesting. But, as I'm sure you're aware, I've been a guest in here for some time. Reason would dictate you've come here about a historic case."

"Actually, no."

Riccio raised an eyebrow. "No? A recent case, then. And you believe I possess some knowledge that might be beneficial."

"I believe you may have ordered a hit on someone."

"A hit. I'm flattered you'd think I still have that kind of pull, Sergeant. However, I can assure you I'm just an old man living out his last few years in solitude."

"Maybe. And maybe not. Forgive me if I

don't find your assurances have much merit."

"An interesting quandary. You've driven all this way for my help but doubt what I'm telling you. I'm curious, who is it you think I want dead?"

"Me."

Riccio's eyes widened in genuine surprise. "You? I've never even met you."

"Why would that stop you?"

"Forgive my impertinence, Sergeant, but you look much healthier than any of my other alleged victims. Perhaps you will enlighten me. Why do you think I'd want to kill you?"

"I'm investigating the murders of several former Portland police officers. Last night, someone tried to push my car in front of a train. Doesn't feel like a coincidence."

"Why would I care about your investigation into the deaths of former cops?"

"These *cops* were all involved in a shootout with three robbery suspects in the mideighties. The robbers in question were suspected of having robbed an armored car during broad daylight in Boston, making off with nearly one and a half million dollars. These police officers were attempting to apprehend the men when the shooting occurred. When it was over, three robbers and one of the officers were dead."

"And? I still don't see how this pertains, in any way, to me."

"You were a made man, Mr. Riccio. Nothing went down in Boston without your say so."

Riccio allowed himself a tight smile. "The legend often exceeds the man, Sergeant Byron. Don't you find?"

"You're saying you weren't behind the robbery?"

"You might be surprised to know not every crime committed in Beantown was connected to me. Let's assume, for argument's sake, I was behind this robbery of yours. It doesn't explain why I'd want you dead."

"There was speculation during the follow-up investigation by the FBI that one of the robbers was related to you."

"Ah, the Federal Bureau of Investigation. So you've turned to the feds for help and they've pointed their far-reaching finger at me. Now you think perhaps I'm seeking to avenge the death of a relative?"

"Something along those lines."

"If you're expecting me to *rat* someone out, I'm sorry to disappoint, you've come to the wrong man. I didn't survive this long in my particular line of work by selling out my fellow man."

"I don't suppose you did."

"Are you a fan of history, Sergeant?"

Byron nodded. "I make my living reconstructing it."

"Touché. Did you know John Edgar Hoover himself, while operating under the color of law, broke more federal laws than I've ever been accused of breaking?"

Byron didn't like the uncomfortable feeling that Riccio had the upper hand. He'd done some research on Riccio prior to coming here but evidently not enough. Riccio didn't act or talk like the stereotypical mob boss. He was articulate and well read, not at all what Byron had envisioned. "I wasn't aware," Byron said.

"It's true. What's the old adage about power breeding corruption? Laws were written to keep the people in line, Sergeant, rather ironic when you consider my alleged job description."

Byron remained silent as he waited for Riccio to finish making his point.

"You've come here seeking information from me, yet I don't expect you'll believe anything I say. You strike me as a man who's good at his job, thorough, a type A personality, like myself. I'll tell you what I think, Sergeant, but you'll have to do due diligence and check the facts yourself. Fair enough?"

Byron nodded again.

"I have no connection whatsoever to the imbeciles who committed the armored car robbery, nor am I responsible for the recent failed attempt on your life. I am, however, aware of things that might assist you. The money you mentioned, was it ever recovered?"

"No."

"This suggests only two possibilities: either the men your officers killed weren't the men who robbed the armored car or the officers themselves took the money."

"There's another possibility. The fourth robber was never captured. We believe he may have gotten away with the money."

Riccio's smile returned. "Making him the luckiest imbecile on the planet."

"What are you saying?"

"Have you read the Bible?"

Byron wondered how it was that even in a federal prison while talking to a convicted murderer and mob boss, he couldn't escape his Catholic upbringing. "Some."

"I read a great deal, Sergeant, always have, more so as of late. Are you familiar with the story of Judas Iscariot?"

"Judas, yeah. Somewhat."

"You may want to revisit that particular

passage. Well, it's been a pleasure meeting you, Sergeant Byron. Best of luck with your investigation. I'll be sure and follow your progress." Riccio looked toward the door. "Guards, we're finished."

Byron walked through the parking, lot toward an anxiously waiting Diane.

"Well, what happened?"

"A mob boss who quotes from the Bible?" Diane said as she turned onto Route 2. "That's whacked."

"He didn't actually quote from it, but yeah, he wasn't what I'd expected."

"Okay, so he threw a bunch of flowery prose at you. Do you believe him?"

Byron shook his head. "I don't know. He did seem genuinely surprised about why I was there. What about his contacts?"

"I had the shift captain pull up Riccio's phone and visitor logs for me. Nothing out of the ordinary. His daughter comes to visit every other Tuesday like clockwork, sometimes brings the grandkids. Every couple of months, his lawyer stops by to update him on the latest appeal attempt. And he gets the occasional call from one of his sons, but that's about it."

"Nothing different as of late?"

"Nope. I looked at his contact logs for the

past two years and nothing stands out."

"Well, one thing's for certain — if my new *paisan* friend is right about Judas Iscariot, my problems are one helluva lot closer to home than Harvard, Massachusetts."

Chapter Twenty-Two

Davis Billingslea sat alone at his computer, typing madly. It was 8:55 and he'd already missed the deadline for tomorrow's edition of the *Portland Herald.* He knew his editor would be all over his ass about it. He was now scrambling for the following day.

The police department had been very tight-lipped regarding the ongoing murder investigation ever since Stanton had gone public. Billingslea had gone to all of his usual police sources, and, as plentiful as they were, none of them had much in the way of specifics. Normally, they'd spew information as fast as he could write in shorthand, but on this particular case someone was playing it close to the vest. He knew Byron was behind this information drought.

Billingslea, forced to employ other methods, had been doing a little surveillance of his own, even resorting to payouts from petty cash, recorded under office supplies. The wagons were circled. It wasn't every day a serial killer set up shop in the Great State of Maine. A killer of former cops.

His desk phone rang, startling him. He considered letting the call go directly to voicemail, but his gut told him it might be important.

"Newsroom, Billingslea."

"Good evening, Mr. Billingslea," a male voice said. "I'm calling to provide you with some information regarding the cop murders."

"To whom am I speaking?"

The caller hesitated. "Call me Hawk."

More like nutjob, he thought. "Okay, Hawk. What can you tell me about these murders?"

"I have it on good authority the cops think the killer is trying to take out all of the former members of their SWAT team."

SWAT? It's SRT, asshole. "Really? And how would you know that?"

"I'm not at liberty to share my source with you."

"Why not?"

"How I come by my information is as sacred to me as how you come by yours, Mr. Billingslea. Let's just say, if I tell you something, you can bank on it being true."

Yeah, right. "Let's assume you do know what you're talking about, how can I confirm it?"

"If you drive out to Stroudwater in Westbrook, you'll see a black Chevrolet Malibu parked down the road from number 875. Inside the Malibu, there's a police officer on assignment."

The hair on the back of Billingslea's neck bristled as he scribbled on a notepad. He didn't care for the caller's tone of voice or the amount of detail he seemed to possess. "And exactly what kind of assignment are we talking about?"

"He's surveilling the home of former Portland Police Sergeant Eric Williams. Maybe you should check it out yourself."

Billingslea opened his mouth to ask another question when he heard the sound of the call being disconnected.

Before leaving his office, he queried the City of Westbrook's online tax records and located a large brick colonial-style house owned by E. Williams at 875 Stroudwater Road in Westbrook, just as the caller had said.

Billingslea couldn't shake the ominous feeling the phone call had given him. Common sense told him to pack up his things and go home. But, as with any reporter worth his salt, the need to know always trumped common sense. Besides, if Byron wasn't going to help him with this story, maybe Hawk, or whoever the caller was, would. He wasn't going to be left out in the cold on the biggest story to hit this town since, well, ever. Breaking this story wide open might get him a desk at the real *Herald,* or maybe even the *Times.* Common sense would just have to wait.

He grabbed a nondescript gray sedan from the newspaper's small motor pool and headed out toward Westbrook. As he passed through the Libbytown section of Portland, the little voice inside his head began to question him. "What do they say about cats and curiosity, Davis?"

"I don't know," he said aloud. "But I sure don't know any cats who've ever won awards for journalism." The little voice went silent.

Billingslea parked about a quarter mile down the road from where he guessed Williams's house would be, hoping the black jeans and dark windbreaker would help to conceal his presence. He locked the car, switched off his cell, and proceeded on foot.

Rookie Portland police officer Anthony Galletti had only been on the job nine months.

He'd taken the overtime assignment because the other guys on his team called it a "cake," the term used for any outside job where you got to wear civilian clothes (or "civvies"), take one of the unmarked cars normally reserved for the detectives, and do absolutely nothing for eight hours, all while earning time and a half. Galletti's girlfriend had initially been pissed, as they'd planned to go out for dinner and a movie, but she was over it quickly after calculating how much extra he would net in the next paycheck.

He didn't understand it. "This Williams guy is supposedly some bad-assed cop, right?" he'd asked one of his buddies in the locker room before driving out to the detail, or "location three" as the dispatcher called it. "So why the hell are we babysitting an ex-cop? Can't he take care of himself? And why can't the Westbrook guys handle it? It's in their city."

Galletti grabbed a tall coffee and some munchies, having decided to spend the night watching movies on his smart phone. By 10:23 he was deeply engrossed in the Steven Seagal movie *Under Siege,* one of his all-time favorites. He'd always fancied himself a bit like Seagal. The rookie was so engrossed in watching Ms. July '89 and

Tommy Lee Jones's band of terrorists step out on to the deck of the USS *Missouri* that he completely missed it as Billingslea, concealed in the shadows, snuck by on the far side of the road.

Billingslea's heart raced with the exhilaration that accompanied going undercover. He wished his job was like this every day, instead of hanging around the police station and courthouse like a stray dog begging for scraps.

The idling Malibu was exactly where Hawk had told him it would be. The officer inside the car gave no indication he'd been spotted. Impressed with his own stealth, Billingslea crawled over a section of cyclone fencing surrounding the Williams's backyard.

"Dammit," he whispered as he heard his pants rip. After freeing himself, he got down on all fours and crawled around a short hedge of evergreens. His position afforded him an unobstructed view of the rear of the house. It was too dark to make out anything except shadows within the yard itself, but he could clearly see inside several of the lighted windows.

He struggled to remain calm, but his building excitement and racing pulse betrayed him. The silence was punctuated only by a symphony of crickets and the sound of a barking dog somewhere down the street. He was extremely grateful the dog did not belong to Williams. A motorcycle roared by on its way toward Portland. A bluish light flickered from one of the home's windows; someone was watching television. Frustrated at not being able to see anything, he decided to move closer. He stood and moved carefully toward the house. A branch snapped beneath his shoe, nearly giving him a heart attack. He exhaled, closed his eyes, and waited for his pulse to slow again. He took another step toward the house, this one much quieter than the last. As he took his third step, he felt something hard press against the back of his head, followed by the unmistakable sound of a hammer being pulled back on a gun. His bladder let go.

Galletti watched intently as the young soldier assigned to guard Steven Seagal began to question his orders. " 'You got shit for brains, Private,' " Galletti said, quoting the lines. " 'I know they brainwashed you at boot camp, but sometimes you gotta question authority. Trust me, boy, that's gunfire. You get me out of here, I'll go take care of it.' " Galletti was reaching into the paper bag for another chocolate chip cookie when he looked up and saw two men approaching his car. One of them had the other at gunpoint. "Ah, shit," he said as he fumbled for the door handle, spilling hot coffee all over his lap. *"Shit, shit."*

Galletti scrambled out of the car and drew his service weapon, a Glock 17. "Freeze," he yelled.

Both men stopped walking. They were only twenty feet away.

"Drop your gun," he ordered.

"Not gonna happen, son," Williams said.

"I'm — I'm warning you," Galletti stammered.

Calmly, Williams continued. "Son, I'm Eric Williams. I'm the guy you're supposed to be watching."

"Drop your —"

"Shut the fuck up, Officer!" Williams yelled, giving the young rookie the equivalent of a psychological backhand. "Now, you listen to me."

Galletti did as he was told, his hands shaking.

"I am the former police sergeant you were assigned to watch. This asshole was sneaking around in my yard and I'm bringing him to you. Do you understand me?"

Galletti gave an exaggerated series of nods.

"I'm going into my pocket to get my identification, nod if you understand."

The rookie officer nodded again. Williams slowly opened his credentials, displaying his badge to Galletti. "Are we good, Officer?"

"Y-yes," Galletti said, wishing with all his heart that he'd turned this job down and gone out to dinner with his girlfriend.

"Say it."

"We're good."

"Glad to hear it. Now, I'll lower my weapon as soon as you get some cuffs on this asshole. Why don't you get on the radio and tell the dispatcher what you have and request a uniformed backup. All right?"

"Okay," Galletti said as he lowered his weapon.

Williams prodded Billingslea forward with the barrel of his gun. "Move it numb nuts."

"Little prick is lucky I didn't shoot him," Williams said to Sergeant Pepin. "How the hell was I supposed to know he was a reporter?"

"I'm glad you didn't," Pepin said, staring at Billingslea, who sat handcuffed in the backseat of a black-and-white.

"That goes double for me," the Westbrook sergeant agreed.

"So," Pepin continued, "aside from criminal trespass, there isn't much I can charge him with."

"I don't want to press any charges, but tell mister pissy pants from the Daily Planet to stay the fuck off my property."

"You got it."

"Look, Sarge, as far as the surveillance detail goes, I appreciate what you're trying to do for me. I get it, but I can handle my own affairs just fine. Junior there would probably be more comfortable watching movies at home anyway."

Pepin glared at the rookie. Galletti, a beaten man, looked down as his feet. "Okay, Rook, he's your collar. I'll follow you in the unmarked to CCJ," he said, referring to the Cumberland County Jail. "Once we get there, you can tell him he's not being charged, but not until. Think you can handle it?"

"Yes, sir," Galletti mumbled.

Pepin turned to Williams and shook his hand. "I apologize again for all the trouble, Eric."

Williams stood on the front porch watching as the parade of police vehicles drove away.

Twenty minutes later, Williams was sitting in the living room watching television when the doorbell rang.

"Who the fuck is this now?" He was halfway to the door before realizing he'd left his .357 on the coffee table. He looked through the front door sidelight and saw a familiar face standing on his doorstep.

He opened the door. "What the fuck do you want?"

"Hello, Eric," the man said before firing two rounds into the ex-cop's chest.

Williams stood there for a moment in wide-eyed disbelief and pain. His mouth opened and closed as if in conversation, but not a word was uttered. He collapsed to his knees. Hawk stepped forward, firing one additional round into Williams's forehead, then calmly turned and walked away.

"213."

The voice of the male dispatcher calling his number over the radio startled Officer Denny Hutchins. He keyed the mic. "213, go ahead."

"213, we are currently on the phone with your target. He is on Curtis Road in foot pursuit of an unknown subject. Do you have a visual?"

"Shit!" Hutchins put the car in gear and accelerated toward the intersection of Summit and Curtis. "I'm en route now, right around the corner." He'd been watching the front of the house and hadn't seen Humphrey leave. "213, what's his 20?"

"He says he's turning onto Abby Lane."

The tires on Hutchins's unmarked squealed and he quickly rounded the corner without slowing. "Does he still have a visual?"

"Stand by. We're trying to get further."

"Give me a signal."

"10–4." The dispatcher quickly sounded the tone. "All units, a signal 1000 is now in effect for 213. Units hold all traffic."

Hutchins made the turn onto Abby Lane, craning his neck trying to see up ahead.

"213."

"Go."

"Target has lost visual in the area of Clapboard Road and Sturdivant Drive."

"10–4. I'll be out with him momentarily. Do we have a K–9 working?"

"Yes, 204 is here at 109."

"Have him start out to this location."

"10–4. 22, copy?"

"22, copied. En route."

"22, do you want additional units?"

"Negative, I don't wanna contaminate the scene for the dog. Get ahold of 720, Sergeant Byron, and let him know what we've got out here."

"10–4, Sergeant."

Byron pulled up in front of Humphrey's house just after one in the morning, and parked the noisy Jetta between two black-and-whites. The sound of a police dog's excited barking came from the backyard. He approached the house and was met by Humphrey and Sergeant Alan Morrell.

"Hey, Sarge," Humphrey said.

"You okay, Ray?"

Morrell answered for him. "He was a little winded when we found him. Maybe less time in the weight room and more time jogging, huh?" He patted Humphrey on the back.

"Did you get a look at him?" Byron asked.

"Not really. A figure dressed in dark clothing near the rear door. I think we startled each other. Whoever that was is friggin' fast."

"Mercer and K–9 Roscoe are starting a track from the back of the house," Morrell said. "I'm sending Hutchins with him."

"What the fuck are you driving?" Humphrey asked.

"It's a long story. Have we alerted the other details?"

"We informed all of them," Morrell said.

"But I'd be surprised if he tried again to-night."

"Even so, let's get a second officer to watch the rear of Ray's house."

"I don't need any more babysitters," Humphrey protested.

"Another officer, Al," Byron repeated.

"I'll take care of it."

The dispatcher's voice came over the radio again, "222."

Morrell keyed the mic on his lapel. "Go ahead."

"Is 720 with you?"

"Yeah, standing right here."

"Have him call the Westbrook shift commander, 10–18."

"10–4. Westbrook wants a call from you right away."

"Now what?" Byron said, gesturing for Morrell's portable mic. The sergeant obliged.

"720. I'm a little busy right now.

"10–4, 720. I think you're gonna want to call them, Sergeant. It's about location three."

CHAPTER TWENTY-THREE

At quarter of two, John Byron stepped out of his car and began walking down the long paved drive toward Williams's house. Flashing blue strobe lights illuminated his path. He stopped at the yellow crime-scene tape marking the perimeter long enough for a uniformed state trooper to record his name in the log.

The gray-and-blue state police evidence unit, a large RV conversion, was parked near the home. Several members of the SP Evidence Response Team (ERT) were busy photographing and marking the scene near the front door. Police floods illuminating the entryway made the dooryard look more like a nighttime sporting event. Byron pulled out and looked at his ringing cell. LeRoyer. He returned the phone to his pocket. The good lieutenant's update would have to wait. He wasn't in the mood.

The person he was seeking found him

first. "John. Over here."

Detective Sergeant Lucinda Phillips, Byron's state police counterpart, was the Major Case Unit supervisor, responsible for all homicides occurring outside of Portland in the southern half of Maine.

"Hey, Luce."

"Sorry about the jurisdictional bullshit. This is most likely your serial."

"No worries. Thanks for involving us. What can you tell me so far?"

"The victim, Eric Williams, was shot as he stood in the open doorway. Close quarters, two rounds to the chest and one to the head, execution style. Looks like he opened the door to the killer." Byron scribbled in his notepad. "I've got one of my folks, Detective Curtis, and your Detective Joyner interviewing Sergeant Pepin."

Byron saw the three of them seated in an unmarked Impala. He had no love for Curtis, having crossed paths with him before, when they were both detectives. Besides the rank, the only other thing they'd shared was a mutual dislike for each other. Byron saw Curtis as an overbearing asshole who thought being a Maine State Trooper made him God's gift to law enforcement. As for what Curtis thought of him, Byron couldn't have cared less.

"Where's the surveillance detail I had assigned out here?" Byron asked.

"Sergeant Pepin pulled it," Phillips said.

His head whipped around in her direction. "Why?"

"I'd better let him tell you."

Byron looked back at the unmarked.

Phillips continued. "My ERT is working the area around the body with two of your people, Pelligrosso and Stevens."

"Any witnesses?"

"Doesn't look like it. The victim was home alone. We've woken up half of the neighborhood canvassing, but most of them slept through it. The ones who didn't weren't close enough to see anything."

"Sounds like you're on top of it," Byron said, trying hard to hide that not being in charge was nearly killing him.

"John, I know this jurisdictional thing is a huge pain in the ass, for both of us. Whatever you need, I'll see to it. I want your people involved in every aspect of this."

"Thanks."

"But remember this when I need your help," Phillips said. "Want to take a look at the scene?"

"Not yet," Byron said. "I want to give the evidence techs a chance to get some of their work done before we start interfering. Think

I'll pop in and listen to what Pepin's got to say."

"Whatever you need, I'll be right here."

Byron knocked on the rear door of Curtis's unmarked. The state police detective waved him inside.

"Andy, how you holding up?" Byron asked Pepin as he climbed into the backseat and sat next to the patrol sergeant.

"I've been better," Pepin said. "A whole lot better."

"I don't want to interrupt," Byron said, turning his attention toward Curtis and Diane, "but I'd like a quick thumbnail of what happened before I start poking around."

"No prob, Sarge," Curtis said as he glared at Byron in the rearview mirror. "We're almost finished here anyway. Sergeant Pepin can fill you in while we write this up."

"What happened? Why did we pull the surveillance?"

"I wish I knew what happened, John. The surveillance pull was my fault. I let Williams talk me out of it. It feels like this whole night was one big setup."

"How do you mean?"

For the next ten minutes, Pepin recounted the story while Byron listened. The two detectives seated in the front of the car worked on their reports and the patrol sergeant's statement. The only interruption was the ringing of Byron's cell phone, which he promptly silenced.

"I was just clearing the jail when I got a phone call from a Westbrook dispatcher telling me they were sending units to the area near location three for multiple reports of shots fired. I drove out here expecting it was kids with fireworks or something, but instead I found Williams dead in the doorway. I was just talking with him, John, not even a half hour before. I shoulda put my foot down about the surveillance. If I had, he might still be alive."

"Maybe, and maybe not, Andy," Byron said, trying to assuage his guilt. "Maybe it wouldn't have made any difference. He might still be dead, and Galletti too."

"I guess."

"What the hell was Billingslea doing here anyway?" Byron asked.

Diane spoke up from the front seat. "Said he'd gotten a tip."

"From who?"

"Told me he didn't know," Pepin said. "Said he got an anonymous phone call."

The gloves are coming off, Byron thought. No way does Billingslea get off the hook that easy. He doesn't get to hide behind that protected source bullshit. Not on this one.

■ ■ ■ ■

·

The following morning Byron, Detective Sergeant Lucinda Phillips, Davis Billingslea, and Everett Goldman, Esquire, were all seated in Portland police CID interview room one while the rest of the bureau was packed standing-room-only into the conference room, monitoring the interview. Goldman was representing the interests of both the *Herald* and their star reporter.

During the prior nine o'clock meeting, which had also included Chief Stanton, his legal counsel, Cross, and LeRoyer, the ground rules for the interview had been established. Both Byron and Phillips knew whenever possible Billingslea and his lawyer would hide behind the rules of confidentiality. The detectives had at least won the battle over recording the interview.

The interview itself was much like a teenager's first time driving stick: lots of stops and starts without much forward progress. Each time they asked Billingslea a question, Goldman interrupted, arguing it was the reporter's privilege not to answer.

Byron was beyond frustrated. "Listen," he said to Billingslea, "you and I have worked together many times before, haven't we?"

You little shit, Byron thought but wisely did not add.

"We have," Billingslea agreed.

"And haven't I helped you out whenever I could?"

"Sometimes, I guess."

"You mentioned a nickname before. So, am I correct in assuming you don't even know who you were speaking with?"

"Davis, don't answer that," Goldman cautioned.

"Think of this as your own little Watergate," Byron continued. "Only instead of Deep Throat sending you out into a murder investigation, it was your caller — a caller who I'm assuming used a different moniker."

"Not sure I'm following you," Billingslea said.

"Neither am I," Goldman agreed.

Byron glared at Goldman, who flinched ever so slightly. It took every ounce of Byron's self-control not to jump over the table and loosen some of the asshole's teeth. He wondered if the pompous attorney would even bother trying to get the blood out of his three-piece suit or simply purchase a new one. He turned his attention to Billingslea. "Everyone knows the Watergate leaks to Woodward and Bernstein came from a person who went by the name Deep Throat, right?"

"Right."

"Okay, so tell me who Deep Throat was?"

"I can tell you who I think it was."

"That's not what I asked you. I asked you to tell me the identity of Deep Throat."

"I don't — I don't know who he was."

"Exactly," Byron said. "You don't, and do you know why? You don't know because all he ever provided was the nickname, Deep Throat. His sole purpose for doing it was to ensure his true identity would not be known. What harm could possibly come from you revealing the nickname your anonymous caller used to hide his identity?"

"Once again, Davis, I am advising you against answering the question," Goldman warned.

"He's a big boy, Everett," Byron said. "He's capable of making his own decisions. Let him speak."

"Sergeant Byron," Goldman began. "May I remind you —"

"No," Byron said, pounding his fist against the table, causing Billingslea to jump. "No, you can't, but let me remind you there are fucking lives at stake."

"Hawk," Billingslea blurted out. "He told me to call him Hawk."

Goldman jumped out of his chair, furious. "This interview is over."

Billingslea sat stunned, unable to believe he'd actually uttered those words.

"Thank you," Byron said.

Byron opened the door to the interview room and he and Phillips walked out.

"This is who we're looking for," Byron said, writing the name on the whiteboard with a black marker. "Hawk."

"How are we supposed to find the guy with only a nickname?" LeRoyer asked, combing his fingers through his hair.

"We know more than that," Byron said. "We know who he's going after."

"Feels like he's trying to send us another message," Diane said.

"Message received. He's a sick cop-killing bastard," Nugent said.

"I think you're onto something, Diane," Byron said. "He's definitely on a mission here. Taking chances by calling Billingslea and sticking him in the middle of this."

"And he's obviously conducting his own surveillance," Diane said. "He waited until Williams called off the detail, then killed him. Pretty brazen."

"He's taunting us," Nugent said.

"Daring us to catch him," Stevens said.

LeRoyer spoke up. "Say you're right and he is trying to send us a message — what the hell is it? So far no one has told us anything different from what we already knew, and they're still dropping like flies."

"What's the one thing all of his targets have had in common?" Byron asked.

They each considered his question before answering.

"They were all supervisors," Diane said.

"Exactly," Byron said.

"Meaning what?" LeRoyer asked. "He's going after the SRT bosses first?"

"Or maybe only the bosses," Diane said.

"But why?" LeRoyer asked.

"Maybe they took part in something the others didn't," Diane said.

"Something Hawk wants to settle," Byron said.

"Say you're right he's only targeting the bosses," LeRoyer said. "Who's left?"

"Only Falcone and Cross," Byron said. "Neither Humphrey nor Beaudreau were supervisors."

"How do we know it's *not* one of the others?" Stevens asked.

Byron returned the marker to the tray. "We don't."

Byron and Diane stood outside of the Williams home, getting a look at the scene by daylight.

"What do you see?" he asked her.

She looked around, taking it all in. "A long driveway, house well back from the main road, secluded."

"What else?"

"No light source in the yard. Easy house to approach."

"Probably how Billingslea got so damned close."

"Steps leading to a front door with glass sidelights. What are you thinking?"

"Do you have the scene inventory?"

"Yup." She pulled out the copy Pelligrosso had made.

"Run down the list for me."

Diane read aloud the list of items recovered, among them a .357 Magnum.

"Hang on a sec." Byron pulled out his cell and dialed Pelligrosso.

"Gabe, it's Byron."

"Hey, Sarge."

"Your list shows a .357 was recovered from the Williams house. The shooter's gun?" he asked hopefully.

"No, not the shooter's gun. The one we recovered wasn't fired. It's registered to Williams. We found it lying on the living room coffee table."

"Thanks, Gabe." He hung up and turned to Diane. "Pepin told me Williams was carrying a .357 last night when he confronted Billingslea, walked him right to the detail officer with it. So why leave it in the living room to go answer the door when he knew someone was gunning for him? It doesn't make sense."

"You're right. It doesn't."

"When you got here last night, was the outside light on?"

"Yes. It was on and Williams definitely should have seen the person standing at the door before he answered it."

"So, either the killer was known to Williams or, at the very least, was someone he didn't see as a threat."

"Like one of the remaining SRT members," she said.

"With the exception of Falcone, they were all under surveillance."

"Were they? We're watching their houses but not the people. How hard would it really be to sneak out and do this?"

"I suppose, but they'd still need transportation."

"They could get around that any number of ways. Taxi or maybe a borrowed vehicle."

"Good thinking," he said, pulling out his cell. "I'll have Tran run down the taxi companies and see if one of them had a fare out here last night. You really think this is a cop?"

"If it isn't, they certainly think like one. And another thing. Who else trains to deliver a double tap to the chest and one to the head?"

He raised his brows. "You're not just a pretty face."

"You're right about that, handsome," she said, giving him a seductive wink.

"What do you mean the surveillance detail is over?" Byron asked, glaring at LeRoyer.

"It's shut down, finished, over. I can't say it any clearer. And don't look at me like that. This isn't my call."

"Whose call is it?"

"This comes from above my pay grade."

"Cross, you mean."

"It doesn't matter who. It's done."

"It sure as hell does matter. You're the lieutenant of CID for Christ's sake. Don't you think policy decisions regarding investigations should be made by you? Doesn't it bother you at all that one of the officers potentially being targeted is making the call to stop surveillance? Don't you have to ask yourself why?"

"He thinks your surveillance is what led

the killer to Williams in the first place. Humphrey too."

"What a crock of shit. Are you kidding me? He certainly didn't have any trouble finding either O'Halloran or Riordan. Or are their deaths my fault too?"

"What would you like me to do, John?" LeRoyer said with a desperate sigh, running his fingers back through his hair.

"How about your job."

"Check yourself, Sergeant," LeRoyer snapped.

"Let me work my case so we can catch this bastard."

"I'm not gonna give you permission to disobey a directive from the chief's office."

"I'm not asking you to."

"What are you asking?"

"Let me do my job. You said you'd let *me* run this case. So let me."

LeRoyer sat there staring at him. Byron knew he was weighing his options. "I've got a wife and two kids to feed, John. My daughter's planning to go to college next fall. Fuckin' Sacred Heart. Do you have any idea what it costs to go there?"

He shook his head. "Nope. I went to Saint Joe's."

"Ha-ha, very funny. I need this job. And I'd like to work here long enough to collect my goddamned pension."

Byron didn't say a word. He'd seen Le-Royer struggle with decisions such as this before. Byron knew if he waited him out, LeRoyer would do the right thing.

LeRoyer slammed his hands down on top of his desk. "Dammit, John. You pull this shit all the time. And you think, what? I'm just gonna give in to your whims?"

Byron kept eye contact and remained silent.

"Okay, Sergeant," LeRoyer said finally, nodding like a bobble head. "Do it your way. You always do. Do whatever you have to do to solve this case. But, if you're planning on doing something you've been ordered not to, or something illegal, I don't want to know about it. You got me? And if either Stanton or Cross finds out, you're on your own."

Byron grinned. "You're the best, Lieu. You know I love you, right?"

"Get the hell out of my office."

Billingslea was pissed. Pissed at Byron for getting him in trouble with his superiors and pissed at himself for letting Byron bully him. Following the interrogation at the police department, he got dressed down again by his editor, like some little kid.

Didn't they understand how big this story was? Couldn't they see what was at stake? Byron certainly could. He paced back and forth inside his small cubicle at the *Herald*. He needed another in on this case. Someone who would give him the inside scoop. Hawk's call had gotten him close but not close enough.

Byron was the problem. *Fucking Byron.* He needed to find someone on the PD who had issues with Byron. Someone with knowledge of the case. Someone who would gladly spill the beans. Billingslea stopped in mid-pace and grabbed for his desk phone. *Crosby.*

"What do you mean he ordered it shut down?" Diane asked. "That's crazy. We need to watch these guys now more than ever."

"And we're going to," Byron said.

Stevens spoke up. "But you said —"

"I told you what Cross said, but now I'm telling you what we're gonna do."

Nugent rubbed his hands together. "God, I love being insubordinate."

Stevens looked over at him. "Makes sense, you're good at it."

Byron sent Nugent to keep eyes on Perrigo, while he drove Stevens and Diane north on

I–295, taking the Yarmouth exit. He back-tracked on Route 1 and pulled into the lot of Royal River Ford.

"You think they're just gonna give us cars to use?" Diane said as they got out of the car.

He turned to her and smiled. "Yup. Watch and learn."

"As I live and breathe, look at what the proverbial cat dragged in. If it isn't my old mate, John Byron," Grayson Timmons said with a fake Irish accent as he stood up and walked around the desk.

Byron gave his old friend a hug. "How are you, Grayson?"

"Never better, never better." He turned his attention to the other detectives. "And are you going to introduce me to these lovely lasses, or do I have to do it myself?"

"Grayson, I'd like you to meet Detective Diane Joyner and Detective Melissa Stevens. This is Grayson Timmons, my old academy mate."

"Nice to meet you," Diane said, extending her hand.

"The pleasure is all mine, lassie." Timmons bent in dramatic fashion and kissed her hand.

He took Stevens's hand next. "Is your accent real?" she asked.

"Nothing about this guy is real," Byron said with a grin. "He sells cars for a living."

"Except for my admiration of pretty ladies," Timmons said, giving Stevens a wink. "It's good to see you, John. Am I correct in assuming this visit is more than a social call?"

"It is actually. We're working a case and are in need of wheels."

"Doesn't the PD still supply you guys with cars, or has the budget gotten that bad?"

"They do," Diane said. "But we need something a little less —"

"Five-O?"

"Exactly," Stevens said.

"Would this be the SRT murders?" Timmons asked.

"It would," Byron said."

"Well, let's take a walk outside and see what we can see."

Timmons set them up with a silver Sentra and a light blue Outback.

"When do you need these returned?" Byron asked.

"When you've finished with them," Timmons said. "They're trade-ins. They'll be going to auction anyway. Afraid I can't help you with plates, though. State's a little funny about those."

"We've got it covered," Diane said as she

pulled two registration plates out of a paper bag.

"Pretty and smart. Looks like you've got yourself some good detectives, John."

"Better than you?" Byron asked.

"Hey, I never said that."

"Thanks, Grayson."

"Bring 'em back in one piece, okay?"

"Trust us," Stevens said with a wink.

Crosby's black Pontiac was parked in the lot facing the Baxter Boulevard running path. Billingslea opened the passenger door, climbed inside, and handed a paper bag to the detective sergeant. The car reeked of sweaty gym clothes and aftershave.

"Thanks for meeting up with me," Billingslea said.

"Don't mention it," Crosby said as he unwrapped the Italian sandwich that the reporter had bought to soften him up, spilling a couple of tomatoes on his lap. "Shit. Grab me a couple of napkins out of the glove box."

"Here. What happened to your face?"

Crosby fixed him with a scowl. "I slipped in the shower."

"Huh," the reporter said.

"So, what can I do for you, Super Sleuth?"

Billingslea realized that he despised this

muscle-bound detective almost as much as he did Byron. But he needed him, and if that meant putting up with Crosby's machismo bullshit, then so be it.

"Byron's fucking up my life."

Crosby laughed, nearly choked on a mouthful of food. "Ha, welcome to my world, sport. What do you want me to do about it?"

"I need information about the case he's working on."

"The murders?"

"That would be the one."

A grin spread across Crosby's face. "Gonna cost you."

"How much?"

"More than this shitty excuse for a sandwich," he said as he shoveled in another mouthful.

"I don't have access to money for sources."

"I'm thinking bigger picture, sport. Some good drug-bust exposure in the press for yours truly."

"You got anything worth writing about?"

"Not at the moment, but I'm picturing a feature story about an up-and-coming drug dick who has aspirations of becoming a lieutenant."

"You help me with this and I'll make you

look like a star."

It was after one o'clock in the afternoon when Diane turned into the entrance to Evergreen Cemetery. She'd been following Beaudreau's Cadillac since he'd left the Unicorn. She picked up her phone and called Byron.

He answered on the first ring. "What's up?"

"I followed Beaudreau to Evergreen Cemetery. You think a guy who owns a strip club eats lunch in a cemetery to get away from all those naked women?"

"It takes all kinds. Maybe women aren't his preference."

"Maybe, but I'll bet you dinner he's meeting someone."

"You sure he hasn't made you?"

"Positive. Looks like he's heading for the duck pond."

"You want backup?"

"I think I can handle this pervo."

"Be careful."

"You're such a nag. I'll call you when I know something."

She pulled off the pavement onto a grassy side drive and parked the Outback. Still a distance from the pond, she wanted to make sure he didn't notice her following. She got out of the car, stretched her legs, pulled up the hood on her sweatshirt, and began jogging toward the back side of the graveyard.

She was making her way toward the pond when she saw Beaudreau. He was standing at the edge on the far side and throwing bread crumbs into the water for the ducks. Diane continued her run around to the rear of the pond, giving him a wide berth. She was beginning to think she might be shelling out for dinner after all when a familiar-looking vehicle pulled up and parked near Beaudreau's Cadillac. The driver and only occupant sat in the SUV for several moments before exiting and approaching the pond. She recognized him instantly. It was Cross.

Diane worked her way toward them, pulling her hood further over her face. She could see the two men were talking. Beaudreau was gesturing with his hands. Whatever they were discussing, it looked like it was getting heated. She ran closer still, hoping to hear what was being said. For one terrifying moment, as she neared them, Cross looked right at her. She was sure he'd made her. Her heart was hammering like it might jump right out of her chest. Then he turned and looked away. He hadn't recognized her. The anxiety left her as quickly as it had come. She continued her jog around the pond and headed toward the car.

The meeting only lasted a few minutes. She watched as Cross drove away. Beaudreau returned to his car but waited several minutes before driving toward the exit. Diane pretended she was stretching near a large headstone as each vehicle passed by.

She quickly dialed Byron. "I don't know what that was all about, but I think I can guess."

"Did he meet someone?" he asked.

"Cross. And it looked pretty heated."

"Interesting. What do you think it was about?"

"I think Beaudreau was pissed about what happened to Williams. I think he's worried."

"Are you still on him?"

"No, I couldn't make it back to my car in time. I was undercover as a jogger."

"Probably just as well. I don't want to burn these cars by having them follow the same person too often. Take a casual spin out by the club. Let's see if he went directly back."

"Will do."

"I'll see if I can find Cross."

CHAPTER TWENTY-FOUR

Byron and Diane were keeping an eye on Beaudreau. They'd stopped at a sandwich shop on Riverside. She ran inside to grab some lunch while Byron waited in the car. Watching her through the store window, he couldn't help but think how quickly things had changed between them.

Sleeping with your partner will do that, John, his little voice said. God, how he despised that voice. He pictured the divorce documents lying unsigned on his apartment counter and felt a twinge of guilt. Maybe he hadn't signed Kay's papers yet, but sleeping with Diane had done more than any signature ever could. He'd pretty much sealed the deal on their failed marriage. It wasn't like there hadn't been a mutual attraction between he and Diane from the start. They'd had plenty of opportunities during their two years of working together, but neither of them had ever acted on it, until now. It was as if the women in his life had grown weary of waiting for him to make a move, any move, and had conspired to force his hand. His thoughts were broken by the ringing of his cell.

"Sarge, it's Mel."

"Hey, Mel. What's up?"

"Perrigo has been acting squirrelly all morning. He's been U-turning me to death, and I'm pretty sure he made me on the last one."

"Where is he now?"

"He pulled into the lot of a Mobile Mart on Route 1 in Yarmouth."

Byron's phone began to chime with an incoming call. "Hang on a sec, I'm getting another call."

He checked the ID. Perrigo.

"Mel, I'll call you right back; it's him."

"Sergeant Byron, Tony Perrigo."

Byron reached through the open car window waving his hand at Diane, trying to get her attention. "What can I do for you, Mr. Perrigo?"

"We need to talk."

"I'm listening."

"Not on the phone. Can you meet me?"

"Where and when?"

Perrigo chose a picnic area off of Route 88

in Yarmouth. Neither Byron nor Diane had any idea what had happened to change his mind, but there was no question he was scared. Perrigo had arrived ahead of them and was already seated at one of the tables as they pulled in to the gravel parking area.

Byron parked Diane's Outback near Perrigo's silver Mercedes, the only car in the lot. "I want to pat him down for weapons or recorders before we start," Byron said as they exited the car.

"You think he's up to something?" she asked.

He stopped and looked at her. "When it comes to this case, you're about the only one I trust." They both unholstered their guns as they neared Perrigo.

"What the hell is this?" Perrigo asked, getting to his feet. "I called you for help."

"And we want to help you," Byron said. "But first I need you get down off the table and assume the position." Perrigo did as he was instructed, placing his hands on the tabletop and spreading his legs out behind him.

"You said I could trust you guys."

"You can, but seeing as how you lied to us the last time we met, you're going to have to earn ours."

Byron holstered his semiauto and nodded

to Diane, who kept hers trained on Perrigo. He moved in and gave the former cop a thorough pat down. The only thing he found were Perrigo's keys, cigarettes, and lighter in opposite pockets of his windbreaker.

"He's clean," Byron said to Diane as he placed the items on the table.

She reholstered her weapon.

"Okay, you can get up."

"May I?" Perrigo asked, sounding indignant. "I called you, remember?" He reached for his smokes and looked toward Byron. "Okay if I smoke?"

"Be my guest."

Both detectives noticed his hands were shaking badly as he lit up. Perrigo kept glancing nervously toward the parking lot entrance.

"Expecting company?" Diane asked.

"I'm pretty sure someone's been following me." His eyes widened in fear. "Who knows we're meeting here?"

"No one," Byron said.

"You didn't tell anyone I called you?"

"No."

"How do you know you weren't followed?"

"We weren't," Diane said.

"Have a seat, Mr. Perrigo."

The three of them sat at a picnic table

near the far end of the lot. Perrigo sat on one side, Byron and Diane on the other, allowing them a view of the entrance. "You said you had something to tell us," Byron said as he pulled out a small digital recorder and activated it.

"You're not taping this," Perrigo said, his eyes darting from one of them to the other.

"Mr. Perrigo," Diane said. "That's how this works. You were a cop. If you want our help, we're gonna need yours as well, and it's all on the record."

Perrigo shifted his gaze to Byron. "You'll protect us? Me and Vickie."

"Who do you need protection from? Do you know who's doing this?"

"No, I don't," he said, taking a long drag off his cigarette and slowly exhaling a cloud of bluish smoke. "But I think I may know why."

"We're listening," Byron said.

"I was a good cop once, a long time ago. I think most of us on the team were. But things kinda got screwed up. I don't know how it happened, but it did." He tilted his head back, closed his eyes, took another long drag and held it in.

Diane leaned over and put a hand on his forearm. "You can do this, Mr. Perrigo."

He opened his eyes and looked at her as

he exhaled smoke from his nose. "We were ripping off drug dealers."

"Who's 'we'?" Byron asked.

"Us, the entire Special Reaction Team. We'd do the raids in conjunction with the drug unit whenever there were warrants for a high-level dealer. At first it was just a little bit and only money, but later —"

"My father was on that team."

"I know. Hey, you asked and I'm telling you."

"Who set up the rips?" Byron asked.

"O'Halloran ran CID. Cross and Williams were running the drug unit. I don't know exactly who made the decisions or where the intel came from, it didn't work that way. Most of us on the team only did what we were told. A need-to-know kinda thing. You know?"

Diane nodded. A gust of wind shook the leaves violently and Perrigo's head whipped around toward the parking lot entrance. "Mr. Perrigo, it's only the wind."

"Tony. Call me Tony, okay?"

"Okay," she said, giving his arm a squeeze.

"You were saying, Tony," Byron said, liking the former cop less by the minute.

"Like I was saying, we only knew what we needed to."

"How much money are we talking?" Byron asked.

"At first it was only a few hundred here and there for each of us, but it got bigger, fast."

"How much bigger?"

"Thousands. And I think some of the guys were skimming drugs as well, but I never had anything to do with that."

"Why not?"

"The rule was, do your jobs and keep your mouths shut. As long as nobody broke the rules everything was fine."

"What do you mean? Did something happen?"

Perrigo stubbed out his cigarette on the ground and lit another. After he'd settled his nerves he started again. "I don't know for sure. It's nothing I can prove, but something seemed wrong a few weeks before we raided the house on Ocean."

"I don't follow."

"I think Gagnon might have gotten on someone's bad side."

"Whose?"

"I don't know. It was something I felt. Some of the others were treating him differently like something was wrong. You ever watch the Animal Planet Channel?"

"I don't watch much television."

"I do," Diane said.

Perrigo looked at her and smiled. She squeezed his arm again.

"I watched a show once about lions of the Serengeti. They travel and hunt in packs called prides. Each pride looks for the weakest or slowest animal in whatever group they're stalking. Once they've identified the animal, they work together to catch and kill it."

"I don't see what that has do with Gagnon," Byron said.

"Sometimes, a rift grows within the pride. Something happens to place one of them at odds with the pride leader. All of the other lions sense the friction and start acting standoffish with the one who's fallen out of favor with the leader. Once that happens, it's only a matter of time before there's a showdown. In the end, the one who fell from grace either becomes the new leader by defeating the current head of the pride, or he's torn to pieces by all of them. It seemed like that with Gagnon. A short time later, he was dead."

"According to the reports, he was shot by one of the armored car robbers," Byron said.

Perrigo looked directly at Byron. "I know what the reports say. But just because it's written down doesn't make it so. I filed a number of reports in my day that were total bullshit."

"Who do you think killed Gagnon?" Diane asked.

"I don't know. Cross, Williams, Beaudreau, and Gagnon went into that house together and Gagnon left in a bag. You do the math. It doesn't really matter what I think, does it?"

"How did you guys get the information about the robbers being on Ocean Avenue?" Byron asked.

"I don't know."

"Was Riccio involved in this?"

"The mobster? If he was, I never knew anything about it."

"What happened the day of the shooting?" Diane asked.

"We'd been training all day, on the range. Afterwards we went out for drinks. It was one of the guys' birthdays, might've been Williams. Next thing I know, we're getting briefed about the robbery and the house."

"Who gave the briefing?" Byron asked.

"I don't remember. It was always one of the supervisors and the intel was always good. It was so good, it was weird."

"How do you mean?" Diane asked.

"It was like we had someone on the inside. Every time we did a rip, we knew exactly how many targets would be there, what they had for weapons, and that there would be a significant amount of money and drugs. We never came up empty. You ever heard of anything like that?"

She shook her head.

"Me neither," Perrigo said. He glanced toward the parking lot again.

"So you knew exactly who you were going to take down on Ocean Ave?" she asked.

"Of course. The armored car robbery had been all over the news. It was all anyone talked about, that and the money."

"One point four million," Byron said.

Perrigo nodded and finished his cigarette. The sound of an approaching vehicle caused Perrigo to leap off the bench. A young woman behind the wheel of a blue minivan drove in and parked on the far side of the lot.

"Take it easy," Diane said.

"Fuck that," Perrigo snapped. "You don't have any idea who these people are."

Byron and Diane exchanged a quick glance.

The woman got out of the van followed by a blond-haired boy, who looked about four, and a butterscotch-colored cocker spaniel.

"It's a family going for a walk, Tony," Diane said. "Relax."

The three of them continued to monitor the activity across the lot. The woman and her tribe headed down a walking path toward the water and out of sight.

"It's okay," Diane said. "They're gone."

Byron checked to make sure the recorder was still working. It was. "Can we continue?"

Perrigo lit another cigarette and sat down. "I don't remember where we were."

"You were about to say something about the money."

Perrigo nodded and fidgeted with his lighter. "After the shooting, we went in and secured the house. O'Halloran had one of the others bring the transport right up to the back of the house and we loaded up the money we'd found in the basement. There were, like, a dozen gym bags."

"Was it all there?" Diane asked.

"No. Only about half. It was really strange."

"What was strange?" Byron asked.

"According to our intel all of the money was there, along with all four suspects. But there were only three guys and only half the money. It was the first time we'd gotten bad info."

"How much did you end up getting?" Diane asked.

"Fifty grand."

"Did all of you get a cut?"

Perrigo nodded silently.

"That doesn't figure. If you divide the money —"

"Whoever said we got equal shares?"

"Who would want all of you dead?" Byron asked.

"I already told you, I don't know. But it's all part of this. I know it. I knew this thing would always come back on us."

"Why?" Diane asked.

"Because, it was the first time anyone died. These were the first guys to go down shooting. We shot a couple of the dealers, but no one ever died. And we never lost one of our own before."

"Why didn't any of the dealers report you for ripping them off?"

"Because it was drug money," he said, blowing smoke from his nose. "Cost of doing business, I guess."

"The dealers report stuff like that now," Diane said.

"Yeah, well back then they didn't."

Byron leaned across the table toward Perrigo, trying to get into his space. "Last time we spoke, at your home, you basically told us to get bent."

"That's true," Diane said. "You couldn't wait to get rid of us."

"What's changed that you're telling us any of this?" Byron asked.

"I can't tell you that. All I can tell you is Vickie and I are in danger and we need protection."

"From who?" Diane asked.

"It doesn't matter."

"It may matter to the prosecutor," Byron said. "You'll be expected to testify."

"Yeah, I figured that much out for myself. But here's the deal, you want me on the stand, you've gotta keep us alive. Both of us."

Byron walked to the far side of the lot and dialed Pritchard's cell while Diane stayed with Perrigo. He watched as she continued to interact with him. It was obvious she'd developed a good rapport with the ex-cop. Her ability to keep him calm and focused might come in handy later on.

"Hello."

"Terry, it's John."

Byron provided a thumbnail version of recent developments, then got right to the point.

"We need to stash this guy someplace safe."

"I can't believe he just confessed to all of that. Do you know how long I tried to get to the bottom of this?"

"I know, it's not really fair."

"Fair? Fuck fair. If you can reel him in, do it. Doesn't matter who gets the credit."

"This has always been your case, Terry. I'm not about to cut you out now. I need your help."

"What can I do?"

"We need a safe house. Did the bureau ever have one around here?"

"I'll call you back within the hour."

Chapter Twenty-Five

Byron and Diane followed Perrigo to his Falmouth home and waited while he and Vickie filled a cooler with food and packed enough personal effects to get them through the next several days.

"You think he's telling the truth about Gagnon?" Diane asked as they waited in the dining room.

Byron shook his head. "I don't know. He didn't give us anything concrete, hard to prosecute based on a feeling. It's bad enough finding out your father was ripping off drug dealers."

Byron had Perrigo secure his vehicles inside the garage, thinking they'd be harder to find if he and Diane transported them to their destination. Leaving the Mercedes parked outside the safe house would be asking for trouble, especially with police officers involved. It would be far too easy to find the car and run the plates.

It was after two by the time Pritchard called with the address.

Billingslea had returned to the office, running queries on each of the names given to him by Sergeant Crosby. He already had a handle on Cross, but some of the others were unknown to him, like the retired FBI agent Byron had helping him. Crosby hadn't known the agent's name, only that he lived locally. Billingslea glanced at the list as he drove over the Martin's Point Bridge into Falmouth. His search of the former SRT officers had yielded addresses all around southern Maine.

The newspaper databases revealed an Anthony and Victoria Perrigo living just off Route 88. He decided to start there. Maybe Perrigo would talk to him. Shed some light on this thing. If not the former cop, then maybe his wife. Billingslea wasn't particular.

About a mile after making the turn onto 88 from Route 1, Billingslea slowed the car, looking carefully at the mailbox numbers. As he neared the address, he caught sight of a familiar face seated in the rear passenger seat of a car pulling out of a driveway several hundred feet ahead of him. He didn't recognize the Subaru Outback but he did recognize Detective Joyner.

"Looks like my luck is turning."

He wasn't close enough to identify the vehicle's other occupants, only that there were four of them. *Coincidence?* He didn't think so. Billingslea slowed as he passed the driveway, double-checking the address. The numbers matched. The driveway was empty. *Perrigo must be with Joyner and probably Byron. But why?* They certainly weren't headed to the PD or they'd have turned toward him.

What are you up to, Detective?

He accelerated, deciding to follow them.

Perrigo sat up front with Byron, while Diane and Vickie shared the backseat for the half-hour trip. Byron caught a glimpse of Vickie in the rearview mirror. She was dressed up as if she were headed to a weekend getaway at some swanky B & B instead of where they were actually going. He was pretty sure she hadn't quite grasped the whole point of their trip.

The safe house was located in the town of Durham, well off a secondary road. Byron followed Pritchard's instructions to the letter, turning onto an unmarked dirt drive and following it about a quarter mile into thick woods. The evergreen boughs reaching out like arms scraped against the sides and roof of the car. At the far end of the drive, the forest opened up revealing a rustic log cabin with faded green shutters. The weathered two-story cottage was situated at the edge of a small pond. Pritchard's SUV was already parked in the dooryard. Byron parked beside it and they all climbed out.

As they were pulling bags from the rear cargo area, Pritchard stepped out onto the porch to greet them.

Byron made the introductions. "Vickie and Tony, this is Special Agent Terry Pritchard. Terry, these are the Perrigos."

"Former Special Agent," Pritchard said. "I'm retired." He shook hands with Perrigo. "I believe we've already met."

"We have," Tony said.

"Sergeant Byron said we can trust you to keep us safe," Vickie said.

"If you do what we tell you, I guarantee no one will find you here," Pritchard said. "Come inside and I'll give you a quick tour."

They followed him up the steps and inside, Byron and Diane behind them.

The first floor was open concept. Living room off to the left, stairway ascending to the second floor on the right, kitchen and small dining area straight back. The vintage avocado appliances took Byron back to his childhood and grandparents' house in

Dorchester.

"It's a little dusty," Pritchard said, breaking the awkward silence. "But it's dry and quiet. I started uncovering the furniture and got the propane back on. Everything here has been converted to run on propane, so it's completely off the grid. The stove, fridge, well pump, even the lights are all gas powered. There's one bedroom and a bathroom upstairs."

"Who else knows about this place?" Byron asked.

"Only a few folks from the bureau, but it hasn't been used in years. You've got everything you should need, minus television and phone."

"We've got our cell phones anyway," Perrigo said.

"I wouldn't suggest using those," Pritchard said. "Everyone knows your numbers. You'd be too easy to track."

"He's right," Byron said. "Diane and I will get you a couple throwaways. Give me yours and we'll take them with us."

Perrigo shook his head. "No way. You get us replacements, *then* you can have these, but not until. You're not leaving us out here without a way to call for help."

"I can run out now and get those, John," Pritchard said. "Probably should pick up some bottled water too. Not sure if the well's ever been tested."

"Thanks, Terry."

"How are you set for food?" Pritchard asked.

"We only brought enough for a couple of days," Perrigo said.

"How long will we need to stay here?" Vickie asked.

Byron noted the concern in her voice, as if Vickie was finally beginning to comprehend their predicament.

"It might take a few weeks for us to get this thing sorted out," Diane said. "Come on, I'll give you a hand getting settled."

"We haven't ID'd the killer," Byron said to Pritchard. "I'll get ahold of the AAG and let him know what we've got. We still need a game plan."

"I suspect they'll want a videotaped confession from you, Mr. Perrigo," Pritchard said.

"In case something happens to me, you mean?"

"If you both do what we ask, nothing's gonna happen to either of you," Byron said.

Pritchard drove off to purchase phones and water. Byron stepped outside to call Ferguson in the AG's office.

■ ■ ■ ■

Billingslea had lost sight of the Outback. Driving on back roads made surveilling damn near impossible. He'd stayed back a quarter of a mile, always keeping a car or two between them. Shortly after crossing into Durham, he had to back off even further after the only car between his and Joyner's turned off. A short time later he lost them. Joyner's car had disappeared around a sharp bend in the road, and, when Billingslea rounded the other side, it was gone.

"Fuck," he said as he brought the Honda to a stop in the middle of the road.

He knew they couldn't have gone far as the road was fairly straight for the next half mile, and he likely would have seen them. He resumed driving, scanning each driveway. Most of the drives continued back into the woods, making it impossible to know what might be on the other end. They had to have turned off onto one of them, but there were too many to know which one they'd taken. After traveling a half mile, he stopped his car and made a quick U-turn backtracking until he came to a mobile home with an empty driveway. He'd wait them out. If luck was with him, no one in the rundown double-wide would be at home, leaving him a perfect spot to blend in. He backed his car in and killed the engine, sliding low in his seat.

"I can't friggin' believe what you're telling me," Assistant Attorney General Ferguson said.

"I know, Jim," Byron said. "It's still a little hard for me to wrap my head around."

"Let me think on this for a minute. We'll need a tape of his confession, of course. Can you do that?"

"We've already made a digital audio recording of Perrigo's confession."

"Where is it now?"

"In my pocket."

"The audio file should be enough for now. We can shoot a video later. Make sure you put it someplace safe."

"I'll make a copy."

"Good. Jesus. Who else knows about this, John?"

"Just Pritchard, Diane, and me. And now you."

"I don't know where you've stashed them."

"Do you want to?"

"No, I think it's probably better if I don't.

How much of this does Perrigo's wife know?"

"We haven't interviewed her yet, but I would assume she knows most of it."

"We can do that later. His statement is the most important. And he clearly says that he was a part of these robberies?"

"Yes."

Byron's phone buzzed with an incoming call. He checked the caller ID. LeRoyer. Perfect timing, as always. The boss would have to wait. He'd fill him in after.

"I'm gonna want a face-to-face with him. Maybe we can videotape him at the same time."

"How soon?"

"Next couple of days. I'll have to clear my schedule and see if I can delay a hearing."

"Well, he's safe here for now."

"So, he confessed to class A robberies, committed by police officers, but there's still the statute of limitations to consider. I'll have to do some research. Which officers did he implicate, specifically?"

"All of them."

"Including your deputy chief, Cross?"

"Assistant Chief. Yes, including him."

"Did he say why he's coming forward with this now?"

"He's scared."

"Sounds like he should be. You think he's holding anything back?"

"Wouldn't you? He's gonna want protection and some kind of deal."

"Don't share this with anyone else, okay?"

"I have other people working on this case with me. I've got to give them enough to keep working."

"Okay, but keep the information compartmentalized. Don't tell anybody more than they need to know. Jesus, John, this is gonna get messy."

"Already is."

"All right, so do we have any idea how this ties in with the three murders?"

"Nothing solid, but ideas? Yes. Looks like someone is either seeking retribution or trying to tie up some loose ends."

"Have you been able to match up the print yet? The one from the O'Halloran scene."

"It's only a partial, and we're still trying."

"Ya know, what we need are cell records. If we could tie Cross to any of the others before you interviewed him, it would at least mean he lied to you about contact. We need to start building a conspiracy case here. If you can do that, you might flush out the killer."

"I'll start on it as soon as I've taken possession of Perrigo's phone."

"Okay, and I'll start trying to plan a legal strategy. Wow. This is unbelievable." Ferguson sounded positively giddy. "Watch yourself, John, and keep me up to date."

Forty-five minutes later, Pritchard returned with the throwaway cell phones and two cases of bottled water. Diane and Vicky uncovered the rest of the furniture and swept out the first floor. Byron had to admit the place was starting to look pretty comfortable. The kind of a place he wouldn't have minded vacationing in. But this wasn't a vacation hideaway, it was a safe house. Period.

Perrigo was the key to unraveling the case, Byron knew it. Tony didn't seem to know enough to lead them to the killer, but maybe he could lead the killer to them.

Byron handed the phones to Perrigo. "Here. They've been activated and we've already programmed all three of our numbers into speed dial. Either of you get any indication something's wrong, you can call one of us."

"What about cell coverage?" Diane asked.

"It's not great," Pritchard said. "But you should have a couple of bars. Enough to get through if you need to."

"I'll take your old phones now," Byron said.

Perrigo handed them over.

"Any questions before we go?"

"I'd feel better if we had a car," Perrigo said.

"We're trying to keep both of you alive," Byron said. "If you're out driving around, someone is bound to see you. We can't chance it. One of us will check in on you daily. If you need anything, we'll arrange it."

"You're gonna be okay, Vickie," Diane said, gently placing a hand on her back.

"Thank you for helping us," Vickie said, prodding Tony.

"Yeah, thanks."

It was getting late. Billingslea had nearly given up waiting when he saw Joyner's Outback pull out of a dirt drive about a hundred yards down the road on his left, followed closely by a dark-colored Lexus SUV that he had seen driving by earlier. He scooted down in the driver's seat, trying to further conceal himself as the two vehicles approached. Joyner was in the passenger seat and Byron was driving. Only two people, he thought. He was positive four had been in the Subaru when it arrived. *Did*

386

they drop someone off? The Perrigos?

He watched the car pass by. Neither detective seemed aware of his presence. He looked closely at the approaching SUV. It was the same older gentleman he'd seen driving away earlier and he was alone. Billingslea squinted at the rear plate and quickly copied it on his notepad. He'd have one of his dispatcher friends run the registration to get an ID on the owner.

He waited several minutes before driving off, making sure that he wasn't seen. As he started the Accord to leave, a gray-primed four-wheel-drive pickup whipped into the driveway, kicking up a cloud of dust and blocking him in. A bearded man of considerable girth, wearing tan Carhartt overalls and a pissed-off look on his face, jumped down from the cab and approached Billingslea's car.

"Can I help you with something, asshole?" Carhartt shouted.

"Fuck," Billingslea said.

"I can't believe all that just happened," Diane said as they drove back toward the station. "It's crazy."

"I know," Byron agreed.

"The entire SRT? What the hell kind of cops were those?"

"Were? Don't forget about Cross."

"Damn, that's right. No wonder he's been stonewalling this investigation. I thought he was just being his usual pain-in-the-ass self. So now what?"

"I've got Ferguson checking to see what kind of charges he can file against all of them, and we've got the Perrigos' cell phones."

"What good is his phone?"

"We can find out who he's been talking to and whether or not any of them lied to us about being in contact. Also, when they discover Perrigo has gone off the grid, they're all bound to get nervous, especially the killer."

"We're using the Perrigos as bait?"

"Not exactly bait, more like motivation. If the killer is connected to the SRT, he's got as much to lose as the rest of them. Turning up the heat might be enough to cause him to trip up. To make the mistake we've been waiting on."

"Why don't I take the recorder," she said. "I'll get Dustin to make a copy and I'll put it someplace safe."

"Guard this with your life," he said, handing it to her. "If Perrigo changes his mind, this recording is all we've got."

"It's in good hands," she said, placing the

digital recorder in her briefcase.

Cross was pulling out of the basement garage of 109 when his cell phone began vibrating with an incoming call. The caller ID showed blocked. He answered, "Chief Cross."

"Remember what I told you?"

He recognized the voice immediately. "I do, and I told you I'm handling it." He waited for a response.

"If you were handling it, would we be having this conversation?"

"Has something happened? Something I don't know about?"

There was another agonizingly long pause.

"Have you spoken to Perrigo lately?"

Nervously, Cross began licking his lips. Perrigo hadn't checked in since his interview with Byron. "Not in the last few days, but he's on board. He won't say anything." *But was he on board?* Cross wasn't sure. Williams had said Perrigo was shaky at best, scared about the murders. But scared enough to implicate himself? It didn't seem likely.

"On board is he? Team player? Why don't you try calling him?"

"I don't want to risk leaving a trail for anyone to —"

The phone disconnected.

"Dammit." He licked his lips again.

Carhartt had Billingslea by the collar of his shirt, bending him backward over the fender of the Accord. "You'd better have a damn good reason for being here, asshole," Carhartt said.

Billingslea scrambled to think of anything that might get him out of his predicament. "It was the cops," he blurted out. He flinched as Carhartt leaned toward him and drew back his meaty fist.

"What cops? I didn't see no cops."

"I thought they were following me. I pulled in here to lose them."

His sweaty brow furrowed. "Why?"

"Suspended license. They catch me again, they'll arrest me." He watched as the big man thought it through. The body odor was making it hard to breathe. Finally, Carhartt's frown disappeared. He lowered his fist and released Billingslea's collar.

"Well, why didn't you just say so?" He laughed and playfully slapped the reporter in the back hard enough to snap his head back.

Billingslea forced a smile.

"Like to drink, do ya?" Carhartt asked.

"Yeah, a little."

"Wanna come inside and have a cold one?"

This is where he tells me he plays the banjo. "Ah, maybe some other time. I'm late for work."

It was after dark by the time Byron and Diane got back to 109. He needed to check in with LeRoyer, who'd left several messages on his phone during the course of the afternoon, but first he needed to see Tran.

"Hey, commander," Tran said. "I was about to call you."

Byron stepped into Tran's office and closed the door, handing him both cell phones. "What's up?"

"Nothing yet on the taxi, but there are so many independents we may never know for sure. As for the rentals, I found fifteen Honda Odysseys leased locally."

"Same time frame as Riordan's death?"

"The week of."

"Any connection?"

"None I could find."

"All right, I've got something else for you anyway, and it's a big one."

Tran held up the cells. "Phone stuff, I'm guessing."

"I need you to download the information from both of those."

"Sure, what am I searching for?"

"I want complete lists of all incoming and outgoing calls along with the corresponding contact phone numbers and duration of the calls."

"Could be quite a list depending on how frequently these are used. How far do you want me to go back?"

"All of the history. If it's on the phone, I want it." Byron provided him with the phone access codes he'd gotten from Perrigo.

"Okay, boss. No biggie. I'm on it."

"That wasn't the favor."

Tran turned back toward him.

"And this one's way outside of protocol." Byron could see he now had the young detective's undivided attention.

"You talkin' black-bag kinda stuff?"

"I'm talking off-the-books kinda stuff. Cell phone records from all of them."

Tran whistled between his teeth. "You know we'd need a court order, right? We could both be up to our gluteus maximus if anyone found out."

"I'll worry about that. Can you do it or not?"

"This is real important, right?"

"I wouldn't ask otherwise."

"Okay. What numbers do you need

checked?"

"I want you to cross-check each of these numbers for calls they might've made to each other," he said, handing him the handwritten list.

"Ah, what you want is a phone tree."

"A what?"

"Phone tree. You want a comparative search done to show who's contacting who, when, and with what frequency."

Byron nodded. He was never quite sure when talking with Tran if the young detective completely understood what Byron needed. But this was exactly what he wanted, and more than he'd thought possible. "Sounds like a phone tree is exactly what I want. Can you do it?"

"It won't be admissible in court."

"I don't need it to be. But I need an edge. I want to know who's had contact with the others and is lying about it."

"How far should I go back?"

"At least a month."

"These numbers are for the former officers?"

"And Cross."

Tran whistled again. "I have an acquaintance who can get me what you want, but there's always a risk of getting caught."

"I'll take full responsibility if that happens. But do me one favor?"

"What's that?"

"Don't get caught."

Tran grinned. "Fear not, striped dude. The D Man is on the case."

Byron headed upstairs to deal with Le-Royer.

"Goddammit, John, I'm your lieutenant. I want to know what's going on with this case. Just once it'd be nice if you could be a team player."

"I told you, I can't give you specifics. I've discussed a number of developments with Ferguson, and he doesn't want me dragging more people into this."

"Last I checked, Ferguson doesn't work for this department, you do."

"But he does have prosecutorial authority over the investigation. Trust me, Lieu, it's better if you don't know everything. I'll fill you in as soon as I can."

The lieutenant's face was flushed as he ran his fingers back through his hair. "This is total bullshit, John. I've got Stanton and Cross breathing down my neck. What the hell am I supposed to tell them?"

"Tell them you gave me the authority to run this free from internal interference. Remember?"

"I'm regretting it more every minute. Can

you at least give me a friggin synopsis?"

"Perrigo turned."

"Turned?"

"Confessed to a bunch of stuff. We stashed him and his wife in a bureau safe house."

"Did he ID the killer?"

"No. He said he doesn't know who it is."

"So what did he give you?"

"Like I said, it's better you don't know."

"This thing's giving me a goddamned ulcer. You'd better get me something, John, and soon."

Billingslea sat at the kitchen table of his in-town apartment, staring at the screen on his laptop, wondering how he had managed to talk his way out of sure death at the hands of his new redneck friend. He dropped the last half piece of pizza back into the box on the floor. Simba, his ten-year-old Siamese, lapped appreciatively at the cheese stuck to the cardboard.

"Hey, old girl, you're gonna end up with high cholesterol. You shouldn't be eating that stuff at your age."

Simba looked up at him and gave a verbal protest.

"Your funeral."

He returned to his Internet search for town properties in the area he had last seen

Byron and Joyner. Tax records indicated that there was a structure at the other end of the road, at the edge of Thompson Pond. The owner of record was listed as the Sin-Tech Corporation.

Simba jumped up in his lap, purring loudly.

He scratched the underside of her chin.

"That's odd, Sim. All of the other properties are listed to individuals or couples. Maybe someone is trying to hide personal property."

He printed the information, then queried SinTech. While scrolling through the results, he slid his notepad closer, flipped to the back page, then picked up his cell and dialed.

"You working?" Billingslea asked the female dispatcher on the other end of the line.

"What do you need?" she asked.

"I need you to run a plate number for me."

"Well? How did you make out?" Byron asked Tran.

"Take a look for yourself," Tran said, pulling it up on the computer screen.

"All I see is a bunch of numbers and lines. Looks like a constellation map."

"This is your phone tree. Each of the

numbers you gave me are shown here. I've included all incoming and outgoing calls for the last thirty days. I've color-coded them with incoming calls showing in red and outgoing in blue."

"It's too hard to decipher what I'm seeing."

"That, boss dude, is because I'm showing you everything for the entire period. Now watch as I remove the calls not pertinent to your query."

"The circle in the middle is Cross's number."

"Correct. And see, his number becomes the focus."

"I'm not following."

"Look here," Tran said, pointing at the monitor. "His number calls the numbers belonging to . . . Williams and Beaudreau. Williams in turn calls Humphrey and Perrigo. Finally, Williams calls Cross again. Cross's number is the epicenter. If this was a drug case or an organized crime case, he'd be your logical boss."

"Looks like he's still running the show."

"According to the phone tree, he is. And didn't you say they all claimed not to have been in touch with one another."

"That's what each of them said."

"Yeah, well their cell records say something very different."

"Thanks, Dustin."

"But remember, you can't use any of this, Sarge."

Byron tousled the young detective's mop of hair. "No worries, D Man."

He left the computer lab and headed upstairs to check in on the surveillance details.

CHAPTER TWENTY-SIX

It was after ten-thirty by the time Diane pulled into the driveway of her Westbrook home. All she could think about was crawling into bed and getting something resembling a full night's sleep. She couldn't remember the last time it had happened.

Like all committed detectives, she knew what real exhaustion felt like. Being so tired that, when the opportunity finally presents itself — or, in this case, your partner makes you — you are unable to actually fall asleep. She hoped it wouldn't be necessary, but, with everything that had transpired over the last twelve hours, she was prepared to pop a couple of little helpers.

Grabbing her briefcase off the passenger seat, she removed her holster and stashed it inside. She pushed the lock button on the remote and made her way up the steps to the yellow ranch's side door. After several moments of fumbling about in the dark, she finally managed to slip the key into the lock. She opened the door and stepped inside.

She laid her belongings on the kitchen table and collected the mail from the floor. As she was sorting through it, she walked around the corner into the living room. Even before turning on a light, she saw it. Someone had been inside her house. Couch cushions and pillows had been thrown about and furniture upended, like they were searching for something. She froze. What if they were still here? Instinctively, she reached for her sidearm, the sidearm she'd placed in her briefcase, which was now lying on the table. *Dammit, girl. You're such a numbskull.* Quickly, and as stealthily as possible, she backtracked to the kitchen. As she reached for the bag, she heard the telltale squeak of the hardwood floor right where it always squeaked at the end of the hallway, where it intersected the kitchen. She sensed as much as heard the rustling sound of something quickly approaching. Her fingers closed around the familiar handle of her Glock. She was turning her head to look when the blow landed.

Byron departed 109 about an hour after Diane, realizing there was little else they could do tonight. The Perrigos were on ice, Ferguson was working on a game plan, and they had two nonpolice surveillance rides for tomorrow. He walked to the rear garage, climbed into his car, and drove home. He was tired and frustrated. They were searching for answers and finding nothing but more questions. Was this really about the money? Were they all as dirty as Perrigo claimed? It was still hard to believe. They were definitely hiding something more than the rip-offs, but what? He didn't believe Perrigo had told them everything. What secret could be so important, they'd risk their lives to keep it?

He parked a block down the street from his apartment in a no-parking zone. He'd forgotten to leave the outside light on again and was fiddling around in the dark with his keys when he realized the front door to his apartment wasn't latched. He might have forgotten the light, but he wouldn't have left without locking up. He drew his gun and nudged the door open with his hip. Reaching around the corner with his left hand, he flipped on the inside lights and forcefully shoved the door all the way open, in case someone might've decided to conceal themselves behind it. The door crashed into the wall, no one there. He entered the apartment with his gun in the lead.

He cleared the entire apartment, ignoring the obvious disarray in which someone had left his belongings until after he'd finished. His apartment was empty. He reholstered his weapon and looked around. The boxes he'd never gotten around to unpacking, in the nine months he'd lived there, had been upended, their contents scattered everywhere. It wasn't exactly the way he'd have done it, but at least they were finally unpacked. The kitchen and bathroom cupboard doors were all standing open, the contents also strewn about. This was more than some neighborhood delinquent looking for drug money. What did he have that someone might be searching for?

The FBI case files. He hurried into the bedroom. The closet door was wide open. Scattered about the room were the contents of both file boxes. There was no way of knowing if any of the files were missing. If someone had wanted the files, they could've taken the boxes. Why hadn't they? The other files were at Diane's. And what had she done with Perrigo's recorded confession? Had she backed it up as he'd asked? *Shit.*

He was reaching for his cell when it began ringing.

"John, it's Marty."

The hair on the back of his neck bristled.

The sense of foreboding was overpowering. He'd known LeRoyer long enough to know the sound of bad news even before it was delivered.

"What happened?"

"It's Diane."

Byron parked in one of the spaces reserved for ambulances, then hurried across the lot toward the emergency room doors. He saw the security guard, who couldn't have been much older than twenty, trying to intercept him from the guard shack.

"Sir. Sir, you can't park there. That's reserved parking for ambulances only."

Byron kept walking, ignoring the guard who was gaining on him.

"Sir, if you don't move your vehicle, I'll be forced to tow it."

Byron stopped suddenly and spun toward the young guard, causing him to take a defensive step back. He stuck his badge about an inch from the guard's face. "I'm a cop. My partner's been attacked. If that's not good enough, then go ahead and tow it," he growled.

Byron continued on toward the emergency room doors.

He found LeRoyer pacing back and forth near the nursing station. "How is she?"

"They're doing a CAT scan."

"Is she conscious?"

"In and out. They gave her something to put her out."

"What the fuck happened?"

"Sounds like she walked in on a burglar."

Byron tilted his head back slightly and closed his eyes, knowing full well this was his fault. He'd made her a target the second he gave her the audio recorder. "Tell me they got him."

"Westbrook PD attempted a track, but the K–9 lost the scent a couple of blocks away. Probably had a car waiting."

"Goddammit!" he said, punching the wall.

The duty nurse turned to look.

LeRoyer continued. "Someone hit her on the side of her head with something. Doc said at a minimum, she's got a pretty nasty concussion."

It took Byron a total of twenty agonizing minutes of pacing like a caged animal, ready to tear into anyone who even looked at him wrong, to realize he wasn't doing anyone any good at the ER.

"I'll be back," he told LeRoyer.

"Where are you going?"

"Westbrook."

Fifteen minutes later, Byron pulled up in

front of Diane's house. Uniformed West-brook officers were still on scene. He looked around for stripes until he found the patrol supervisor.

"You the guy in charge?" Byron asked.

"Jim Rodway. You must be John Byron." Byron gave him a puzzled look. "Your lieutenant called ahead."

"Take me through what happened."

"Well, the victim, your partner, called 911 and told the dispatcher she'd been attacked in her home and she needed an ambulance. My officers got here as quick as they could. They found her lying on the kitchen floor. She was really out of it. Someone clocked her pretty good. We swept the entire house, but the perp had already fled. We helped the paramedics get her into the ambulance. They tell you about the track?"

Byron nodded. "You think whoever it was got into a car?"

"Yeah. The dog was really pulling. Good strong scent, then nothing. The track ended at the side of the road, couple of blocks from here."

"Did Diane give a description of her attacker to your dispatcher?"

Rodway shook his head. "She did well to call for help. We had to trace the location of her cell to find her. Your PD gave us the exact address."

"Mind if I take a look inside?"

"Be my guest. But be careful, one of yours is still inside processing everything."

"One of mine?"

"None of our E.T.'s were available to-night. Officer Pelligrosso responded."

Byron stepped inside the kitchen door and stopped. "Gabe."

"In the living room."

Carefully, he stepped around the blood stain on the floor and entered the living room. Pelligrosso was dusting for prints.

"How is she, Sarge?"

"Too early to tell. They're still running tests."

"This fucker better hope I don't find him."

Byron could see by the look on Pelligrosso's face that he meant it. Get in line, he thought. "Any luck?"

"I'm lifting a bunch of good prints, but there's no way to tell yet whose I'm getting. Might only be hers."

Or mine, he thought, wondering how he'd explain the ones undoubtedly left in Diane's bedroom.

"What can you tell me so far?"

"There's no sign of forced entry. They either had a key or picked the lock."

Exactly like my own apartment.

"As far as what's missing, I've no idea. Looks like they turned the place upside down searching for something. I can tell you what they didn't take. They didn't take her gun, her phone, her pocketbook, her money, or her jewelry. Everything you'd expect to be missing is still here."

A knot tightened in Byron's stomach. He knew exactly what they were searching for, and it wasn't the FBI case files.

It was nearly four A.M. by the time Byron returned to the hospital. Diane had been wheeled to a quiet room in the ER. Her head was bandaged and there was an IV connected to her arm. She was sleeping. He couldn't help but be reminded of the scene inside O'Halloran's bedroom. LeRoyer was seated in a bedside chair, trying desperately to stay awake.

"How is she, Marty?" Byron whispered.

"I haven't had a chance to talk to the doc yet. They're working a cardiac patient an EMS transported in from Falmouth."

"How long has she been back?"

"About twenty minutes. What did you find out about the break-in?"

"Not much. Gabe finished processing and headed to 109 to go over the prints. I called

Mel in to help him. Didn't think you'd mind."

LeRoyer nodded. "Any idea what they were after?"

"I might."

"What?"

The ER doctor came to the door and signaled for them to come out into the hall. "Sorry to keep you two waiting. It's been a little crazy this morning."

"What's the prognosis, Doc?" Byron asked for both of them. "Is she gonna be okay?"

"She's your partner?"

"Yes."

"She's suffered a fairly serious concussion. Somewhere between what we refer to as stage two and stage three. I was told she was struck in the head. Do either of you know what she was struck with?"

"No, only that she was attacked in her home by an intruder," LeRoyer said.

"Why?" Byron asked.

"The reason I ask is because I've seen injuries similar to the one suffered by Detective Joyner when someone is pistol whipped. Her CAT scan was inconclusive. But I want to monitor her closely. She might still experience some swelling of the brain near the impact point. If that happens, we may have to drill a small hole to relieve the pressure. It's too soon to say."

Byron felt the knot in his stomach tighten.

"I've consulted with the on call neurologist, Dr. Iselbach, and he'll be taking over her treatment from here."

"When do you expect her to wake up?"

"We're intentionally keeping her under for the time being. If we brought her around right now, she'd be very agitated and have one hell of a headache. Best if we let her rest now. We'll be moving her to the Special Care Unit shortly."

"How long do you think before we can speak with her?" LeRoyer asked.

"I wouldn't plan on talking to her for at least eight hours."

Byron sighed and stood looking in at her from the doorway.

The doctor placed a hand on Byron's shoulder. "Look, it's still too early to give you a definitive answer, but if I were a betting man, based on her age and physical condition, I'd say she'll probably be fine."

"Thanks, Doc," LeRoyer said for both of them.

Byron left the hospital pissed off, at himself mostly. He never should've handed over the recording to her. But who was the burglar? Certainly not the killer, or she'd be dead.

This felt like someone else. Someone trying to prevent them from uncovering the truth. Diane's attacker was most likely a cop. But who? Only a handful of people even knew about Perrigo. He needed answers and fast. He drove to 109 to check in with Pelligrosso and Stevens. At the moment they were his best hope.

He took the stairs two at a time to the third floor. As he reached the landing, he stopped. His head was spinning. He realized he'd missed another night's sleep and couldn't remember the last time he'd eaten anything. He waited for the feeling to pass, then unlocked the steel door to the third-floor hallway.

"Well?" Byron asked as he entered the lab. "What have you got?"

"How is she?" Stevens asked, looking concerned.

"They're keeping her sedated until the swelling goes down, but the doc thinks she'll probably be okay. How are you two making out?"

"Well, I lifted a shitload of prints from every room in her house," Pelligrosso said. "We also took elimination prints from the Westbrook officers who entered the house."

"And I pulled Sergeant Joyner's to rule her out," Stevens added.

"You'd better pull mine for elimination as well," Byron said.

Stevens raised an eyebrow but said nothing.

Byron pretended not to notice.

"You know this is going to take us a while, right?" Pelligrosso asked.

"Take all the time you need. This takes priority over everything else. If her attacker wasn't wearing gloves, we may get lucky." Although he knew it was a long shot.

"You think this guy could be our serial?" Stevens asked.

"I don't know, but if you find one that doesn't belong to any of us, make sure you check it against our partial. Call me if you get anything."

Byron waited until six before calling Pritchard. He wasn't sure what kind of hours the retired agent kept but he figured six o'clock was late enough. Pritchard was already awake and readily agreed to meet him for breakfast.

Byron was on his second cup of coffee, wishing like hell it was whiskey, when Pritchard walked into the Foreside Diner on Main Street in Falmouth.

"John, you look like hell," Pritchard said as he slid into the booth across from Byron.

"At least my outward appearance matches how I feel."

"When was the last time you got any sleep?"

"Been a while. I'll rest after we catch this son of a bitch."

"How's Diane?"

"Sedated. Doc said she suffered a pretty serious concussion."

"What the hell happened?"

"Someone broke into her house and turned the place upside down. Looks like she surprised them and got bashed in the head for her trouble."

"She get a look at who did it?"

"Don't know. She was barely able to call for help."

"Think it's related?"

"I know it is. They went through my apartment as well."

"What do you think they were searching for?"

"The recording we made of Perrigo's confession."

"Tell me they didn't get it," he said, signaling the waitress with his mug.

"Won't know for sure until I can speak with her."

"How would anyone even know about it? Who else knew you had the recording?"

"Besides the three of us, only AAG Jim Ferguson and Lieutenant LeRoyer."

"You think one of them is in on it?"

Byron considered his question. His brain was fuzzy. He didn't know what to think at this point. "I don't know. The only remaining member of the original team still working at the PD is Cross. *Shit.*"

"What is it?"

"LeRoyer might have told Cross. Dammit, I shouldn't have told the lieutenant anything."

"What exactly *did* you tell him?"

Byron tried hard to focus. "I said we got one of them to flip. Told him that we stashed the witness in a safe house."

"A *bureau* safe house?"

"Fuck. I'm not sure. Maybe."

"You think Cross might be the killer?"

Byron shook his head. "No. But I think he might be trying to tie up loose ends and Perrigo is a loose end."

"Have you checked in on him?"

"Not since —" Byron's eyes widened. "Fuck." He pulled out his cell and dialed Tony's number. If someone had gone to all that trouble to get at the recording, wouldn't the Perrigos be next? "Pick up, come on." He let it ring a dozen times but there was no answer.

Byron grabbed his jacket and threw a five on the table for the coffee. "He's not answering. Let's go."

Pritchard hopped in with Byron, continually trying both cell numbers while Byron focused on the driving. It took the better part of twenty minutes to reach the safe house. They were still several hundred feet short of the driveway entrance when they were flagged down by a man wearing a reflective jacket and holding a flashlight. Byron could see a kind of glow above the tree line. He stopped the car and lowered his window.

"Sorry, folks, but you'll have to turn around. Road's blocked up ahead."

"What's going on?" Byron asked.

"Got a structure fire down the road apiece. Used to be somebody's camp. Three alarm," he said proudly.

Byron didn't know exactly what a three alarm meant in firefighter parlance, but he knew it wasn't good and there was only one camp he was concerned with. He displayed his ID and explained where they were headed.

"Down here on the right, you say?"

Byron nodded.

" 'Bout a quarter mile off the main road?"

With a sinking feeling, he nodded again. "Yes."

"Sounds like the place."

Byron parked the car on the shoulder and they made their way in on foot. The two men walked in silence. Gradually, the dark shadows of the wooded driveway were replaced by dozens of angry-looking red high-intensity strobes. It looked as if the entire fire department had come out for this one. The air was thick with the acrid smell of wood smoke and diesel exhaust from the idling trucks.

They stopped and stared at the smoking remains of the camp. It was a total loss. The roof and second floor had collapsed. Blackened timbers poked out of the pile at impossible angles, resembling some twisted pyro's version of the game Pick Up Sticks. Several firemen wearing bright yellow coats and helmets stood around the steaming pyre directing streams of water here and there.

Byron grabbed one of the young volunteers who was running by and identified himself. "I'm looking for the chief."

The fireman turned around, pointing across the yard. "Parked over there, in the red SUV."

Byron and Pritchard both introduced themselves to the fire chief. "Wayne Fifield," he said as he shook hands with both men. "FBI?" he asked, sounding surprised.

"Retired," Pritchard said.

"What can I do for you guys?"

"Were there any survivors?" Byron asked.

"Didn't know anyone was staying here."

"Yes, a husband and wife," Pritchard said.

"We haven't seen anyone, but we never got inside. The roof had already started to collapse by the time we got here. Had a bitch of a time getting our trucks down this narrow drive. Took us some time to get the lines run out. We had to pump from the pond. No hydrants around here."

Byron could tell the chief felt bad as he rattled off his list of excuses, but it didn't change anything. None of this was Fifield's fault. This was all about loose ends.

The chief was still spouting technical jargon about how they'd fought the blaze when Byron cut him off. "How long before we can go through the rubble and find out if they are still in there?"

Fifield turned around and surveyed the ruins. In spite of the water volume, flames kept them at bay, reigniting in several different spots. He turned back to them. "Afraid it's gonna be a while. I just got off the horn with the State Fire Marshall's Office, said they'd have someone down here by lunchtime."

"Thanks," Byron said. "We'll be back."

"Friends of yours?" Fifield asked.

Byron considered the question. "Acquaintances."

"Well, their car wasn't here. Maybe they left for the night," Fifield said, trying to sound hopeful.

"We'll be back," Byron said.

They trudged back toward the main road in silence.

Byron felt like he'd won the bad-luck trifecta. In one fell swoop, all of their momentum was lost. He was pissed at himself for making mistakes, exhaustion was no excuse. He had to consider every possibility. Ferguson knew about the Perrigos, but his knowledge of the case was limited, and he worked out of Augusta, not exactly nearby. Obviously Pritchard knew, but he'd been the one to actually get them into a safe house, and he had no connection to any of the Portland officers. LeRoyer knew, but Byron had worked with him for far too long to suspect the lieutenant. Byron was pretty sure he knew LeRoyer better than anyone. He still didn't know who was responsible, but he was beginning to think there might be more than one killer.

The silence continued as Byron drove

Pritchard back to his car.

"What do you need me to do, John?" Pritchard asked as he climbed out of the Jetta.

"Meet me back at the safe house at noon."

"Okay. Where are you going?"

"The hospital."

"Want me to come with you?"

Byron shook his head. "Thanks anyway, but I need some time to think."

"All right. I'll see you later."

Pritchard had started walking toward his car when Byron stopped him. "Hey, Terry."

"Yeah?" he said, turning back.

"How are your surveillance skills?"

"A little rusty I imagine, but still better than some. Why?"

"Someone just took out my partner. I might need your help."

Pritchard nodded. "Anything you need."

Byron backed out of his space and drove toward Portland.

CHAPTER TWENTY-SEVEN

Billingslea drove his aging Honda up Deering Avenue toward Maine Med. His editor had phoned him at home about an overnight attack on an off-duty police detective in the town of Westbrook. A Portland police detective named Joyner.

He'd jumped into the shower almost before hanging up the phone. He was already imagining headlines for the unwritten story as he quickly dressed, then headed out to the car.

Did it have something to do with yesterday's clandestine meeting in Durham? Or Terrance Pritchard, former FBI agent and registered owner of the Lexus he'd seen coming out of the driveway behind Byron and Joyner? He'd have wagered a week's salary it did.

He sat in traffic at the intersection of Deering and Congress, his fingers impatiently drumming on the steering wheel.

And what about SinTech Corporation? He'd spent an hour online and managed to find out zip about the company. SinTech's website was one of those designed to look professional while saying absolutely nothing about what the company did. There were no pictures aside from stock images, probably copied from a photo site; and no phone numbers, only an email and a post-office box in Manhattan. He wondered if this mysterious company had something to do with the FBI agent. And what, if anything, did it have to do with the murders?

Billingslea drove around the block, finding an empty space two blocks up from the hospital. He fed the parking meter with the loose change he scrounged from his console, then hoofed it to the main entrance. He breezed past the friendly smile of the elderly female manning the information desk and headed toward the Special Care Unit (SCU).

It was almost ten by the time Byron made it back to 22 Bramhall Street. He parked the beat-up VW in a no-parking zone near the hospital's main entrance, hoping someone would tow it. Once inside, he made the long walk down the hospital's central corridor past the Richards Wing to the Bean Building where SCU was located.

He made his way to the SCU nursing station. He was about to ask what room Diane was in when someone called out to him.

"Sarge."

He turned and saw Stevens and Nugent walking in his direction. Mike was holding a bright-colored bouquet of artificial flowers.

"Hey, guys," Byron said. "How's she doing?"

"Still sedated," Stevens said. "We're headed up to the cafeteria for coffee, then we'll check back. Care to join us?"

"What's going on, Sarge?" Nugent asked. "The LT told us someone broke into both of your places last night."

Byron looked around and observed a number of people staring in their direction. "Why don't I meet you guys in the cafeteria? I'm gonna stop in to see her for a sec."

"We'll see you there," Stevens said.

"Which room?" Byron asked.

Before either detective could answer, a middle-aged woman working at the nursing station spoke up. "Detective Joyner's in room 1043, Sarge," she said with a wink.

He turned to Stevens and Nugent with raised eyebrows. "Looks like I'm headed to 1043."

A uniformed female officer Byron didn't

recognize was seated in the hallway beside the door to Diane's room. Her auburn hair was tucked up underneath her hat. She didn't look old enough to drive let alone be a cop. He flashed her his badge and they exchanged nods.

"You're Sergeant Byron?" the officer asked as she stood.

"I am."

"I'm supposed to give you this," she said, handing him a slightly crinkled business card.

It was Billingslea's.

"Has that piece of shit been in there?" Byron demanded.

She shook her head. "No, sir. I wouldn't let him."

"Good. Under any circumstances. Did he ask you anything?"

"He wanted to know if the attack on the detective had anything to do with the murder investigation."

"What did you tell him?"

"I told him — 'No comment.' He started whining about freedom of information. I told him to call the shift commander if he wanted information."

Satisfied, Byron opened the door to 1043, then paused to look at the officer. "Thank you, Officer. If he bothers you again, arrest him."

A faint smile appeared on her lips. "Yes, sir."

The window drapes had been closed in Diane's room. She was the sole occupant. Byron pulled a plastic chair over to the side of her bed and sat down, listening to the steady cadence of her breathing. She looked so peaceful except for the large bandage taped on the left side of her head. Once again the image of O'Halloran came to him. The IV tube inserted into her arm, the hospital bedding, it was all too close to home for his liking. *What was it she had said? "Relax, silly. I'm not looking for a relationship."* Neither was he. It was the last thing he needed as his twenty-year marriage to Kay was ending. But here he sat, knowing he was already in over his head. Complicating his life even more. It wasn't just sex. It never was. That was only a lie some guys told themselves. Truth was, he cared deeply for Diane.

His eyes were watering as he reached out and gently took her hand. "This isn't your fault." He sniffed loudly and wiped his bloodshot eyes with the back of his hand. "I'll make this right, I promise. I'm gonna get this fucker if it's the last thing I do."

Ten minutes later he entered the elevator and was turning to push the button for the cafeteria level when he was nearly overcome with dizziness. He reached out for the wall and closed his eyes until it passed. When had he eaten last? He couldn't remember. When had he slept last? Also a distant memory. He couldn't do anything about the sleep, but he could eat.

He grabbed a random assortment of food from the warming trays. After being rung up by the cashier, he walked to the table occupied by Nugent and Stevens, observing that Tran had joined them.

Tran greeted him in his usual manner. "Hey, striped one, we saved you a seat."

"Thanks." Byron sat down carefully, not wanting to repeat his earlier trick in the elevator, and unwrapped one of three lukewarm breakfast sandwiches on the tray.

"You don't look so good yourself, Sarge," Nugent said.

He finished chewing, then washed it down with some harsh black coffee before he answered, giving himself time for the witty comeback he didn't have. "This coming from a guy toting a bouquet of plastic flowers?"

Nugent frowned and looked at Stevens. "Mel wouldn't let me leave them in the room. Said we have to give them to her personally."

Stevens laughed, playfully punching Nugent in the shoulder.

"They bring out your sensitive side, Nuge," Tran said, grinning.

"Watch it, pencil neck."

"What's up with the burglaries, Sarge?" Stevens asked.

Byron swallowed the last bite of the sandwich and unwrapped the next. Having something in his stomach made him feel a little better. "This thing is getting really messy. I've been trying to protect you guys from it as much as I can. What happened to Diane last night is precisely why."

"The hell with that, Sarge," Nugent said. "We're a team here, good or bad."

Stevens chimed in. "Nuge is right. What's going on?"

Tran nodded in agreement.

Byron felt an overwhelming sense of pride as he looked at the three of them. He took a large swig of coffee, then filled them in on the events of the last sixteen hours. He told them about Pritchard and about Perrigo's confession and the safe house.

"Holy shit," Nugent said when Byron had finished.

Stevens looked over at her bald partner.

"Eloquent as always, Nuge. But I gotta say, 'holy shit' is right. These guys were ripping off dealers? I thought I'd seen everything."

"Are you sure the Perrigos are dead?" Tran asked.

"At this point, I'm not sure of anything," Byron said. "But I'm betting I already know what they're gonna find at the safe house."

"You really think Cross is behind this? Stevens asked.

"Maybe not all of it, but he's involved." Byron looked directly at Tran. "Did Diane ask you to copy anything last night?"

Tran shook his head. "No. Should she have?"

Byron's heart sank. He shook his head. "Doesn't matter."

"This is probably as good a time as any to tell you this," Tran said. "I found another connection to the armored car robbery suspects late last night."

They all looked at him.

"Well? Spit it out," Byron said.

"I did some cross-checking on each of their criminal histories."

"I thought you checked those already," Nugent said.

"I did, on what we got from Triple I," Tran said, referring to the Interstate Identification Index. "But not every state reports arrests and convictions to the feds, so I checked further. Andreas, the missing robber, was arrested in Massachusetts in 1982 for trafficking in cocaine. He got hooked up by a drug task force after they found him in possession of nearly a kilo of cocaine. His charge was reduced to simple possession and he was given one year of probation."

"What the fuck?" Nugent said.

"Sounds like they got him to flip on someone," Stevens said.

"That's what it sounded like to me," Tran said.

"I'm not following you, Dustin," Byron said. "What's the connection to this case?"

"The arresting officer was on loan from our department. Guess who?"

Byron shook his head. "I'm too tired for guessing games. Just tell me."

"Detective Reginald Cross."

It was eleven-fifteen by the time Byron departed from the hospital. He'd stayed as long as he could, but Doctor Iselbach had decided to keep Diane sedated a little longer. He headed off to meet Pritchard with the promise from Stevens she'd let him know if anything changed, and a promise from all of them they wouldn't discuss the new information with anyone.

He dialed the number for Pelligrosso. "Gabe, it's Byron."

"Hey, Sarge. How's she doing?"

"No change. Listen, I want you to double-check something for me. Did you compare the partial from the O'Halloran scene with Cross's prints?"

"Yeah. Didn't match."

"You're sure?"

"Not even close. Why?"

Of course they didn't, he thought. It would have been too easy. "And we ruled out Andreas too?"

"Yup."

"Who haven't we been able to eliminate?" He listened as Pelligrosso shuffled some papers.

"Looks like the only people I don't have prints from are Falcone and Humphrey. You told me not to worry about Falcone and my request for Humphrey's haven't come back from the state."

Had he intentionally been overlooking Ray as a suspect in all of this? Was he so blinded by his friendship, he hadn't wanted to look? What had Arthur Conan Doyle written about eliminating the impossible? "I'll get them for you, Gabe."

The road was no longer blocked and the crowded driveway had cleared as Byron navigated his way toward what remained of the camp. He recognized Pritchard's Lexus parked beside the bright red SUV belonging to the state fire marshal. What he no longer recognized was the pile of blackened timbers and ash where the FBI safe house had stood the previous day. He'd hoped not to see anyone wearing a rock concert T, but alas there was Ellis, in classic Def Leppard, poking around with a shovel, assisted by a young man wearing yellow fireman's pants, red suspenders, and black rubber boots.

"Hey, John," Pritchard greeted. "Afraid it's bad news."

"So I gathered. How many bodies?"

Pritchard held up two fingers.

"Dammit," Byron said.

"How's Diane?"

"Still under."

"Sergeant Byron," Ellis hollered over. "Top o' the afternoon."

Byron forced a smile as he made his way over. "Hey, Doc."

"You know Fire Marshal Cody?"

"Don't think we've met." Although, they could've been related for all he knew. The sheer exhaustion was beginning to affect his recall.

"Steve Cody," the soot-covered marshal said as he jumped down from the pile, removed a glove, and extended his hand. "You're Byron?"

"I am." He paused to look around. "I don't see the state police here. Didn't anyone call them?"

"I did, a minute ago," Cody said. "Agent Pritchard told us these were witnesses on a case of yours, so we held back on notifying them. Wanted you to have a chance to see it for yourself first. Sorry I don't have better news."

"Any idea what caused the fire?" Byron asked.

"Tough to say when there's this amount of destruction. Old place like this is a tinder box. As far as the propane tanks go, it looks like they exploded because of the fire, not the other way around. Had Daisy go through the debris already."

"Daisy?"

"My partner," he said, pointing to his vehicle, where the smiling, panting, and drooling head of a lab was poking out of a window.

"She find anything?"

"Didn't hit on any of the usual accelerants."

"Meaning?"

"Meaning, if an accelerant was used it was something exotic, something Ms. Daisy isn't trained to detect."

"Heard Perrigo was a smoker," Ellis said.

Byron nodded, shooting a glance at Pritchard. "Pretty much of the chain variety as of late."

"Looks like they might've been in bed, John," Ellis said. "Seen a lot of smoking-in-bed deaths. They fall asleep with one lit and next thing you know the bedding is on fire and it's already too late. You wanna take a look?"

"Sarge, I've got extra gear in the truck if you wanna climb up and have a look," Cody said.

"Think I'm gonna pass," Byron said. "The way this day is going, I'm liable to fall and break my neck."

Ellis and Cody climbed back into the ruins and resumed their careful digging.

"What's the plan, John?" Pritchard asked.

"I'm working on it. Got some interesting news, though."

Pritchard raised a brow. "Oh? Do tell."

"My whiz kid detective found a link between Cross and one of the armored car robbers. Cross busted Andreas around '82 for trafficking coke."

"Coincidence?"

"No way. I don't believe in them. Cross was part of a regional DEA task force and

Andreas got caught holding a lot of weight. A few months later, Andreas gets probation on the reduced charge of possession."

"He flipped?"

"Most likely."

"How did that not show up in our investigation?"

"The bust was in Massachusetts and they don't report to you guys. Even if you'd checked Triple I, it probably wouldn't have shown up. Besides, Cross worked for Portland. You wouldn't have been looking for him to be involved in an out-of-state grab."

"Still, I can't believe I missed it."

Byron's cell rang. Anxious for news on Diane, he pulled it out and checked the caller ID. It wasn't Stevens, only LeRoyer again. He ignored it, returning the phone to his pocket.

"The boss?" Pritchard asked.

"Who else?" he said. "I gotta head back to the barn. I'll check in with you later."

"And where the *hell* have you been?" Le-Royer barked at Byron from behind his desk. "Don't you ever return messages? Cross and Stanton have been all over my shit. And what's this about you investigating an out-of-town fire and two bodies? The colonel of the state police just reamed me a

432

new one. Something about jurisdiction. Or doesn't that mean anything to you?"

Byron waited until the lieutenant had finished his rant before speaking. "May I say something?"

"You'd damn well better."

"Cross is involved in this."

LeRoyer stood there staring at him to see if Byron was serious. "Can you prove it?"

"Who did you tell about my witness?"

"Only Cross."

"Fuck, Marty!"

"He ordered me to. I only said you'd gotten someone to turn, and that you'd stashed them in some FBI safe house around here."

"You used the words 'FBI safe house'?"

"Yeah, I think so. Maybe."

"Well, that's just great. The fire you asked about was my safe house and the bodies were my cooperating witness and his wife."

"Shit."

"Yeah, Marty, shit."

"Come on, John, even if you're right about Cross, he couldn't have known the location. Right?"

"How many safe houses you think the bureau has up here?"

"You've still got Perrigo's recorded confession."

"No, I don't. Why do you think someone

broke into my apartment and Diane's house last night?"

"Shit," LeRoyer said again. He stared down at the top of his desk and ran both hands back through his hair. He removed a large bottle of antacid from his desk drawer and took a gulp. "What do you want me to do?"

"Stop talking to Cross! I need you to run interference for me. If you really want deniability when this thing breaks, then stop asking me questions. I need you to trust me, Marty. I'm gonna turn up the heat."

"You sure you know what you're doing?"

The truth was he wasn't sure. But he was tired of feeling like he was always a step behind the killer, constantly playing catch-up. It was time to push some buttons and make something happen. It was time to take the gloves off, time to go on offense. "Trust me."

Byron's cell rang. He answered it without checking to see who it was. "Byron."

"Sarge, it's Mel. Diane's awake."

"On my way."

Byron was heading for the door when LeRoyer stopped him. "Here," he said, tossing him a set of keys.

"What's this?"

"Keys to the maroon Chevy repaint

parked in the back garage."

"Thought you didn't have anything else for me?"

"Take care of this one, John. We just had it painted."

Byron's mind was racing as he drove toward the hospital. How had things changed so fast? In the past twenty-four hours, he'd gone from breaking the case wide open to losing everything. The confession was gone, the key witness, all of it. It was as if someone knew his every move. But who? Only a handful of people knew about stashing the Perrigos at the safe house. Diane hadn't given herself a concussion, which pretty much ruled her out. Pritchard had helped him place them at the safe house, and he'd been the primary robbery investigator for the bureau. Besides, Pritchard had no connection to Portland, and this was a Portland case. The SRT, Cross, everything pointed to Cross. But there was something else. Someone else. Something he was still missing.

LeRoyer said he'd told Cross that Byron had gotten someone to turn. Would Cross have known who? Would he really have gone in search of them? Or would he have gotten someone else to do his bidding? Humphrey? But Humphrey hadn't known about Perrigo turning. *Not unless Cross had told him.*

Byron parked the Chevy in front of the hospital's main entrance and got out.

"There's a sight for sore eyes," he said as he walked into Diane's hospital room.

"Hey, John," she said, still sounding a bit groggy.

"How you feelin'?"

"Like someone used my head for batting practice. Jeez, John, you don't look so good. When was the last time you slept?"

"Can't remember," he said as he pulled a chair up beside the bed and sat down.

"I could call room service and have them bring in a cot."

"Don't bother. They'd only charge you for a double. When are they releasing you?"

"Doc said if I make it through the night okay, I might be able to leave here tomorrow."

"I'll have someone bring your car up and some clothes."

"Thanks, but I've already got that covered. I'm not staying here one minute longer than I have to."

"Everyone was worried about you."

"Aw, even you?" she said.

"Of course."

"You big softy."

"Anyone fill you in yet?"

"Not all of it. They said you would. Did you catch the asshole who tuned me up?"

"Not yet," he said with a concerned look on his face. "Did you get a look at who attacked you?"

"No."

"Perrigo's dead."

"What? How?"

"Someone torched the safe house. We found two bodies in the rubble."

Diane stared at him, as if he was joking.

"We don't even have the confession," he said.

"What are you talking about?"

"The recording. I checked with Dustin. He said you never gave it to him to copy."

"I didn't. I decided not to involve anyone else, so I copied it to my computer instead."

"Where's the recorder?"

"Under the spare in my unmarked."

"Oh, man, I thought we lost it. I could kiss you right now."

"What's stopping you?"

Byron spent the next twenty minutes bringing Diane up to speed on the fire, the break-ins, and the links to Cross.

"This sounds more like a friggin' mystery novel," she said. "What did Ferguson say?"

"I spoke with him on the way over here.

He said even with the recording, minus a witness, it's only hearsay. No judge in their right mind would ever think about issuing a warrant based on what we've got. There's no way of proving what Perrigo told us wasn't bullshit. Not unless we can turn one of the others. Get someone to confirm what Perrigo said."

"I'd say we can rule out Cross as ever being helpful. What about Beaudreau or Humphrey?"

"Beaudreau's as greasy as they come. Ray may be our only shot."

"What does Terry think? Any chance this is still Andreas?"

"I highly doubt it. Terry's pissed about missing the link between Andreas and Cross. I think Riccio was right. The weeds are growing right in our own backyard."

"What are you gonna do?"

"I've got an idea."

"Care to share it?"

Byron headed home to get a few hours of sleep. On the way he called Nugent.

"Mike, it's Byron."

"Hey, Sarge. Heard the patient is alive and well."

"She's gettin' there. Listen, I need you to do me a favor."

"Name it."

"Find Mel and grab the two cars we got from Royal River Ford. I want you to locate and stay on Beaudreau and Humphrey." He checked his watch, nearly three. "Humphrey will most likely be at his office on Commercial Street and Beaudreau should be on the way to his club in Westbrook."

"What about Cross?"

"I'll worry about Cross."

"Want me to let Westbrook PD know what we're up to?"

Fresh off the loss of a witness, one he was supposed to protect, the last thing they needed was more people knowing what they were up to. "No, I don't. And stay off the radio. Keep in contact with each other by phone only. Let me know if either of them move."

"You got it, boss."

"Nuge."

"Yeah."

"Keep your eyes open."

Byron hung up and was about to pocket the phone when he stopped. Something about the Perrigos was nagging at him. A loosely formed thought, as discorporate as mist but still troubling. He had attempted to place them out of harm's way only to see both of them dispatched as swiftly as if he'd shoved them in front of a speeding bus. O'Halloran, Riordan, Williams, and now Perrigo, four ex-cops had been murdered so far, the last two while in his care. Someone was toying with him, always a step ahead. But who? He kept thinking about something Perrigo had said about their intel.

"It was like we had someone on the inside," Perrigo had said. *"We never came up empty. You ever heard of anything like that?"*

Byron never had. He dialed the PD's computer lab. There was something else he wanted Tran to check.

CHAPTER TWENTY-EIGHT

Through gauzy layers of sleep, Byron's conscious mind gradually became aware of a phone ringing. He struggled to open his eyes and sat up, knocking his cell off the bedside table. "Fuck," he said as he scrambled onto the floor after it. "Byron."

"Top o' the evening to you. Hope I'm not interrupting anything."

Ellis. "No, Doc, you're good. What's up?"

"Well, I finished emergency surgery on Mr. Anthony Perrigo, but in spite of my best efforts he didn't pull through. Think it might have something to do with the burn he got."

Byron checked the time, impatient for Ellis to get to the point. It was nearly seven. He stood and was shuffling toward the bathroom when his stubbed his bare foot on a picture frame lying upside down on the floor. He reached down, picked up the frame, and turned it over. Beneath the broken glass was a photo of him and Kay, mugging for the camera. They had taken a Caribbean cruise to celebrate their fifth wedding anniversary and Byron's promotion to detective. A painful image from his past, cast aside like refuse by a recently departed burglar.

"John, you still there?"

"Right here, Doc, but I'm pressed for time," he said, gently placing the picture atop an overturned cardboard box and continuing toward the bathroom. "Do you have a cause of death or not?"

"You're the kind of guy who reads the last page of a book first, aren't you?"

"I'm begging you," he said as he reached into the shower and turned on the water.

"Oh, all right. He was dead before the fire."

"How?"

"Gunshot to the head. Close range."

"The wife?"

"Haven't done hers yet."

"Caliber?"

"Can't say with any certainty because we didn't recover the round or casing, but if I had to hazard a guess, I'd say a nine millimeter."

The same caliber that killed Williams.

After the call with Ellis, and a hot shower

that did little to wake him up, he checked in on Stevens and Nugent. According to Nugent, Beaudreau was still at the club. Stevens reported Humphrey had driven home around five-thirty, before leaving again twenty minutes ago.

"Where is he now, Mel?"

"I followed him into town. He stopped at the 7-Eleven on Washington, came out carrying a paper bag, and drove up to CB Circle," she said, referring to the nickname given to the intersection of North Street and the Eastern Promenade.

"Is he still in the car?"

"Nope. He locked it up and walked down the hill toward the highway. Do you want me to go and look for him?"

Humphrey had made the surveillance. Byron knew the significance of that location and was pretty sure Ray was sending him a message. "Stay put. I'll be right there."

Byron turned into the circle, the headlights of his Chevy illuminating Humphrey's empty SUV. He parked behind it and got out. About a hundred feet down the embankment, he found his former detective, mentor, and friend seated on the darkened hillside in the grass.

"Sarge." Humphrey greeted him without

turning.

"Ray."

"I wondered how long it would take for you to show up. Pull up a seat, best view in the house." He handed Byron a bottle. "Here. Bought a six pack, thought we could split it."

Byron took the cold beer and sat down on the grass. He paused before opening the bottle. It was the first alcohol he'd had in days, and he wasn't sure he wanted to push his luck. He twisted off the cap but didn't drink.

"Beautiful, isn't it?"

Byron looked out over Portland's skyline. From their vantage point, they could see the entire north side of Portland's peninsula, Back Cove, and the edge of Deering. Far below, the interstate wound toward them, the cars resembled lightning bugs on a racetrack. "It is."

"Fort Sumner once stood here. Built in 1794 under orders from George Washington. It was Maine's first federal fort until it was torn down in the 1840s. Lotta history here, Sarge."

"So you've said."

"Seeing the city from up here, you'd never guess anything was wrong out there, would you? It's so damn peaceful."

Byron knew Humphrey only came up here when he had something weighing on his mind. They'd come here together after Reece's suicide and again when Ray's wife died. "What's going on, Ray?

"Your dad and I used to come up here all the time. Did you know that?"

"You told me."

Humphrey nodded. "Reece was the one who taught me to take a step back when shit got too heavy. He said coming up here always put it back into perspective."

"Is shit getting too heavy, Ray?"

Humphrey ignored the question. "You ever imagine your life turning out differently, Sarge?"

"There's only the two of us here, Ray. Why won't you call me John? We go back a long ways. You trained me, for Christ's sake."

Humphrey looked at him. "I trained you to be a good detective. You became a good sergeant on your own. Had nothing to do with me."

Byron didn't feel much like a good anything at the moment. "I had some help there too."

"Maybe, but you've earned the respect some never do. You earned my respect, and you'll always be my sergeant. No matter what." He took another swig of his beer.

"So, did you?"

"Did I what?"

"Ever hope it would be different."

"What are we talking about, Ray, regrets?"

Humphrey nodded.

"I guess. Always thought I'd be a better husband than my old man was."

Humphrey looked over at him.

"Definitely didn't fuck up my kids, though. Not having any took care of that."

"I know you don't believe this, Sarge, but Reece was a man worthy of respect. Taught me a lot about being a cop."

"Reece Byron was a fucking coward. Suicide? Really? Who did he think would find his body?" He eyed the open beer again, fighting the urge to gulp the entire bottle. "That's not something a teenaged son is supposed to see. That's not something anyone should see. Don't call me John if you don't want, that's fine, but don't lecture me about my goddamned father. Okay?"

For the next several minutes neither of them spoke. They sat listening to the sounds of the night while watching the flow of traffic on the highway below. Nearby crickets kept cadence. Somewhere in the distance a siren wailed.

"How long have you known about the surveillance?" Byron asked.

"Mel? Ah, she's a good kid. Don't be too hard on her. It's pretty tough to tail a cop." Humphrey finished his beer, tossing the empty into the bushes. He grabbed another and handed it to Byron.

"I'm still nursing this one."

Humphrey shrugged. "Suit yourself." He opened it and took a long drink before continuing. "Me, I've got a boatload of regrets."

"Like?"

"I wish I'd been a better husband to my Wendy."

"I know the feeling," Byron said.

"You ever fuck around on Kay?"

"Not until after we separated. But, I guess I cheated on her plenty, all the same."

"I don't follow."

"The job. Like having a girl on the side, isn't it? Think about her all the time, can't wait to get back to her, sneak out to see her when she calls in the middle of the night. Maybe you don't come home to your wife for days."

"Never thought about it like that."

"Maybe it's not infidelity in the physical sense, but it's still cheating."

Humphrey nodded his understanding. "I guess I fucked around on my Wendy plenty, then. Between the ponies, the job, and the women. I still miss her, Sarge. She didn't deserve to suffer like that."

"Nobody does."

"Fucking cancer. Not one of God's better ideas."

Byron considered telling him God probably had nothing to do with it, but decided against it. "How about the job, Ray?" he asked, trying to get him back on topic. "Any regrets?"

Humphrey looked over, studying him. "Plenty."

"Like?"

He turned his head to look out at the skyline and changed the topic. "Think you're getting close to solving this case?"

"Feels like something's gonna break soon."

He nodded, giving Byron a knowing glance, and took another long drink. "You know, you've always been like a son to me. The son I never had."

"I know about the money, Ray. And about the drug rips." He waited for a reaction but Humphrey remained silent. "Perrigo told us everything. Why, Ray? How could you be a part of that?"

"Is that really the question you want to ask?"

"I know you were with Riordan the night

he died," Byron said, bluffing. "I know about the rental car. Tell me you're not the one doing this."

Humphrey stood up, finished the remaining half of his beer in three quick gulps, and carefully placed the empty in the cardboard holder. "You're a good detective, Sarge. No denying it. You'll figure this thing out. Forgive me for leaving you here, but it's been a long day. I'm going home."

He waited until Humphrey had departed before taking the brown paper bag out of his pocket and unfolding it. He hadn't gotten the answers he'd wanted, but he had managed to accomplish one thing. Carefully, he placed Humphrey's empty into the bag, then dumped his own beer in the grass. As he walked back to his car, he phoned Stevens, instructing her to follow Humphrey home and to await word from him. His next call was to Pritchard.

"You still want in?" Byron asked.

"Point me in the right direction."

During his short drive to 109, he filled Pritchard in on the latest developments, including the blown surveillance on Humphrey.

"You think it's Humphrey, John?"

"I should know pretty quickly. Can you tail him without getting made?"

"Like the man said, it's tough to tail a cop, but I'll do my best."

"Send me a text when you're in position and I'll pull Mel."

"Okay. What are you going to do?"

"After I check out these prints, I'm gonna pay a visit to Diane at the hospital. Then I think I'll pay one to Cross and totally fuck up his night."

"Well?" Byron asked.

"Take a look for yourself," Pelligrosso said, rolling his chair away from the lab's computer screen.

Byron bent forward and examined both images. They looked similar, but he didn't know a whorl from a loop. "Are they from the same person?"

Pelligrosso used the mouse to drag one image over the other. "You tell me."

"They look identical."

"They are. Maybe not good enough for the court's standard seven-point comparison, but they'll pass my common sense test any day. So, you gonna tell me where you got the bottle?"

"Those are Ray Humphrey's prints."

"So why wouldn't Ray tell you about visiting O'Halloran?" Diane asked.

"Maybe because he killed him," Byron said.

"John, how long have you known him? Do you really think he could kill his old friends?"

"I'm not sure how close any of these guys really were, Diane. And I don't think he went over to O'Halloran's intending to kill him. I think something happened."

"Like what?"

"O'Halloran was dying. He knew it. Maybe he wanted to get something off his chest. Something he shared with Ray. Maybe he confessed to something Ray didn't already know."

"Something that pissed him off enough to put a pillow over the man's head and suffocate him?" she asked.

Byron nodded. "Might be that simple."

"And what could've been bad enough to make him start killing the guys he worked with?"

"I don't know. But this is about a lot more than money. Whatever's happening here, Ray and Cross are the key, I'm sure of it."

"But what about the attempt on Ray? Who was the police dog tracking from Ray's house?"

"I've thought a lot about that. What if the K–9 was tracking Ray?"

"Huh?"

"Who else saw the suspect Ray described at his back door?"

"The officer on the detail. Ah, Hutchins."

"No, he didn't. I reread Hutchins's report. He reported what Ray told him, but he never actually saw the other person. The K–9 tracked from the house right to where Hutchins picked Ray up." Byron gave her a minute to process what he'd told her. "I think Ray may have been attempting to supply himself with an alibi for Williams."

"He has an alibi, John. He was home when it happened."

"Was he? Hutchins didn't even know he was out of the house until the dispatcher told him. Why couldn't he have slipped out earlier and come back right after killing Williams?"

"But what about Riordan? There's nothing linking Ray to his murder."

"Maybe there is. Ralph Polowski, the bartender from the AMVETS. The guy he saw with Cleo may very well have been Ray." Byron studied her face. A face he now saw differently. Even the harsh hospital lighting couldn't hide it. She was beautiful. He would have given anything to be with her at that moment, but he still had a job to do, and at least one killer to catch. He bent down and kissed her cheek. "Gotta run."

"Be careful, John."

It was after ten when Byron pulled in and parked in the dirt lot across from the Washington Avenue chapter of the AM-VETS. As he exited the car, he wondered if Humphrey had also parked there. Before leaving 109, he'd made copies of the Bureau of Motor Vehicle photos of the remaining SRT members. It wasn't nearly as good as a photo array would have been, but it would have to do. Time was running out.

He was preparing to cross the street when his cell rang. "Byron."

"Sergeant, it's Davis Billingslea. You got a minute?"

"Not for you. And stay the fuck away from Detective Joyner."

"I know about the fire in Durham."

"What?" Byron snapped, momentarily taken aback by the reporter's comment.

"The state police said there were two victims."

"I don't know what the hell you're talking about —"

"Was it the Perrigos? Does this have anything to do with Detective Joyner being attacked?"

"Listen, Davis. I don't know where you're

getting this crap, but I'm warning you — stop fucking around with this case or I swear to God you'll be sorry we ever met."

Byron hung up. "Fuck." This was not what he needed right now. Billingslea snooping around again could really screw things up. *Did Davis actually know about the Perrigos or was he guessing? Looking for a reaction. And if he did know, who might he have told?*

He pocketed the phone and opened the door to the AMVETS.

The bar was thick with cigarette smoke and noise. Unlike the last time he'd been here, there were actual customers, about forty by his estimate. Ralph Polowski was right where Byron had hoped he'd be, tending bar. Not wanting to draw any attention, Byron sat down at an empty stool near the end of the bar, waiting until Polowski saw him.

"Evenin' friend."

Byron looked over at the inebriated old-timer sitting to his right. The man had spittle forming at the corners of his mouth and breath that could stop a truck. "Evening, yourself."

"Hey, don't I know you?" the drunk asked.

"I don't think so."

"You ever serve?"

He thought about it for a moment before

answering. "Every day."

"What can I getcha?" Polowski asked before recognizing him. "Hey, Sarge. Didn't think I'd see you again. I haven't seen the guy you were askin' about. The one who came in with Cleo."

"Actually, that's why I'm here. I've got a few photos I want you to look at." He set them on the bar in a stack, intentionally putting Humphrey's at the bottom. "Take your time and tell me if you recognize anyone."

" 'Kay." Polowski flipped each picture face down as he finished with it. He either shook his head or said nope after each one. "I don't think you — Wait. This is the guy." He repeatedly tapped the photo of Humphrey with his index finger. "This is the guy who came in with Cleo right before he died."

"You're sure?"

"Yeah. Had a goatee and was wearing a hat, but this is the same guy. I'm almost positive."

"Almost?"

The bartender pursed his lips and looked back at the picture of Humphrey. "Ninety percent."

Byron left the bar feeling very conflicted. With Polowski's ID, he had now linked

Humphrey to two of the murders. Closing in on a killer usually came in the form of an excited knot in his stomach. While he definitely felt something in the pit of his stomach, there was nothing exciting about it. The thought that Ray was capable of murdering his fellow cops was sickening. He still couldn't connect him to Williams or the Perrigos. He'd have to push forward with what he had. His first call was to Nugent.

"Stone, homicide," Nugent said, jokingly.

"You still got eyes on Beaudreau?"

"Yup. He's still at the club. You want me to stay on him?"

"Right on him. Let him know you're there. When he leaves tonight, be on his bumper. Park right in front of his house."

"Uh, okay. You're the boss."

"Trust me, Nuge."

Byron made the second call after receiving Pritchard's text.

"Mel, it's Byron."

"Hey, Sarge. Nothing happening here."

"Listen, I need you to pull off Humphrey and sit on Cross's house."

"What about Humphrey?"

"I got it covered."

"Okay," she said. "He made me, didn't he?"

He could hear the disappointment in her voice. "It's okay, Mel. Don't beat yourself up about it. No one's harder to surveil than a former cop."

"I'm sorry, Sarge."

"Don't be, just get over to Cross's and let me know if he moves. Oh, and one more thing. He'll be getting a surprise visit later."

"From whom?"

"Me." Byron ended the call. *Time to poke the bear.*

CHAPTER TWENTY-NINE

Byron alternated between pounding on the front door and ringing the doorbell until he finally heard Cross lumbering down the stairs to the first floor. The porch light came on as Cross looked through the sidelights at Byron. Cross opened the door, his black semiautomatic firmly in his right hand.

"Jesus Christ, John, you scared the shit out of me. What the hell are you doing here?" Cross asked as he slid the Glock inside the pocket of his robe.

"Didn't think I'd find out, did you?" Byron asked.

"I don't know what you're —"

"Don't play stupid with me, Reggie."

"Sergeant, in case you need reminding, I'm still Assistant Chief of Police and I don't care for your insolent tone or your accusations." Cross's ever-expanding forehead reddened in anger.

"And I don't appreciate being lied to."

"And what is it you think you know?"

"I know about the dealers you were ripping off. I know about the money from the armored car robbery."

"Keep your goddamned voice down."

"Afraid your wife will find out?" Byron said, glancing up the stairs.

"She's not here. I sent her to her mother's. Figured she'd be safer there."

Byron stared at Cross, sizing him up, waiting for any tells in his demeanor. A twitch of the lips, a break in eye contact, anything that gave him away. Then he saw it — Cross's Adam's apple bobbed up and down as he swallowed nervously. Byron pushed ahead. "Did you really think you'd get away with it?"

Cross dropped both his gaze and the bullying façade he'd unsuccessfully attempted to use. Byron saw a beaten man standing in front of him. "Come inside, John."

Cross turned and shuffled slowly toward the dining room. Byron stepped inside, closed the door, and followed Cross. As they reached the dining room, Cross removed two glasses and a bottle of Jameson's from a large antique mahogany hutch.

"Have a seat," Cross said as he sat down at the dining room table and poured whiskey into both glasses. His hands were visibly shaking.

Byron remained standing, averting his eyes from the whiskey. "You've known what this was about the whole time, haven't you?"

"You're right about the money, but I have no idea why we're being killed," Cross said, taking a sizable swig out of his glass. "I've been sleeping with my gun under my pillow for two weeks."

"Why the hell didn't you say something? Do you have any idea how many people might still be alive if you had come forward?"

"And told you what? We took some money? Please. What difference would it have made? You still don't have a clue who's after us. Please, sit down."

Byron didn't budge.

"Please," Cross said, gesturing toward a chair.

Byron reluctantly sat in one of the chairs across the table. Cross no longer bore any resemblance to the overbearing second in command of Maine's largest municipal police agency. He looked like a scared old man whose years of lying and secrets had finally caught up with him.

"How did you find out?" Cross asked.

"The FBI provided me with the case files from the armored car robbery. It wasn't too hard to figure out what had most likely happened. But I wasn't a hundred percent sure until Perrigo spilled his guts."

"Perrigo, huh? Funny, I always thought it would've been Beaudreau who'd shoot his mouth off." Cross pulled a glass ashtray over in front of him and reached into the pocket of his robe.

Byron sprung up out of the chair and drew his gun, pointing it at the chief.

"Jesus Christ, I'm only reaching for my cigarettes. You mind not pointing that thing at me?"

"Not at all, Reggie. You mind taking your hands out of your pockets? Slowly."

"Take it easy. I'm on your side," Cross said as he set both of his shaky hands on the table in front of him.

"I doubt that," Byron said. "Someone connected to the SRT is killing cops, Reggie. How do I know it isn't you?"

"If you want my gun, take it."

Byron walked behind him and removed the gun from the pocket of Cross's robe.

"Stand up so I can pat you down," Byron said. Cross did as he was told. Byron found a pack of cigarettes in the right pocket of the robe and a lighter in the left, but nothing else.

"Here," Byron said as he tossed the cigarettes and lighter on the table in front of Cross.

"May I?" Cross gestured to his chair.

"Certainly."

Byron holstered his own weapon, then removed both the magazine and chambered round from Cross's gun. He laid them on the table, far from Cross, taking some pleasure in watching Cross make several nervous attempts at lighting up before he was finally successful. It was amazing how quickly command presence dissipated when the suit was replaced by a bathrobe. Byron wondered if this was what it was like for Cross, watching his subordinates fumble about during CompStat each week.

Cigarette finally lit, Cross inhaled deeply, closing his eyes like a junkie getting his fix. The nicotine seemed to have the desired calming effect. He opened bloodshot eyes and looked across the table through a haze of bluish smoke, awaiting Byron's questions.

"Okay, Reggie, let's say it isn't you. You must know who it is."

"I honestly don't know."

Byron had been at this a long time, and if there was one word criminals loved to throw around, it was the word *honestly.* "Are you gonna sit there and tell me you had nothing to do with the death of the Perrigos?"

"I didn't, John. I swear to you."

"Marty told me you knew about the safe house."

"He told me you'd stashed a witness in a safe house, but I didn't know who it was or where."

"He said he told you it was an FBI safe house."

"Which means what to me?"

He studied Cross's face. If the chief was lying, he was good at it. His nervousness was obvious, but beyond that Byron couldn't get a read.

"What have you been telling Billingslea about this case?"

"The *Herald* reporter? Nothing. Why?"

Cross appeared legitimately surprised at the question. Byron let it drop.

The chief had finished his glass of whiskey and was eyeing Byron's untouched glass. "Are you going to drink that?"

"Be my guest," Byron said, sliding the glass toward him.

Cross took a large gulp before resuming his story and his cigarette. Byron was growing impatient, waiting for the chief to help him put the pieces together. "Tell me about the night of October nineteenth."

"There were so many things that led to what happened," Cross said. "I guess what I mean to say is, it wasn't just one event gone wrong, John. It's important for you to understand that. We were good cops, but back then none of us made much money. Christ, the rookies coming on the force were eligible for food stamps. Can you believe it?"

"And that's supposed to make it all right?"

"No. I'm only telling you how it was."

"As you know there were ten of us on the Special Reaction Team in 1985. Jim O'Halloran was the Lieutenant, Riordan, Williams, Falcone and I were the sergeants, the rest of the team was comprised of Officers Dominic Beaudreau, Ray Humphrey, Anthony Perrigo, Bruce Gagnon, and your dad, Reece Byron. Our core group had worked together for a long time, John. Years. We knew we could count on and trust each other no matter what. The only new addition was Gagnon. He'd only been with us a year."

Cross lit another cigarette.

Byron knew the chief was stalling.

"We'd been training all day. Everyone was in great spirits. We were celebrating Eric's fortieth birthday. We starting talking about the Boston armored car robbery. It was all anyone was talking about. Grabbing almost a million and a half in broad daylight. These guys had huge balls. We were joking about it over beers down at Sporty's, on Congress Street. You remember that place?"

"The Sportsman's, yeah, I remember."

The Sportsman's had been the popular Congress Street haunt for Portland cops until closing its doors in 1999. Many officers would bring their families to eat at the restaurant on their off time, while others used it only for blowing off steam, proceeding directly to the bar side of the establishment following a "late out" shift (midnight to eight), where they would imbibe, sometimes until two or three in the afternoon. Byron's own father had frequented Sporty's, the bar side.

"Anyway, we were playing the 'what if' game. What if they fled to Maine? What if we were called to take them into custody? At first that's all it was, talk. You know, the macho bullshit that comes out of all of us when we get together. But later on, well, some of us began talking about what we would do if they still had the money on them. I mean the money was insured, right?"

Byron said nothing.

Cross stubbed out what was left of his cigarette, finished off his whiskey, and poured another glass. Byron began to worry the chief might not remain coherent enough to finish the story.

"O'Halloran got a phone call after which he pulls Williams, Riordan, and me aside and tells us he's got an informant who knows where the robbers are hiding, right here in Portland."

"And you don't know who the informant was?" Byron asked with incredulity.

"Good CI's are hard to come by, you know. The lieutenant wasn't sharing the source and we knew better than to ask."

"What happened?" Byron asked.

"We rounded up the team and headed down to 109 for a briefing. Unmarked units from CID were already sitting down the street from the house. The black-and-whites all knew about the intel on the bad guys, but they'd been ordered not to make any attempt at either approaching the house or apprehending the robbers. This arrest was ours. The consensus was these guys were too unpredictable and too dangerous to fuck around with. The guys we were looking for were Warren, Ellis, Andreas, and Rotolo. I think the house on Ocean belonged to Warren's girlfriend. Anyway, it was pretty standard. The detectives and MedCu staged down the street at a makeshift CP. Beaudreau, Humphrey, and your dad were our

466

snipers. Perrigo and O'Halloran had containment, and the entry team consisted of me, Riordan, Williams, and Gagnon."

Byron remembered Williams's account of the event had been identical. A near impossibility even for officers at the same incident. People, as a result of their life experiences and individual biases, always tend to see things a little different. Byron was now sure that what he was hearing was the lie that the group had concocted thirty years ago. One big lie with enough sprinkles of truth to make it easy to remember.

"We took the door, used a stun grenade, and made entry. At first there was nothing as we cleared several rooms. But then I heard the sound of a shotgun blast coming from one of the bedrooms. The firefight started. They'd been lying in wait. It was crazy, it seemed like the shooting went on forever. When it was over, I found Williams kneeling over Gagnon's body. Rotolo shot the kid in the throat with a shotgun. Eric's hands were covered in Gagnon's blood. I'll never forget it as long as I live."

Byron watched with fascination as the cigarette in Cross's hand burned down to his fingers. There was an ash stump several inches in length protruding from what was left of it. The chief was so lost in his memories, he didn't notice.

Cross took a moment to get his thoughts in order before continuing. Byron remained silent. The house was eerily quiet, Byron could hear the sound of a clock ticking in a nearby room.

"So O'Halloran came inside. We told him Gagnon was dead, along with Warren, Ellis and, Rotolo. Andreas was in the wind."

As he spoke, Cross fortified himself with the Irish again.

"Tell me about the money."

"We tore the place apart searching for it. Found nearly half of it. They'd hidden it everywhere — basement, attic, kitchen cupboards, and bedroom closets. Everywhere. I'd never seen so much money, none of us had. O'Halloran had your dad and Humphrey bring the SRT transport to the house. The rest of us loaded the money into our equipment bags and carried them out to the truck."

Cross was clearly trying to elicit a reaction from Byron. He didn't get one.

"After that, we split the money. In all we recovered a little under seven hundred grand. Everyone assumed Andreas must have gotten away with all of it. But if he did get away, he only got half."

"You're telling me this is the reason

468

someone's trying to kill all of you?"

"I'm not telling you anything. I'm only telling you what happened. It's the only reason I can think of."

"What about Gagnon?"

Cross's eyes narrowed. "What about him?"

"Perrigo thinks you killed him."

"That's ridiculous."

"Is it?"

"Why would we kill one of our own? Sounds like you've been talking to someone who's still pissed about not getting an equal share of the money."

"Does Stanton know about this?"

"Of course not."

Byron slowly shook his head for effect. "I can't believe you assholes actually thought you'd get away with it."

"Hey, news to you, we did get away with it," Cross said, his arrogance returning.

"Really?"

"You've no proof of anything. The money is long gone and most of the guys who benefited from it are dead now, anyhow. Maybe you need to brush up on your Criminal Code, John. The statute of limitations on a class A crime has long since expired."

"Not on murder."

"You can't prove I had anything to do with

any of these deaths. Tell anyone about the money and I'll only deny it. It'll be your word against mine."

"What about Perrigo?"

"What about him?" Cross asked with a knowing smirk. "Thought he was dead."

"I've still got his taped confession."

Cross's smirk vanished.

"Why are you telling me any of this?" Byron asked, knowing that Cross was still trying to play him. He'd never seen Cross do anything without some kind of angle from which only he would benefit.

"Because, I need you to catch whoever is doing this. For Christ's sake, I may well be their next victim."

"You deserve to be the next victim." Byron stood up abruptly, intentionally knocking his chair into the wall.

"What are you gonna do?" Cross asked as he stood and followed.

"My job."

"Before you go and do anything stupid, Mr. High-and-Mighty, don't forget your father took his share of the money too." Cross smiled, having played his ace in the hole.

Byron stopped as he reached the front door and turned to face Cross. "It's not my father I'm coming after." Byron stormed out of the house and down the front steps.

Cross paced back and forth nervously, trying to decide what to do. He poured himself another whiskey to calm his frazzled nerves. He picked up his Glock from the dining room table, reinserted the magazine and chambered round before placing it back into the pocket of his robe. He lit another cigarette, grabbed his cell phone, and dialed.

He sat down at the table, closed his eyes, and rubbed his temples, listening to the distant ringing. At last the person on the other end of the line picked up.

"I thought my instructions were clear. You were never to call me unless it was an emergency."

Cross exhaled the smoke he'd been holding in. "We've got a big problem."

Byron drove to 109. He had done all he could to set things in motion. All of his remaining targets were covered, at least he hoped they were, and he'd poked the proverbial bear with a stick to see what would happen. He liked Humphrey for the first two murders, but a partial print and a drink with a friend would hardly make the case. They were in fact the kinds of flimsy circumstantial evidence any first-year court-appointed hack would poke holes in. They needed more, something concrete. Besides, he was certain something else was happening here, something he still couldn't see.

Byron didn't realize he'd fallen asleep until his cell phone rang, startling him. He looked around the conference room, trying to get his bearings. The clock on the wall read two-fifteen. "Byron," he mumbled as he sat up in the chair, rubbing his stiff neck.

"Sarge, it's Mike. Looks like Beaudreau and his old lady are heading out of town."

"Where are you?"

"I'm on ninety-five southbound, following his Caddy. We just passed the Saco exit. I was watching the club when I saw someone come outside and load a couple of suitcases into the trunk. I started following them about ten minutes ago. What do you want me to do?"

Byron tried to clear his head as he thought it through. They had no legal reason to detain either of them. Beaudreau wasn't a suspect in the murders. If anything, he was probably wise to get out of Dodge while the getting was still good. But Beaudreau had lied to him, he was sure of it. And after losing Perrigo, he needed another source. Someone he could keep alive to testify.

"Sarge, you still there?" Nugent asked.

"Nuge, do you have Statewide Car-to-Car on your radio?"

"Think so."

"Get ahold of the nearest trooper on the turnpike. Tell them you need a car stopped. I'm leaving 109 right now. Text me with your location as soon as they're pulled over."

A light rain was falling as Byron pulled up behind Nugent's unmarked and a light blue state police unit, a mile south of the Kennebunk service area. He could see a figure silhouetted in the backseat of the trooper's Chevy. Nugent and the trooper were standing beside the light-colored Caddy, talking with a very animated female. Byron stepped out of his car and approached them.

"Is that him?" the intoxicated female yelled. "Are you the fuck-stick who ordered this?"

Byron saw Nugent lean in close to her and say something back. Whatever he'd said quieted her, for the moment. Nugent left her in the trooper's care and walked back to meet Byron.

"Beaudreau's girlfriend?" Byron asked, recognizing her as the party girl from the Unicorn.

"In the flesh. Belinda Gee, and she's a piece of work."

"What's Beaudreau told you?"

"About the case, nothing, and Belinda's shit-faced. She offered to perform a service if I let her go, but I turned her down."

"Wise decision."

"I thought so. Evidently, she doesn't hear the word *no* very often. She's called trooper Edwards and me every name in the book and threatened to sue us at least a dozen times."

"What about Beaudreau? Why is he in the backseat of the cruiser?"

"Ah, Dominic was threatening to kick our asses. We had to restrain him. You wanted them, they're all yours."

"What the fuck gives you the right to detain me, Sergeant?" Beaudreau barked as he stepped out of the state police car.

"We're gonna sue all of your asses," Belinda shouted.

"Belle, shut the fuck up," Beaudreau yelled back.

Byron remained calm. "You're right. I don't have a good reason. But we've been working hard to keep you alive. You leaving town will make that impossible."

"I already told you, I don't want your help. Besides, you haven't exactly done a bang-up job keeping all of us alive, have you?"

"You also said you didn't know why someone was trying to kill each of you. But we both know differently, don't we?"

Beaudreau shook his head in denial. "I don't have the slightest idea what in hell you're talking about. I'm telling you, for the second time, I don't know why this is happening. But I'm not stupid, Sergeant. I'm not gonna wait around and become the next victim."

"I know about the money," Byron said, trying to gauge his response. Beaudreau's eyes widened ever so slightly. A reaction Byron might've missed in the flashing light of the trooper's strobes, had he not been watching for it.

The former cop returned Byron's stare. "What money?"

"The drug rips, the armored car money. Perrigo told us everything."

Beaudreau broke eye contact, unconsciously rubbing the stubble on his chin.

"I can't help you unless you talk to me."

Beaudreau's eyes locked back on Byron's. "Let's assume that we had anything to talk about, how does that help *me*?"

"Give me your statement, tell me everything that happened, and I'll get you into protective custody."

"Sounds more like being *in* custody to

me." Beaudreau looked back toward Belinda.

"At least you'll be alive," Byron said.

"Why do you think I'm leaving this Christly state? Seems like that might keep me alive too."

"You really think you can hide from this? You know who you're running from. How far do you think you'll get. Talk to me, Dominic. Let me help you."

Byron saw Beaudreau's expression soften. The former cop, no longer adversarial, looked scared.

"What if — ?"

"How much longer are you guys gonna stand around pulling your puds?" Belinda yelled. "I gotta pee."

Beaudreau turned briefly to look at her before turning back. Byron could see the fear was gone. The spell was broken. Whatever momentary progress he'd made toward gaining Beaudreau's cooperation had disappeared, thanks to Belinda's big mouth.

"I think we're done here, Sergeant Byron."

"Cross told me everything," Byron said in a desperate attempt to pull Beaudreau back.

Beaudreau stared at him, unblinking for several seconds, before his mouth curled up into a knowing grin.

Byron knew instantly he'd overplayed his hand.

"Now I know you're lying," Beaudreau said. "Are you charging me with something or not?"

Byron shook his head. "No."

"Good, so you've got no reason to detain either of us. We're leaving." Beaudreau turned and walked toward his car. "Come on, Belle. We're going." Nugent looked at Byron for guidance.

"Let 'em go," Byron said with a backhand wave.

Bathed in flickering blue light, the three cops stood in the breakdown lane of the Maine Turnpike and watched as Beaudreau and Belle drove away.

Byron knew he'd almost had Beaudreau. He'd come so close to reeling him in, only to lose him. Maybe for good. Beaudreau hadn't believed for a second that Cross had come clean.

"Well, maybe your killer won't get to him if he's out of state," Trooper Edwards said.

"Don't think it's gonna make much difference," Byron said.

"Why not?" Nugent asked.

"The way this case is going, he's dead already."

■ ■ ■ ■

Byron sent Nugent home to get some sleep, then drove to his own apartment, hoping to squeeze in a two-hour nap. He set the alarm on his nightstand for six o'clock along with a cell phone backup.

He awoke a couple of minutes before either alarm went off. His internal clock keeping him on edge in spite of his exhaustion.

Wipers on high, Byron drove through a torrent of rain, his mind replaying the previous night's interactions, first with Cross, then Beaudreau, and the ever so-charming Belle. First stop the drive-through at D & D for an extra-large dose of caffeine, then on to 109.

He was attempting to catch up on his reports when he got a call from the chief's secretary, summoning him to Stanton's office. He knew precisely what it was about and wasn't surprised in the least when he found Cross and LeRoyer already seated there. Cross smirking was bad, but LeRoyer staring at the floor was worse.

"Have a seat, John," Stanton said in a warm and inviting way that could only signify he wanted something.

Byron sat down apprehensively as Stanton got up and closed the door to the office. The chief returned and sat down with the others in one of the brown leather guest chairs, effectively removing the obstacle of his mahogany desk. Byron knew the game as well as anyone. He could see where the whole show was headed, entirely scripted and designed to convince him to play ball.

"How are you, John?" Stanton asked, removing his glasses and placing them in the pocket of his dress shirt. "Case going well?"

"I'm fine, thanks," he said, attempting to remain calm. Byron despised Stanton's manipulative and cozy use of his first name. Being referred to as sergeant suited him just fine. "We're making progress."

"Good. I'm glad to hear it. John, I won't beat around the bush."

Sure you will, he thought. It was the name of this game, after all.

"I understand Assistant Chief Cross shared some sensitive information with you last night in an attempt to help you with your case."

"Is that your understanding, Chief?" Byron asked, his sarcasm obvious.

LeRoyer shifted uneasily in his chair. His gaze moved from the floor to Byron.

"I also know he entrusted you with some dirty laundry from a long time ago, which might not be sitting all that well with you."

"Dirty laundry, Chief? Is that what we're calling it? Funny, I would've thought the theft of over a half million dollars in evidence might warrant a more fitting description." Cross glared at him. LeRoyer went back to studying the carpet.

"We all know you're an ethical man, John, and as such I'm sure this is difficult for you. The story Chief Cross shared with you happened in a different time, back when the police, even your own father, sometimes operated outside of the law in order to get the job done."

"Leave my father out of this," Byron snapped.

"I'm afraid he's not a separate issue," Cross said calmly, shaking his head.

"What's important now," Stanton continued, "is that we all stay focused on this case and stopping this lunatic before he can kill again. Airing out some moldy old skeleton from the Portland Police Department's historical closet won't do anybody any good. It'll only serve to distract people from what's really happening here."

"Are you ordering me to cover up a crime, Chief?" Byron asked.

"I'm doing no such thing, Sergeant.

"What I am asking is for you to see the big picture, and to use a bit of discretion."

Byron wordlessly stared at him.

"I know this isn't a small thing I am asking."

He had that right, suggesting Byron become a co-conspirator was no small thing. And bringing his father into it wasn't helping Stanton's cause or Byron's mood. But the chief wasn't finished. "I need you to do me a personal favor and keep the past to yourself."

"Why would I want to do that?"

"You might find yourself in need of *my* help one day, and I'll be sure to remember what you've done for me, and for the department."

Byron wondered if Stanton knew the difference between a bribe and a threat.

"Do we have an understanding, Sergeant?"

Byron looked over at Cross, who was smirking at him once again. He wondered exactly what kind of dirt Cross had on the chief. Byron looked back at Stanton. "I guess we do, Chief."

"Good. I'm glad to hear it," Stanton said, giving Byron a phony grin.

"So that's it? We're finished?"

"That's it," Stanton said as he stood, sending a clear signal to all that the discussion was over. "This chapter of our history is closed. No good can come from digging up the past and possibly tarnishing the reputation of some damn fine police officers. Let's keep our eyes on the prize, shall we? And catch us a killer."

Byron stood up and headed for the door, Stanton followed, clapping Byron on the back as he opened the door. "Keep up the good work, Sergeant."

Byron left the office quickly, before saying or doing anything he'd regret. He was trying very hard to outwardly appear unshaken, but inside he was knotted up and ready to punch something, or someone. He heard the door to the chief's office close behind him. *Post strategy session.* The point at which Stanton would threaten LeRoyer's position as the head of CID, and likely Byron's job as well, unless he could get his rogue detective sergeant under control. The political game was as predictable as it was timeless.

What had just happened? Was Stanton only protecting the department's reputation or was there something else happening? Had Byron missed some connection to Stanton?

He pulled out his cell and dialed Pritchard.

"Morning, John," Pritchard said, sounding chipper.

"Making sure you're still awake."

"Still on the case, my friend. No movement here," Pritchard said. "You?"

"Let's just say I've done everything I can to stoke the fire. Now we wait. You need relief?"

"Nah, I've had so much coffee I wouldn't be able to sleep now anyway. I'm good for the time being."

"Okay, keep in touch," Byron said.

"Will do."

Byron hung up and headed for the stairs. *Time to relieve Stevens.*

CHAPTER THIRTY

It was nearly one in the afternoon. Cross got up from behind his desk, walked over and closed the office door. He returned to the desk, picked up the phone, and dialed Ray Humphrey's cell.

"Hello," Humphrey said, answering on the first ring.

"We need to meet."

"I was wondering when I'd hear from you, Reg."

"One-thirty."

"Where?"

"Fort Williams."

"How will I find you?" Humphrey asked.

"Walk to the ruins. I'll find you. Come alone."

Cross returned the phone to its cradle. He reached into his top desk drawer and removed his snub-nosed .38. He held it in his hand and flipped open the cylinder. Fully loaded. He snapped it shut and slid it back into its holster.

"One way or another this ends today."

Byron's phone rang. It was Pritchard. "Talk to me, Terry."

"Anything on your end, John?"

"Yeah, Cross is on the move. He just left 109. I'm following him south on Middle Street, but I've got no idea where he's going."

"I think I know. I just tailed Humphrey out to Fort Williams. Pretty sure something's about to go down. Looks like you're right about them being in this together."

"I'll keep you posted."

Byron hung up and dialed Nugent.

Nugent's cell rang a dozen times. Byron was about to hang up when his groggy-sounding detective answered.

"Nugent. This better be good."

"Mike, it's Byron. Get dressed."

Normally, Fort Williams Park made a great public meeting place. It was safe, open, and well populated by locals and tourists alike, all coming to see the famed Portland Head Light, but not today. Byron knew the combined effects of it being midweek, post Labor Day, and wind-swept with rain meant the ninety-acre park would be deserted. If this was a trap, he wondered which one of them had set it.

All of the evidence, circumstantial as it was, pointed to Humphrey as the murderer. But Byron knew that Cross was still somehow part of what was happening. Based on Tran's phone tree, Cross might have been the one giving the orders to kill, but nothing linked him directly. The unanswered question bothering Byron the most was why? If Byron was interpreting this correctly, if O'Halloran had said something to Humphrey that made him kill the old man, setting this whole thing in motion, what was it?

He hung back several hundred yards, taking care to keep a handful of cars between them as he followed the SUV across the Casco Bay Bridge into South Portland. Tailing Cross was much easier when he already knew where the Ass Chief was likely headed. He lost sight of the SUV only once as it passed through a curve on Shore Road, the winding thoroughfare that led to the park. As Byron rounded the corner, he saw the black Mercury already halfway down the park's main road. Byron drove past the entrance, pulling into a U-shaped private drive about a hundred yards further down Shore Road, and stopped. If he followed him in, Cross would make him easily. Besides, he knew Pritchard already had eyes on. He removed his Glock from its holster, double-checking both the magazine and chamber as he waited for Terry's call. He was returning the gun to its holster when his cell rang. It was Diane.

"John, I got your message. I'm leaving the hospital now. What's up?"

"They released you already?" he asked, sounding surprised.

"Nope. I released myself. Tell me what's going on."

"It looks like Humphrey and Cross are about to meet up."

"Where are you?"

"I don't suppose I can talk you out of coming here?

"Not a chance. Where?"

"Fort Williams."

"On my way. Is Pritchard with you?"

"He's already inside the park. He followed Humphrey here and I tailed Cross to the same place. I'm waiting on his call."

"I can't believe this is really happening. You think they're both responsible for these murders?"

"Either that or only one of them is, and this thing's about to come to a head. We'll know soon enough. Nugent is headed out here too." Byron's cell vibrated with an incoming call. Pritchard. "Terry's calling, I gotta let you go."

"John, please be careful."

"You too."

Cross arrived a little past one. The rain had let up some but it was still falling steadily as he pulled into the deserted lot nearest the ruins. Further up the hill, in the other parking areas, only a handful of cars were scattered about. He checked his weapons before exiting the SUV. He lifted the hood on his parka and headed toward the ruins on foot.

Cross heard the automated foghorn moaning in the distance as he entered the woods. He was searching for a secure spot to hide, hoping he had beaten Humphrey to the park, when he heard someone approaching from behind.

"That's Goddard Mansion, built in 1857. Named after Colonel John Goddard, First Maine Cavalry. Did you know the First Maine fought in more campaigns than any other regiment in the Union Army? Thirty-five battles to be exact."

Cross, recognizing the voice, slowly inched his hand toward the Glock on his belt.

"I wouldn't do that, Reggie."

He heard the familiar metallic click of a

hammer being pulled back. Cross dropped his hands back to his sides.

"I see you haven't lost your flair for the dramatic, Ray. Now what?"

"Now you'll slowly take out your gun and toss it on the ground."

Cross did as he was told.

"Now your cell."

Again Cross complied.

"Don't forget the .38 you always carried in your ankle holster."

"I'm not wearing it."

"Pardon me if I don't believe you. But I don't. Now lose it."

"Had to try, didn't I?" Cross asked.

"I'd have been disappointed if you hadn't."

He reached down, lifted his right pant leg, unholstered the revolver, and tossed it on the ground. "That's the last of them."

"Is it? Let's see. Step two paces forward, get down on your knees, put your hands behind your head, and interlock your fingers. You know the drill."

"Is all this really necessary?"

"No. We can skip right to the good part if you'd like."

Cross followed his instructions and Humphrey recovered the guns and patted him down.

"Well, well, well. What do we have here?" Humphrey asked as he removed a stainless Raven .25 semiauto from the inside pocket of Cross's raincoat.

"You never said anything about that one."

"Didn't I?" Humphrey pocketed the Raven while keeping his own firearm trained on Cross. "Stand up. Let's take a walk."

Byron pulled into one of the upper lots and parked beside Pritchard's Lexus. The former special agent was already out of the car and waiting for him.

"Any chance he made you?" Byron asked.

"None." Pritchard pointed toward one of the lower lots near the water. "That's Cross's SUV parked down there."

"Where is Ray's car?" Byron asked, looking around.

"Up there behind us. Humphrey walked down toward the ruins and into the woods about ten minutes ago. Cross went in the same way."

"You want to call in some backup?" Byron asked.

"Who do you trust at this point?"

"Fair enough." Byron unlocked the trunk and reached inside. "I brought an extra vest for you."

Pritchard looked at the offering and shook

his head. "No, thanks. I appreciate the offer, but after retiring I told myself I'd never
wear one of those damn things again."

Byron looked down at his own vest. After
brief consideration, he tossed both vests
back into the trunk and slammed the lid.

"How do you want to do this?" Pritchard
asked.

"Hoods up. Neither one of them will
recognize us if we're seen. We'll look like
two people just out for a stroll. Make sure
you kill the ringer on your cell — we'll text
if we get separated."

The two men started down the hill toward
the ruins.

"Haven't done this in a while, John," Pritchard said with a grin.

"How's it feel?"

"Didn't realize how much I missed it."

"So what do you want, Ray? More money?"

Humphrey laughed. "You trying to buy
your way out of this, Reg?"

"What then?"

"Justice."

"Justice? For who? The three shit-heads
we killed?" Cross said. "Maybe you need
reminding, you were in on that too. If
memory serves, you didn't have any problem taking your share of the money either."

"That was before I knew you killed one of ours."

"What are you talking about?"

"I know what you did, Reggie. I know you killed Reece. O'Halloran told me everything."

Cross stopped walking. "Reece Byron was gonna blow the whistle, you fucking idiot. On all of us. I did what I had to."

"You didn't have to murder a cop. He was one of us."

"That's pretty rich coming from you, Ray. How many cops have you killed now? I've lost track."

"Keep moving," Humphrey said, prodding Cross in the back with the barrel of his gun.

"I should have known it was you all along," Cross said as he resumed walking, stumbling slightly on an exposed tree root.

"Why's that?"

"Because you always were a fucking coward."

Humphrey grinned. "Keep walking."

Cautiously, Byron and Pritchard advanced down the muddy path with guns drawn, under a canopy of trees, past the ruins, toward the ocean. Byron could see two figures walking about fifty yards ahead. Byron recognized Cross's burnt orange parka. The other had to belong to Humphrey. They were headed directly toward the fort's main battery. The rain was still falling, pattering on the leaves, although it was now more of a drizzle.

Byron's overtaxed brain raced through the facts of the case. He was having trouble focusing again. *Had Humphrey and Cross been together on this thing since the start? Had they turned on each other? Was this about money or revenge? Who else was involved?* There were still too many unanswered questions. He felt as if he were still missing something. Something important.

Byron felt his phone vibrating. He pulled it out and checked the ID. Tran. *Now's not the time, Dustin.* Whatever it was, it would have to wait. He pocketed the phone.

Byron and Pritchard continued forward, stepping silently and carefully like two hunters tracking their prey, along the rain-slicked trail.

Diane paced nervously back and forth in the paved lot near Byron and Pritchard's cars. Neither of them were anywhere in sight. Her stomach was in knots and her head was already throbbing. *Where the hell was Nuge? He should have been here by now.* She pulled out her phone and dialed Nugent's cell. The call went directly to voice-mail.

"Damn it."

She thought about calling police dispatch to request backup but remembered what John had said about involving anyone else. He was right. Cops were being killed, and now it looked like two of their own might be responsible.

She checked her cell, hoping for a text from John. Nothing. She was looking in the direction of Cross's SUV when she saw it. In the distance, two figures exiting the woods, walking toward the battery. One wearing an orange jacket the other dark green. Diane pocketed her phone and hurried on foot toward the battery.

The two men had moved around to the ocean side of the battery at the edge of the rocks when Humphrey ordered Cross to stop. "That's far enough," Humphrey said, motioning with his gun. "Turn around."

"What are you gonna do, shoot me and leave me here?"

"Nope. I got something else in mind," Humphrey said. "Something I've always wondered about."

"What?"

"Whatever happened to Andreas, Reggie?"

"Where the fuck do you think the safe house information came from?"

"So *he* was your informant? You killed him, too, didn't you?" Humphrey said.

"I didn't see you complaining when you took your share of the money."

"I didn't know we were murdering people for it."

Davis Billingslea tailed Diane out of the hospital. A Westbrook cop had given him the details about the break-in at her house. Billingslea's keen investigative instincts told him it was most likely related to the murders. He'd sweet-talked one of the night-duty nurses into telling him when Detective Joyner might be released, then he waited, knowing if something broke she'd likely lead him directly to it. He'd followed her into South Portland and out to Fort Williams.

Billingslea had driven up the hill past Joyner's parking lot to the next and was now sitting in his Accord, watching her pace back and forth.

What are you up to, Detective?

As if in answer to his question, she took off toward the Goddard ruins.

Billingslea jumped out of his car, locked it, and hurried after her.

■ ■ ■ ■

Byron and Pritchard concealed themselves in the bushes on the ocean side of the battery, off the path, as they observed both men stop. Cross was facing Humphrey. They'd managed to close the gap without being detected and were now within fifty feet. It was obvious that whatever Humphrey had planned for Cross was imminent. Byron knew he was close enough to shoot if he had to, but not close enough to guarantee he wouldn't miss once he'd settled on a target. They'd need to leave cover. He turned to Pritchard and whispered. "Hang back for a minute, Terry. Let me make the initial approach. If things go to shit, you'll have my back."

"Your show, John. I'll be right here."

Quietly, Byron moved closer.

"What did you do with Andreas?" Humphrey asked.

"What difference does it make now?"

"It doesn't, I guess. It's almost funny, really. The feds have been searching for the guy for over thirty years. Did you bury him? Or maybe you weighed him down and dumped him in Casco Bay?"

"We buried him all right, in the Ocean."

"What?"

"Ocean Avenue. The landfill."

"You're shittin' me?"

"Nope. Not that hard to get rid of a body, Ray."

"What if they'd developed the area? They might've dug him up."

"Yeah, and I'd have known about it in advance, wouldn't I?"

"I suppose you would've. Okay, turn around and face the water," Humphrey ordered.

Cross did as he was instructed. "Not very sporting of you, Ray. Shooting an unarmed man in the back. Like I said, you always were a coward."

"You've got no imagination. Here," he said, handing Cross's Glock back to him. "I've emptied the mag but you've still got one round in the chamber."

"What am I supposed to do with this?" Cross asked.

"I think you know."

Byron crouched as he made his way out onto the rocks, trying to make himself as small as possible while positioning himself directly behind Humphrey. He was now within twenty feet of the two men and completely exposed. The crashing waves were helping to mask his approach and forcing Cross and Humphrey to speak with raised voices.

"And if I don't?" Cross asked.

"Then I'll kill you myself," Humphrey said.

"What if I use it to shoot you instead?"

"That would be some trick seeing as how I'm pointing my gun at the back of your head."

"Drop it, Ray!" Byron yelled.

Diane walked as fast as she dared, not wanting to give herself away by inadvertently stepping on a fallen branch or, worse still, slipping on the wet uneven ground and landing on her bruised head. Her gun was out and her eyes were darting in all directions. The legs of her pants were soaked from brushing up against the skeletal remnants of goldenrod and bittersweet vines. She looked down as her cell began to vibrate, it was Tran. She quickly answered it. "Can't talk right now, Dustin."

"Don't hang up. I can't reach the Sarge. Where are you?"

"Fort Williams. It's going down right now. Humphrey and Cross are meeting."

"Is Pritchard with you?"

"He's up ahead with John. Why?"

"Listen to me. Cross and Pritchard know each other."

"Yeah, of course they do. Pritchard investigated the robbery shooting."

"That's not what I mean. I mean, they served together."

"What?"

"In the army, Diane. I'm looking at their service records. They're both out of Fort Bragg, 101st Airborne. Both deployed to Vietnam in 1971. They knew each other *before* the robbery."

"Oh my god." She pocketed her phone and ran toward the battery.

"I can't do that, Sarge," Humphrey said.

"Shoot him," Cross shouted, hiding his own gun from sight. "Ray's the killer."

"Trust me when I tell you he's got it backwards," Humphrey said.

"Ray, don't make me shoot you," Byron said, pleading with his friend.

"By all means, shoot him," Cross said.

"Sarge, you don't know what's happened," Humphrey said.

"Put your gun down and you can fill me in," Byron said.

"They murdered your father," Humphrey said. "They killed Reece."

"What are you talking about? My dad killed himself."

"For Christ-sakes, Sergeant," yelled Cross, "shoot him. That's an order!"

"Shut the fuck up, Chief," Byron snapped. "Ray, what the hell are you talking about?"

"We stole the money from the robbery, all of us. You were right about that. Your dad was gonna go to the feds and they killed him for it."

Byron's legs felt rubbery, the gun suddenly much heavier. "Who killed him?"

"Cross found out your dad was going to turn himself in to the FBI. They went to see Reece at his house and try and talk him out of it."

"Who went to see him?"

"All the supervisors — Cross, O'Halloran, Riordan, Falcone, and Williams. And when your dad wouldn't back down, Cross shot him and made it look like a suicide. O'Halloran told me everything."

Byron struggled to stay focused. It all made sense. Cross had been the sergeant who assigned a detective with no experience to investigate his father's suicide. Here Byron was pointing a gun at his mentor and friend while trying to save the life of his father's killer? He couldn't imagine a more twisted irony. "Please, Ray, just put the gun down."

"Cross is armed, Sarge."

Byron's eyes focused on Cross's hands. The left was empty, but the right was hidden behind his body. "Let me see the other hand, Chief," he demanded.

Cross slowly moved the gun into sight.

"Both of you put them down," Byron said. Now!"

"Perhaps you should put yours down, too," Pritchard said calmly from behind him.

Byron's heart sank, but he kept his gun fixed on Humphrey. His suspicions about FBI involvement had been justified after all.

"Kill them, Terry," Cross yelled, spit flying from his mouth.

"Shut the fuck up, Reggie," Humphrey said.

"Ray's right, Reg," Pritchard said. "I think you need a new line. You're starting to sound like a parrot." He turned his attention back toward Byron. "Sorry about this, John. I never wanted it to go down like this. I was hoping these two would kill each other before we got here."

"You know, I didn't want to believe it, Terry."

"Thought you might've figured it out after

the safe house."

"There were a couple of times when I wondered if maybe you were somehow mixed up in this," Byron said. "But it seemed too farfetched."

"You should've trusted your instincts, John. You were right not to trust anybody. Guess you should have called in some backup after all. If it makes you feel any better, your dad's instincts weren't too keen either. Turns out he left a message with the wrong guy."

"But you were the robbery case agent," Byron said, stalling for time.

"Got myself assigned to the case. I was the hot-shot agent, remember? Great clearance rate. Made my boss look good. Had him wrapped around my finger." Pritchard chuckled. "Sound like anyone you know?"

"But why? Why risk everything?"

"The usual reasons. Money. Power. They're both powerful drugs. This wasn't the only time I crossed the line, John."

"Did you kill my father?"

"Nope, Ray's right, that was Reggie. One of the few things he managed to do right."

"Stop fucking telling them everything, Terry," Cross said.

"Or what, Reg? Seems like the least I can do is set the record straight."

Byron felt the rage welling up inside like water coming to a boil, but he needed to massage Pritchard's ego, keep him talking. "Why even pretend to help us?" Byron asked.

"I had planned to reach out to you after Riordan ended up on a slab. But you made it easy by contacting me. Figured I could stay up on the case and make sure that the killer, your pal Ray, didn't find out about me. I rather like breathing. The problem was working itself out until Perrigo opened his big mouth."

"So you killed the Perrigos?" Byron said.

"They were becoming a considerable liability."

"I can help you kill them, Terry," Cross said.

"Doesn't look like you're in a position to help with much of anything from where I'm standing," Pritchard said. "You know, you've kinda become a liability here yourself, Reg."

"I can still help you, Terry," Cross pleaded. "No one will have to know. We kill them and pin it all on Ray."

"Or, better still, I kill all of you and still pin it on Ray," Pritchard said. "I warned you about what would happen if I had to get involved. Now, John, put down the weapon."

"Drop it!" Diane yelled, partially concealed behind a stand of flame-colored sumacs.

Terry lowered his gun slightly and glanced back over his shoulder. "Well, if it isn't the hardheaded detective. Shit, John, I guess you didn't quite trust me. Called in some backup after all. Any chance we could get a few more cops out here? You know, we might actually have quorum."

"Terry's part of it, Diane," Byron said. "He killed the Perrigos."

"I know," Diane said. "I'm not kidding, Terry. Drop your gun."

"Forgive my lack of PC, Detective, but it looks like we've got ourselves an old-fashioned Mexican standoff. Wouldn't you agree?"

"Put it down, now," Diane said.

"Or what? You're gonna shoot a decorated FBI agent in the back? Might be a little difficult to explain."

"Not when she tells them what you and Cross were into," Byron said.

"It will be my word against yours."

"Last chance —"

Something landed with a loud thud behind Diane. She instinctively turned her head.

"Fuck," Billingslea said after tripping over a rock.

It was all the distraction Pritchard needed. He moved fast, surprising Diane, spinning to his left and firing two quick rounds, striking her in the thigh and chest. She cried out and returned fire, hitting him twice in the torso before she collapsed. Byron turned his attention from Humphrey and Cross long enough to get out of the line of fire, jumping down to a lower ledge and taking cover. Cross used the commotion to his advantage, shooting Humphrey in the chest with his one bullet, dropping him to the ground. Byron opened fire at Cross, hitting him multiple times, knocking him from the rocky ledge into the ocean below.

Byron peered over at Humphrey, who was lying face up on the ledge.

"Diane," Byron yelled.

"I'm hit. Fucker got me in the leg."

Byron looked back toward where Pritchard had been standing but didn't see him. "Where is he?"

"I don't know," she said. "I think I got him."

"Stay put."

Cautiously, Byron crawled over to Humphrey and retrieved his gun. Humphrey was aspirating. Cross had managed to send his one round into Humphrey's left lung. The rain, mixing with rivulets of blood, had created a crimson pool on the rocks beneath the burly former detective. Byron covered the wound with Humphrey's parka and applied pressure, attempting to seal it.

"Aw, Jesus, Ray. What the hell?"

Humphrey looked up at him in obvious pain, bravely trying to smile as blood bubbled from his mouth. "Sorry, Sarge."

Humphrey reached into his unzipped parka. Byron, thinking he was going for another weapon, grabbed his hand. Humphrey removed a small wireless transmitter and his keys, handing them to Byron. "The receiver is in my car. It's all recorded."

Byron looked at the wire. "Why, Ray?"

Humphrey grabbed Byron's forearm, squeezing as the pain got worse. "Couldn't let 'em get away — with it. Tried to make it right."

"I know you did, Ray. I know."

"I swear I didn't know what they'd done to Reece." His breathing was coming in ragged gasps. "Never thought they'd go that far. You believe me, don't you?"

"Yeah, Ray. I do. Lie still. Save your strength. Help's coming."

The gunshot was deafening, the round finding its mark. Humphrey's head.

"I don't think so," Pritchard said.

Byron looked up from Humphrey's lifeless body to find the former FBI agent standing with his gun trained directly at him. Pritchard's parka was flapping open in the wind, revealing the Kevlar vest he wore beneath it. His left hand, pressed against his abdomen, was covered in blood.

"Thought you never wore a vest," Byron said.

"I lied," Pritchard said through clenched teeth. "Pass me the keys and the transmitter, John."

"That looks bad, Terry," Byron said, ignoring him.

"I appreciate your concern, Sergeant. Now hand them fucking over."

"Freeze," Diane yelled from behind him.

Pritchard lowered the gun and sighed heavily. "You know, Detective, you're becoming rather tedious."

Byron locked eyes with Pritchard.

Pritchard's lips spread into an evil grin.

Byron knew what was coming even before the retired agent raised his gun hand. "Vest," he yelled to Diane.

As Pritchard aimed the gun at Byron, a single shot rang out. The top of Pritchard's head flew off like a toupee. His body fell forward, as rigid as a tree, landing face-first on the rocks.

"Freeze asshole," Nugent said, pointing his gun at Billingslea cowering on the ground with his hands over his head.

"Please don't shoot me."

"God damn you, Davis," Diane shouted before turning her attention to the most recent arrival. "Nice of you to join us, Nuge."

"Hey, I got stuck on the wrong side of a train. Sue me. Either of you hit?"

"Yeah," Diane said as she plopped down heavily on the ground. "I took one in the leg and one in the vest."

"How 'bout you, Sarge?" Nugent asked.

"I'm okay. Get an ambulance out here."

"I'm on it." Nugent holstered his gun and fished out his cell, turning his attention toward Billingslea. "Make yourself useful, numb nuts. Go wait for the paramedics and direct them in here."

The young reporter staggered to his feet, staring wide-eyed at the scene before him.

"Now!" Nugent said.

Wordlessly, Billingslea scurried back into the woods.

Byron squatted next to Diane. "How bad is it?"

"Hurts like a sonofabitch, but I don't think it's too bad. Where's Cross?"

Cross. He'd nearly forgotten about him. Byron got to his feet, moving carefully toward the water's edge where the ocean was crashing against the rocks. Twenty feet below, Cross's lifeless body was floating face down in the surf as waves washed over it, moving it back and forth.

"Cavalry's on the way," Nugent said.

Byron turned and headed back to Diane.

Byron and Nugent stayed with Diane as paramedics prepped her for transport.

"How the pain?" Byron asked.

"You kidding? I've had cramps worse than this," Diane said, gritting her teeth.

Both men grinned.

"I'm sorry about your friend, John," she said.

Byron's smile faltered. He wasn't sure which was worse, finding out that Ray was the killer they'd been chasing or that his father had been murdered by Cross. What was obvious, was how much Diane cared. In agony from a bullet wound yet still concerned about him. "Let's worry about getting you patched up, all right?"

Byron and Nugent assisted one of the EMTs and a young, wiry Cape Elizabeth cop in carrying Diane's stretcher up the uneven path toward the parking lot to a waiting ambulance. Red and blue strobes reflected off every wet surface like rabid fireflies. More sirens coming.

"You gonna be okay?" Diane asked Byron as they slid her into the back of the transport.

"Yeah. Gonna be a bitch explaining all of this, though."

Byron looked up to the sound of tires skidding to a stop on the wet asphalt. LeRoyer's Crown Vic.

"We gotta go," the bearded MedCu attendant said to Byron.

"I'll be up to see you later," Byron said, stepping back from the ambulance.

"Good luck," she said as the attendant closed the doors.

"Take good care of her," Byron said.

The attendant nodded, then hurried to the front of the truck.

Byron walked toward the lieutenant's car as the red and white MedCu unit pulled away.

"John, what the fuck happened here?" LeRoyer demanded as he jumped out of the car.

"Cross, Pritchard, and Humphrey are dead. Diane was shot."

LeRoyer stood in obvious shock, his

mouth agape. "Jesus Christ. Where's the shooter?"

CHAPTER THIRTY-ONE

The fourth floor of 109 was a flurry of activity, more closely resembling the start of a workweek than seven o'clock on a Thursday night. Every available detective had been called in, along with the president and vice president of the Superior Officers Benevolent Association (SOBA), two SOBA attorneys, the FBI, and several members of the Attorney General's Office, including the Maine attorney general herself.

Byron sat in interview room one. Alone and tired, he was sitting on a side of the table he'd never seen. Mike Nugent brought him a change of clothes and a coffee. Stevens and Pelligrosso had taken his damp clothing, gun, and spare magazines. Everyone wanted a piece of him. He knew there was legal wrangling happening in another room, most likely the conference room. He knew all too well the questions that would be asked. Did you have to shoot Cross?

Wasn't there a better course of action you could have taken? What about the bad blood between you and Assistant Chief Cross? Why involve your already injured detective in this? Why didn't you follow department protocol and notify your superiors about the meeting? Byron knew he had much to answer for, but he didn't care. He knew he wouldn't have done anything differently. Except maybe he wouldn't have involved Diane. If he hadn't given her the heads-up, she wouldn't have gotten shot. *Christ, Diane shouldn't have even been out of the hospital yet.* He should have called Stevens instead.

Why had he trusted Pritchard in the first place? *Because you needed him.* He supposed that was true. He had needed Pritchard. Pritchard was the case agent, and any good investigator would have gone to him. Besides, Byron had no reason to suspect him of being involved. At least initially.

But what about Humphrey? Hadn't he overlooked Humphrey's possible involvement? Hadn't he let their friendship cloud his judgment?

How could Cross have killed his father? They were partners. Exhaustion was muddling his thoughts again. His inner voice needed a nice big cup of shut-the-fuck-up.

Byron should've been at the hospital checking on Diane, not stuck in a six-by-six room, waiting to be interrogated like a criminal.

He was gazing up at the camera, wondering who might be watching him on the closed circuit monitor in the other room, when someone knocked at the door.

LeRoyer cracked the door open and stuck his head in. "Hey. Thought you might want this," he said, handing Byron a mug of coffee.

"Thanks, Marty."

"How you holding up?"

"Going a little stir crazy in here. Any word on Diane?"

"She is going into surgery now. Doc thinks she'll be okay. The bullet passed right through her leg, missed the bone."

He nodded and sipped.

"Can I get you anything else?"

"No, I'm good. Thanks."

"Fucking Billingslea. We should be charging that little prick with something. Obstructing maybe."

Byron hid a grin behind his mug.

"Shouldn't be much longer. I think the attorneys are working out the final rules of engagement for your statement. You sure you want to do this right now? You know you can wait."

Byron looked up. "You asking me as my lieutenant?"

"As your friend, John. Your lieutenant wouldn't try and talk you out of giving a statement."

Byron nodded. "I want to."

LeRoyer closed the door behind him, leaving Byron alone once again.

He wasn't sure why he'd agreed to the interview. All he really wanted was to get up to the hospital and check on Diane. In spite of all that Humphrey had done, Byron couldn't help but think of him as a friend. What would Byron have done if put in a similar situation? He didn't know. He only knew that his father had been murdered by the very men he trusted. Yes, Humphrey had killed those men, but he'd been trying to right a wrong. In his own twisted way, Humphrey had believed that what he was doing was just. Byron couldn't quite condemn him for that.

Someone else knocked on the interview room door.

"Come in," Byron said.

Tran poked his head in. "Hey, striped dude. This a bad time?"

Byron smiled weakly and shook his head. "No. Come in."

Tran stepped into the room and closed

the door. He glanced up at the camera. "I assume we've got an audience."

"I'd say that was a safe assumption. Did you get it?"

"Right here," he said, handing Byron several compact discs. "I made multiple copies. These are yours."

"Did you get a chance to listen to any of it?"

"Most of it. Everything you'll need is here. Cross, Pritchard, Humphrey, all of it."

"Thank you, Dustin," he said, slipping the disks into his jacket pocket.

"I'm sorry about not making the connection sooner between —"

Byron cut him off. "You're a good detective, Dustin. Thank you."

At seven-thirty Assistant Attorney General Eugene Marchand entered the interview room, followed by SOBA Attorney Jack Bennett. Bennett sat next to Byron while Marchand, clearly announcing his side, sat across from them.

"Gene," Byron said.

"Sergeant Byron," Marchand said, already cloaked in formality. "Do you need anything before we start?"

"I'm fine."

Byron knew when he agreed to give his

statement directly to an AAG today, instead of waiting to speak with an investigator in a couple of days, that he wouldn't get Ferguson, especially since Ferguson had been working this case with him. But he had hoped to draw someone from the pool a bit more fair-minded than Marchand. Unlike Ferguson, Marchand's every move was designed to increase his value in the mind of the attorney general. Byron figured Marchand most likely even had aspirations to one day place his rotund backside in the big chair.

"For the record, Sergeant, you are here voluntarily to answer my questions, correct?"

"Yes."

"And you have been advised by union counsel that you don't have to do this right now?" he asked, nodding toward Bennett.

"He has," Bennett said.

"I have," Byron agreed, "but I'm ready to proceed."

Marchand activated the digital recorder and set it on the table between them. Byron glanced at the camera again, wondering how big the audience was in the other room.

"The time is 7:33 P.M. Today is Thursday, October the eighth, 2015. My name is Eugene Marchand, assistant attorney general for the state of Maine. Also present is John Byron, detective sergeant for the Portland Police Department, and Attorney Jack Bennett, representing Sergeant Byron on behalf of the Portland Police Superior Officers Benevolent Association. We're here on the matter of the shooting death of Reginald Cross, formerly the assistant chief of police for the Portland Police Department. Sergeant Byron, for the record, would you please confirm you are here voluntarily to give your statement concerning the shooting of Assistant Chief Cross."

"I am here voluntarily."

"And are you ready to proceed?"

"I am."

"Sergeant Byron, would you please tell me how it was you came to be at Fort Williams Park this afternoon?"

"I was conducting surveillance on Assistant Chief Cross."

"Was this surveillance department sanctioned?"

"No. I was conducting it on my own."

"Why were you surveilling your chief?"

"The surveillance was part of my investigation into the murders of several former Portland police officers."

"Were you conducting surveillance on any

518

other individuals or just Assistant Chief Cross?"

"Yes. I was also running a surveillance detail on one of my former detectives, Ray Humphrey."

"Why were you surveilling one of your former detectives?"

"I had come to believe Ray Humphrey might be a suspect in an ongoing murder investigation."

"Did you share your suspicion with anyone else?"

"Yes. My detectives, Diane Joyner, Mike Nugent, and Melissa Stevens, also former FBI Special Agent Terrence Pritchard."

"You were working this case in conjunction with the FBI?"

"Not formally. Agent Pritchard is retired. He was the primary on a related case from years ago."

"Would that be the First Bank of Boston armored car robbery connected to your murder investigation?"

"It would."

"And was your involvement of Pritchard department sanctioned?"

"No." Byron waited as Marchand scribbled something on his notepad.

"Where were you surveilling Humphrey?"

"The surveillance had been ongoing but

began today at his place of employment on Commercial Street in Portland. Around one o'clock this afternoon, Agent Pritchard informed me that he'd followed Humphrey to Fort Williams Park in Cape Elizabeth."

"And how did you come to be at Fort Williams?"

"I followed Assistant Chief Cross from Portland police headquarters to the same location."

"Did you also consider Cross a suspect in your murder investigation?"

"No. I'd considered him a possible target."

"Why?"

"Because he was a part of the department's Special Reaction Team from thirty years ago, and the killer was targeting members of that team."

"Was Detective Humphrey a part of that team?"

"He was."

"What did you think when you found out Cross was meeting Humphrey?"

"Several possibilities occurred to me. I thought either Cross was in danger or that he and Humphrey might be in collusion."

"Did you notify your department superiors?"

"No."

"Did you notify the Cape Elizabeth police

department, in whose jurisdiction you were operating?"

"No."

"Did you notify the Maine State Police?"

"No, I didn't."

"Why didn't you share any of this information with your superior, Lieutenant Le-Royer?"

Byron leaned across the table toward Marchand. "There were only four people with whom I shared my suspicions regarding Humphrey: Detectives Joyner, Nugent, Stevens, and former Special Agent Terrance Pritchard."

"You didn't trust the other officers?"

"Someone was killing former cops — it's a little difficult to fully trust your own when you think one of them might be responsible."

"What happened next?"

"Agent Pritchard and I met up after Cross entered the woods on foot near the ruins. Pritchard informed me that Humphrey had gone into the woods about ten minutes before Cross."

"Then what happened?"

"We followed them into the woods."

"Did you call for backup?"

"I had already notified Detectives Joyner and Nugent about what was happening.

They both informed me they were en route to our location."

"Detective Joyner was your backup?"

"Her and Mike Nugent. Yes."

"Why didn't you wait for them?"

"I had no idea what I was walking into, and I was afraid if we waited another cop might be killed. Also, I figured if my detectives were behind us, they'd be in a better position to back us up if we got into trouble."

"Did you find Cross in the woods?"

"Yes. We located Cross and Humphrey behind the ruins, walking toward the fort's battery."

"What happened next?"

"We followed them. They stopped upon reaching the water. Humphrey stood behind Cross, pointing a gun at him."

"What did you do?"

"I had Agent Pritchard hang back while I approached with my gun drawn. I ordered Humphrey to lower his weapon."

"Did he?"

"No."

"Did Cross have a weapon?"

"Not that I could see at the time. But, yes, he did."

"Why didn't you shoot Humphrey? He was threatening your chief with a firearm."

"I didn't shoot him because of what Humphrey was saying."

"You sure it wasn't because of your hatred of Cross?"

Byron looked across the table at Marchand, making direct eye contact. "Absolutely not."

"You're saying you didn't hate the assistant chief?"

"He was an asshole and you're right, I didn't care for him, but that's not the reason I didn't shoot Humphrey."

"Why, then? Was it because you allowed your friendship to cloud your judgement?"

"I didn't shoot Humphrey because he was trying to get Cross to admit what he'd done."

"What he'd done?"

"Humphrey said he'd found out that Cross had murdered my father."

"Your father was murdered?"

"Officially, my father committed suicide, or so I'd thought. Reece Byron, also a member of the SRT, was reported to have committed suicide by his own gun shortly after a police-involved shooting thirty years ago."

"So Humphrey told you Cross murdered your father. Is that why you shot Cross?"

"No. I shot Cross because he shot Humphrey."

"You shot Cross because he shot the man who'd assaulted him and was holding him at gunpoint?"

"Humphrey had lowered his gun before Cross shot him. Cross was trying to silence him. Don't you want to know about Special Agent Pritchard, the man who shot Detective Joyner?"

"The FBI agent killed by Detective Joyner, right? Maybe she was accidentally struck by rounds meant for Humphrey?"

"You can twist this any way you want, Gene. But that isn't what happened. You weren't fucking there."

Bennett placed a hand on Byron's forearm, which Byron promptly shook off.

"I would've liked to question Assistant Chief Cross about what happened," Marchand continued. "But I can't now. Can I?"

Byron glared at Marchand. He wondered if Marchand was only trying to rattle him or if he was doing Stanton's bidding — the chief's attempt at preserving his career in the face of a public scandal. "No, I guess you can't. And I think we're done here," Byron said as he stood up.

"I'm not finished with you, Sergeant."

"That's too bad, because this was voluntary, remember? And I'm finished with you, Gene."

Byron whipped the door open, banging it against the wall, and stormed out of the interview room. Bennett chased after him. All eyes were upon Byron as he marched through CID toward his office.

Byron was packing up some personal belongings as Bennett walked in accompanied by LeRoyer.

"What the fuck was that?" Byron snapped, directing his question at the lieutenant.

"John," Bennett began, "I have to advise you against saying anything that could be used to —"

"Great, you've advised me." He turned back to LeRoyer, "Well? Did he really just ask me if I fucking murdered Cross?"

"John, look, I know you're upset but —"

"You've already got my gun, might as well take this too," he said, unclipping the badge from his belt and tossing it at LeRoyer.

"John," LeRoyer said, putting a hand out to try and prevent him from leaving.

"Save it," Byron said as he walked out of his office and out of 109.

CHAPTER THIRTY-TWO

"How's my favorite patient?" Byron asked as he peered around the curtain.

"You're lucky I wasn't in the middle of a sponge bath," Diane teased.

"My timing's never been that good." Byron leaned over the bed and kissed her. "How're you feeling?"

"Like I got shot."

"Nice outfit," he said, poking fun at her pink johnny.

"You like it? You oughta see it from the back."

Byron surveyed the brightly colored bouquets lining the windowsill and floor beneath.

She followed his gaze. "It's a little much, I know."

"Nonsense. They look great. Almost makes the hospital room bearable. By the way, I brought you a present," he said, handing her a white box with a red bow.

"Ooh, you got me a going-steady ring?"

"Better."

Diane removed the box top and looked inside. She reached in and held up a ballistic breastplate.

"Your old one has a big dent in it from Pritchard's forty-five," Byron said.

"Ah, that would match the big-ass bruise on my chest."

"Thought you might want a new one."

She batted her eyes at him. "You're such a romantic."

"I read somewhere if something doesn't kill you, it makes you stronger."

"Oh, so now you're a reader?"

"Well, okay, maybe I saw it on television."

"Thank you," she said, setting the gift on the bedside table, wincing as she did so.

"Hey, have I thanked you for saving my life?"

"Nope. Not since yesterday, you unappreciative bastard."

"Thank you, again," he said. "Maybe I'll show you some proper appreciation once you're out of here."

"Promises, promises. Anyway, you'd have done the same for me."

"Stanton just had his big dog and pony show at 109."

"Sorry I missed it," she said, rolling her

eyes. "What'd he say?"

"Called you a bona fide hero."

"Not sure I want him discussing my bona fides in public."

"How is it you can even make that sound dirty?"

"It's a gift. So the chief decided to spin this in his favor. How do you like that?"

"Not like he had a choice."

"What do you mean?"

"Ray's recording and statement. I handed them over to the FBI. Special Agent Sam Collier, to be exact."

"The feds took the case from the state attorney general?"

"Yup. The U.S. attorney general himself. Evidently, they'd been trying to get something on Pritchard for years, while he was still on the job. They're searching his old files and his house."

"Stanton must be livid."

"I hope so."

"What about Beaudreau?" Diane asked.

"Feds picked him up in Pennsylvania and he's talking like there's no tomorrow. From what Sam told me, it looks like Beaudreau confirmed that Andreas, the missing robber, was one of Cross's CIs. Following the armored car robbery, Andreas got cold feet. He contacted Cross about giving up the other three robbers in exchange for half of the money and a way out of the country. Cross contacted his old army buddy, Pritchard, after he learned they were hiding out in Portland."

"Holy hell."

"Pritchard posed as a money launderer and Cross introduced him to Andreas. They killed Andreas and got half of the money before the SRT raid even happened."

"What about Andreas?"

"The feds are planning to search the old Ocean Avenue landfill for his remains."

Diane looked puzzled. "There's still one thing I don't understand."

"What's that?" Byron asked.

"How did Dustin make the military connection between Cross and Prichard?"

"After the Perrigos were murdered, I asked him to go through everything again. Looking for any link between the FBI agents who originally investigated the shooting and the SRT. Collier provided the bio stuff, including the DD214s on all the agents, and Dustin compared military records for everyone who'd served. They met at Fort Dix, advanced infantry training, then on to Fort Bragg as members of the 101st Airborne."

Diane shook her head in disbelief. "Jesus."

"Even deployed to Vietnam together."

"You suspected Pritchard might have been involved?" Diane asked.

"Since our witnesses were killed at the safe house, I suspected someone from the bureau might be. I'd hoped I was wrong about it being Terry."

"So, then you knew you might be walking into a trap at Fort Williams?"

Byron shrugged. "It was a possibility. But I knew you and Nuge were coming."

"Jesus, John. That's pretty reckless."

She was right, of course. It was reckless. Maybe he'd been too tired to think it through. Or maybe that was just a convenient excuse. Maybe he'd been so hell-bent on catching the killer and on finding out what role his father had played that he had acted recklessly. Endangering all of them. "I had to know the truth."

Diane shook her head again. "I still can't believe it." She reached for the plastic water cup and took a sip from the straw. "So you're still working?"

"Of course not. I killed the Ass Chief, remember? Suspended with pay, at least until the AG's office announces their finding. They're also pissed about the feds taking the case, so it might be a while."

"I'll bet they are. How are you doing,

John? Really?"

He looked down at the floor, trying to avert his eyes from her prying ones. "Still trying to wrap my head around everything, I guess."

"You thought about talking to someone?"

"I'm talking to you."

"Ha-ha. I mean someone trained to help you through it."

"Therapy?" He shook his head dismissively. "Not really my thing."

"There's nothing wrong with getting at little —"

"Please, don't run that 'strong people ask for help crap' on me. Okay? This is something I'm gonna have to work through on my own. I've spent the last thirty years believing my dad was a coward and that Ray was a good man. It's gonna take me some time."

Diane smiled and slid her hand over his. "You know, I read somewhere if something doesn't kill you, it makes you stronger."

He grinned. "Oh, so now you're a reader?"

She returned the smile and stared into his eyes. "John, I think maybe I'm falling —"

"Hey, lady."

They both looked up and saw Melissa Stevens standing in the doorway.

"Hey, Mel!" Diane said.

"Catch you guys at a bad time?" Stevens asked with a knowing grin as she looked from one to the other.

"Not at all," Byron said, sliding his hand out from under Diane's. "I was just leaving."

"Where are you going?" Diane asked.

"I've got a few things to take care of."

EPILOGUE

Byron stood at the nursing station where a woman in her late fifties, wearing a crisp white uniform, was busy berating one of the young orderlies about maintaining her room schedule instead of sneaking outside to call her boyfriend. He waited off to one side, pretending to read something on his cell phone. When the supervisor had finished properly chastising her subordinate, the young woman with the ponytail returned to her rounds.

Byron approached the counter and the nursing supervisor turned her attention toward him.

"Kids," she said, flashing a knowing smile, which he returned. "May I help you?"

"I hope so," he said as he showed her his credentials. "I'm a police officer and I'm looking for Christopher Falcone's room."

"Of course. He's in room 121. Take this hallway down to the end and turn left, fifth door on your right. Can't miss it; it's the one with the police officer seated at the door."

Byron thanked her and headed toward Falcone's room. He wasn't expecting much, having had his detectives already attempt an interview. They reported during their previous visit that his Alzheimer's was in the advanced stages.

If there was one place Byron did not enjoy spending time, aside from the chief's office, it was nursing homes and homes for the aged. What the hell did that mean anyway? Wasn't home for the aged really a fancy way of saying we're waiting for you to die? And would you please step it up, there's a waiting list for your bed.

The facility reminded Byron a little too much of his last visit to his mother. The hallway was painted the same depressing pale blue and tiled with the same stark white-speckled linoleum. The air smelled strongly of bleach, masking the faintest hint of urine. He forced his mother's image from his head.

At the far end of the corridor, he turned left as the nurse had instructed. A uniformed Maine State Trooper was seated in the hall, flipping through a magazine.

"Help you?" the trooper asked as Byron

approached. He stood, facing Byron in a bladed position, gun hip turned away.

Byron identified himself, explaining that he only wanted a couple of minutes with the old man.

"My instructions are not to let anyone in there other than FBI."

"He's in your custody, right?" Byron asked, hoping to gain his trust.

"Right."

"I'm not taking him anywhere and I'm not here to fuck with the FBI's case. Just wanna talk with him."

The trooper looked down the hall nervously, then back at Byron. "You're gonna get me in trouble."

Byron could tell the trooper wasn't a rookie. There were some miles under his campaign hat. "Look, how many times have the feds muscled you aside on a state police case?"

The trooper stared at him, unblinking. Byron could see the wheels turning.

"I just need a few minutes with him. This may be my last chance to find out something I need to know, about my father."

"You got five minutes."

Byron walked through the open doorway and saw the old man, dressed in blue pajamas, dozing in one of two adjustable beds. Falcone's torso was raised slightly. The room was a two-person, but Falcone was the only occupant, situated in the bed nearest the window. The wall-mounted television was on, but muted. Byron quietly entered the room and sat down in one of the bedside chairs. Falcone was frail. He couldn't have weighed more than a hundred pounds. A plastic tube had been inserted into his left nostril, the other end of which was connected to a large green oxygen tank. Falcone looked nothing like the young man he had been in the SRT team photo.

A woman and her two children walked noisily by the door, carrying yellow flowers and a bright red balloon. Party for the dying, he thought. When Byron looked back, Falcone was wide awake and had fixed his eyes upon his visitor.

"Mr. Falcone," Byron began as he reached into his jacket pocket for his identification. "I hope I didn't wake you. My name is Detective Sergeant John —"

"I know who you are, Sergeant," Falcone said, gruffly cutting him off.

"You do?" Byron asked, surprised at the old man's response.

"Yup, I do. I watch the news, ya know. Got nothing else to do. Well, except for waiting around to kick the ol' bucket."

Byron supposed it was probably true, given the way he looked.

"Congratulations on killing that fucking psycho bastard."

"Ray Humphrey? But I didn't kill him."

"Not Humphrey. Cross. Figured whoever was doing it would get to me eventually. Maybe a pillow over the face or a needle in my IV bag, like in the movies. Guess I'll sleep a little better now. Been expecting you, actually."

"The police, you mean?"

"No, you personally, Sergeant Byron."

"Why me?" Byron asked, proceeding cautiously. Normally, he was in control when conducting an interview. Falcone had somehow gained the upper hand during what should have been a surprise visit.

"Because I knew you either wouldn't or couldn't let it go. You're here about your father, right?"

"I am."

"And you want me to tell you what really happened?"

"Guess that's true as well, but I thought you —"

Falcone cut him off again. "You thought I was bat-shit crazy with Alzheimer's, right?"

"I wouldn't put it quite like that, but yeah, that was my general impression."

"Ha," Falcone cackled. "Well, sometimes I am, I guess. Fucking can't remember periods of time, though some days I'm still pretty good, like today. But I can still pretend if I don't want to do something or if I don't want to talk to someone, like when your detectives were in here." Falcone grinned, revealing several blackened teeth. "That Joyner, she's a pretty one. Wouldn't mind seeing her again," he said, raising his eyebrows. "Back along, we didn't have too many women on the job."

"What can you tell me about 1985, Mr. Falcone?"

"Enough with the Mr. Falcone crap, okay? It's Chris, for Christ's sake."

"Okay, Chris. What can you tell me about 1985?"

"Guess I can tell you the whole damn thing. Not like you're gonna arrest me. Feds already got me anyway."

Falcone proceeded to tell the tale to Byron with surprising clarity. He confirmed almost everything Byron had learned about the robbery, the call-out, the money, and subsequent cover-up. Falcone only got emotional once, while describing the death of Officer Bruce Gagnon. Falcone's eyes were red and his voice cracked. He stopped talking and looked out the window.

Several minutes passed. Byron began to worry Falcone's mind might have slipped from the here-and-now into that place where the shroud of Alzheimer's was impenetrable. At last, he spoke again. "I'm sorry about your dad, son. I didn't have anything to do with that. It was Reggie Cross who pulled the trigger. I thought we were going over there to talk some sense into him. I've had plenty of time to think about that night. I think Reggie planned to kill him all along."

Byron continued to listen, saying nothing.

"I did more than my share of bad shit over the years, Sergeant. I'll admit it and I'll take whatever punishment the Almighty sees fit to bring down on me. Guess I got it coming. But I never did anything like that. My life turned to shit the day he killed Reece. I blew my share of the money, my wife left me, and my kids haven't spoken to me in years. It was like Reggie cursed all of us. I hated that son of a bitch."

"Why didn't any of you do something?" Byron asked. "Why didn't you come forward?"

"We almost did. A couple of us talked seriously about coming forward and giving the money back, and turning states evidence, but we couldn't do it."

"Why not?"

"Because we were all fucking scared of him, even O'Halloran was. That's the God's honest truth. Reggie was a bully. He had stuff on all of us — well, almost all of us. He never did manage to get anything on your dad."

"Perrigo told me you'd been ripping off drug dealers, even before the armored car robbery."

"Some of us had. When we could get away with it. Your dad never knew about those and he never took a cent until the robbery shootout."

"If that's true, why involve him at all?"

"This wasn't like taking down a drug dealer. We needed the whole team for this one. I guess Reggie probably figured there was so much money, everyone would go along with it."

"But everyone didn't," Byron said.

"No, everyone didn't. That money was the only money your dad had ever taken, and he was going to turn it over to the feds. Reece Byron was the only guy I ever knew man enough to stand up to that asshole, and it got him killed."

Byron leaned forward in the chair, forearms on his knees. He looked down at the floor as his eyes welled up. He felt a single tear run down his cheek, and he quickly wiped it away with the back of his hand.

Falcone reached over the bedrail and gently placed a weathered old hand on Byron's shoulder. "Son, your dad was a good man, an honorable man, and one of the best cops I ever worked with. Somewhere along the way, I guess we just forgot what being cops was all about.

Byron lifted his head and looked at the old man.

"Your dad never did."

Byron parked out in front of Kay's office on Meeting House Hill in South Portland. He picked up the manila envelope from the passenger seat and opened it. He pulled out the papers and looked at the cover sheet. It looked the same as it had each of the previous times he'd looked at it during the course of the morning, and there had been at least a dozen. He slid the documents back into the envelope and stepped out of the car. He climbed the office steps and went inside.

Byron didn't recognize the attractive young receptionist. She was new.

"Can I help you, sir?" she asked.

"I'm dropping something off for Kay Byron."

"Dr. Byron is in session, but she'll be done

in about ten minutes, if you'd care to wait."

He glanced beyond the lobby into the empty waiting room, considering it. "Thanks anyway, but I can't stay. Would please you make sure she gets this?" he said, handing her the envelope.

"Certainly. May I tell her your name?"

"Tell her it's from John."

Byron grabbed the brown paper bag off the passenger seat, then ducked under a damaged section of cyclone fencing separating New Street from Evergreen Cemetery. Neighborhood kids had most likely vandalized the rusted barrier, which now served as a cut through.

He walked slowly but purposefully toward the back corner of the property, attuned to everything around him. The smell of freshly cut grass and rotting leaves filled the air. He heard the sounds of kids playing, the twitter of birds, and a power mower.

It had been decades since he'd been to the grave, but he still remembered the way. The area looked vastly different. The maples and pines had grown along with the number of stones. A chilly breeze rustled through the leaves, making a whispering sound. He no longer felt like a man in his late forties. It was as if the last thirty years never happened and he was once again a teenager sneaking into the cemetery to drink beer with his friends from the Hill. He felt vulnerable and unsure as he approached the marker.

A simple granite stone, nearly obscured by debris, was embedded in the turf. He knelt in the grass, removed a small branch, and brushed pine needles from the grave. Reece James Byron 1939–1985. A lump formed in his throat and his eyes watered as he tried to speak.

Memories came flooding back after years of repression. Good memories. Playing catch on the Eastern Prom, fishing off the docks on Commercial Street, riding in the police cruiser. He reached into his jacket pocket and removed a faded picture of them. Reece was in uniform, holding a young John Byron on his lap. He was wearing his father's police hat, awkwardly cocked to one side. They were both smiling and happy.

He pulled a brand-new bottle of Jameson and a single shot glass from the bag. He twisted the cap off the bottle, catching a whiff of the Irish, filled the glass, and placed them gently upon the stone, then he leaned the photograph against the bottle. Wiping his eyes with the back of his sleeve, he sat down cross-legged in the grass.

"Thought it was about time we had a talk, Dad."

ACKNOWLEDGMENTS

Among the Shadows is the culmination of a long journey, from my first days attending the University of Southern Maine — to study writing — through nearly three decades in law enforcement. I am eternally grateful to a number of people instrumental in my transition to published novelist. You'll forgive me if I've left any of you out, it was certainly not my intention.

Kate "Doc" Flora for your friendship, sage advice, counsel, ruthless editing, and ongoing psychotherapy as I blindly navigate my battered dory through the forbidding, shark-infested waters of writing and publishing. And for pushing me to reach beyond while talking me off the ledge.

The many writing teachers who've inspired me, among them Scarborough High's Gerald Hebert, Eileen Matrazzo, and Deborah Kerr.

My proofreaders, critics, and fact-checkers: Nancy Coffin (my mom), Michael Cunniff, Sherry Simons, Jen Printy, Judy Ridge, Barbara Nickerson, Marge Niblock, Lee Humiston, Cindy Swift, and Inger Cyr.

Fellow crime writers Brenda Buchanan, Dick Cass, Kate Flora (yes, again), Al Lamanda, and Rick Simonds.

My immediate family and friends for their constant encouragement and support along the way.

Dave and Theresa Cote for providing me with an opportunity.

The many men and women in the field of criminal justice, true professionals I was fortunate enough to have served with, whether municipal, county, state, federal, corrections, prosecutors, defense counselors, or magistrates. I will always consider each one of you my extended family (Wouldn't that make for a great tax deduction?).

My agent, Paula Munier, at Talcott Notch for believing in me.

Nick Amphlett, my editor at Harper-Collins, for allowing me to stick my foot in the novel publishing door and for prodding me to reach further. And Patrice Silverstein, my copyeditor, for catching what I missed.

Lastly, and most importantly, my wife, Karen, for her love, support, inspiration, infinite patience, and for believing. Without you in my life there would be no story.

ABOUT THE AUTHOR

Bruce Robert Coffin retired from the Portland, Maine, police department in 2012, after more than twenty-seven years in law enforcement. As a detective sergeant, he supervised all homicide and violent crime investigations for Maine's largest city. Following the terrorist attacks of September 11, he worked for four years with the FBI, earning the Director's Award (the highest honor a nonagent can receive) for his work in counterterrorism.

Bruce's fiction has been shortlisted twice for the Al Blanchard Award. His story *Foolproof* appears in the Level Best Books anthology *Red Dawn, Best New England Crime Stories,* 2016, and in Houghton Mifflin Harcourt's *Best American Mystery Stories,* 2016. He is currently writing the sequel to *Among the Shadows.*

He lives and writes in Maine.